The PROMISE

By Addison M Conley

2024

Butterworth Books is a different breed of publishing house. It's a home for Indies, for independent authors who take great pride in their work and produce top quality books for readers who deserve the best. Professional editing, professional cover design, professional proof reading, professional book production—you get the idea. As Individual as the Indie authors we're proud to work with, we're Butterworths and we're *different*.

Authors currently publishing with us:

E.V. Bancroft
Valden Bush
Addison M Conley
Jo Fletcher
Helena Harte
Lee Haven
Karen Klyne
AJ Mason
Ally McGuire
James Merrick
Robyn Nyx
JP Preston
Simon Smalley
JJ Taylor
Brey Willows

For more information visit www.butterworthbooks.co.uk

CATALOGING INFORMATION
ISBN: 978-1-915009-70-8
CREDITS
Editor: Nicci Robinson
Cover Design: Nicci Robinson
Production Design: Global Wordsmiths

Acknowledgements

I want to thank my editor, Nicci Robinson, also known as the authors Helena Harte and Robyn Nyx, and her wife, Victoria Villaseñor. *The Promise* and my previous novel, *Cabin Fever*, would not have been possible without their help. Yes, Nicci did the heavy lifting of editing and cover design while Victoria worked with other clients. But Nicci and Victoria's enthusiasm for WLW literature and tireless work running Butterworth Books have made a difference in my life and work. They organize and run writing retreats, which are fun and challenging. I've cherished the occasional early morning when Victoria has shared coffee with me, virtually ensuring I didn't sleepwalk the entire day. And I'll never forget that day in the bakery, Vic. I learned a lot from you that day. I'm amazed at your kindness.

I'm privileged to call the other authors at Butterworth Books my friends. Our bond has strengthened as we've shared our work in progress at the retreats. I deeply appreciate their kindness, wit, and spirit. I'd visit them more often if it weren't for the plane ride. Their dedication to their craft and their unique perspectives have been a source of inspiration for me.

I'm immensely grateful to my friends, Lyn and Gill, for their keen eye and attention to detail. Their ability to catch errors that the rest of us miss dazzles me.

In my personal life, I'd like to thank Pamela and Judy for their friendship and encouragement in our small country town. To Paul and Trey, I admire your energy, tenacity, and love for all. And to the many friends I don't see often—a special shoutout to Joanna and the old bus stop gang—thank you for the good times.

Finally, I love you, K and J. Your life is in your own hands now that you've navigated your teenage years. K, I'm proud of you. You've shown a lot of responsible independence and are a beautiful young woman.

Dedication

To Grandma Ruth, Uncle Ronnie, Aunt Sandy,
and Uncle Richard. There was so much I never
told you, but you meant the world to me. I miss you.

To my teachers who made a huge impact on me,
especially Mr. Henry.

Their presence in my life and their
kindness made me want to live.
Love can be so powerful.

Youth is the gift of nature, but age is a work of art.
Stanislaw Jerzy Lec

"In youth, we learn; in age, we understand."
Marie von Ebner-Eschenbach

Chapter One

MIKA LAVIGNE LOVED HER family, but with everyone cramped around the dining room table, the chatter was loud enough to shatter the windows. Mom's sister, Aunt Val, was a no-show, which made Mom sad, but Grandpa and Grandma Hayden didn't seem to care. Mika didn't know what the deal was with her mysterious aunt or why everyone but her parents hated her.

"Michaela, pass the turkey platter, please. How's school?" Grandfather Lavigne asked.

She grabbed the plate and placed it beside him. "I got a B in English but As in everything else."

"Excellent, Michaela."

She clenched her jaw and smiled tightly. None of her grandparents would use the name she wanted them to. *Old fogeys.* While the adults talked at one end of the table, Mika and her cousins sat at the opposite end. She mostly kept her mouth shut and communicated with her slightly older cousin, Jenn, through facial expressions, shrugs, and some hand gestures they'd developed as code. Carla, Jenn's younger sister, was shy and didn't talk much.

"Jenn, dear, your mom told me about your New Year's Eve dress. Maybe you could give some tips to Michaela," Grandma Hayden shouted over the granddads talking football with Mika's dad.

"I'd love to." Jenn grinned.

Freakin' traitor. She thought about throwing the spoonful of mashed potatoes at her.

"Mother, what Mika wears to any party is fine with me," her mom said.

Mika glanced at her mom proudly. Over the years, she'd become more progressive and stood up more to Grandma too.

Grandma Hayden puckered her lips. "I think Michaela's blouse goes well with her jeans, but it'd go better with a skirt. She should dress up more."

"I'm not going to the New Year's Eve party or any other party soon. If I do, then I'll think about getting dressier," Mika said, harsher than she'd intended.

"Oh, you should come to our club's New Year's Eve party. And I have the perfect dress for you." Jenn gave her a big shit-ass grin and twirled her hair around her fingers.

"Thanks." Mika glared at her. *But if I go, I'm not wearing a damn dress.*

"Pass the stuffing, please," Grandfather Lavigne shouted. "You know, I don't care about young women's clothes. Dress pants are fine with me." He plopped a dollop onto his plate after Grandmother handed him the bowl. "What bothers me is all this liberal crap, especially the gays. I don't know how we're supposed to get America great again."

Here it comes. When it came to politics and social issues, both sets of grandparents were the opposite of Mika's parents, and they acted like they were living in Russia.

"Father, nothing will change unless people vote," Aunt Pauline said.

Of course she would throw some gas on the fire. Jenn rolled her eyes. Thank God her cousins weren't anything like their mother.

"My point exactly," Grandfather Lavigne said.

"I don't know what it's like in Wyoming, but we have a problem in New York. Ithaca and the state have become too left-wing. People need to stand up and stop the homosexual agenda being pushed by the woke." Grandpa Hayden pounded his fist on the table.

"I agree," Grandfather Lavigne said.

Mika stabbed a piece of turkey and smeared it in gravy. Her grandparents would have a fucking heart attack if they knew she dreamed about Willow Parker every day.

"Let's not talk politics at the table, please," Mika's dad said.

Aunt Pauline let out an exaggerated sigh. "Andrew, it's getting out of control. Mother and Father have it better out West. And the new thing now is letting kids choose their gender *and* letting them go into the wrong bathroom. I've never heard such nonsense."

Mika focused on her meal, trying to tune it all out. Why couldn't people just *be*? She jumped when her mom slapped her hand on the table.

"Enough!" her mom yelled. "Andrew and I disagree," she said more softly but gave Aunt Pauline and the oldies a hard stare. "Love is love, and I'm happy to live in a progressive state. No more political talk, or you're out the door."

Mom hardly ever raised her voice, and Mika had to bite her lip to keep from smiling. *Well done, Mom.*

"I wholeheartedly agree," Mika's dad said. "Let's focus on the common good and count our blessings."

Everyone went silent briefly before sliding back into idle chatter. Then Grandma Hayden started questioning Mika about dating and what she liked in boys. Mika froze, and Jenn smiled wider. Mika chugged some water. She had no interest in guys and didn't want to talk about it with anyone.

"Mother, stop pestering her."

Yes! Mom to the rescue again.

"Hannah, she's almost seventeen. Why not talk about it now?" Grandma Hayden elbowed Mika in the ribs gently. "How many boys have you kissed?"

"Mother! That's none of your business."

The mashed potatoes that Mika had scooped into her mouth lodged in her windpipe, and she couldn't breathe. She coughed, swallowed them down, and gulped more water.

"You okay, sweetie?"

"Yeah, Mom. Just took too big of a bite." Mika forced a smile and ignored Grandma's question.

"Hannah, she hangs around that Latin boy all the time. It's time you had a good talk with her."

"Benjy's not Latin. His mother is Indian, and his father is Dutch American." It wasn't any of Grandma Hayden's, or anyone else's, business who she hung around with.

"He does seem like a nice kid," Grandpa said then looked at Mika. "But he is a little too dark."

"Dad!"

Fuck, did he really go there? She'd never heard a racial slur from them before, but she wasn't going to let it slide. "He's my best friend, and we've known each other since elementary school. He was born in Syracuse, and English is his native language, but he also speaks his mom's language of Gujarati fluently. Please don't talk about him like he's less than you or me."

Grandpa Hayden barely nodded and continued to eat. Her dad winked at her and smiled.

"It's dessert time. I'll grab the pies." Mika's mom rose. "Sweetie, please help me in the kitchen."

"I'll help too," Grandma Hayden said.

"No, Mom. I think you've helped more than enough today," Mika's mom said. "And when we return, no politics, no religion, and no slamming our friends."

Mika followed her mom into the kitchen. When they were alone, she gripped Mika's shoulders.

"I'm sorry about that, sweetie. You know we love Benjy and his family. And when you date, all we hope for is a good person who cares about you."

Person? Did that mean her parents didn't care whether she dated a girl or a guy or anyone else? That'd piss off her grandparents. But she hoped her mom didn't mean Benjy. Sure, he was a handsome guy with his mom's gorgeous dark hair and chocolate-brown eyes, but it was gross to think of dating him. Mika turned toward the basement stairs as her mom cut the apple pie. "I'll get the ice cream."

"It's up here."

"I like the French vanilla better," Mika said over her shoulder as she practically ran down the stairs. At the bottom, she took a deep breath before going into the storage room and yanking the freezer door open. When the alarm beeped, she snatched the ice cream, slammed the freezer door, and slowly climbed the stairs.

She wasn't sure how to handle her feelings for Willow. They were on the swim team together, and damn, no one looked as good in their team swimsuit as Willow, but they rarely talked to one another until they started working in the library together. Now Mika found it hard to breath when Willow was around, and the tingling throughout her body was unstoppable, especially between her legs. Why would a popular, cute senior be interested in a junior who was a math and science geek? Fuck it. Dreaming about more wasn't going to change anything. Willow was straight and would probably run if she knew Mika liked her. Why did life have to be so difficult?

Chapter Two

Early December

MIKA WANTED TO PLAY online games over the weekend, so she had to get ahead of the curve with homework. Tapping her pencil on the desk to "Karma," she glanced over her finished calculus assignment. When she played against Benjy, they alternated their playlists because music was the only thing they disagreed on. Taylor Swift was her favorite, but he liked hard rock. So they mixed it up to come up with playlists that included artists they both liked.

Satisfied with her math, she slipped it into her binder and switched to English—the subject she couldn't stand. She was behind on a critique of another boring *classic*. What was it with teachers calling a book classic just because it was written at the beginning of time? She slowly began scribbling ideas down. Maybe she'd wait until tomorrow. No, she shouldn't. Benjy was good at pulling things out of his ass at the last moment but not her. Mika liked to be on top and go beyond what was expected. *Fuck it.* She slammed the book shut. Her right earbud was tugged out, and she turned.

"No wonder you didn't answer."

"Sorry, Mom." Good thing she hadn't cursed. It would've gotten her kitchen chores for a week. She shut off the music and removed the other earbud. "What's up?"

"Grandma Hayden says they're going with Aunt Pauline to Wyoming—"

"Dope. Christmas at the Lavigne Ranch would be lit." Mika smiled widely. "I want to go. If you and Dad are busy, can I still go with them?" Mika tossed her pencil down. She loved the ranch and riding horses with her cousins, especially in the snow. The couple who took care of her grandparents' horses knew all the incredible trails. And the house was humongous. Even with Carla tagging along, she and Jenn could stay out of their grandparents' hair, and with any luck, they wouldn't have to listen to them throwing shade like they'd done at Thanksgiving.

"I wasn't talking about us going too." Her mom sat on the edge of the bed.

"But I haven't been to their place for an age."

The glint of emotion in her mom's eye and the short silence that followed didn't look promising.

"I'm sorry to say no. I've invited Aunt Val for Christmas."

"That's mid." Mika huffed and rocked back in her chair.

Her mom arched her eyebrow. "Mid?"

"Boring," Mika said and rolled her eyes at having to explain. "She hasn't visited since the last Ice Age."

"Her job keeps her very busy. You know your great-grandmother died of cancer—"

"Yeah, and Aunt Val works for a drug company trying to find a *miracle cure.*"

"Please watch your tone and stop cutting me off."

Her mom stood to her full height, which wasn't much compared to Mika, and put her hand on her hip: code for *this conversation is over.*

But Mika wasn't done talking. "Sorry, but I don't get it." Her mom and dad always defended Aunt Val, the missing-in-action family member, and it really ticked Mika off. "I can count on one hand the times she," *the family sow,* "has visited." Jesus, one of these days, she was going to mess up and blurt a nickname she'd given her aunt. "You and Dad won't tell me the full story about why Grandma and Grandpa Hayden treat her like the plague. Is that why they're leaving town? To avoid their youngest daughter?"

Her mom sighed and glanced away with that strange look she always got when Mika mentioned the unspoken tension.

"Sweetie, it was a stupid argument a long time ago. And you know Grandma and Grandpa are stubborn. It's been a long week, and it's getting late. Lights out in half an hour, please."

Mika crossed her arms as her mom left the room. She would be seventeen this summer, old enough to know the full story. Whenever Aunt Val was mentioned, Grandpa Hayden always turned away and immediately shifted the topic like he hadn't heard the question. Dad's side wasn't any better. Aunt Pauline's eyeballs would bug out like she had a mouthful of razor blades. What the fuck did the entire family have against her mom's sister?

Mika pulled some old photos out of her desk. The ones at her first birthday used to make her laugh but as she got older, she noticed something seemed off. In the picture of her in a high chair with cake smeared all over her face, everyone was laughing, but Aunt Val was looking down at Mika with a sad face.

She tossed the photos back in her drawer and reluctantly cracked open her English book again. Whatever the family problem, it wasn't hers. Mika's problem was not being able to get Willow out of her head. After thirty minutes, she tossed the book in her bag, brushed her teeth, and slid into bed. She tried hard *not* to think about Willow and her perfect smile as she dozed off.

Chapter Three

"No," Mika mumbled as her phone alarm woke her from a deep sleep. She snuggled deeper under the blanket and tried to fall back to sleep, but the urge to pee pulled her out of bed. Panic struck her when she saw the time. Instead of her usual morning exercises, she threw on clothes, brushed her teeth, and ran her fingers through her hair. The messy look would have to do. She groaned. Today was Mom's volunteer day at the hospice care center, so it'd be a cold walk to school. She grabbed her backpack, bolted down the stairs and nearly ran smack into her dad.

"Slow down before you break your neck," he said.

"Huh?" She turned around. "What are you doing here?"

"Good morning to you too."

"Sorry. Good morning, Dad," she said, matching his formal tone. "What's up?"

"I'm free for breakfast because my first two clients rescheduled. I was about ready to wake you since I kept hearing your alarm, then you tackled me like a linebacker." He grinned.

She grinned too. "Sorry."

He was the coolest dad. Everyone always remarked on their smiles and hazel eyes being so much alike. Grandma Hayden said Mika's straight dark brown hair and darker complexion came from her southern Italian relatives, and that Mika's mom's fair complexion and green eyes were from Grandpa's Irish side. Even though the comparisons didn't make sense because Mika was adopted, she still liked them.

"I'll drive you to school after breakfast."

In the kitchen, the smell of his famous strawberry pancakes

made her stomach growl. He plated a small portion for himself and a larger one for her.

"Did you take your pill?" He held up the bottle.

"Not yet." She reached out, and he shook a Zoloft into her hand. "Hey, I overheard someone talking about you and your firm." Her attempt at seriousness failed as the grin she so desperately tried to hide spread across her face.

"And what sordid detail did you hear?" He eyeballed her playfully.

"That you're a fair guy and not a shyster."

"Yeah, I did flunk Shyster 101 in law school. But family law is emotional enough. When people are hurting, they shouldn't have to fight or worry about finances. I've shown a few lucrative clients the door because they wanted to cause their soon-to-be ex as much pain as possible."

Mika looked down at her plate. "Does it bother you that I don't want to be a lawyer?"

"No, sweetie. I want you to find whatever makes you happy and go for it." He softly tipped her chin up with his fingertips and looked her in the eye. "Life presents opportunities. Sometimes you go for something and it's scary, or it doesn't turn out as expected, but I personally think that more good happens if you follow your heart and run with it. And whatever happens, don't waste your time with woulda, coulda, shoulda. Move on. Regret over the past is just wasted energy."

She thought about the conversation with her mom a few nights ago; *that* hadn't made her happy. "Hey, Mom said Val might come home for Christmas."

"Respect, please. She's Aunt Val to you."

"Sorry. So Aunt Val is visiting?"

"I certainly hope so. We haven't seen her for too long, and you weren't home the last time she popped in. It'd be nice to be together again." He rose and took his time getting the cream from the refrigerator and pouring more coffee.

Mika didn't understand why her dad either said good things or just deflected whenever they talked about Mom's sister. "She moved back from Germany a year ago and hasn't visited once. Do you really think she'll make it?"

He slowly placed the spoon in the sink and turned to face her. "Her job is very demanding."

Mika would fucking scream if she heard that one more time. She tossed down her napkin and stared at him. "If Mom's parents and your sister are visiting your parents in Wyoming for a Lavigne Christmas, then why are we staying up here for Mom's sister when she might not even bother to turn up? Why can't we just invite her to Wyoming?"

He took a sip of his coffee. "If she doesn't make it, then I promise we'll go see her in Boston before you go back to school."

With that look in his eyes, Mika should have backed off. God, she hated confrontation with him. And why would he think that visiting the aunt who didn't seem to care about her would make up for missing out on ranch time? "Nope." She crossed her arms. "Tickets to see the New York Rangers beat the Bruins in TD Garden would be a better deal."

He chuckled, and she relaxed.

"Are you sure you want to be a scientist? Maybe you *should* be a lawyer."

She scarfed down the last of her food, and they headed out the door for the short drive to school.

"Hey, Dad, when are you going to give me more driving lessons?" she asked when they were about a block from their house. "We've only done half of the daytime driving and nothing at night."

He glanced at her before refocusing on the road. "You didn't want Mom taking you out, and my schedule's tight."

"I know, but most of my class has their junior driver's license and a state approved class for their senior license lined up in the New Year." She clasped her hands together.

"My schedule lightens up in a couple of weeks. We'll do more driving then. And when it's time for your class, I suppose you want me to find one that lets you drive my Mustang and not your mom's SUV." He winked.

"You got it. But not because it's a sports car. EV's are the future, and I need to learn about the battery and charging for scientific purposes."

He laughed. "Right."

She'd won enough points with him today. It was best to move on. The rest of the way they talked about sports.

"The drop-off lane's full. I can get out here. Thanks for the ride, Dad. I love you."

"I love you too, kiddo."

He didn't call her that a lot since she'd become a teenager, but she still liked to hear it. She waved as he drove away, then ran toward the door.

"Lavigne, where have you been?"

She looked across the lot to see Benjy walking toward her. "Sorry. I overslept."

"No wonder with four days of swimming starting at the butt crack of dawn. That should be a fucking crime." He brushed his hair out of his eyes.

"Swimming's over, but my sleep's still all over the place."

"Want to come over for dinner tomorrow night? Mom's fixing some bussin' Tongan fish dish. She's featuring South Pacific dishes on socials next month."

"I'll try, but I'm halfway through an English paper."

Benjy's mom was a blogging superstar, and Mika loved taste-testing her recipes. Even when Benjy's mom said she'd screwed it up, her food was tongue-tingling heaven. Shame Benjy hadn't inherited the talent; he couldn't cook to save his life. "I love your mom's spicy dabeli. Any chance of talking her into fixing it if we play at your house on Sunday? I'm coming back from my cousins' around three."

"Only if you let me win." He laughed. "And I can show you the new woodworking project me and Dad are doing."

"You got me, bro. How's your dad's shop doing?"

"Crazy busy, but he still has time to train me. And he's not pressuring me to go to college or take on the family business." Benjy shrugged. "Which is great, 'cos I don't know what I want."

"It's okay." Mika punched his bicep. "I've got plans, but who knows? I might change my mind. So, don't stress. Take your time. You'll eventually do whatever makes you happy."

"Yeah." A grin the devil would be proud of spread over his face. "Hey, I got a CyberPower PC Xtreme for Christmas."

She grabbed his arm. "No fucking way."

He laughed. "It's last year's model and not the newest processor–"

"Who cares? It's a screaming machine. Wait a minute. Your parents gave you your gift early? I'm dead."

"No." He lightly smacked her shoulder. "I unwrapped and rewrapped it. They'll never know."

"You've got balls, dude."

They laughed and entered the noisy hallway. She saw Wes and Tiana, her other online gaming friends. Well, they were her only friends period, besides Benjy.

"Hey, Mika. How's it going?"

She and Tiana fist bumped. "Good. I plan to jump online Friday night, but I can't the rest of the weekend."

Benjy gave her a look, but she wanted to keep their Sunday plans between them.

Wes squeezed in. "Hi, Mika. Want to come over whenever you're free?"

Benjy stepped back and to the side. He pointed at Wes' back and silently mouthed, *He likes you.* Mika shot him a glare.

"You've already seen the new game I found, Benj. You too, Tiana. It's the one I showed you online." He looked at Mika again. "How 'bout it?"

"Thanks, but I'm busy." Mika adjusted her backpack and shifted from foot to foot. This was going to get awkward fast if he didn't get the hint. Why couldn't the guy wake up and see that Tiana was the one who liked him? And Mika had no idea why Tiana hadn't said anything yet.

"I can help you fine tune it," Tiana said.

The five-minute bell for class rang, saving her from Wes.

"See you later, guys." Mika shuffled down the hall, dreading English, her first class of every day and the enemy of her perfect grade point average. She hated grammar but was good at it, and creative writing was fun sometimes, but the required reading was mid, and she tuned out. If English didn't fry her brain cells, then the next period would—history and economics alternated days of the week. They were easy but boring. The economics teacher's monotone voice put everyone to sleep. And if it wasn't for Benjy and his weird fondness of history, she'd zone out completely. The rest of the day was tight: library duty, lunch, then her favorite subjects, chemistry, AP math, and gym. The locker room sucked, but other than that, she loved gym.

Mika slumped in her chair and chewed on her fingernail. The morning dragged on, but when the bell sounded for third period, excitement coursed through her, and she jumped up and headed to the library. She'd been drafted by her English teacher, who'd hoped that shelving books would magically instill some passion for literature and pull her grade up to an A. Mika smiled. Or maybe it was punishment because of her occasional use of profanity in her papers. Whatever, it was the best thing that ever happened to her because she could avoid the study hall, where idiots passed notes and gossiped, and best of all, it meant she could be near Willow.

Mika had always been at the bottom of the popularity food chain, but something had shifted in the Universe, and the chance to be around Willow was like magic. Mika could never have imagined in a zillion years that she'd become friends with Willow Parker.

Mika's pulse increased when she caught sight of Willow's

sandy blond hair and big, honey-brown eyes. "Hi." Her face felt like it would crack in two from smiling, but she couldn't help it.

"Hey, I see you survived your boring morning. What's on the agenda today?"

Mika melted at Willow's smile. "Not much to shelve." She pointed to the cart and grabbed the first book.

As they went along the stacks, Willow glanced at Mika repeatedly, looking like she wanted to say something but couldn't. Mika's heart sank. Maybe Willow had heard the rumors and was figuring out how to say that she didn't want to hang around with her anymore. Mika always kept her head down and never bothered anyone, but that didn't stop the slams. After they'd finished shelving, they studied and didn't talk.

Willow drummed her nails on the table, and Mika's jitters soared. *Here it comes.*

"Um, I'm..." Willow stopped tapping and stared at Mika with wide eyes. "I'm flunking trigonometry." Willow put her hand over her eyes. "I have enough credits to graduate, but Mom thinks a bad grade jeopardizes my admission to college."

"I can help you." Mika reached out to touch her but withdrew at the last minute.

Willow straightened up. "That'd be great. You're in advanced math. Aren't you doing calculus?"

Willow looked so scared but relieved at the same time that Mika wanted to hug her. "Yeah, but I love trigonometry."

"Thank you. You're such a good friend."

Friend wasn't what Mika wanted, but it was better than nothing. "You're welcome." She scooted her chair closer, maybe a little too close, but hardly anyone came in around lunchtime, so nobody would see. Not that there was anything *to* see. "Show me what you're working on."

Willow leaned toward her with the assignment sheet, and their arms brushed together briefly. All Mika could think about was how soft the touch was and how Willow's perfume smelled so nice.

She didn't know what it was, but she'd bet that it smelled better on Willow than on anyone else.

"What do you think?" Willow asked.

Good thing Mika was a math whiz because her daydream mode would have sunk anyone else. She could do these equations in her sleep. She explained each step, then made up some samples for Willow to solve. But Willow bombed every single one. The library period was nearly over by the time she got one right.

"I did it!" Willow grinned.

"Girls. Quiet, please." Mrs. Simmons looked at them over the top of her glasses before a small smile cracked her stern expression.

"Thanks, Mika," Willow whispered.

"Gucci. I'm happy to. I'll make up some more equations for you tonight." *Like I don't think about you enough...* "It's like swimming. Keep at it, and it'll flow."

Willow rose and gathered her books. "I need to go. See you later?"

Mika waved and smiled, but it faded when Willow was out of sight. Mika used to wonder if she was asexual or something until she and Willow started talking. Her small crush grew until it was like a tsunami washing through her body. But she couldn't talk to anyone about her feelings. Bullies had landed enough hits over the years that she'd more or less given up on making friends. She didn't think Benjy would understand, and she couldn't risk losing him. Talking to her parents would be uncool, not to mention downright embarrassing. Dad would probably take it well, but would Mom? Her grandparents would probably disown her. And she didn't really know how to put her feelings into words. She just wasn't ready.

Mrs. Simmons tapped her watch, interrupting Mika's thoughts. "There's not much time left before your next class."

"Oh, yeah." Mika crammed her books in her bag and hurried out of the library. *Why can't I say it?* The faster she walked, the more she realized it didn't matter. Willow was straight, and nothing could happen between them. And she wasn't about to risk her new friendship over a clumsy mistake.

Chapter Four

DIVING WAS DOPE. SYNCHRONIZING in a rhythm necessary to approach the board, feeling its flex, and getting that perfect spin and landing excited her. She'd started lessons at Jenn's private club last year, but she didn't think her sporadic visits were enough to refine her skills. But today, the club's dive coach said her technique had improved dramatically.

Jenn waved her hand in front of Mika's face. "Earth to Mika."

"Yeah?" She plopped down on the bean bag in Jenn's bedroom, and her cousin smirked. "What? Why are you looking at me that way?"

"Are you gay?"

"What?" Mika's stomach muscles tightened. "No." Why had Jenn popped that question out of nowhere? Had she done something stupid that Jenn noticed?

"It's okay if you are."

"What makes you think I'm gay?" If Jenn had figured it out, who else had guessed?

Jenn eased down onto the other bean bag. "You know I don't believe in all that Catholic conservative crap like Mom and our grandparents. They'd jump in front of a train if the priest told them to."

"I know you're not like them. But why ask that?" Mika held her breath.

"Your jeans and T-shirts are plain like a dude's. Your hair's short." Jenn laughed. "You exercise a lot and have muscles as big as most of the guys your age. And your posters—"

"What about my posters?" Her mouth went dry.

"You have posters of Megan Rapinoe and other fit women. You've got some on your computer screensaver too." Jenn nudged her knee. "You never talk about guys, and I catch you glancing at the girls in their swimsuits." She grinned wider. "Never the guys."

"I'm sizing up the competition, that's all."

Jenn grinned and grabbed Mika's phone. "Nice home screen of the beach. Love Hayley Kiyoko's swimsuit."

Damn, she should have locked the screen. "Give it back." She yanked it out of Jenn's hand.

"Have you ever had sex?"

"What the fuck, Jenn? Just because you've been smashing your boyfriend for two years doesn't give you the right to get your ass all up in my business." Mika pushed up from the floor so fast that her balance briefly wavered. She'd shared so many things with her cousin, but whatever she shared would be her decision and not Jenn's.

"Hey, I'm sorry, cuz." Jenn stood. "I just want you to know that I don't care how you identify. I'm there for you. Everyone should be free to be who they want. And I know your best friend is Benjy, but trust me, you don't want to talk to dudes about sex."

"Great. If you're done with your speech, let's work on your project."

"It's not due until mid-January. Like, who the hell assigns homework over the holidays? And I'm not going to work on it in Wyoming."

"Don't remind me about Christmas. I'm jealous enough." Mika sat at the desk and typed in Jenn's password. "Let's get on with it because I'm betting you haven't started." When it came to school, Mika had no idea how her cousin would graduate when she did so little work.

"It's Saturday. Let's watch a movie, geek." Jenn punched her shoulder.

"But—" The Lavigne Family Tree suddenly filled the screen. "What's this?"

"My assignment."

Mika narrowed her eyes and glared at Jenn. "I thought you had a history assignment."

"I do. We're supposed to create a simple family tree and pick an ancestor, then write about the region they're from and any historical events, but the tree's already done." Jenn grinned. "Mom opened the account a long time ago. She's horrible with basic computer skills, and she screwed it up by adding some relatives twice and linking a son as someone's spouse. So she paid me to fix it, and she's been paying me to research and add ancestors. It's not too hard."

"Let me get this straight. You say you hate history but have no problem going through historical records."

"There are hundreds of DNA matches, and Mom pays me to match each one and dig up stories and info. I've linked tons of Lavignes in the US and Canada to our tree," Jenn said. "So my homework is nearly complete." Jenn took the mouse from Mika and brought up DNA matches for Mika's dad. "It's easy, but most matches past third cousins are a dead end because people sometimes list wacky user names or don't share any information."

Mika tensed her muscles while a million thoughts ran through her mind. "Can you test me?"

"I hate to point out the obvious, but you're adopted."

Mika tuned out Jenn's chatter as she flipped through tabs, not wanting to hear why she didn't fit in...*again*. Jenn's yacking came to a screeching halt.

"Oh, I get it." Jenn's eyes lit up. "Maybe your bio family has tested. But why are you so interested? Your mom and dad are great."

Jenn wasn't being judgmental, but Mika looked down. "They are. I couldn't have asked for better parents, and I love them, but I've always wondered about things. Like, do I look like my bio family? Why did my mom give me up? Maybe she was a single teenager." *Or maybe she just didn't want me.* Mika shrugged. "You know, stuff like that."

"Your parents never talked to you about it?"

"I asked Mom a couple of times. She said she doesn't know anything about my birth parents." Mika rubbed her neck. She bolted upright and waved her hand. "Forget it. Your mom will find out, and I don't want her telling my parents."

"Dork. She'd never know. Mom handed the site over to me. There's a feature to run reports, and that's all I show her." Jenn rubbed her nails on her shirt and blew on them. "I know you're awestruck by my genius."

"What would it take?" Mika chewed on her fingernail.

"A simple cheek swab." Jenn snapped her fingers. "I have a kit because Mom ordered extras."

"Test me," Mika blurted out. "But I'm not eighteen, and my allowance isn't even close to yours."

"Don't be a chicken. I'll pay for it, and we can make up a name and an age for you."

"No. We can't lie."

Jenn frowned. "Why not?"

The only thing Mika didn't like about Jenn was her easy ability to lie. But Mika wanted some answers, and this was the only way she could get them. "You're sure your mom won't see it?"

"Stop being so paranoid." Jenn rolled her eyes. "She left her freaking notebook full of passwords with me to take a phone call and didn't ask for it back until the next day. She thought I'd only use it to access this site, but I saved them all." Jenn laughed and bumped Mika's shoulder. "I've been ordering things for a couple of years using her credit cards, and she's never noticed."

Mika's dad was a successful lawyer, but he never flaunted his money like his sister, who was drowning in cash since her divorce from Jenn's dad. Her Lavigne grandparents were more than comfortable, and their large Wyoming ranch did really well.

Jenn snapped her fingers. "So whatcha gonna do? Come on. No one will find out."

The possibility of discovering her birth parents and where she came from was too much of a temptation. "Okay, let's do it."

After they'd done Mika's DNA test, Jenn picked up her car keys to drive them to the post office. That was another difference between them. Jenn had her driver's license and a car while Mika was still hoofing it. But she shouldn't complain. Her twenty-minute walk was only torture in the winter when she couldn't get a ride with her parents.

"Mom, Mika and I need to go out and grab a book from a classmate. We won't be long."

Aunt Pauline nodded. "Okay. Be home before ten p.m."

Later that night, they watched a movie and went to bed around midnight. Mika snuggled into the trundle bed while Jenn carried on about her favorite actors. This one had abs of steel. That one had a mustache that she wondered what it would feel like to kiss since she'd only kissed guys with a clean-shaven face. Mika tried to discuss the movie's plot, but nothing shifted Jenn's focus from drooling over the guys.

"What about you? Any actor or actress catch your fancy?" Jenn rolled over and looked down at her.

Jesus, she wasn't giving up with her crowbar. "It's late. I want to sleep."

Aunt Pauline burst into the room, and the hall light shone around her like a spotlight from behind. She looked at Mika. "Girls." She rubbed her hands up and down her arms. "Come downstairs, please." Her voice cracked then she put her hand over her mouth and cried.

"What's wrong, Mom?" Jenn threw back the bed covers as her mom turned and hurried out of the room. "Get up, Mika." Jenn tugged her arm.

Downstairs, Aunt Pauline paced back and forth as she continued to cry. Mika's heart pounded as she sat with Jenn on the sofa and waited for her aunt to calm down. Finally, she sat beside Mika and placed her arm around her shoulders.

"Honey..." She pulled Mika in tighter.

Mika's stomach rolled. What the hell had happened, and what did it have to do with her?

"A truck hit your parents' car."

The room spun out of focus. This couldn't be real. Mika felt Jenn's hand over hers, but it did nothing to comfort her. "What hospital are they in?"

Aunt Pauline squeezed her shoulder and kissed her cheek. "I'm so sorry, honey." Her bottom lip quivered. "They didn't make it. Neither did your grandparents."

"What do you mean?"

"They died," her aunt said between sobs.

No, no, no, no. Mika struggled to breathe. Tears clouded her eyes. "You're wrong. They can't be dead."

"I wish I were."

"No." She pushed her aunt away and stood. "We have to call the police. Tell them to double check. It's a mistake." She sank to the floor and buried her head, which felt like a giant weight. She rolled to the side and sobbed. "This can't be real."

Chapter Five

MIKA'S EARS RANG, TEARS blurred her vision, and snot oozed down her face with each heave of her chest. This fucking nightmare couldn't be true. Watching her parents' caskets being lowered in the ground was like a scene from a movie she was watching from above. It was too much.

Aunt Pauline held out a tissue, but she didn't take it. Aunt Val put her arm around her and held out a rose, her mom's favorite flower. Mika gripped it above the cloth wrapped around the stalk, and the thorns cut into her skin. The pain was nothing compared to her raging sorrow.

"Sweetie," Aunt Val said, "hold the rose at the bottom. You're bleeding."

Who the fuck cares? And don't call me sweetie. Mika wiped her sleeve across her eyes and nose.

"It's time to say goodbye, honey," Aunt Pauline whispered and pulled Mika forward.

No! But her weak legs made resistance useless. Her body shook with heavier sobs, and she collapsed to her knees as she tossed the rose onto her mother's casket. How was she supposed to carry on when her parents had been ripped away?

Her aunts helped her stand. When Aunt Val tried to hug her, Mika stepped toward Aunt Pauline instead. Mika held her tight for several minutes, then she hugged her dad's parents.

"Honey, you're freezing. It's time to go home now," Aunt Pauline said.

Mika stumbled against the wind as she walked to the car, and Aunt Pauline wrapped her arm around her waist. Halfway there,

Mika saw Willow, Benjy, Tiana, and Wes standing together. She lowered her head, not wanting them to see her like this. When they reached the long line of vehicles, Aunt Pauline led her to Aunt Val, who was holding the passenger door open. Mika glared at her. "I'll ride with my cousins."

"Honey, you're going home with Aunt Val. You can visit us soon." Aunt Pauline gently shoved her toward Aunt Val's BMW.

"Fine." Mika looked back as Aunt Pauline slid behind the wheel of her Cadillac Escalade. Her grandparents glared at Aunt Val before getting inside. Not once did the grands talk to her.

Everyone had been surprised that her parents had chosen Aunt Val to be her guardian. Surprised didn't cut it for Mika; she was fucking pissed. What the hell were they thinking? She knew Aunt Pauline, and she'd bothered to spend time with her, unlike Aunt Val. Mika balled her hands into fists and stepped toward Aunt Val, ready to tell her exactly what she thought, but two elderly women walked up. One of them looked about a hundred years old.

"We're sorry for your loss," one of them said. "Your mother and I played pinochle with the other women after church for almost thirty years."

"Very sorry." The other woman reached out with a shaky hand and lightly touched Mika's cheek before she looked at Aunt Val. "Your daughter looks just like you."

"Oh, dear. Please forgive my mother. She's dealing with some memory loss." She gestured toward them. "Mother, this is Mary Hayden's daughter, Val, and her niece, Michaela Lavigne. Andrew and Hannah Lavigne were Michaela's parents."

The older woman scrunched up her face. "Who?"

Mika jumped in the car and slammed the door. She couldn't block out her aunt's muffled apology for her behavior. She could behave any way she goddamn liked; her parents were dead. And why did she have to live with Aunt Val anyway? She hadn't cared enough to visit for years, and now she was supposed to be Mika's guardian. Fuck that.

The silent drive home was a killer. Mika stared out the side window and gritted her teeth to stop her crying, but tears still ran down her cheeks.

"I think it would be good for you to see a therapist. Pauline agrees with me, so I made an appointment for you." Aunt Val pulled into the driveway. "How about I order us a pizza for dinner?"

"I'm not hungry." Mika jumped out and slammed the door as hard as she possibly could, and the car rocked. Mika ran up to her bedroom. Yeah, her fucking world had crashed, but what gave her aunt the right to make an appointment with a shrink without asking her?

The next day, Mika got up late. Needing to work some kinks out of her body, she stretched briefly then turned on some music to distract her thoughts and began her workout. She went past her usual fifty push-ups and didn't stop. The pain burning through her shoulders and biceps was nothing compared to the pain crushing her heart. She collapsed face down. Her muscles quivered as her tears soaked into the throw rug. Several minutes passed before she stood and wiped her eyes.

Her stomach growled. After skipping dinner last night, she should try to eat something. She put her ear to the door to make sure her aunt wasn't around, then tiptoed down the stairs. She glanced around the corner into the living room, and when she didn't see anyone, she hurried into the kitchen.

She wanted a coffee, but she bet that Aunt Val would think she was too young for the caffeine. She'd likely pour her apple juice and want to make fucking Mickey Mouse pancakes. Mika popped a coffee pod in the machine anyway and pressed the button, hoping the Keurig wouldn't bring her aunt running. She went to open the fridge and almost tripped on one of the cats. They rubbed against her legs and begged for food.

"All right. I'll feed you, furball whiners." Mika opened a can of wet food, and the family's pudgy tabby and humungous blue-gray Maine coon rushed to their bowls. Mika took a deep breath and held it, but it did no good. Her eyes filled with tears. She knelt and petted the lovable beasts as they gobbled down their food. They were like extra messy kids, and now they were the only family Mika had. She sniffled. Missy, the tabby, was Mom's favorite. Mom had saved her from the animal shelter. The Maine Coon put up with Mom and Dad but took a liking to Mika. She'd spotted him in the pet store and begged Dad to adopt the tiny kitten. Then the little booger doubled his weight twice before his first birthday, and they renamed him Mr. Big. She loved the furballs, but she thought of her parents every time she saw them.

She wiped her eyes with her sleeve, then turned back to breakfast. With her coffee mug in one hand and hard-boiled eggs in a bowl in the other, she carefully walked out of the kitchen.

"Good morning," Aunt Val called out from the living room. "Is this your phone? It's really nice."

Mika silently swore for leaving it downstairs. She probably had a billion texts from Jenn and Benjy. And now there was no way to avoid her aunt. "Yeah." She put her bowl on the end table and held out her hand. "I need it back."

"Sit down for a minute, please." Her aunt handed it over. She looked at Mika's mug and raised her eyebrow.

Busted. There's no mistaking the smell of coffee, but Aunt Val didn't say anything. Mika sat in a chair farthest away. "I'm gonna eat while you talk." If her aunt was going to deliver a long *I care about you* speech, she didn't need it.

"I have a meeting with the lawyer tomorrow to go over the estate. There are some critical papers I need to sign. Marianne will be here. Her two employees will clean the house, but she mentioned baking cookies with you."

"Yeah, right. Like I've ever made cookies with her. I'm not a kid that needs babysitting." This was bullshit. "Just because our neighbor owns the service doesn't mean she comes over with her employees. She only does that if there's a problem."

"Okay. Then you can listen to music or whatever you like to do."

Mika leaned her elbows on her knees and stared at her aunt. "What is it with you? Why have you left your freaking queen's throne in Boston just for me? Oh, I get it. Dad made lots of money, and this big house is in the best part of Ithaca. I don't know real estate, but I'm sure our wooded six acres near Cayuga Lake is worth a lot of money. I bet that's what you're after."

"No. How could you think that?"

"There's no reason for you to be here now." Mika looked hard at her and ignored the look of horror on her face. "You don't care. You last visited when the dinosaurs roamed the earth." She bolted out of the room.

"Mika, please—"

"Save it," she yelled as she ran up the stairs to her bedroom. She pushed her dresser in front of the door just in case Aunt Val had followed. Tears clouded her eyes.

"Mika." Her aunt lightly tapped on the door. "Please talk to me."

"Go away." She dove under her bedsheets to muffle her crying. Nothing she could do would bring her parents back. The dresser scraped across the floor. "Stop, or you'll scratch the hardwood." Mika looked over to see Aunt Val stick her face through the crack of the door.

"I regret letting my job take up my life and not visiting often. I miss my sister, and your dad meant a lot to me too," Aunt Val said in a choked voice.

"Sure. Just leave me alone now." After the door closed, she pulled the pillow over her head and sobbed. The pain just wouldn't go away. The things she'd shared with her parents would never happen again. They wouldn't be there for another swim meet or to see her graduate. Hiking would never be the same without them. Her mom used to go on and on about birds and flowers with Mika zoning in and out. But now, she'd give anything to hear the excitement in her mom's voice. And the observatory visits wouldn't be the same without her dad.

She pounded her fist on the bed. Eventually, she stopped

crying. Her eyes were sore, and she didn't have the strength to raise her head. She didn't want to sleep either, but her body and soul were so drained that she couldn't get out of bed.

Her eyelids slid slowly shut, and a memory of her dad came into focus. *Goodnight, kiddo. Don't worry about the woulda, coulda, shoulda. Move on. You're strong, and you'll make it.* She hoped that was true, but it was so fucking hard.

Chapter Six

THE COLD FROM THE wooden bench seeped into Mika's bones. If someone came up and tapped her on the shoulder, she felt sure her brittle body would break into a million pieces. It'd been days since the funeral. She couldn't remember exactly and didn't give a fuck. Tonight, she had to get out of the house. Death hung over the place and smothered any happy memory that popped into her mind. The truck driver had also died when he took her family's lives. It was bad karma, but she wished his family just as much pain as he'd caused her.

Benjy strode up to her. "Lavigne, what the hell are you doing?"

She slumped over with her elbows on her knees and regretted calling him. "Why did you come?"

"Because I'm your friend. You do know the park closes at ten, right?" He sat down beside her. "I can't imagine how you feel but freezing your butt off isn't going to help."

She nodded and wiped her tears away with her jacket sleeve.

"You said that you might move in with your dope cousins. I wouldn't see you much if you did."

"No. I thought about it because I can't stand being in my house right now." She rolled her lip between her teeth and sniffled. "Jenn and I are close, and her private club with its Olympic pool is fun. But Aunt Pauline is too uptight and nosy. Plus, I'd have to go to the Catholic Girls' School. No fucking way am I wearing a dress uniform and taking religious lessons."

Benjy laughed. "Yeah, you'd look pretty weird in a dress, but if you're thinking of going to church, you know you're welcome at mine anytime."

"The UU Church is cool, and I like going with you guys. But after what's happened," Mika tightened her jacket around her, "I'm not sure there's a God anymore."

"Fair enough. Is your setup with your other aunt better?"

"It's okay." Mika had tried to give Aunt Val a chance, but her words sometimes pulled the scab off Mika's wounds. "I hate it when she tries to talk about my feelings. She was never there before, so fuck her; why does she suddenly care now? When I go to college, she can keep the house going and shut her mouth."

"Damn, that's extra, even for you. Didn't you say she was a workaholic and her lab's cancer drugs have improved peoples' lives by years? That's some high-key shit."

Mika shrugged and wiped her tears again. Her parents would have been shocked at her bitter, ugly words, but they weren't around, and Aunt Val could never fill the space they'd left.

"She's turned up for you now. That's gotta be something, right?" He leaned down inches from her face. "Look, I get it. You're angry, but don't let that drown you. And maybe you shouldn't take it out on your aunt. There's got to be a reason that your mom picked her to be your guardian."

Mika shrugged. "Yeah, but I don't know what. It's annoying as shit that there's a secret everyone's keeping from me. Like, why did Grandpa and Grandma Hayden hate her so much?"

"Whoa. Hate's a strong word." He bumped her shoulder. "You should talk to someone that's outside your family, like the school counselor. I heard it helps to shout out your anger and stuff when it's someone who doesn't know your family."

She sniffled. "She's made me an appointment with a therapist near Cornell University. I don't know what I'll say or do. I'm not going to kill myself. It just fucking hurts. All the time."

"Can I give you a hug?"

She looked at him, unsure for a moment, then nodded. His arms around her felt good, and she let her tears fall. "Don't get any ideas. We're just friends."

He laughed. "You're safe. I don't think I'm your type anyway. Now, let's get the hell out of here. I'm cold, and you're a popsicle."

A chill ran through Mika and not from the cold. Jenn and Benjy dropping hints about her made her want to hide even more. She loved them, but who she liked was no one's fucking business.

"Come on." He bumped her shoulder. "I'll walk you home."

"Okay. But I don't wanna talk anymore," she said, and they headed home in silence.

"We've been best friends since we were kids," Benjy said when they neared her house. "I know girls don't like to talk to dudes. But hey, you know I'm chill. You're like my sister."

Mika teared up. He really was the best friend anyone could ask for, and she felt guilty for getting angry earlier. "Thanks, Benjy." She was grateful when he didn't say more. She watched him walk away, then turned to the house. Aunt Val'd probably be pissed that she left, but she wasn't a baby.

Mika opened the door gently and shut it quietly. Her aunt sat on the sofa with her laptop. Straight ahead, in the living room, was the family's twelve-foot-tall Christmas tree, taunting her to be shiny and happy when all she wanted to do was destroy the world.

Aunt Val looked up. "I didn't know you were out. It's getting late."

Mika didn't answer and just stared at that fucking tree she and her parents had decorated, like they had every year...but like they'd never do again. Every time she came in, that damn tree was in full view. Christmas was next week, but she didn't want any part of it. There was nothing to celebrate, and she didn't care if she ever saw another Christmas. And what the fuck was she supposed to do on her mom and dad's birthdays?

"Where have you been? You're cold."

She felt her aunt's hand on her arm, but Mika continued to stare at the tree. *Fuck Christmas.* She ran full force at it and pushed the tree over, knocking over a lamp and other knick-knacks in the process. She kicked a gift across the room.

"STOP."

She ignored her aunt's tug on her arm and further pleas and continued to stamp and kick the presents. They'd all been so neatly wrapped, but her life had come undone. When Aunt Val managed to yank her off, they both fell on their asses. Mika jumped up, ran upstairs to her room, and slammed the door. Aunt Val was right behind her and opened it before she could lock it.

"What are you doing? This is my bedroom." Mika slumped on her bed, too spent to shove her aunt out of the room.

"We need to talk." Aunt Val sat beside her.

"Get out."

"Listen to me, sweetie."

"Don't call me that. Only my mom calls me that." Mika shoved her aunt hard, and she fell, her head missing the desk by a foot. Mika blinked through her tears and looked at her hands as if they'd acted without her consent.

Aunt Val rose, her eyes wide. "I know you're hurting but lashing out at me won't help." She sat back down next to Mika and rested her hand on Mika's arm.

"Leave me alone." Mika wiggled away. She rolled onto her stomach, buried her face in the pillow and sobbed. "I...I miss them. It's so fucking unfair."

"I miss them too."

Several seconds of silence passed, and her aunt remained on the edge of her bed.

"You need to find a way to channel and process your pain. It's too late now, but I'll try and schedule an appointment with your therapist tomorrow."

Mika sat up. "I'm sorry that I pushed you."

She brushed Mika's hair back. "I know. I hurt too, but it's even harder for you. You should have had so many more years of happiness with them. I could never fill their shoes, but I'm going to try my best to help. I'll listen when you want to talk. And I won't lie; the pain you're going through will take some time to lessen, but there'll come a day when you can look back at the good times and laugh and find happiness."

Something in the sound of Aunt Val's voice moved Mika. But if she cared so much, why had she been like a ghost? "You didn't get along with anyone in this family. Why did you leave Boston to come here? There's no way this compares to being the top dog of a major company."

Tears welled in her aunt's eyes. "I needed a break, but I'll go back part-time in January—online. That'll give me the flexibility to stay in Ithaca because I want you to be near your friends. As for my disagreements with your parents, I made up with them years ago."

"So why didn't you visit then?"

Aunt Val swallowed. "I was wrong, and that will forever haunt me. But I can't change the past. We can only go forward."

Another bullshit deflection, just like everyone else had given her. "I want to go to bed now. Please leave me alone." Mika curled up on her bed and faced the wall. Why was everything such a mystery? She wasn't a baby. They were all hiding something from her, and she was damned well going to figure it out.

Chapter Seven

COMFORTABLE CHAIRS AND LOTS of fancy paintings, some with neon colors, couldn't change how Mika felt—like shit. Why did she have to see a shrink? She sure as hell didn't want to talk to some stranger, but Aunt Val made the appointment and Benjy said a counselor might help, so she'd promised to go. Fine, she'd give it a shot for a little while to keep the peace and drop it if she didn't like it.

The door opened, and a woman with long dark hair smiled and stretched out her hand. "Hello, Mika, I'm Dr. Iliana Papadopoulos. Feel free to call me Iliana."

"Hi." Mika sighed, then slowly shook her hand. It was kind of weird calling the doctor by her first name. Was she that friendly? Or was it some sort of technique to get people to quickly trust her? Whatever.

As Iliana said hello to Aunt Val, Mika looked into her pretty face. She sure wasn't what Mika expected. She thought the doctor would be older with gray hair. But Iliana was probably about her aunt's age, and her accent was slightly British. Not real strong, but Mika could pick it up after watching all those *British Bake-Off* episodes with her mom. She never did get better at making German chocolate cake, and now she never would. Mika swallowed hard and closed her eyes; she wouldn't break down right out of the gate.

"Shall we?" Iliana gestured to her office.

"I guess."

More paintings hung inside Iliana's office. A desk was in front of a wall lined with books from the floor to the ceiling. Mika would be okay if they could talk about rockets and science fiction. Two lounge chairs, a sofa, and a coffee table were opposite from the desk. Gee, was Iliana going to serve tea too?

"Sit anywhere you'd like. I have a fridge with soda pop, water, and juice. Would you like something?"

Mika sat in the middle of the sofa. "Pizza and a lemon lime."

Iliana laughed. "Sorry, it wasn't a pizza night. Maybe next time." She poured a water for herself and handed Mika a Sprite. "Mika, our conversation is confidential. I won't tell your aunt anything we discuss unless I believe your life is in danger." She took a drink, then sat in one of the chairs and crossed her legs.

She had nice long legs. "Yeah, I bet you two never talk." Mika stretched out with her arms resting on the back. She crossed her ankle over her knee.

"Your aunt had to give me some initial information, but anything between us is safe. I'm here to help." The doctor placed her drink on the coffee table, put on her reading glasses, and picked up a pen and pad of paper. "Would you tell me a little about yourself?"

Mika chugged some soda then put the can down. "Nope. You first. You sound British, but your last name sounds Greek. Why?" She bit her lip to keep from smiling when Iliana raised an eyebrow and also seemed to suppress a smile. She'd make a nice warrior princess in one of the online games Benjy was working on. So let the games begin, princess.

"These sessions are about you, not me, Mika."

"I filled out your form." *After* Aunt Val bugged the crap out of her. "If you want me to be comfortable and call you Iliana, tell me something about you."

"Fair enough." Iliana smiled. "My father's third generation Greek-American, and my mum is British. I was born in England, and we moved to the US when I was young. My bachelor's degree is from the University of Cambridge, and my medical degree is from Harvard."

"Impressive." Mika stared for a few seconds. "Why did you decide to be a psychiatrist? Aunt Val gave me your bio, but I didn't read it. Does she think I need meds?" She picked up her soda can and watched Iliana's face as she drank.

"No, she didn't mention medication. I chose this career because I wanted to help young people who'd been through traumatic events. Mika, just because I'm a psychiatrist doesn't mean you need additional medications." She leaned over and looked Mika in the eye. "As an MD, I have access to your medical file and know that you've been on a low dose of anti-anxiety medication for panic attacks for a while now. You've refused prior therapy back in junior high school. It'd help if you told me why the panic attacks started, because your recent trauma could make things worse."

Mika swallowed. "I was being bullied at school, but I can handle it."

"Do you want to talk about it more?"

She gritted her teeth. "No."

"Okay. So what should we talk about?"

"You know what I've been through. Have you ever been through anything like that?" She placed her soda can down hard and crossed her arms. She bet the well-educated doctor had only read case studies.

"No two people are alike. Trauma comes in many forms and magnitudes, and each person reacts differently. Some bounce back quickly, while others struggle throughout their life. For most people, the pain never goes away, but it lessens over time. They learn better ways to cope, and they find happiness again. And yes, I've suffered trauma over the loss of my mum." Iliana paused. "I feel sad on her birthday and sometimes at Christmas, but I've found ways to manage my pain, and my extensive training has enabled me to help others. I want to help you. Your aunt says you like sports and online gaming. Tell me about that." Iliana smiled again.

Mika cracked her knuckles. Okay, she could do this. She talked about swimming but didn't mention Willow. She was a secret treasure whom Mika didn't want to talk about with anyone, so she talked about Benjy instead. "I love to watch hockey." She bit her lower lip. That was her and Dad's favorite. Flashes of her parents invaded her mind.

"Sounds fun. Do you play hockey?"

"No. I just love to watch it. I prefer swimming because there's less chance of getting my teeth knocked out."

Iliana chuckled a second, then several seconds of silence passed.

Mika had to change the subject before she broke down and cried. "Oh, I do a lot of exercises to keep my body in shape." She felt like Iliana was a scientist studying her like a bug that caused disease.

"When do you exercise?"

"Whenever I feel like it." Morning, before lunch, and night. Mika didn't really keep track. Why the fuck did it matter anyway?

"Physical exercise doesn't usually affect sleep, but there is an exception. New studies have found that high intensity exercising late at night makes it difficult to fall asleep and results in poorer sleep quality. So, you might want to work out earlier."

"I suppose." *And should I drink warm milk too?* Mika played with the tab on her can.

"Are there any nights you don't sleep?"

Mika tightened her jaw. "Yeah."

"How many hours do you typically get?"

"Maybe four." Mika wiggled the pop can tab until it broke off. She tossed it on the table, plopped the can down, and a little spilled over the edge.

"Okay. I'd suggest you try journaling. Write down how much you sleep every night, what you ate for meals and snacks, and what makes you happy or sad."

And that was exactly why Mika didn't want to come here. Like some extra English paper was going to make her feel better.

"Start off basic, then try to add a little more detail every few days. And Mika, I don't expect you to read it to me. It's only for you. Of course, you're welcome to share if you want, and you can talk about anything, but it's your choice."

Mika bit off her hangnail. "Sure." No way was she going to do that.

"Your aunt mentioned the Christmas tree. Would you like to talk about it?"

"It's fucking Christmas, and my family's dead!" She bolted up, walked to the window, and rested her forehead against the glass. "What the fuck do you want me to say?" Her time had to be up; she spotted her aunt's car in the parking lot and wanted to leave so bad, but she stood there, watching the wind whipping the snow around. It reminded her of the burial. She bit down on her lip, but this time, it didn't stop the tears from falling. The taste of blood filled her mouth. It wasn't the first time, and it wouldn't be the last. She pulled a tissue out her pocket and dabbed her eyes and mouth. "Sorry. I shouldn't be nasty to you."

"You can say anything you want in here, including fuck."

Mika couldn't help but laugh. "Sounds funny in your accent."

"As long as you're not violent, I don't have a problem."

"Violent like me kicking down the tree or pushing Aunt Val? Did she tell you about that?"

"Yes, she did, but she made it clear that her concern is for you."

Mika closed her eyes. What she'd done was awful. "I should apologize."

"I'm sure she'd appreciate that."

Mika sat again on the sofa. Shit, she was a total disaster. "I'm not normally this angry."

"You're under a lot of stress. It's hard to express feelings, even for adults. Sometimes anger just spills out. You're safe in here. Yell if you want. Pound your fists on the cushions. We're okay as long as you're not destructive toward yourself, me, or the things in my office." Iliana held a box of tissues out for her.

"Thanks." More blood oozed from Mika's lip; she held the fresh tissue in place.

"Your aunt was shaken up last night, but she's worried about you. She wants to help you." Iliana put her paper and pen down.

"I hope you'll come back after this session. Your pain and anger are real, and you'll have to fight to stop those demons from overwhelming you."

"She said this would be twice a week."

"That's what I recommended, but it's the holiday season. We wouldn't meet again until the first week of January. Will that be okay?"

Mika nodded.

"Good." Iliana pulled one of her business cards off the stack on the coffee table and wrote a number on the back, then held it out to Mika. She tapped the written number. "I don't think you're suicidal, but please call the crisis hotline if you experience those feelings. Now, our time will be over soon. Is there anything else you want to talk about before you go?"

"No." Mika stood and walked toward the door. She paused and swallowed. "I should probably clean up the tree mess."

"That would be a kind gesture to your aunt."

"Bye."

"Goodbye, Mika."

After a deep breath, Mika opened the door. Aunt Val was waiting for her, but they didn't talk as they walked out to her car.

"I'm craving ice cream. Do you want to go to the drive-thru? A big scoop of chocolate with salted caramel on a sugar cone sounds like heaven right now," Aunt Val said.

"Nope." Their awkward silence returned. "Salted caramel in a cup with chocolate drizzle and coconut flakes is much better."

Aunt Val chuckled. "You're right."

Mika turned and looked out the side window. She would apologize eventually because her aunt was clearly trying. And even though Mika would clean up the tree, she still didn't want to celebrate Christmas. Tears trickled down her face. Her parents were gone, and the joy of her favorite holiday had gone with them.

Chapter Eight

MIKA'S PHONE VIBRATED ON her desk, but she ignored it. She was playing a game against AI opponents because she wasn't ready to face her friends just yet. She finally paused her computer after the billionth ping and saw a text from Jenn.

hey, answer. dont u want to talk.

Mika groaned. *Busy Saturday, and I'd like to play my games. Later.* Her stomach growled. She'd only eaten toast for breakfast. When Aunt Val tried to get her to come down for lunch, all she grabbed was a banana. But she was really hungry now. She tossed down her phone and took off for the kitchen, trying to ignore the fucking Christmas tree and her aunt sitting on the living room sofa. "I'm getting a snack."

"I made eggplant parmigiana. It's in the fridge. I'll pop it in soon."

"Great." Mika flashed a fake smile. Once she was out of sight in the kitchen, she opened her mouth, stuck her finger in the middle, and made a gagging sound. "Eggplant and not chicken. Yeah, every teenager's favorite," she mumbled. Eating the cat food would be better than eggplant.

The front door bell sounded as she turned to go back and hide in her bedroom. She heard Aunt Val answer it, and then the smell of curry wafted through the air. Mika rushed into the foyer. Mrs. V and Benjy were at the door.

"Hello, Ms. Hayden. I'm Shabana Van Aken, and this is my son, Benjy. I hope we're not disturbing you." Mrs. V held a tray with two dishes while Benjy held one.

"Not at all. Please come in." Aunt Val stepped back to let them enter.

"I've come to pay my respects. I was out of town on family business at the time of the funeral. My apology that my husband, Garrett, isn't here. He's working." Mrs. V turned to Mika. "Hello, young lady. I made your favorite foods, including murgh makhani."

Benjy's mouth twisted, and Mika was surprised he didn't laugh out loud. No way in hell was she ever a lady. "Hi, Mrs. V. Hey, Benjy. Thanks for the food." And thank God for Indian buttered chicken instead of eggplant.

"Hey."

Mika high-fived him a little too hard, and the dish that he had in his other hand wobbled.

"Thank you so much. It smells heavenly," Aunt Val said. "Can I carry something?"

"We've got it," Mrs. V said.

"Let's put the food on the dining room table. I'm sure Mika will want to eat soon." Aunt Val glanced at her.

"Oh, yeah. No one can cook like Mrs. V." Mika had missed seeing them.

As they walked toward the dining room, Mrs. V stopped at the living room door. "Oh, goodness. What happened to the Christmas tree?"

Embarrassment flooded through Mika.

"Just a small accident. We haven't had time to clean it up," her aunt said.

Mika had to give Aunt Val credit for covering up their argument. But she could hear the disappointment in her voice.

"This holiday season will be tough, but it'll get better," Mrs. V said.

"Thank you." Aunt Val turned to Benjy. "Are you in college?"

That was a stupid question. Okay, so Benjy's goatee made him look maybe twenty, but... God. Was Aunt Val thinking he was her honey boo? That thought was just gross.

"We're both juniors. I've known Mika since third grade." Benjy jammed his hands in his front pockets.

"I remember seeing you at the burial. Thank you for being there for Mika."

He nodded. "That's what best friends are for."

"I am so sorry for your loss." Mrs. V's expression was filled with compassion. "I can't imagine what you're going through. May I hug you?"

Mika saw Aunt Val hesitate then nod. She hoped her aunt wasn't a racist like her grands. Mrs. V hugged her. Benjy's mom was so full of kindness, and her hugs were the best, just like her food.

"I'm sorry too," Benjy said.

If Mika didn't turn this conversation around, she'd be in a pool of tears. "This is bussin'. I haven't been eating much, but you know I love your food, Mrs. V." She smiled through her tears. "Let's eat now."

"The food is just for you and your aunt," Mrs. V said.

"Please stay. Everything smells so wonderful," Aunt Val said.

"It would be an honor." Mrs. V bowed slightly with her hands together in prayer.

"Mika, could you please set the table while Shabana and I relax in the living room?"

"Sure." Good thing the living room was large, so the tree mess didn't take up the whole room.

"I'll help." Benjy followed her into the kitchen.

"Hey, grab the water glasses and fill them." She pointed to the cabinet. "I'll gather the plates and silverware."

"Wait a minute. What the hell happened to the tree?" Benjy whispered.

Mika hung her head. "You know I was sad at the park the other night. Well, I came home and saw the tree and got mad at that asshole who hit my mom's SUV head on." More tears clouded her eyes. When was all the pain going to end? Her eyes were permanently puffy. "Anyway, I don't want to have Christmas without Mom and Dad." She swallowed. "So I kicked it over."

He gently placed his arm around her shoulder. "You can't go around destroying stuff. That's not you. It all sucks, but you've got to talk to me. Is this why you haven't answered your phone?"

"Yeah." That and she didn't like crying in front of people. She grabbed a napkin to wipe her eyes. "Let's set the table before they come in here and get the wrong idea." She pushed Benjy's arm away and tried to laugh. "Hey, the adults can eat at the table, but let's do some gaming."

"I don't know."

Mika nudged his shoulder. "We always do when you come for lunch. Why should dinner be different?" She needed some fun and time away from the mysterious aunt who came in from nowhere.

After they set the table, Aunt Val and Mrs. V took a seat at opposite ends, clearly expected Mika and Benjy to join them. Her aunt looked confused when Mika and Benjy loaded their plates but didn't sit.

Mika stuck her fork in her pocket and grabbed her water glass. Benjy glanced at his mom, then looked wide-eyed at Mika. No way was she going to let him chicken out. "We like to play games and eat." She headed toward the basement, and he followed.

"Excuse me?" Aunt Val asked.

Mrs. V cleared her throat and glared at her son.

"You two can do grown-up talk while we eat in the basement. Look, I haven't played games with Benjy like forever, and gaming makes me feel better. Can we please go to the basement?"

The hard look Aunt Val gave her could've been *hell no* or *maybe*, but Mika didn't know her that well. She hoped her aunt wouldn't chew her ass out in front of Mrs. V. "Please?"

Aunt Val sighed.

"I kicked down the Christmas tree, Mrs. V." Mika looked up at her aunt. "I'm sorry. I promise to clean it up tomorrow. And I'll load the dishwasher tonight. May we please play games?"

Aunt Val's expression softened. "Thank you for taking responsibility. And I appreciate the apology."

Mika shifted on her feet, waiting for her aunt to give her permission to go downstairs.

Aunt Val steepled her fingers and tapped them together. "It's okay with me, but only if Shabana approves."

"Sure. Then I can share some juicy stories about the shenanigans these two pull," Mrs. V said.

"Great." Mika faked a laugh and left with Benjy behind her. Mrs. V was sweet and liked her. Hopefully, she wasn't going to tell her aunt too many embarrassing stories.

Walking down the steps, Mika thought about how Benjy's family had been so kind to her. And Mrs. V was the only one of Mom's friends that had stopped by or called since the burial. Did people just want to give her time? Or maybe they all knew why Grandpa and Grandma Hayden never talked about Aunt Val. Sooner or later, Mika was going to figure out her aunt's secrets.

The next day, Mika got out of bed early. Well, nine was early for her on a Sunday. She did some push-ups and sit-ups. But to get on Aunt Val's good side, she needed to get her ass downstairs and clean up the Christmas tree. She grabbed her phone and opened her bedroom door. A note was taped to it.

We're low on bread and out of eggs and milk. I'm going to run out quickly. Be back soon. Love, Aunt Val.

Mika looked back at her desk with breadcrumbs scattered everywhere. A bowl piled high with eggshells sat next to the nearly empty gallon of milk. She sometimes had midnight snacks but never this much. She couldn't remember when she'd snuck downstairs, cooked the food, and brought it up to her room. Her body froze with panic until she remembered cleaning the kitchen. Her phone dinged, and she looked at Benjy's text.

Hey stupid. I'm here to help with the tree. Let me in. 😉

She went to the door just as he knocked. "Morning, dude."

"Don't you look pretty in your PJs?"

She gave him the finger without turning around as she headed to the living room.

"My dog woke me up, or I wouldn't be here this early. Hey." Benjy gently grabbed her arm. "You should try working out your anger in the gym or something. This is fucked up."

"I know." She hated admitting mistakes, but there was no way she could hide from him.

"You're lucky it's fake, or there'd be needles everywhere."

After they'd stood the tree upright, they began putting the ornaments on it, though some had broken in the fall. Tears filled Mika's eyes when she found some with extra sentimental value. One was a paper heart she'd made in third grade with the words, 'I love you, Mommy and Daddy.' It was partially torn. "I need to get some tape." She held the ornament. "I'll be right back."

Mika barely made it to the kitchen before breaking down. She leaned against the cold granite countertop and sobbed. Like the heart, she was broken and felt empty.

"You okay in there?" Benjy called out.

"Yep. Just searching for the tape." She grabbed a piece of paper towel and wiped her eyes, not caring that it was rough against her skin. That was nothing compared to the fact that her whole life had been turned upside down. She found the tape and gently mended the heart, wishing it could be that easy to do the same for her own.

When she returned, Benjy gave her a long look. He couldn't miss her red, swollen eyes, but he didn't ask.

"You should open your presents with your aunt."

Mika hung her head. "It hurts too bad."

"I know, but your parents wanted you to have these gifts. They were cool parents like mine. And your aunt is trying her best."

When Aunt Val came in the front door and saw the Christmas tree, her mouth hung open for a second. "Thank you," she said softly.

"I'm sorry for what I did." Mika hated that she'd lost control. Everything was so fucked up. Lately, she behaved more like a junior high kid and not someone turning seventeen. But every day was a battle with pain and anger that lingered like food poisoning in her stomach.

"Apology accepted. Did you help, Benjy?"

"Yes, ma'am."

"Thank you so much." Aunt Val smiled. "Would you like to join us for brunch? I was going to fix omelets and pancakes."

"I gotta go, but thank you for the offer, Ms. Hayden. Here, let me help with the groceries. Mika's still half asleep." He took the bags and dropped them in the kitchen.

"You have a good friend there."

"Yeah. He's the best." Mika could feel her face flush.

"I'll see you at school soon. But you better hop online for games and stop by the house some time." Benjy bumped his fist to hers.

"Yeah, I'll play this Wednesday. I'll enjoy kicking your butt."

"In your dreams." He smiled then turned to Aunt Val. "Goodbye, Ms. Hayden."

"Take care, Benjy. You're welcome any time."

Mika opened the door for him and waved goodbye. *Shit.* She still had to survive this fucking holiday. She wished she could skip the whole thing and go back to school. She felt trapped in the house and needed to get out. Her classes would be a good distraction. More importantly, she wanted to see Willow. Even if they only shelved books and didn't talk, that'd help Mika feel better.

"How do you like your omelet?"

Mika took a deep breath. "Ham, cheese, and mushrooms. You don't need to fix pancakes, but thanks."

"Are you sure? I could make chocolate chip or strawberry pancakes."

Mika swallowed. *Don't cry.* Her dad was the master of strawberry pancakes. "Mm, strawberry would be great."

Aunt Val hugged her, and this time, Mika didn't raise a fuss. Having an aunt who hadn't been around for eons suddenly show up and take an interest was taking some getting used to. But sometimes, Mika couldn't help herself.

She remembered a moment with her dad. They were alone

and talking about swimming, and she was complaining about not beating the school's record the day before in the butterfly. He was fixing his famous Sunday pancakes when he turned and said, *Woulda, coulda, shoulda. Move on.* She wished moving on was as simple as saying those words.

Chapter Nine

Christmas Eve

MIKA SHUT OFF THE annoying alarm and glanced at her iPhone. Right above the time was the date–December 24th. *Fuck Christmas Eve. Fuck Christmas.* Her body was fatigued from night after night of falling asleep past two or three a.m., but she rolled out of bed, did a few stretches, and started her routine of sit-ups, lunges, and push-ups. Only she didn't stop at twenty reps each. When her muscles trembled under the strain, she collapsed on the floor and sobbed. Several minutes passed before her tears slowed. *I need fresh air.* She ran down the stairs and threw on her coat.

"Hold on." Aunt Val came out of the kitchen wearing an apron.

"I'm going for a walk."

"Where?"

"Look. I said I was sorry for kicking over the tree. I'm just going to the park. I'll be back soon." Mika yanked the door open.

"Okay, but please –"

Mika slammed the door. Her fast walk soon became a run, and she pushed herself harder. Her legs burned, and her chest heaved with each stride. Her tears became a river, and she collapsed on a park bench. The cold from the metal slats went right through her jeans and stung her skin.

How could she even think about Christmas without her parents and grandparents?

She pulled her knees up to her chest and buried her head. Her body shook from her sobs, and she'd messed up her coat from rubbing her nose on the sleeve. Gross, but she didn't have any tissues. Then she felt a blanket over her back. It smelled like the one that she'd just folded from the dryer.

"I'm sorry to invade your privacy, but I was worried about you. It's freezing out here." Her aunt pulled out a pair of gloves and tissues from her coat and held them out.

Mika took the tissue and blew her nose. Her hands trembled. They were fucking freezing. She didn't want to celebrate Christmas, and she didn't want to talk. Thankfully, Aunt Val didn't say anything else, and they sat in silence for a couple of minutes.

"I know it's hard for you to face the tree and decorations you put up with your family, but I also know that your parents loved you. Whether you believe in spirits or not, they're crying right now seeing you in so much pain."

Mika pulled the blanket up over her head. *You're not my mom. Go away.*

"To help you through today, I invited your Aunt Pauline and cousins over for lunch. I'm sorry, I should have told you, but I wanted to surprise you. They'll be here at twelve thirty. Why don't you come back, take a shower to warm up, and maybe take a nap? I'll wake you when they arrive."

Aunt Pauline had delayed going to Wyoming for Christmas for her? It would be good seeing them. She pulled the blanket back. "Thanks. I know you hate Aunt Pauline."

"I don't hate her. We have our differences, but we get along at times."

"You mean tolerate one another?"

"She loves you. Your cousins love you. Come home, please." She squeezed Mika's shoulder.

Mika blew her nose again.

"I'm cold to the bone, despite my extra padding," Aunt Val said. "You're so lean; you must be frozen. Mika, please. I'm so sorry that I wasn't around more. I love you."

Her aunt sounded like she was about ready to cry.

"I loved your parents. Yes, we fought sometimes, but we did

love each other. I miss them too." Her aunt held out her hand. "Sitting out in the cold and refusing to go on with life isn't what they would have wanted. Please."

Mika got up, and Aunt Val looped her arm through hers. She almost pushed her away, but she remembered Benjy telling her to give her aunt a chance. He was usually right about most things. They walked to the parking lot in silence. When she slid into the car, the sound of the seat belts snapping into place reminded Mika of the accident. She turned her head away and squeezed more tears out of her eyes. She had to think of something else before she was a puddle of snot again. "How'd you know where I was?"

"Don't be mad. I called Benjy's house. He told me this was your favorite park. Then I saw you running when I came close." Aunt Val began driving. "You should join the track team with your speed. You're like lightning."

Mika lost it. "Mom was on the track team in high school," she said even though her head and throat were clogged from all the tears. "She ran almost every other day, and I'd join her sometimes."

Aunt Val placed her hand over Mika's. "I'm sorry. I wasn't thinking."

They didn't talk for the rest of the trip home.

"I'm going to shower." Mika slowly moved up the stairs and stopped. She turned around. "Were you on the track team too?"

"No. Softball and tag football were my favorites."

"Yeah, they're fun, but I like swimming and running. I guess I like solo sports where I get to smoke the other girls."

Her aunt smiled. "I liked to smoke the other girls when we played dodgeball, especially the mean ones."

Mika laughed. "Me too. But now the gym teacher has to let any girl that doesn't want to play sit on the sidelines or do something stupid like dance or shoot baskets if the other court's open." She jammed her hand in her pockets. "I'll come down and help out after my shower."

"I'd like that very much." Aunt Val smiled.

Upstairs, Mika took twice as long in the shower, letting the warm water rinse away more tears. Damn, she could fill Cayuga Lake with as much as she had cried. She slowly dressed and made her way to the kitchen, where her aunt was sprinkling fried onions on top of the green bean casserole.

"Can I help?" Mika asked.

"Yes, thank you."

Mika busted up the cooked sweet potatoes with a hand masher then spread brown sugar on top. Mom liked them cut up in big pieces with a little sugar, but she mashed them and put in extra sugar because Dad liked them that way. Mika added even more sugar. *For you, Dad.*

Aunt Val gave Mika a one-arm hug. "Thanks. Looks perfect."

"No problem." Mika heard the front door open and shut. Dad's family never knocked.

Jenn burst into the kitchen. "We're here. I hope that food's edible since you're helping out." She bear-hugged Mika, and they swayed for a minute.

"You know that I only put poison in yours," Mika said.

"Love ya, cuz. It'll be all right," Jenn whispered in Mika's ear. She let go and waved to Aunt Val. "Merry Christmas."

"Merry Christmas."

Aunt Pauline hugged Mika but barely glanced at Aunt Val. Carla hugged them both. She was way better in school than Jenn, but she was too damn quiet for a sixth grader. Sometimes, it freaked Mika out.

The food was great, and Mika ate more than she had in the past couple of weeks. It was good to have her family around. Too bad her Lavigne grands couldn't stay for Christmas, but then they'd probably get into an argument with Aunt Val on social issues. "Could you pass the ham?" Fuck, she needed to change her attitude. "Sorry, please."

"Here you go. Save some room for Aunt Pauline's pie." Aunt Val winked.

"Oh, you're right. I'll take a slice each of pumpkin and cherry, please."

"I'm on it." Aunt Pauline rose and returned swiftly. "Take as much as you want. You're young and will burn it off."

Mika glanced at her aunts. It was no family secret that they didn't like each other, but strangely, they seemed to put their shit aside for tonight. Maybe it was all a show of unity for her.

Jenn served the pies and started telling funny stories and jokes. She and Mika laughed, but Carla only smiled. Maybe she felt left out by her extra-social sister. Seven years between her and Jenn was a lot.

"Hey. Got any jokes, Carla?" Mika asked.

She swallowed her food, then cleared her throat. "What did the duck say when he bought ChapStick?"

"I don't know. Do you, Jenn?" Mika hoped Jenn wouldn't roll her eyes or say something mean.

"No clue," Jenn said.

"Put it on my bill." Carla smiled brightly.

"That's a good one." Mika and her aunts chuckled, while Jenn just nodded. Geez, she didn't like to share the spotlight.

"Girls, let's go open presents." Aunt Val stood up. "I started a fire before our meal. The living room should be nice and toasty."

Shit. This was the moment Mika dreaded. Could she do this? It hurt so fucking bad, but she knew her mom and dad would want her to carry on.

"Let's go." Jenn jumped out of her chair like a Pop Tart coming out of the toaster. She left Mika and Carla sitting at the table.

"I don't know what I'd do if I lost my parents. They don't fight as much as they did before the divorce." Carla took Mika's hand. "It sucks what happened to your parents and your mom's parents. But we're here for you. And I bet they're watching you unwrap your presents from heaven."

"Thanks, Carla." Mika smiled through tears. So Carla had a super power after all. She was thoughtful, and kind, and a lot smarter than Jenn gave her credit for. Mika intertwined her fingers with Carla's, and they walked into the living room together.

Unwrapping the presents was a roller coaster between joy and sorrow. Mika tuned out a lot of the conversation and nodded every now and then. Her parents had given her a new MacBook, a pair of cozy UGGs, and a few gift cards. One card was from Java Heaven. Mika loved their croissant sandwiches and cupcakes. The last time she'd eaten in the place was with her mom in November.

"These are from me." Aunt Val handed her two boxes.

"I didn't get you anything." Heat creeped up her neck and filled her cheeks. Aunt Val always sent her a present every year, but Mika never did anything for her, not really. She'd pick one of the presents her mom had suggested, and her mom wrapped it and put Mika's name on it. But her mom hadn't gotten around to buying all the gifts, so there was nothing at all for Aunt Val.

"It's okay. Go ahead." Aunt Val shook the box gently.

Mika tore the paper off to see an ordinary box. But other wrapped boxes were inside. She looked up. "Looks like it's going to take me a century to unwrap." She ripped off the wrap and stared at the boxes that contained an SLR camera and expensive lens. "Wow. You even bought me a telephoto lens."

Aunt Val knelt down and rubbed her back. "Right after Thanksgiving, I was talking with your dad on the phone. He mentioned borrowing his friend's camera and how excited you got taking pictures. So I thought you'd like your own equipment. He said it was too expensive of a gift, but I insisted."

"Thank you." Mika wiped her eyes. She quickly let go and unwrapped the second box, which was a padded camera backpack with plenty of room for extras. "It's perfect." She checked the battery charge on the camera, then turned to Jenn and Carla. "Let's go outside and take pictures."

"You're kidding. It's cold." Jenn moved closer to the fireplace.

"I'll go." Carla jumped up.

Mika looked at her aunts. "I'll watch Carla. We won't be long."

"I'll leave the decision up to Aunt Pauline."

"Don't stay out too long," Aunt Pauline said.

"Great. Carla, you can take some pictures." Mika placed everything in the backpack. As she and Carla put on their coats, Jenn joined them.

"I'll go for a bit." Jenn crossed her arms.

"Chicken." Mika grinned.

Jenn, as usual, did most of the talking, but she headed back to the house after a block. It was too quiet without her. Mika broke the silence by giving Carla a few tips that she'd learned from her dad's friend, and Carla seemed like a natural. Mika was impressed with her shots of winter birds on the telephoto. Sure, her eleven-year-old cousin could be annoying at times, but Mika had underestimated her. "You're good. I'll bring the camera next time I come to your house. We can take more pictures."

Carla's face brightened. "You mean it?"

"Yep." Mika held up her hand for a high-five.

"Thank you." Carla slapped her hand. "You're way cooler than Jenn."

"Thanks."

"Do you know why I hate Russian dolls?"

Mika stopped. "No. Why?"

"They're so full of themselves." Carla grinned. "And so is my sister."

Mika burst out laughing. Who knew that today would end with her being almost happy? She put her arm around Carla's shoulder. "You're hilarious. Maybe you should be a comedian when you grow up. But don't tell your sister that one. She'll kill you for sure."

"Nah. Not over that joke, but she will when we get home." Carla grinned wickedly.

"Why?"

"Because she pissed me off. So I stole all her underwear, soaked them, and put them in the downstairs freezer."

That had Mika doubled over. "Oh. My. God. She'll kill you.

You've got guts. Sometimes, I wish I had a sister. Even one like you." Mika rubbed the top of Carla's head, like her mom and dad used to do to her. "Thanks for sharing Christmas with me, cuz."

"Thanks for taking me on a walk, big cuz." Carla slipped her arm around Mika's. "I'm trying not to be too much of a brat."

"You're not a brat." *Don't lie.* "You can be a little, ah, much at times, but you're cool."

"Really?" Carla's smile beamed under the street light.

Mika nodded. Her younger cousin hadn't ratted on her and Jenn for a while. Maybe she was changing for the better.

"I want to be like you when I get older."

"What do you mean?"

"You know. You seem to have everything together. You're smart and know what you want to do with your life."

Mika didn't think she had her shit together. "You're smart too, and you've got an eye for photography. Maybe one day your photos will hang in a famous museum."

"Thanks." Carla's face glowed.

They continued home in silence. Mika looked up to the snow-filled sky and sighed; she had to believe that her parents were in heaven. *I miss you so much, Mom and Dad.* There were times she was so lonely and felt out of control. Sure, she had family and a small group of good friends. But would that be enough when the darkness threatened to eat her alive?

Chapter Ten

"Yes, I got your ass again," Mika yelled into the computer mic and grinned. Although Benjy's menacing look might fool his classmates, she knew he was a softie. "Yo, bro, stop screwing up your face so tight, or you might end up permanently looking like that."

Tiana and Wes laughed.

"Dude, she's stolen your resources three times, and you never saw her coming?" Wes banged his hand on his desk and laughed.

Tiana threw up her hands. "Hey, man, move your mic. Every time you hit the desk, you bust my ears."

"Sorry. Are we playing again?" Wes sounded miles away.

"Now the mic's too far from your mouth," Benjy said. "Well, you fu—"

Mika saw Mrs. V enter the room over Benjy's shoulder.

"You've been video chatting and playing games long enough." She said hello to Mika and the others, then she removed the dish towel from her shoulder and flapped it at the back of Benjy's head.

Mika had seen Mrs. V do it a thousand times. She never hit very hard, and all it ever did was mess up his hair.

"Yes, Mom." He looked at them, his mouth shaped in a cocky half-smile.

"I asked you an hour ago to walk Toto. Now, I'll give you five minutes to stop and go get some fresh air," Mrs. V said.

When Benjy's mom left the room, Mika, Wes, and Tiana cracked up.

"Your dog's name cracks me up," Tiana said between chuckles.

"Yeah, is the *Wizard of Oz* your favorite movie?" Wes pounded the desk.

Benjy gave them the finger. "What about you, Mika? Any comments?"

"What were you about to say when your mom walked in?"

"I was about to say, I need to go, you fuckers."

The door flew open behind him, and his eyes widened as his mom walked in. She glared at him with her hands on her hips then looked at everyone else on Benjy's screen. "I know you teenagers curse, but I wish you wouldn't use that word." She crossed her arms. "And while you're at it, Benjamin Van Aken, Mrs. Henry needs help moving a piece of furniture."

"Yes, Mom. Bye, guys."

"It's been fun, but I have to go too," Tiana said. She waved, leaving Mika alone with Wes.

"So, it's just you and me. Ready to rumble?" He wiggled his eyebrows.

No way. Wes had been hitting on her since mid-November, and her subtle brush-offs hadn't worked. "I've got some chores to finish. Bye." After she'd signed off, Mika flopped on her bed and stared at the ceiling.

Now what was she going to do for the rest of the day? Maybe she should take her new camera outside. It was such a thoughtful gift. It hit her that she hadn't said another word of thanks since Christmas Eve and worse, she'd been holed up in her room or the basement the whole holiday. She just didn't want to talk about her painful reality.

Mika grabbed her camera and decided to ask Aunt Val to go for a walk with her. Maybe it'd help them get closer. She looked around downstairs, but her aunt wasn't in her usual spot. Mika went back upstairs and walked down the long hallway toward the guest room where her aunt was staying. It was next to her parent's bedroom and their adjacent study. Nothing had been cleaned out as far as she knew, and Mika wasn't about to go in there. As she got closer, she heard faint crying.

Mika pressed her ear against the door, and Aunt Val's cry ripped through her gut. She needed to do something. But if she knocked, her aunt would probably just muffle her crying and say everything was okay. Mika slowly turned the door knob and cracked the door.

"I've never told anyone but you, Amanda."

"It's going to take time, Val. You and Mika have an incredible amount of grief to manage."

Who was she talking to? Mika gritted her teeth and took a deep breath through her nose. Her aunt had no right to talk about her.

"I wish I could do more for her."

"Val, you're doing the best you can, and you're not Wonder Woman. You need to take care of yourself too."

"I know." Her crying turned to sobs.

Mika's anger melted. Her aunt was just as broken as she was. Then Mika remembered Aunt Val saying how she needed a friend too, and this Amanda sounded like she had good advice.

"Thanks, Amanda. You're the best therapist, but I...I just feel like some days are too much." Aunt Val blew her nose.

So not a friend. She slowly began to shut the door.

"Hannah and Andrew said Mika was doing well, but they didn't brag enough. She's such a bright young woman, but she's been crushed by this, and I feel so useless. How am I supposed to help her piece her life back together?"

Hearing her parent's names squeezed the air out of Mika's lungs, and tears clouded her eyes. When the door closed, she wanted to run away fast, but she couldn't let Aunt Val hear her heavy footsteps. Eavesdropping wouldn't earn her any brownie points, no matter how bright Aunt Val thought she was.

When she got far enough away, she ran down the stairs and grabbed her coat. She jogged to Stewart Park and spotted an empty bench between the willows. She sat on the top of a park bench with her feet on the seat. Her tears almost froze the instant they rolled down her cheeks.

A wind gust blew through, and the branches of the weeping willow swayed to a virtual snapping point. Crusting ice coated the southern part of Cayuga Lake, and gulls gathered in an unfrozen spot. Mom and Dad always warned her to stay off the ice, even the layers close to shore.

She sniffled. New Year's was two days away. Yesterday, Aunt Val had said something about going out for lunch, but Mika blew her off. She should reconsider after hearing how sad her aunt sounded but celebrating without her parents seemed wrong. She just wanted this damn holiday to be over with. Getting back to school would help channel her jumbled mind and hopefully help steady her emotions. The constant swinging between feeling okay and being slapped back down to reality was exhausting.

With a deep breath, she looked out at the lake again and let more tears fall. There wasn't anywhere—the lake, a park, a theater, a café—that she could go without memories of her parents, and it hurt like fuck.

Chapter Eleven

The alarm sounded, and Mika bolted out of bed. The holiday had passed, and it was time to go back to school. She needed to get busy with classes, but she also needed to see Willow. Nothing was going to erase December, but being around Willow would help her feel hope again. It was like everything stopped whenever Willow was around. And the slight touch of their hands caused Mika's heart to beat faster and her skin to tingle. But the best was looking into Willow's eyes and seeing her smile. It always made Mika feel warm and safe, and she needed that feeling now more than ever.

After her morning exercises and shower, she set about choosing something that expressed who she was in a way that would get Willow's attention. That meant going into *that* side of the closet. Taking a deep breath, she slid the door open to the left side and tried to ignore her black dress pants that would forever represent that fucking awful day. She grabbed her newest pair of blue jeans and searched for her Baby Queen T-shirt, then stopped. Tears came to her eyes, and her fingers trembled on the hanger holding her Taylor Swift Eras Tour long-sleeve T-shirt.

It was late May, and Taylor was playing in New Jersey, but Mika and her mom couldn't get tickets. That afternoon, Mika came home from school in a lousy mood. When she kicked off her shoes by the front door, her parents came through to the foyer. Mom was wearing a gray Taylor crewneck, and she held up a black, long-sleeve Taylor T-shirt. Dad was holding suitcases.

Mika would remember Mom's words forever: "This is for you. Sorry I couldn't get tickets. How about a weekend in the city?" That had been the best weekend with her mom in Mika's life. They didn't argue, Mom acted like a big sister, and they had a ton of fun.

Mika dropped to the floor, drew her knees to her chest and cried. She'd never have fun with her parents ever again. She crawled to the bathroom and stuck her head in the toilet. After she'd finished throwing up, she dragged herself up to the sink and washed her face again.

When she looked half-decent, she went back to the closet. She practically ripped a plain T-shirt off the hanger. She swallowed and looked at the Taylor tee again, remembering the time she told Benjy how one of the school bullies had made fun of her for being a Swiftie. Later that night, Mom had confessed she'd overheard their conversation. She told Mika not to listen to them, and said, "You know the woman is a genius."

Mika tossed the plain tee down and took her Taylor T-shirt off the hanger. As she pulled it over her head, her phone alarm sounded. Damn, she was running late. It'd be a grab and go breakfast.

Aunt Val was reading the *New York Times* in the kitchen. "Can I cook you some eggs?"

"Thanks, but toast is fine. I need to get going." Mika grabbed the loaf of bread and popped two slices in the toaster.

"I'll drive you—"

"No, it's a short walk." January had slammed in with freezing temperatures. Her parents used to drive her during extreme temperatures, but it'd just feel too weird with Aunt Val. And everyone at school was probably already talking about her new mysterious aunt. Mika buttered her toast, filled her water bottle, and grabbed an apple.

"Are you sure?" Aunt Val looked at her phone. "My app says it's twenty-six degrees with a windchill of sixteen. I should drive you."

"No, I'm fine. It's a short walk. Bye." Mika put her coat on and hustled out the door before her aunt could argue further. The cold wasn't what she was worried about today. The road to the high school went right past Lake View Cemetery. Her parents were buried in Frear Memorial Park, but seeing any cemetery would tear her up. Walking around the backside of the football stadium and through the back parking lot was her only option to avoid it.

She chewed her toast as she fast walked, trying to push away the negativity and concentrate on seeing Willow's sweet face. She'd seen Benjy a couple of times and played online with her gaming friends, but she hadn't seen Willow at all.

Benjy wasn't outside when she arrived. She took a breath and entered. The noise in the hallway sounded a hundred times louder than ever before as she edged her way to her locker. She accidentally bumped a few shoulders and muttered, "Sorry."

"There goes Moron Mika. But I guess she's Mourning Mika now."

She shuffled along but glared over at Jackson Thornton, aka Jack Daniels Thornton. She wanted to punch him in the face, but that would only get her suspended, and he wasn't worth it. The dumbass was a total plastered prick. She didn't know how the two connecting brain cells he had got him through school.

"Hey, don't listen to that jerk." Willow draped her arm around Mika.

The noise around them faded, and Mika's pulse increased with Willow's casual embrace. Willow had never done that before. And Jesus, she did it in public. Her touch was like a jolt of high voltage electricity. Mika had walked into school feeling miserable, hoping she could make it through the day without breaking down. But one touch from Willow and somehow, everything was a little brighter.

"I'm so sorry about your family." Willow bear-hugged her, then stepped back and entwined their fingers. "Come on."

A full hug and handholding were also a first. The softness soothed, electrified, and terrified Mika, but she felt like a thousand pairs of eyes were staring at them. "You need to get to your classes." She dropped Willow's hand and opened her locker, half-hoping Willow would stay. When she turned, they briefly stared at one another without a word. She always got lost in the kindness and warmth in Willow's soft brown eyes, but today there was a sadness in them too. The first period bell rang and broke the moment. "Go. I'll be fine. If I'm late, they'll forgive me. Everyone knows about my family." She stuffed her books into her bag.

"I'm worried about you. Where are you eating lunch?" Willow placed her hand on Mika's shoulder.

Oh, God, she's touching me again. If this continued, Mika feared she'd slip up and tell Willow how she really felt. *Yeah, telling Willow she's gorgeous and how much I want to kiss her would go so well.*

"You do know that reading science books doesn't qualify as a nutritious lunch, right?" Willow said and grinned. "And one of these days, you'll get caught hiding in the auditorium backstage."

How'd Willow know she sometimes hid back there and *read* through lunch?

"Meet me to the right of the cafeteria entrance, and I'll have lunch with you."

"Really?" *Oh God, could I have said anything more stupid?*

"Yes, really. Bye, Mika."

"Bye." She sucked in a breath and admired Willow's confident strut down the hall before fear hit. God, they'd be seen by hundreds of students who'd gossip about why a popular senior like Willow was having lunch with a nerdy junior. Mika had to stick to her normal school act: eyes down and pretend not to be affected by all the cute girls around, especially Willow.

But wow. One of the most popular girls in school was going to have lunch with *her*, Math Geek Mika. The excitement temporarily distracted her, but then the sadness crept back like a cold claw to scoop out her insides. Her parents were dead, and a mountain of hugs wouldn't bring them back. She squeezed her eyes shut to hold back the tears and continued to class.

Mika went through the day on auto, her attention weaving in and out, and her feelings rolling like a coaster from excitement to sadness and back again. At lunch, she waited at the cafeteria entrance with her hands crammed into her jeans' pockets, worried that Willow was playing a joke. Working together in the library was one thing, but eating lunch together was something else.

"Hi, Mika."

She gave Willow a wide smile. "Hi."

"Ready for some gourmet food?" Willow laughed.

"After you." God, she was so cute. Mika could stare into her face and listen to the sound of her voice all day.

While they ate lunch, it seemed like everyone was staring at them, either with puzzled looks or smirks. She thought the attention would make Willow cut things short and make some excuse to leave...but she never did.

"Do you have Netflix?" Willow asked.

"Yep."

"Have you ever watched *Riverdale*?" Willow took a bite of her chicken salad sandwich.

"No." She wasn't going to admit that *Heartstopper* on Netflix was her favorite. That'd be like standing on top of the table and shouting her gayness. "I watch *Stranger Things*."

"That's a bit too dark and scary for me. But I can see why you'd like it, science nerd." Willow nudged her and laughed.

Mika nodded. If anyone else had called her a nerd, she would've given them a rash of shit. But Willow saying it only made Mika dizzy with plenty of butterflies in her stomach. "What do you like about *Riverdale*?" It was probably all the face-sucking. She shoved rice into her mouth.

"Sex, murder, and mystery. You know, the typical teenage life." Willow laughed.

Her laugh made Mika's pulse tick a mile-a-minute. The bell rang. How had the time gone by so quickly? She hoped they'd have lunch again. "Thanks for having lunch with me."

"It was fun. We should do it more often." Willow dumped her trash and tossed her tray on the kitchen conveyor belt. "What time do you drive to school?"

Mika wet her lips. "I don't have my driver's license yet." *Shit, that's embarrassing.*

"Oh. How about I pick you up at seven thirty?"

"Ah, sure." She was getting a ride from Willow Parker!

Willow handed over her phone. "Stick your deets in here."

"Okay." Mika's body shook inside, and she hoped that it didn't show. Their fingers touched when she handed Willow's phone back. Curious onlookers whispered, but it didn't seem to affect Willow.

"See you tomorrow morning. Just no math lessons while I drive, or I'll wreck the car." Willow waved and headed off to class.

Mika headed to her class in the opposite direction. Willow had friended her, not in the library with a handful of people, but in front of the entire cafeteria. It all seemed too good to be true.

"Hey, Mika."

Mika turned to face Willow, and so did just about everyone.

From halfway down the hall, Willow cupped her hands and yelled, "Great T-shirt. I'm a Swiftie too."

Then reality hit again, and Mika's stomach twisted, and she felt like she'd been thrown into an oven. When Willow turned and walked away, Mika ran into the bathroom where she nearly knocked over Ashley Devins, her fucking nemesis.

"Hey. Watch it, bitch."

Mika rushed inside a stall and banged it shut. She muffled her cries until she thought Ashley had left, then she dropped to her knees and heaved into the toilet. It didn't matter how good the past hour felt, her parents were dead. Nothing could change that—even time with sweet Willow. When she opened the door, Ashley was leaning against the wall with her arms crossed.

She jutted her chin toward Mika's stall. "Better clean up after yourself, freak. You stink."

Ashley strutted out of the bathroom like she was some fancy queen. Of all the people to run into, why did it have to be her? Ashley was on the relay team with Willow, but she was stuck-up and ran around with a gang of ultra-popular kids.

Mika washed her hands and face. She stood still for a few seconds and let the water drip off into the sink. Tomorrow, she'd be riding to school with Willow. Screw all the bullies.

Chapter Twelve

MIKA CREPT DOWN THE stairs and into the kitchen. She came to a standstill when she gazed out the window. The bird feeders were full, and a bright purple finch pecked away at the feeder while smaller birds ate on the suet. They scattered when a blue jay swooped in to eat. Beyond the bird feeders, dormant plants with bare stems stuck out of snowy ground in the big backyard garden. Mom loved that garden, and she was always pointing out birds and wildflowers when they went hiking. Mika placed her hand over her mouth and held her breath, willing the tears to stop.

One of the cats rubbed against her leg, and she looked down to see Missy. "Breakfast time, girl?" She grabbed a napkin and wiped her eyes and face. Missy purred warmly as Mr. Big pranced in like he was the king of the Universe. "Hey, big boy." After feeding them, she opened the refrigerator and grabbed the milk jug.

"Good morning. You're up early."

How could she sound so cheerful? Mika chugged some milk, only stopping long enough to fill the toaster with bread.

"Please pour your milk into a glass next time. Drinking out of the jug can easily pass along a cold to me or visitors."

"Oh, sorry." Mika turned her back.

"You should eat something besides toast. Let me fix you some eggs."

"I'm fine." Mika jammed her water bottle and an apple in her backpack and slathered the toast with butter. She wrapped one piece in a paper towel and chewed on the other as she hurried toward the door.

"Wait. Where are you going? School doesn't start for over an hour."

"The gym opens early." That wasn't a lie, but she wasn't going there.

"I'd like to drive you to school today."

"I've got a ride." Mika bolted out the door and jumped into Willow's cute little Toyota. She waved at Aunt Val as they pulled away, but boy, she looked pissed. What was her problem? A ride was no biggie. Mika turned to Willow. "Thanks for texting me."

"I can't believe you wanted to go with me at seven a.m. to drop off Mom's design. I could have picked you up afterwards." Willow laughed.

Mika admired Willow's beautiful profile. "I want to keep you company. I can't believe your mom's an architect."

"Nope. They call her a designer. After ten years, she almost has her degree. She's juggled the house, her job, and me since my dad left."

"I'm sorry about your dad." Mika swallowed.

"Doesn't bother me. I was little."

Mika had heard people say you shouldn't have a favorite child or a favorite parent, but Mika had always favored her dad. He was her buddy as well as a gentle enforcer when she messed up.

At the stop sign, Willow handed Mika a to-go-cup. "Not sure what you like. Caramel macchiato's my fave, and I had a coupon."

"Perfect. Thanks." Mika took a sip.

"You're welcome." Willow smiled and turned on the music.

Mika would love to kiss the dimple in her cheek. As the acoustic version of Taylor's "Lavender Haze" played, Mika sat in awe as Willow sang along.

"Sing with me."

Mika matched Willow's loud voice, but she couldn't match her perfect tone. "Why aren't you in the choir?" she asked when the song ended.

"I'm not really that good. Plus, I'm busy with ten billion other things."

"So not true. Your voice is great." Mika melted when Willow winked at her before taking a sip of her coffee.

The next song started with violins and sounded sad but then kicked into a club beat. The singer had an accent, so Mika had to listen closely to the lyrics. Willow dancing in her seat made Mika's temperature spike. The tingly feeling that had been low-key shimmering through her body since she'd gotten in the car exploded.

"Did you like it?"

"Yeah, who's the singer?"

"Aryra Starr. She's from Nigeria. The song's called 'Bloody Samaritan.' It's like her saying 'Fuck the world, you won't tell me who to be.' That's my interpretation anyway. Come on. You can dance in my car." Willow scrolled through her playlist and hit the next song.

This was way better than a dream. Mika danced in her seat. She couldn't believe Willow listened to Baby Queen, and the lyrics to a "Quarter Life Crisis" were so lit. Mika first heard it on Netflix's *Heartstopper*, which was full of gay characters. If Willow had watched the TV series, she would've said so the other day.

"Damn, the British are killing it with upcoming new artists. But we've got badass artists too." Olivia Rodrigo's "bad idea right?" began playing, and Willow pumped up the speakers. Once the song finished, she drove up to a big country house south of town and turned down the sound. "I'll just be a minute."

The smell of Willow's perfume lingered, and Mika breathed it in as she watched her walk away. She couldn't help but admire her round ass in those skinny jeans. *What the hell? Friends. She's my friend.* But when Willow came back and gave Mika a mega-watt smile, she swore she'd died and gone to heaven.

After dancing in their seats to another Olivia Rodrigo song, Willow pulled the car over into the park. "We're still early for school. Let's finish our coffee." She grinned. "What's on your phone. Play something that might surprise me. Oh, let me pick something." She held out her hand.

Mika froze for a second with the cup raised to her mouth. She took a big swig, then licked the caramel flavor from her lips. "Okay." Her hand trembled as she pulled her phone from her pocket and handed it to Willow. *Breathe*.

"Let's see." Willow scrolled through Mika's phone. "Recently played... a song by Sarah Jeffrey. She and Olivia were in Disney productions but didn't work together. I've never listened to Sarah, but she must be good since her song is your top favorite." Willow looked up and grinned wide.

Mika muscles tensed. Shit, this was a bad idea.

Willow hit play, and Mika took a deep breath and closed her eyes as "Even the Stars" played. Tears burned the back of her eyes. *Don't cry, don't cry, don't cry.* She gripped her legs. When the song ended, Willow's warm hand was on top of hers.

"Mika, you're digging the shit out of your thighs."

That did it. She couldn't stop the tears.

"I think you need a big hug."

Mika didn't say a word, and when Willow stretched over the console, she fell into her arms and cried harder. "I'm...I'm not okay most of the time. I hate the dark. I hate the pain. I try to crawl out of it, but I can't. My grands were a little wacko but okay. I just miss my parents. They were awesome. It hurts so fucking bad that I'll never again hear their voice or get to tell them how much I love them." Mika pulled back and wiped her tears. "I'm sorry to dump on you."

"It's okay." Willow rubbed Mika's shoulder. "You've had a fall over a gigantic cliff. By the way, that song's really cool, and it tells me you haven't given up trying to climb out of the pain. You're stronger than you think, Mika. So keep climbing, and please let me help."

"Thanks." It was hard to breathe. There were several questions Mika had been dying to ask for months, like whether Willow was bi or gay, but no way in hell was she going to ask that now. *Stuff it away.* "Aren't you friends with the popular gang?" She swallowed.

"Like with the Ashley and Carrie crowd."

"No. Yeah, we were together on the relay team. Swimming's over, thankfully. I tried to be polite and congratulate them when they swam good, but I don't hang with them." Willow rolled her eyes. "They're two-faced bitches who throw shade on people just to pump themselves up. I cut them off or walk away if they do it around me. Some of their minions are in my classes." She draped her arm across the steering wheel. "There are two jocks who annoy the piss out of me. They're always hanging all over me in the halls. All they want is to get into my pants. They can fuck off."

"Didn't you date that—"

"Fuck Levi. Yeah, he became a convert to the gang, but dating him wasn't that great before."

"I'm sorry to make you angry," Mika whispered.

"You didn't," Willow said. "He did. They did. Sure, I'm a senior, but I'm tired of all the shade and lies. I've heard they bully you. Don't listen to them. They're not worth your time. Now for more music."

They sang to more songs, then Mika's alarm went off.

"What's that for?" Willow asked.

"To tell me classes start in fifteen minutes in case I get too involved in working out...or something else." Or *someone* else.

"Crap. Detention is not what we need." Willow started the car and pulled into traffic. "I always drive the limit, but I think this calls for going five miles over. Let's hope I don't get my first speeding ticket."

"Thanks again for the ride, the coffee, and friendship. It made me feel better." You *make me feel better.*

"Any time." Willow smiled then turned her attention back to the road.

And just like in Sarah Jeffrey's song, Mika felt a little light shining through the dark.

"Oh, I almost forgot. I can't give you a ride home. I have to leave early for a doctor appointment," Willow said.

"Are you okay?" Mika asked softly.

"Yeah, it's routine. I had to reschedule, and when Mom called, the only thing they had was on a school day," Willow said. "Thanks for today. I'm happy we spent some time together outside of school. Maybe we could grab a pizza sometime."

"Yeah. I'd love that." Mika was too scared to ask if they'd go as friends or if it'd be a date. What was she even thinking? Willow hadn't done anything that a friend wouldn't do. *Friend. Period.*

She had to keep her true feelings buried. When she wasn't drooling over Willow, her anxiety kicked in, and she was scared that Willow would reject her. Maybe one day she'd feel whole again and come out of the shadows to someone. Maybe that someone would be Willow.

Chapter Thirteen

THE LAST BELL RANG, and Mika took her time to get to her locker while everyone else rushed past her. All day, she'd thought about Willow. The ride to school had been lit. When Willow listened to "Even the Stars," it was like she saw into Mika's soul. They had a connection. Willow was real. She wasn't faking any crap. Too bad they weren't doing it again tonight.

Mika squeezed by the other students and saw Ashley and Carrie by the main doors. She doubled back and headed to the gym. The girls' varsity basketball team had to be changing, so Mrs. Horowitz likely hadn't come out, and the teacher coaching wrestling didn't pay Mika much attention.

"Hello, Mika. Did you forget something?"

Just a few more steps, and she would have gotten through the door. Mika took a breath and faced Mrs. Horowitz. "You know I love to run outside."

"And?"

"Yeah, so I was walking all over the place yesterday and came by the school. I had an old wallet on me. Not much money in it, but I think I lost it on the road behind the gym. I just wanted to check." Heat crawled up her neck and covered her face. From the expression on Mrs. Horowitz's face, this wasn't working. She needed to play the sympathy card and cry a little, which wasn't hard because she always teared up any time she thought of her parents. She squeezed out a few tears and hung her head. "I came here yesterday because it's quiet on New Year's Day."

Mrs. Horowitz sighed. "This door is only for emergencies, but I'll allow it this one time—*if* you tell me why you really want to go out that door." She folded her arms.

Mika towered over Mrs. Horowitz by at least six inches, but the woman wasn't called Commander Shorty for nothing. "I don't want to face some of the kids near the main door."

"Bullies?"

Mika nodded.

"Who are they?"

Mika lowered her head. No way was she going to spill the tea, even on those assholes. They'd know it was her and come after her harder.

"Are you talking to anyone?"

"I'm seeing a therapist about everything." Her voice shook, and tears rolled down her face. This time, she wasn't faking them. Out of all the teachers, she trusted Mrs. Horowitz and Mrs. Simmons the most, but she just wanted to get the hell out of here.

Mrs. Horowitz stepped closer. "Here." She held out a tissue. "Take it. It's clean." Then she punched in a key to turn off the alarm and opened the door. "Just this one time."

"Thanks." Mika stepped outside. Instead of going home, she walked through the neighborhood to the Fuertes Observatory. She looked across the snow-covered ground at the building and held her breath. Her emotions wouldn't hold back for this.

Dad took her most Fridays to gaze through the rooftop telescope. Her fascination with viewing the planets, galaxies, and stars had only grown as she'd gotten older. She used the last of the tissue for her nose and used her coat sleeve to wipe her tears. Getting the hell out of high school and studying physics was her goal.

She turned toward home and stopped at Sunset Park on the way. When she was a little girl, they'd come up here in the summer, sit on the stone wall, and watch the sunset. She sniffled and brushed away more tears. Even in the winter, it was still beautiful.

She made it home fifteen minutes later and went behind the house, but the light was on in the sunroom. The foyer light wasn't on, so maybe she could go through the front door and sneak up to her bedroom. When Mika opened it, she came face-to-face with Aunt Val and almost knocked her down. "What the hell?"

"Michaela Lynn, it's not okay that you just ran out to your friend's car this morning. And it's certainly not okay that you didn't come straight home at the end of school. It's dark and almost five thirty. Where have you been?" Aunt Val put her hands on her hips.

"I went for a walk." When Mika shot past, Aunt Val lunged and grabbed a handful of Mika's tee, pulling it off of her shoulder. "Stop, you're gonna rip my shirt." Mika smacked her arm away and ran up the stairs.

"Stop!" Aunt Val caught her arm and didn't let go. "I'm your guardian. I need to know that you're safe, and you need to show me some respect."

"Willow has an awesome car, and I don't want you driving me around." Mika glared at her and shook off her grip.

"I'm sorry. I didn't mean to hurt your shirt. The point is, you're a minor under my care. I want you to be safe. You took me by surprise this morning. I know nothing about your friend, including her driving experience. You should've introduced us to be polite at the very least. And it would have been better if you'd asked me the night before if it was okay to ride to school with your friend."

"Fine. Got anything else to say?"

"Why didn't you call if you weren't coming straight home from school? I tried to call you and was worried sick when you didn't answer."

"I don't need a babysitter." Mika crossed her arms. "Besides, I'm not supposed to have the phone on in school. I forgot to turn it back on when I left."

Her aunt sighed. "Okay. In the future, please tell me when you change plans. I didn't fix dinner because I was so worried. Let's go to that new diner. I heard they've got great mac and cheese and lots of desserts."

"Crashy." Mika huffed. "In case you haven't noticed, I'm not ten. You know, the age that I last saw you." She turned and slowly climbed the last steps. But Aunt Val was on her heels and caught her bedroom door before it shut.

"We need to talk." Her aunt gently placed her hand on top of Mika's shoulder. "Please look at me."

Mika turned, trying not to cry by gritting her teeth. She'd already cried so much that Ithaca would soon have a new waterfall to name after her. "You never cared before, so why do you care now? You haven't been in my life for six fucking years."

"I'm sorry for the years I didn't visit. But the past is exactly that, and we can only move forward. I know you're hurting." Aunt Val's eyes filled with tears. "And while you don't understand the disagreements that separated me from the family, I loved them too. You're not the only one who feels the sharp pain of loss. Please don't shut me out. Sulking in your room and refusing to talk or snapping at me isn't helping either of us. I'm trying my best. Please meet me halfway. And I want to get to know you better, but I can't read your mind. Please tell me about your friendship with Willow and where you went tonight."

Mika broke down into ragged sobs. She tried to speak but couldn't. When the tears slowed, she sat on the bed. "I...I can't stand being in the house at night. I can't sleep."

Aunt Val handed her a tissue and sat beside her. "I understand. It's going to take time." She brushed the hair out of Mika's eyes. "I guess I'm paranoid now because of that damn drunk truck driver. Willow might be great behind the wheel, but there are so many crazies are out there."

"Willow's not a bad driver. She's careful. Look, I'm sorry I pushed you the other night."

"Thank you for your apology. I'm not the enemy. And I never imagined something like this would happen to our family. I think we need each other to make it through." She rubbed Mika's shoulder.

Emotions ripped through Mika. Maybe now would be the time that Aunt Val would tell her everything. "Why are you my guardian and not Aunt Pauline?" A few seconds of silence passed.

Aunt Val took a breath and sighed. "Your parents didn't want to take you out of your home and away from your friends. You can still visit your cousins and Aunt Pauline. Binghamton's only an hour south."

Mika thought about Jenn and the DNA testing. "Do you know who my real parents were?"

Aunt Val's face turned pale like she'd seen a ghost. Holy shit. The knot in Mika's stomach clenched tighter.

"I know that your parents wanted you so bad. You were a beautiful baby, and they raised you with love." Aunt Val swallowed hard and stood. "I'll microwave the leftover chicken and broccoli pasta." She walked away.

Mika followed her downstairs and into the kitchen. "Why did you move here? I googled it: a lab director of any medical research firm makes six figures."

Aunt Val leaned against the counter. "It would have been difficult to handle my grief and keep working all the insane hours that the position demanded. My moving helps us both, but you're the primary reason. Look, Mika, I'm trying my best. You need to try too. Maybe you could start by showing me some respect."

Mika nodded and stuffed her hands in her pockets. "Um, I have a driver's learning permit. I did some driving with Mom and Dad, but they wanted me to wait until I was seventeen for my junior license. I still need thirty-six hours of supervised driving with fifteen hours of night driving before I can even apply." She cleared her throat. "Will you take me out driving or get me into a class?"

"Sure. I'll check on what classes are available for your level, and then we'll talk over the options."

"Thanks. I'll set the table."

During dinner, her aunt asked what movies she liked. It seemed like a safe topic.

"You go first," Mika said.

"Science fiction. My top two favorites are *The Martian* and

Interstellar."

"For real?" Mika sat up straighter in her chair.

"Yes. Why are you surprised?"

"I just figured you'd be into romance."

"Happily-ever-after movies are okay every now and then." Her aunt swirled her wine then took a sip.

"Sci-fi is the best," Mika said. "*Stowaway*, *Rebel Moon*, and *Simulant* are cool. I love the TV series *The 100*. Netflix has a lot of old good stuff like *The Martian*."

"Old?" Aunt Val raised an eyebrow. "Are you calling me old?"

Fuck, she'd pissed her off without even trying.

Aunt Val laughed. "Just kidding."

Mika laughed too. Her aunt didn't seem so bad, and her parents must have trusted her plenty to make her Mika's guardian. But it bothered her that Grandma and Grandpa Hayden held some mysterious grudge against their younger daughter. Mika didn't want to be like them. *I'll try harder.*

Chapter Fourteen

MIKA NEEDED TO SPILL her guts to someone, and Iliana was sort of cool. The art in her office was definitely lit. Each artist had a unique technique. Some were colorful, and others were drab. It was like a parade of all human feelings. Mika had drifted away from the session; chewing on her fingernail and looking at the paintings was easier than working out her emotions while Iliana sat down with her cup of tea.

"I'm afraid the tenants might complain." Iliana took a sip of her tea.

What the fuck did that have to do with anything? "Why?"

"Because you're bouncing your leg a hundred times a minute." Iliana crossed her leg.

"Oh." Mika looked away and crossed her ankle over her knee. When she looked back, Iliana smiled at her, then Mika noticed her foot. She put her hand over it to stop the bouncing. "I'm nervous."

"Why?"

"You're a doctor, and I feel like I'm under a microscope when I come in here." Mika cracked her knuckles.

"I don't mean to make you uncomfortable. How was your holiday?"

"Right before Christmas, I spent most of the time alone in my bedroom." Mika cracked her knuckles again and put her hands by her side on the sofa. "I didn't want to see anyone, not even my friends, so I played video games against AI opponents." She looked down and noticed she was tapping her fingers on the sofa. She stopped and cleared her throat. "According to the game rewards counter, I jumped up four levels by playing twenty-six hours. I ate in my room, and I didn't exercise or shower for two days." *Why'd I tell her that?*

Iliana's expression remained neutral. "Gaming is a common coping mechanism for many, and it's healthier than drinking or drugs. It only becomes a problem when it interferes with socializing, school, and sleep. You need adequate sleep, or the anxiety and pain will only get worse."

"Okay. Anyway, Christmas was better than I thought it was gonna be. My cousins came over, and Aunt Val bought me a great SLR and lens. Then on New Year's Day, I played online with my friends. It felt pretty good."

"Great."

More moments of silence passed, and Mika glanced at the paintings again. Some looked like photos, but she liked the ones with chaotic patterns and colors. They matched her life now, which was like trying to find her way out of a maze. Some days she thought she'd make it through, and other days, she crawled over obstacles, but she hung on tight. Her parents had taught her never to give up.

"How was the first day back in school? Are the bullies still coming at you?"

Mika shrugged. "There were a few looks, and they're still throwing shade but..." Mika remembered reconnecting with Willow and how sweet she'd been.

"That must be a pleasant memory from the smile on your face."

The rattle when Iliana put down her cup snapped Mika back to the present. Shit, she'd walked into that one. *Watch the pronouns.*

"Ah, there's this person that I like. And they were really nice to me and gave me a ride on the second day. We work in the library and study when we aren't shelving books."

"That's wonderful."

"Yeah." Mika stared at the floor. "I'm sad, then happy. Rinse and repeat. My feelings are like a spinning top that never stops. How can I be happy for an hour or a day, then flip the other way?"

"Because you've undergone some serious shit."

Mika looked up. That was the second swear word Iliana had said during their sessions. She never imagined the refined woman, let alone a doctor, sitting in front of her would curse.

"You're also going to feel guilt with sadness, but that's normal. Try to hang on to the good, but always remember that it's okay to be all over the place when you've had such severe trauma." Iliana crossed her legs.

Mika had to look at the paintings again. Staring at Iliana's lovely legs was not okay, especially when she was twice her age. Damn, she felt like a creep. She pointed at one painting. "What's that one?"

"It's a reproduction of Claude Monet's Leicester Square at Night. He liked to capture the nuances of light and color, but the reproduction is more vivid. What does it mean to you?"

"The colors conflict. Bright yellow and orange against blues and purples." She looked at the floor. "You mentioned guilt. Sometimes, it's so painful that I wish I'd died with them. Other times, I just push on."

"How do you feel right now?"

Smack. She kept walking into it deeper. She'd be lucky if Iliana didn't press a button for some guys to bust in and put a straitjacket on her. "I mean, the sadness can last for hours, but I don't really want to die." She glanced at the clock on the wall and stood. "There are only a few minutes left, and honestly, my mind's empty for the day."

"Remember my card."

"It's in my wallet, but I'm not suicidal."

"It's just best to be prepared." Iliana walked her to the door. "This is only our second session, but you've opened up quicker than some of the adults that come in and see me. Everyone's different and that's okay, but I want you to know that I see a strong young woman who's a fighter."

"Thanks."

The session had been a mixed bag, and the times Mika thought about the doc's legs was so embarrassing. She hoped that Iliana didn't catch on. Mika sighed and walked out into the sunlight and toward the coffeehouse. Having Aunt Val in the waiting room made her feel even more like an unwilling specimen, so she'd asked to be dropped off, then she promised to meet her at Java Heaven afterwards. Once inside, Mika stood at the back of a long line.

"Oh, that's funny."

Mika looked in the direction of her aunt's voice. She was at a table not far away with another woman who had long reddish-brown hair. Aunt Val clearly hadn't noticed her come in.

As they laughed, a man rushed in the door and up to their table. "Brie, Jack's car broke down, and he can't make it in. Could you please help?"

The woman sitting with Aunt Val looked up. "Who's in the shop now?"

"Shelly's staying a little longer, but you know we're both mammal and reptile people. The tanks need maintenance."

"Sure, I'll be there in five," the woman said, and the man rushed out.

"Sorry about this," the woman said to Aunt Val.

"Reptiles and tanks? Are you a snake charmer, Brie Owens?" Aunt Val smiled.

What the fuck? She's acting like December never happened. What gives her the right to be happy?

The other woman laughed. "I'm an accountant with my own business. I started helping my friend Jack a couple of hours a week at his pet shop, but his wife just had a baby, which means my freebie work just spiked."

"That's terrific," Aunt Val said.

Mika turned slightly away. *That's terrific*, she mimicked and sneered.

"I mean it's terrific that you're an accountant. I just happen to need one. That is, if you can fit me in between the reptiles and fish." Aunt Val laughed again.

"Sure. Here's my card."

Mika was fucking pissed. No one needed to rub elbows with their accountant unless they wanted a super sweet deal. And Aunt Val's laughter made Mika sick. She turned her back as the woman walked out, then Mika pivoted to leave and almost ran into another customer.

"It's your turn," the man said. "Do you want a coffee or not?"

"Mika, I didn't see you come in. Would you like a drink?"

She turned to the barista. "A large, iced caramel latte, please." *To throw in my aunt's face.*

They stepped over to the pickup area.

"I met an accountant. I need help with my taxes and getting the estate finances together."

"Yeah. I'm sure it's all confusing," Mika mumbled.

"Her brother owns this shop. She was helping him out today and sat down with me during a slow period."

"Oh." That made sense, except the chummy part and the laughter. Mika balled her hand into a fist.

"I'll get my bag while you wait for your drink."

"Large, iced caramel latte," another barista called out.

Mika sipped her drink, but the cold liquid did little to numb her emotions. She wanted to scream but stuffed it inside. Maybe she'd say something at home. Aunt Val joined her, and when they stepped outside, Mika just began walking.

"My car's this direction."

She snapped around and walked alongside her aunt, hoping for silence.

"How was today? You don't have to tell me details. Was it thumbs up?"

"Yep." Mika stopped and glared. Her gigantic ball of anger would explode if her aunt didn't keep her mouth shut. "Look, it's Saturday, and I just want to go home and salvage what's left of the day. Maybe game with my buddies."

Aunt Val rubbed her forehead and sighed. "I've felt regret for so many things. Hannah and I were just beginning to heal some old wounds, and I was looking forward to visiting and doing things with her, you, and Andrew again. Meeting Brie today helped with my sadness. It's nice to make a new friend. Adults need friendship too."

Her aunt's words punched through Mika. Fuck, what was she thinking? Just because she was hurting didn't give her the right to make an assumption and jump down Aunt Val's throat, even if she'd only done it in her head.

Mika swallowed. "I get it. I'm sorry that I'm in a bad mood."

"Give therapy some time. I think it will help. If you can't get comfortable with Iliana, then we can look for another one. And just so you know, I had a therapist for several years. I called her recently. Adults need help sometimes too."

Aunt Val always looked strong and confident. She had to be shattered inside too. How did she keep it together?

"Oh, I almost forgot. I found a driver's ed school. Their only opening is eight a.m. until noon for the next two months beginning next Saturday."

"I can do that. But will it give me enough hours?"

"I'll make a deal with you. Stick with therapy, and I'll take you out to complete your remaining time. Then you should be able to apply for your junior license."

"Sweet." She'd finally be able to catch up with her classmates. "And I do like Iliana. It's just kind of hard sometimes. Thanks. Can I drive home now?"

Aunt Val took a breath, then slowly blew it out. "I'll drive us out of town to Hanger Theatre. We'll go over the features of my BMW, then you can drive us north on Taghannock Blvd up to Glenwood Pines."

"Can we go out in the Mustang tomorrow?"

"If you drive cautious today."

"All right!" Mika twirled around. When they reached the car, she pointed to the radio. "Do you mind?"

"Go for it."

Mika turned on Sirius XM and "Snow on the Beach" began playing. She knew the lyrics by heart since she'd listened to the album and watched the video numerous times. The video was the only one of Taylor Swift's where it looked like two women were in love. At least, that's how Mika saw it. She began singing and imagined that Willow was there, singing to her. She hoped that someday it would come true.

Chapter Fifteen

February

It was another boring Monday as Mika walked to gym class. The indoor track sucked because the entire gym had been newly painted and stunk. It was warmer, so hopefully Mrs. Horowitz would let them run outside.

Once the class assembled, Mrs. Horowitz blew her whistle, and a few troublemakers rumbled. They always complained about something. Mika ignored them. She placed her hand on her hips and gave Mrs. Horowitz her full attention.

"The outdoor track is clear of snow, thanks to Mother Nature and the maintenance crew. Go put on your sweatpants and grab your jackets. Hustle."

"It's still cold even with the sun shining..."

The whiners just wouldn't give it up.

"Now, ladies," Mrs. Horowitz yelled.

Mika loved taking in the fresh, cool air. While hockey had been her and Dad's thing, running on the weekends with Mom had been their thing. Mika hadn't run much since the accident, except to run away from her feelings and Aunt Val. Deep down, Mika needed to feel the burn in her legs. She needed to clear her mind and a good run on a sunny day in the fresh, cool air was perfect.

Outside, she surged ahead and ran extra laps while others walked. Then someone let off a string of curse words in front of Mrs. Horowitz, and they were ordered back inside. Mika couldn't believe how dumb some of her classmates were. Now, they groaned like dying cows because Mrs. Horowitz had a reputation of being hell personified in a track suit when she got pissed off.

Mrs. Horowitz blew her whistle. "Twenty push-ups and sit-ups. Not one word, or you'll be doing a lot more."

Mika didn't mind the extra reps. They seemed to take away some of her pain. The mats were comfy enough on the gym floor, but the horrible paint smell made her nauseous. Still, she dropped and began to exercise. The gym walls reminded her of when Aunt Pauline suggested she should paint her room. "Give it a try. Maybe, it'd help you move on." Yeah, like a good slap of acrylic would erase her pain. Funny how she was noticing her dislike for Aunt Pauline more and more. The main reason she didn't want to paint her room were the lingering scents of her mom's perfume and her dad's cologne. She missed them coming into her room and checking on her. Fresh paint would wipe those memories away.

"Mika, you can stop now," Mrs. Horowitz said. "I blew the whistle minutes ago. Everyone else has already gone to the shower."

"One more rep." Her muscles burned, but no matter how many she did, the nightmare remained hiding in the back of her head.

"Would you like to talk?" Mrs. Horowitz softly asked.

"No, ma'am." Mika rose and forced a smile, then headed toward the locker room. As always, she kept her gaze on the floor. She didn't need the headache of someone accusing her of checking them out.

She took a deep breath and pushed open the main door. The janitors had drenched the place in too much chlorine, though it was a much better smell than the paint. She spun the dial on her lock, intentionally messing up before getting it right. Most of the girls in her locker row had grabbed their towels and moved on. A few lingered, chatting. The thought of getting naked pricked her skin with fear. She didn't like others seeing her body, and the bright fluorescent lights shone a spotlight on her every flaw. She didn't have the curves most girls had. Her body was muscular, her shoulders were broad, and her boobs were small. She didn't hate her body. She was just different, and sometimes, she wished that she looked more like a girly-girl to stop the bullying.

Shower, get dressed, and get out as fast as possible was her typical MO but today, she was extra jittery and switched up her strategy. She stopped playing with the lock and hid in a bathroom stall for several minutes, hoping most of the girls would finish showering before she emerged.

She stepped out, grabbed her towel and stuff, and slowly moved to the communal showers. She didn't look at anyone's face, not wanting to see the sneers. Not all bullies called her names, but their over-the-top facial expressions and hand gestures hurt just as much. Damn, most of the showers were occupied.

"Hi, Mika."

She looked up into Willow's usual cheery face before quickly glancing at her body. *Stop looking.* Maybe Willow hadn't noticed. She'd never seen Willow naked. In swimming, their lockers were at opposite ends of the room, and the seniors always showered first before anyone else. "Ah, you're not in my gym class." *Smooth. Stop looking.* But Willow's near-perfect body made it difficult. And her breasts were just right—not too big and not too small.

Willow laughed with that tone that always made Mika mushy in the right spot and put a smile on her face. But smiling at a naked girl wasn't a good idea. Quickly, she averted her eyes to her soap and bumped the plastic bottle. The cap popped off, and what little bit remained in the bottle spilled out.

"Use mine." Willow held out her shower gel bottle.

"Thanks." Mika caught another glimpse of Willow's breasts as she took the bottle, and her body quivered. She had to get out of here before she fainted, or slipped, or something. She squirted gel into her hand, set the bottle on the ledge, and lathered up furiously. She didn't dare look back at Willow.

"I'm ahead in English, so the teacher let me come for extra swim lessons for the next two days," Willow said. "There are a few other girls too."

"Cool."

"Why are you in such a hurry?" Willow asked.

"I'm behind on this research paper. I have to get to the library." She hoped that didn't sound as lame as she thought it did and turned the shower off. "See you around."

"Oh, Mika."

"Yeah?"

Willow laughed. "It's the end of the day, and only the study hall is open after school. Unless you mean the public library. Need any help?"

Stupid. "Ah yeah, the public library, but I'm good on my own today. Thanks. Bye."

"Oh, okay. See ya."

There seemed to be sadness in Willow's voice, but the sooner Mika got out of there, the better. The other girls had left the row when Mika reached her locker. Toweling off, she stopped. Was she having her period? She pulled the towel out and touched between her legs. It felt slick, like when she masturbated. She wadded up the towel, threw it down, and dressed faster than ever. If she had this type of reaction to just seeing Willow's breasts, what would happen if she ever got to kiss and touch her?

That night, Mika tossed and turned, torn up with thoughts of agony and embarrassment on one side and Willow's perfect breasts on the other. They hadn't talked much before working together at the library, but now that Mika thought about it, Willow sometimes stole glimpses of *her* during swim season. *Nah, I'm dreaming.* But Mika frequently glanced at Willow, just enough so she didn't catch on. The swimsuits they wore compressed their breasts, but boy, did she love what she saw today. She'd known for some time that even the slightest hint of breasts turned her on. Now all Mika could think about was touching Willow's body. That wasn't happening any time soon. She'd never even kissed anyone, and telling Willow how she felt would probably scare her away for good.

Mika finally got up, went into the bathroom, removed her nightshirt, and faced the mirror. She didn't hate her body, but she didn't love it either. She stared at her breasts. They were small, but she didn't want them to get any bigger. She didn't like wearing makeup, painting her nails, or curling her hair. She liked to see it on cute girls, but it just wasn't for her. What was the point of taking all that extra time? Running her fingers through her hair did the job. What she hated the most was her period. But none of that meant she wanted to be a guy.

Fuck the haters who said she wanted a dick. She couldn't wait to get out of high school and away from them. Sure, people like that'd be in larger towns too, but a city had more diversity. She'd likely find friends and people would like her more easily, people who didn't care how different she looked. All she had to do was hang on a little longer until closer to spring graduation, then she'd tell Aunt Val. Surely, she wouldn't stop Mika from graduating early since the top colleges in California had already accepted her. She still hadn't gotten a letter from Columbia University, and though California would be cool, New York City was closer to home. *And that weekend with Mom was the best.*

She sighed, flicked off the bathroom light, and returned to bed. All Mika knew was that she was different, probably too different for Willow. But she was falling hard for her. Still, Mika could dream of one day when Willow was hers, right?

Chapter Sixteen

MIKA MARCHED OUT OF her cousins' house toward their SUV. The weekend had started well but had collapsed into a disaster. She wanted to get home and confront Aunt Val as fast as possible.

Jenn ran after her. "What the hell's wrong?"

Anger blinded Mika. She gritted her teeth and didn't say a word as she grabbed the rear door handle and yanked. It didn't open, and she almost pulled her arm out of its socket. "Who the hell locks their vehicle on five acres of land with a gated driveway in a nice neighborhood?"

The car beeped, and the SUV door unlocked with a click.

"You're sure you want to go home now?" Aunt Pauline stood on the porch.

"Yes."

"Very well."

Mika hopped inside. Aunt Pauline locked the front door and marched toward them, looking pissed. Mika didn't care that it was an hour's drive. She wanted to go home. Jenn joined Mika in the backseat while Carla sat in front with their mom.

Mika's phone vibrated. She glanced at Jenn. Why couldn't Jenn mind her own business? She kept poking, physically and with texts. Mika looked at Jenn's text.

i'm sorry about looking at ur phone. i'm sorry about ?s on willow. i like her pic. she's cute.

After the billionth text, Mika responded. *How many times do I have to tell you? It's not you. I overheard your mom say something.* Mika shook her head and turned to look out the window, but Jenn kept texting.

it's ok if u like her. don't ignore her. maybe she's the 1. kiss her. how else are u going to figure it out?

Kiss her? Mika could barely talk to her sometimes. *Don't start.*

admit it. U LIKE HER. ur really happy every time U say her name. & her text didn't sound so innocent to me--hi, Mika. i miss you. when are we going to study again?

Mika glared at her. Jenn just wouldn't let up. *Fine. I like her. But I wasn't going home because of you. Now STFU.*

When they got back to her house, Mika ran up and opened the door. She faked a smile and waved at her aunt and cousins from the threshold. After making sure they were out of sight, she went in and slammed the door.

"Mika?" Aunt Val called from the kitchen.

She marched in and threw her duffel bag onto the island. It landed with a thud and knocked over the salt and pepper shakers.

"What's gotten you ticked off now?" Aunt Val washed her hands.

Mika was so fucking mad. She wanted to pound the countertop. She stared her aunt down, afraid she'd punch her once they started talking.

"Aunt Pauline called. She thinks you and Jenn were fighting. Care to tell me what's going on?"

Mika gritted her teeth. "You were my dad's lover."

"What? No!"

"Jesus Christ. Why can't you just tell me the truth? That's why the family hated you, isn't it?"

"Do you honestly think your mom would've appointed me as your guardian if I had an affair with your dad?" Aunt Val placed her hands on her hip.

"Fuck your shitty lies. I know why Aunt Pauline hates you. I overheard her talking to a friend about you and *Andy.*" He preferred Andrew, but his family called him Andy as a child. Mika hated the way Aunt Pauline used his childhood name when she talked about him with friends. Like she was still the big sister. *Focus.*

I'm angry with Aunt Val. "She can't forgive you for your affair. Ho bitch." Mika grabbed her bag then ran upstairs.

"Wait. You've got it all wrong."

She heard Aunt Val behind her, but Mika didn't give a shit anymore. How could her dad have chosen her over her mom? "Go away! I fucking hate you. Slut!"

"Don't you dare use that tone and those words with me!" Aunt Val stuck her foot in the door and somehow grabbed Mika's arm with a death grip. "Follow me. I have something to show you that will clear everything up."

Mika had had enough of Aunt Val's secrets and lies. "Let go of my arm."

When her aunt let go and stepped back into the hallway, Mika slammed the bedroom door. Aunt Val probably envisioned herself as some sort of hero caring for poor little Mika. All she was really doing was hiding the truth. *Fuck her.* Mika left the door unlocked and silently dared her to enter.

After a few seconds of silence, Mika pulled out a suitcase and another duffel bag from her closet and started stuffing clothes inside. She didn't want to leave Ithaca but couldn't live in this house with Aunt Val. Mika needed at least a week or two. If Aunt Val confessed and apologized, maybe she'd move back, but she didn't ever want to talk to her again. She stopped at the sound of tapping on the door.

"Come out. Let's talk. Please," Aunt Val said quietly.

Anger ripped through Mika, and she jerked open the door. "I told you to leave me alone!" She clenched her hands into fists. But she didn't have a clear shot at Aunt Val's face. The slut held up some damn book between them.

"This is my high school yearbook when I was a senior." Her aunt thrust it forward, tapping her index finger on a picture of a girl.

With as much sarcasm as Mika could muster, she said, "Charming."

"Read her name."

"I don't have time for games. I'm packing and going back to Aunt Pauline's." Mika would call soon and give Aunt Pauline her victory lap, at least for a little bit. Maybe she could go live with Benjy.

Aunt Val lowered the book, her eyes full of tears. "Say her name out loud, please."

"Fine." Mika leaned over to get a better view of the picture. *Oh fuck. Is that what I think it is?* She squinted and reread the name. "Andrea Kingston."

Aunt Val flipped to a pink sticky note and tapped the picture. "What's this one say?"

"Homecoming Queen, Andi Kingston." Damn, she hadn't seen that coming. Her arms dropped. "You're gay?"

"Yes."

Mika swallowed. She was the one who was an ass, not Aunt Val. Too late to take back all the shitty names, but she had to try. "I'm sorry. What's the story? I mean, Aunt Pauline lives in Binghamton. How would she know about your high school years?"

"May I come in and sit?"

Mika sat on her bed and gestured toward her desk chair.

"Andi's family moved to Binghamton after our graduation. I didn't know she worked with Pauline or that they'd become good friends. Anyway, years later, we met again at a party. She was with her husband—"

"You messed around with a married woman?" Mika bolted upright. "Sorry. It's none of my business. You were both adults. But I thought you didn't live here after college."

Aunt Val sighed. "That's correct. The party was in Toronto, where I worked. It was my first job after college. Anyway, she was planning to leave her husband and file for divorce by the time we got involved."

"Dad and Mom's families weren't gay-friendly. More like nail 'em to the cross. And they'd tell Mom and Dad all the time that I should move to a private Catholic school because they thought

Ithaca had turned too liberal and had a lot of bad influences. Wait. If you lived in Canada, how'd they find out?"

Aunt Val rubbed her forehead like she had a headache. "The relationship heated up, and I started visiting Ithaca more."

"Oh, someone saw you two together." That was pretty stupid.

"Your mom and Pauline caught us together."

What had her mom seen? Fooling around with kissing or— "Holy shit. They caught you screwing?" Her words were out so fast, and she could feel her eyebrows shoot up to the top of her hairline.

"Andi lied to cover herself. She claimed that I seduced her and talked her into the divorce." Aunt Val ran her fingers through her hair and sighed. "Up until then, no one knew that I was gay. But Pauline went on the warpath, telling everyone. Mom and Dad couldn't deal with it. Your dad tried to settle everyone down, and your mom was in shock, not so much that I was gay, but that I'd had an affair." Aunt Val pulled a tissue from her pocket and wiped her eyes.

Mika shouldn't press further, but she couldn't help herself. "Was she your only married lover?"

"Yes." Aunt Val glared at her. She put her hand up. "Sorry. I shouldn't have answered with that tone."

"Sorry I asked. It's just...interesting." *Oh my God.* What other damn thing was going to drop out of her mouth spontaneously? "Are you just into women? Or are you bi?"

"Do you have a problem with that?"

"Nope. Just curious." It was cool to learn her aunt was gay, and Mika felt more of a connection with her, but talking to her would be like talking to a parent. "Look, I'm sorry I called you names and went crazy. But you're my guardian." This was awkward. Maybe this was the secret that everyone was hiding from her. But Mom and Dad weren't homophobic like the grands. So maybe this shit was deeper. Mika had to be careful how she phrased things. She didn't want to make things worse. "You've told me this much, you might as well help me with research for sex ed class. Don't worry. I won't use your name." Mika cracked her knuckles.

"Class research, huh?"

"And to get to know you better. It's only fair. You're not hiding, are you?"

"No, I'm not hiding. It didn't come up before, and I'd assumed that you already knew." Aunt Val relaxed her stance. "I'm physically and emotionally attracted to women, and I identify as a lesbian. I am who I am, and I'm not ashamed of it. But it tore the family apart." She choked up again and wiped a tear from her eye. "Your parents were in the middle, but we got past it. It hurt that Mom and Dad never could. Mom was just cold. When Dad found out I was with a woman, he said that I was an abomination and that I was dead to him."

"Grandpa Hayden said that?" Mika knew her grandparents thought gays were destroying traditional marriages but never guessed they'd turn their back on their kid. *Fuck, this was intense.*

"Yes."

"And that's why he never talked about you?"

"Yes. Everyone but your parents believed Andi's side of the story. After everything fell apart in the family, I got a job offer in Boston. I wanted a fresh start in a new city, and I liked the company."

"I get my parents forgave you. They asked you to come home a lot, but you didn't. Why?"

"I tried last summer, but you went to Wyoming with your cousins."

Mika felt terrible because Aunt Val looked like she was on the verge of crying again. "Sorry. Mom tried to get me to stay, but I wasn't going to pass up horseback riding at my grandparents' ranch." She took a deep breath. "And it seemed kind of stupid to hang around to meet an aunt I didn't know and who I thought didn't care about me."

Although teary-eyed, Aunt Val cracked a smile. "I missed you, but I probably would've gone too if I were in your shoes. Horseback riding is fun, and the Wyoming mountains are beautiful."

"You still haven't answered my question. Why didn't you visit more?"

Aunt Val closed her eyes and rubbed the bridge of her nose. Her face seemed to turn into stone. "Mika, I spent long hours at work building my career. The higher I got, the more I worked, and when I did vacation, it was never back here." She choked up again but wouldn't look at Mika. "Believe me, I'm really sorry. I missed you growing up, and I missed time with my sister." She got up and went to the door. "I'm making your favorite chicken pot pie. I'll call you when it's done. Maybe we can play ping pong or something afterward."

Gee, Aunt Val was just like Mom when she threw up a wall and diverted. "Wait." Mika ran after her and caught up at the bottom of the stairs. "Do you have a girlfriend now?"

Her aunt raised her eyebrow.

"Um...just curious. You should get a girlfriend. Someone to hang out with and have fun." Maybe she should take her own advice and tell Willow how she felt.

"I'm not in the habit of telling my niece when I date."

"Sorry."

"If I get serious with someone, I'll be sure to introduce you." Aunt Val continued to the kitchen.

"Gucci."

Her aunt briefly turned and looked puzzled. "You want to go shopping for expensive clothes?"

"Gucci. It's another word for cool." Mika smiled. "Do you need help in the kitchen?"

Aunt Val stopped and blinked. "That'd be lovely. Mika, this..." she waved her hand back and forth between them, "is all new to me. I'm trying my best."

"I'll try too."

"Thanks."

In the kitchen, Mika crammed her hands in her pockets. "Um,

you wear dresses, and Andi looks really glamorous in those photos." She swallowed her embarrassment; she wanted to know more about Aunt Val being gay.

Her aunt raised an eyebrow then smiled. "There's no rulebook about how a gay person should dress. Thankfully, the cookie-cutter bullshit of the past is fading."

"Did you know who you were in high school or when you were younger?" She wished she hadn't asked. Her interest was coming off way too high-key.

"I had this massive crush on Mrs. Buckley in junior high school. Oh my God, her long wavy blond hair and curves." Aunt Val's smile widened, and she fanned herself. "But it was hard to admit it to myself. The pieces slowly fell into place in high school when Andi and I grew closer. I finally became comfortable with myself when I moved away to college. Mika, life is all about change, and I learn something new about myself and the world every day. Sometimes it's small, and sometimes the significance hits me later. Change is inevitable. It's not always bad and being different isn't bad. You don't have to have everything planned out in detail by the time you're eighteen." She placed her hand on Mika's shoulder. "I want you to know that you can ask me anything if you have any questions about dating or sex. I won't judge. And when the time comes, please practice safe sex. Have you had those discussions in school?"

Now besides burning up, Mika's mouth hung open. All she could do was nod. Everyone knew that embarrassing teens was a sport to parents and relatives, but shit, this was her damn fault. She'd walked into the mess by asking Aunt Val all those questions. At least, she could hide in the back of the room in sex ed class. She couldn't do that now.

"Do you have any questions about sex?"

Mika swung around and stuck her head in the fridge. "I thought we were going to prepare food. It's a little gross to be talking about that stuff so close to dinner, don't you think?" She grabbed a handful of carrots and celery. "I'll cut up the vegetables while you make the pie crust."

They worked in silence. Suddenly, the thought slammed into Mika's brain. Why didn't her parents say Aunt Val was gay? The knife slipped in her hand and cut her finger.

"You're bleeding." Her aunt pulled her over to the sink. "Rinse it good. I'll get some antibacterial ointment and a Band-Aid."

Mika swallowed hard while Aunt Val ran out for the first aid kit. *Shit. Shit. Shit.* Her parents must have guessed she was gay. That would explain why they chose Aunt Val as her guardian. And didn't all gay people have that radar thing? All of the fucking trauma probably threw Aunt Val off, which meant it was only a matter of time before she saw that Mika was gay too. Though Mika wasn't even sure who she was until she met Willow. But Aunt Val was gay. She shouldn't care. Should Mika tell her? *NO.* Mika liked Willow, but maybe the attraction was to her personality. She was kidding herself; it was so much more than that. But she definitely didn't want to give her aunt a reason to launch into a lengthy sex ed discussion. God, her mind was so jumbled with thoughts.

Aunt Val came back and dressed her cut. "Better?"

"I'm glad you told me," she said softly and really meant it.

"Me too." Aunt Val smiled and tucked Mika's hair behind her ear.

But that was enough, and the topic had to be shut down before her aunt started asking questions about her stuff. She turned and opened the refrigerator again. "I've taken some private diving lessons at Jenn's indoor pool and was thinking about signing up for lessons after school."

"Do I need to sign anything?"

"Probably, but I haven't decided yet."

"I'm so sorry I didn't see you swim during the regular season."

Mika took a juice out of the fridge. Warmth and sadness shone in Aunt Val's smile and eyes. "Aunt Pauline's club is having an invitational in April. They invited me to swim with the team. All the profit goes to charity. Want to come?"

"That sounds good."

Aunt Val's smile dropped at Aunt Pauline's name, and she looked away. She didn't have to spell it out. Aunt Pauline held grudges. A chill ran down Mika's spine. Jenn didn't have a problem with her being gay, but all hell would break loose if her mom ever found out. Aunt Pauline would probably stop Jenn from seeing Mika.

"You should finish dinner. Don't want to cut myself again." Mika placed the chopped vegetables into a bowl and handed it to Aunt Val. She didn't say anything, and Mika hustled out of there fast.

Upstairs, Missy and Mr. Big had taken up the center of her bed.

"Get off." Mika gently shoved them, but they didn't move. Missy yawned and closed her eyes, and Mr. Big stared at her, as if daring her to move him. His big, round eyes were wideset and creepy as hell. But he was a sweetheart as long as he was fed on time. Otherwise, he jumped up where he shouldn't and knocked things down. They each had their favorite hiding spot, but if Mika left her door open, they'd come in and make themselves at home. She squeezed in next to them and petted their soft fur, then texted Jenn. *Does your mom have access to your phone?*

no way. she doesn't know the passcode. why so tense?

You know your mom doesn't like gays. Now I know why. Mika paused and erased the sentences. It wasn't her business to out Aunt Val. *I'm sorry for storming out of your house. I was mad at Aunt Val, but we got things settled. I was wrong about a lot of things. We ok?*

yeah. i was hurt because u always talk to me. but lately ur in the clouds.

Sorry.

uv been thru a lot. i should be kinder.

Mika was lucky to have Jenn as her cousin. They could talk about things she didn't want to bother Benjy with. Dudes just didn't understand sometimes. *Do I look gay?*

well u got more muscle. u don't wear makeup or dresses. but its not about ur clothes. like i said u glow when u say willows name. what do u like about her? if u say it to me, maybe ur brain & heart will catch fire.

Mika wasn't sure she wanted to go that far, but then after a second, she answered. *Her eyes are beautiful, like I could stare at her all day. She wears lip gloss or lipstick, but she doesn't put on a ton like some girls. She wears nice clothes but doesn't act like she's a princess. Her wavy blond hair looks great. And she's really nice to everyone.*

&

& what? Mika knew what Jenn was getting at, but why was it so hard to say?

do i have to hit u over the head? does ur body tingle?

Mika sucked in a breath of air and blew it out. What did her dad always say? "In for a penny, in for a pound." *Yes. Gotta go.*

oh no u dont. tell me then u wont be such a scared little kid. its okay to be queer.

Not everyone thinks so.

huh? is some dick cappin u? assholes don't define u. ur dope. don't forget it.

Thanks, cuz. So far, the bullying hadn't gotten bad, but she didn't want to get into the details with Jenn. *Hey, almost forgot. Heard anything about my DNA test?*

not yet. they get swamped around xmas. proly valentines day too. now what about willow?

Mika slowly typed out the response and reread it. *The shape of her body. I didn't want to let go the first time she hugged me.* She swallowed and added, *I dream about kissing her and touching her. Her breasts are perfect. The right size and shape.* She hit send.

what??? how do you know about her breasts?

Fuck. Mika tossed the phone aside, but Jenn blew it up. After a while, Mika couldn't stand the chiming from Jenn's bombardment. She typed, *Sweaters. She fills them out nice.*

i smell shit miles away. dish.

Fuck. Fuck. Fuckity fuck. *Okay, I saw her naked in the gym shower.*

wow. im proud of u.

Thanks. No more questions. Please.

k. lmfao because ur prob red as hell. but its freeing to say it out loud. bet u feel better.

Jenn was right; she did. *Yeah. Bye.*

bye, cuz. luv u even tho ur weird.

What do you mean?

in a good way ur a luvable geek. sports. ur super brainy & super kind.

I love you too, Ms. Nosey. Later. Need to help with dinner.

One more little white lie didn't hurt. Geez, what was it with their families? White lies seemed to be the crowning family jewel.

The air whooshed out of Mika as Mr. Big relocated to her stomach. She pushed him off. His hair was so soft, and it made her think of Willow. Yeah, she wanted to touch Willow's hair, run her fingertips along her jaw and down her body. She wanted to kiss her and hear her moan. But what if she was bad at it? And even if Willow was gay, would she want Mika? *Shit, face it. I want her and can't stop thinking about her.*

Mika curled up around the cats and closed her eyes. When her thoughts continued to swirl, she grabbed her earbuds and listened to one of her playlists. Her muscles began to relax, and her breathing slowed. Madison Beer's "Make You Mine" began to play, and Mika's mind surged to thinking about Willow again. The lyrics perfectly matched her feelings. *Please pick me.*

Chapter Seventeen

WILLOW WAS ALREADY IN the library when Mika arrived. For a minute, she watched Willow's beautiful face as she read a book. Mika shook out of her haze and sat down next to her. "Hey, can I talk to you for a minute?"

Willow closed her book and rested her chin in the palm of her hand. "Sounds serious. What's up?"

"I had a bad fight with my aunt." Mika explained what had happened but left out the part about Aunt Val being gay. "I acted like a jerk and called her some nasty names. Dad liked to be called Andrew." Her stomach flipped. It hurt so much that he was gone. "His family called him Andy as a kid. So, when Aunt Pauline said Andi, I thought she meant Dad. But now I know different." She took a deep breath, relieved it was all out, and hoped to get some advice. But Willow remained quiet for a minute.

"You shouldn't jump to conclusions like that."

"I know. I was an ass." Mika folded her arms on the table and lowered her head.

"There's a lot of hurt inside you and your aunt. You need to find a way to make peace."

"How'd you get so smart?" Mika looked into her poker face, then Willow smiled, and Mika felt a hundred times better.

"Being an only child whose father ditched us. Mom made sure I worked hard. And if I acted up and sassed back, we'd have a talk about what I did wrong and how to correct it. Then she'd give me lots of extra chores to rethink everything I'd done."

"What happened to your dad? Does he ever send you cards or gifts?"

"I never hear from him. He abandoned us when I was two. I've always known Mom has worked hard for us, but I'm just now realizing how much she's sacrificed."

"Sorry." Mika had the world's greatest dad. Why was life so unfair?

Willow lightly rubbed her forearm. "What happened to you is so fucked up, but your aunt came here to help. I know you'll find a way to make it up to her because you're a good person," she said softly. "And remember, the small things from the heart are the best."

"Thanks." Mika sniffled. Four kids who had been sitting in the corner laughed, and Mika looked in their direction, but they weren't laughing at her and Willow. They dumped about a zillion books on the table as they left.

Willow tapped Mika's hand. "Is there any chance you could come over to my house on Sunday and help me with math?"

"Sure." That'd be one of Mika's small dreams coming true. The big one would be Willow being her girlfriend.

"Let's do homework, then we can shelve books." She held up *The Great Gatsby*. "I read it a couple of years ago, but to help you, I've been speed reading it again."

"I'm glad one of us can." Mika slumped in her chair.

"Are you almost finished? We could talk about ideas for your paper."

"I've only read four or five chapters." Mika wet her lips. "I've been busy with physics and math."

Willow shook her head. "Okay, let's talk an abbreviated version to get you started but promise me you'll finish it."

When Willow held up her little pinky, Mika hooked hers with Willow's. "I swear."

"Can I have my finger back now?" Willow asked.

"Ah, yeah." Mika released her hand.

"Goofy." Willow nudged her, her eyes sparkling.

The more Mika got to know Willow, the more she craved being with her. When Mika realized she was staring, she quickly opened her spiral notebook before Willow caught on to how turned on she was. "I'm ready." She scribbled notes as Willow talked about the overall plot, but her mind kept drifting to Willow's lovely face. With every word coming out of Willow's mouth, Mika's pulse increased, and she thought about what it would be like to have Willow's soft lips on hers.

Too soon, the period bell rang, and they had to split off to their separate classrooms. She had her favorite classes in the afternoon, but she kept daydreaming about Willow. At the end of the day, reality struck. Mika had to apologize to Aunt Val. Willow said to do something small but thoughtful from *the heart*. An idea came to her, and she texted Willow. *I need a favor.*

The next morning, Mika got up super early and quietly rushed downstairs to beat her aunt. She turned and smiled when Aunt Val entered the kitchen. "Good morning."

"Good morning." Her aunt raised her brows. "Anything special happening at school that I should know about?" She glanced down at her PJs. "I'm obviously not dressed."

"Nope." Mika smiled, and thanked her lucky stars that Aunt Val hadn't seen Willow's car moments ago when she dropped off the bakery bag.

Her aunt opened the cabinet and stretched for a mug.

"Oh, your cup's ready to go." Mika held up a large mug. "One packet of sweetener and almond milk, just how you like it." She placed Aunt Val's cup under the machine and popped in a K-cup. "Here you go."

"Thank you so much." Her aunt took a sip.

"How does it taste?"

"Perfect. But I could have sworn I smelled cinnamon and thought maybe it was in the coffee. I guess I'm half asleep. But you are Mika and not an alien, right?" Aunt Val smiled.

"Didn't you know? I'm a changeling." Mika chuckled. "And you're welcome." She handed her aunt a plate of toast and a hard-boiled egg. "I don't really cook much, and so I thought this'd be the safest." Mika folded her hands behind her back. "I'm sorry about the other day, especially about calling you names."

"Thank you. That means the world to me."

Mika fixed her own toast and sat down. "It's super cold today, and you said you had an afternoon appointment with an accountant. Can I catch a ride with Willow, please?" When Aunt Val arched an eyebrow, Mika thought she'd blown it. "That's not why I fixed you breakfast. I just needed to apologize since I was totally wrong."

"Okay. Promise me that you'll buckle up. I want you to be safe."

Mika grinned. "No drag racing? You're no fun. Can I have her teach me to drive?"

"No." Aunt Val returned the smile.

"Okay." Mika winked. "Thanks. And don't worry. Willow's a careful driver."

"How's the photography going?"

"It's great. I've snapped images of the deer at the park."

Her aunt grabbed her empty plate and stood.

"No, let me get the dirty dishes. Would you like another coffee?"

"Yes, please, Ms. Changeling."

"Here's your newspaper." Mika grinned at the look on her aunt's face. She didn't know someone could raise their eyebrows that high and open their mouth that wide at the same time. "I can be nice, you know." She took the plates to the sink. While the coffee brewed, she removed the treat out of the bakery bag. Carefully, she placed the coffee and a heart-shaped cinnamon coffee cake in front of her aunt. "It's a few days before Valentine's Day and your birthday, but happy birthday, Aunt Val."

"Thank you, sweetie." Her aunt jumped up and hugged her.

"You're welcome. But you don't have to squeeze me to death."

"This is the biggest and most thoughtful surprise in my life." Aunt Val rubbed her thumb across Mika's cheek, then her smiled dropped. "I'm sorry. I forgot that you don't want me calling you sweetie."

"I don't mind now that we've gotten to know one another. Sit and enjoy." Happiness spread through Mika. They were on the right path now.

After putting her plate in the dishwasher, Mika turned back around. "Oh, I'm tutoring Willow in math. She's asked me to come over to her house this Sunday." Mika bit her lip, wanting to grin. Aunt Val would find that weird and ask her why she was so excited. Her aunt might be gay, but Mika didn't want any dating advice.

"I don't see a problem with that." Aunt Val put on her reading glasses and picked up her phone. "I'll put it in my calendar."

"Great!" She said that a little too enthusiastically because her aunt looked at her as if she somehow knew. "I gotta get ready." Mika hurried out of the kitchen and up the stairs. Her entire body felt super-charged, and that amazing tingling feeling grew. Hot damn, she was going to Willow's house.

Chapter Eighteen

MIKA CLENCHED HER BOOKBAG to her chest as they drove the short distance to Willow's house. Tutoring Willow in the library was nerve-racking and exciting enough, but this was overload. She was scared she'd do something wrong, excited at the chance of another hug, and desperate for her first kiss... God, Willow was so cute. *But what if I'm stuck in a dream?*

"You're extremely quiet," Aunt Val said. "Are you nervous?"

Tons. "Ah, a little."

"Your teacher said you were excellent at trigonometry. You'll be fine."

"Yeah." Mika smiled but curled her fingers tighter around the bag. It wasn't the math she was nervous about, but she couldn't tell Aunt Val that. She couldn't say that she wanted to be more than friends with Willow. But maybe Willow was only being friendly because she desperately needed help in math. Mika mentally slapped herself. Willow was *real*, and she was the nicest person Mika had ever met. And if Willow was gay, then she was the prettiest girl in the Universe who was gay too.

Her aunt pulled the car into the driveway, and Mika hopped out.

"What are you doing?" Mika asked when Aunt Val got out of the car too. She slung her bag over her shoulder and crossed her arms. Aunt Val needed to get her ass back in the car and drive home.

"I'd like to meet Willow's mother."

"Do it another time. I'm not a baby, and this isn't a play date."

"It's impolite for me to leave without saying hello." Aunt Val walked toward the house.

Mika sighed heavily and followed. Willow opened the door, smiling and looking pretty in light blue jogging pants and a cream-colored sweater that clung to her breasts perfectly. Mika's throat went dry. She wanted to kiss Willow all over.

"Hi, Mika," Willow said.

"Hey." Mika tightened her grip around her bag.

Willow's smile widened. "And you must be Mika's aunt, Ms. Hayden. I'm Willow Parker."

"For heaven's sake, open the door and invite them in. It's cold outside," Mrs. Parker called as she approached them.

"This is my mom, Naomi."

"It's finally a pleasure to meet you in person, Val." Mrs. Parker gestured them inside, then shut the door.

"Good to see you too, Naomi. I've enjoyed our phone conversations." Aunt Val held out her hand.

What the fuck did they have to talk about? Mika's stomach roiled, like she was going to vomit.

"Me too." Mrs. Parker shook Aunt Val's hand. "I made us some coffee and a pound cake. Come on in and get comfortable."

"Thank you." Her aunt sat on the sofa next to where the cake and coffee were already laid out. They immediately started chatting and laughing.

The two looked like they'd be talking forever. *This can't be happening. Shit, shit, shit.*

"I made spinach dip for you girls. It's in the downstairs fridge, and there's a bag of tortilla chips on the table," Willow's mom said.

"Thanks, Mom." Willow grasped Mika's hand and led her to the basement.

Mika emptied her book bag, and her pulse ticked up when Willow positioned her chair beside her. Wow, she smelled extra great. "What's that perfume?" Heat crept up from her neck to her face. How did that thought slip out of her mouth?

Willow smiled. "Ariana Grande's Cloud. Do you ever wear

perfume or cologne?"

"No. I'm saving my money." Mika looked away. "We should start." Hell, she wouldn't know what to wear. She often got ugly looks when she shopped around the men's cologne counter. *Wait a minute. She asked if I wore perfume or cologne.* Mika liked Willow more and more.

After an hour of studying, Willow threw her pencil down and buried her head in her hands. "I hate logarithms and quadratic relations. I feel like an idiot." She turned and put her hand on Mika's forearm. "But you're a great tutor. I didn't understand half of this mess until you started helping me. Thanks."

"You're welcome. And you're not an idiot. I'll catch you up before the next test." Her face was so close to Willow's. She glanced down at her lips then bolted out of the chair and began packing up her things. "Aunt Val should be here soon." *If she ever left.*

"Want to see my bedroom?"

Mika froze. "Ah, sure."

Mrs. Parker was alone when they went back upstairs. "Mika, your aunt should be back in about twenty minutes. She had an errand to run, and I told her to take her time."

"Thanks." Not only was Mika grateful for the extra time, but Mrs. Parker also didn't seem to freak out that they were heading to Willow's room. Yet another sign she wasn't gay.

Willow swung the door open and stepped aside for Mika to enter first.

Mika was blown away. The ceiling looked like the sky, and it had a cheerful sun peeking out from behind white puffy clouds. The walls were one big mountain scene with animals and birds hiding in the bushes or trees. "This art is fantastic. Who painted it?" Mika turned, and Willow's bright smile took her breath away. "You did this?"

"Uh-huh. I'll study art in college." Willow's smile faltered. "I missed out on a scholarship to one of the better schools, but I won one at the City University of New York. I need a decent grade to keep it. I think you've helped with that."

"You're welcome." Mika glanced around the room again. "You're super talented." She stared into Willow's beautiful face, and that mysterious weightless feeling and tingling took over her body.

"CUNY's a great public school, but my budget's tight for NYC living expenses. Mom tells me not to worry. She's been working extra hours and says she's got it covered. What about you?" Willow asked.

"Physics, maybe astrophysics. The University of California Berkeley and Cal Tech accepted me, but I'm waiting to hear from Columbia. That's my top choice." And now it was even more important to get there. Her and Willow in the same city, with no adults or guardians? That sounded like heaven.

"Columbia University in New York City?" Willow's mouth popped open.

Mika nodded. Then realization of her family's wealth compared to Willow's suddenly knocked the wind out of her. Mika had the choice of all the top schools, and Columbia was the most expensive.

"That's fire." Willow's face lit up with a wide smile. "I'd heard about how good you were in math and science before we met." She put her hands on Mika's arms. "I really hope you get into Columbia. We could hang out since CUNY's only a short subway ride away."

"Yeah." Mika zoomed from feeling shitty to feeling like she'd won the Breakthrough Prize in Quantum Field Theory. Damn, this day couldn't get any better. Her pulse skyrocketed as Willow's touch lingered. "I have enough credits to graduate this year." Mika cleared her throat. "I haven't told my aunt yet. I want to look at my options and decide on my own."

"I get it. I love my mom, but her constant opinions on what might be best for me are annoying."

"That's what I'm afraid of." She had to keep this a secret until the last minute. Her mom thought she was too young to graduate and move to the city, and Aunt Val would probably think the same. But if Aunt Val stood in her way, Mika would fight like hell.

"It'll work out for you too." Willow threw her arms around Mika and hugged her.

But this one was different from the hug after her parents' death. Her body was strong, yet so soft. Mika wrapped her arms around Willow and inhaled the sweet smell of her skin. When Willow stepped back, she had the cutest blush.

"Thanks for everything, Mika."

"Sure." Now, what would they talk about? Mika jammed her hands into her jeans' pockets and scanned her suddenly empty brain for a topic. "I could join the college swim team, but I won't have much time with my major."

"That's too bad. You're the best on our team in fly, but I think you're good overall. Some are jealous of you. I've heard them throw shade." Willow rolled her eyes and crossed her arms. "They're the basement of mid."

"Yeah. Not all the girls on the team are nice like you." Mika didn't know how Willow could be so nice to idiots like Ashley and Carrie, but she was.

"Forget them. You're smart, a good person, and a great swimmer." Willow gently grasped her hand.

Willow's compliment, her unwavering gaze, and the touch of her hand caused Mika's body to tingle all over. Should she kiss her? She moved a bit closer, and Willow didn't step away.

"Mika, your aunt's here."

Mika flinched and jumped back at Mrs. Parker's voice. "I'd better go." Her insides trembled. What was she thinking? She'd almost kissed Willow right in front of an open door.

"Thanks for coming over. I don't hate math as much when I'm around you."

"No problem."

"Um, could you tutor me twice a week for a while?"

"Sure," Mika said, almost choking around her response. She

wasn't about to turn down the opportunity to spend more alone time with Willow. "I'll talk to Aunt Val and text you. Better go." She raced down the stairs.

"I was telling Mrs. Parker about my new work schedule," Aunt Val said. "Beginning next week, I have an eight a.m. video conference call every day."

"And I'm out the door at six," Mrs. Parker said.

Aunt Val looked at Willow. "Your mother assures me you're a good driver. Would you mind giving Mika a lift to school?"

"Sure." Willow bumped Mika's shoulder and smiled. "We like the same music. Should be fun."

Holy shit. This day was turning out great. On the way home, Mika stuck her earbuds in and tapped her thumbs against her book bag to the rhythm of the music. She'd never kissed anyone, but she bet Willow's lips would be soft and sweet. Could she get that happy ending to all her dreams? Her aunt patted her shoulder, and Mika removed her earbud. "Yeah?"

"How did the tutoring go?"

"Really good. But we might have to meet twice a week. Do you think that's possible?"

"I'll talk with Mrs. Parker. I don't see a problem as long as your grades and other activities don't suffer."

"Great." Mika smiled at the thought of another Willow super hug. But she had to curb the affection that bubbled below the surface. She didn't want to embarrass herself or drive Willow away. Willow's friendship felt good, not as good as it would be if they were...*more*, but close.

As Mika was putting her earbud back in, Aunt Val took a drink from the red Yeti that Mika had given her mom last year for Christmas. Mika turned away and pressed her face against the cold window. *If Mom was here now would I tell her? Or would I be too fucking scared?*

She thought her parents had guessed. Sometimes, they just said stuff that hinted at it. But now she'd never know, and that hurt so fucking bad. Goddammit. Her grief came out of nowhere and smashed her good times and happy feelings. She closed her eyes, refusing to cry.

Chapter Nineteen

March

MIKA GATHERED HER BOOKS into her backpack and walked down the school hallway. It was nearly empty since school was over, but the last thing she needed was to get into trouble from running inside. She flung the doors open and ran toward the pickup zone.

"Mika, wait up!" Benjy called out.

She turned around, walked backward, and yelled, "My aunt is picking me up." She hurried on, but he soon caught up with her.

"You haven't been online much recently. What gives? You've got plenty of time to talk with Willow."

Mika stopped. Was Benjy jealous or something? "So I can't have any other friends that don't game?"

"You know that's not what I meant. I'm glad she's your friend, but I miss gaming with you." He grinned. "And you can be fun to talk to sometimes."

Mika's phone pinged, and she glanced at it. Good, Aunt Val was running late too. Mika stared at the pavement as she began walking at a slower pace. "I'm just busy." She hadn't told him about tutoring Willow in her house. She kind of wanted to spill the tea, maybe just a little. But she also wanted to keep Willow to herself.

"You were on fire in the games, but when Willow came into the picture, I started beating your ass badly. Then you dropped out. Is Willow...different?"

She kept moving but gave him a sideways glare. "What are you getting at?"

"It's okay. My cousin is bi. He's coming out to his parents soon."

Benjy bumped her shoulder. "Most people don't give two shits. Only a few stuck-up assholes care."

Mika thought about her Hayden grandparents; how they'd treated Aunt Val was fucked up. They'd probably disown her too if they were alive. Fear crept up her spine. Her Lavigne grandparents and Aunt Pauline were just as bad with their homophobe jabs. And what about the other students? Ashley and Carrie would love having something else to mess with her.

Benjy grabbed her shoulder. "Are you into Willow?"

"So what if I am?" she said in a low voice and pushed his hand away. Jenn had guessed she was gay and now Benjy was digging. Who else? It'd suck if Ashley's full gang of ten came after her.

"Hey, I'm happy for you, and I hope she feels the same way because you're super cool." Benjy lightly smacked her back. "Playing online with people outside our group is dope, but I miss you. Hey, hop on tonight. And Sunday, the youth group at church is going ice skating. Come with me."

"I'm busy, and I'm just not into religion." Damn, there's that Benjy puppy dog face that tore her apart. "I'll think about gaming tonight. Depends on how much homework I get done." In truth, she'd probably rush home and spend most of the night texting with Jenn and Willow. She heard a car approaching and turned to see Aunt Val. "I have to go."

Aunt Val lowered the window. "Hi, Benjy. Can I give you a ride?"

"Sweet." Benjy hopped in the backseat before Mika opened the front passenger door.

Shit. He'd better not say anything about Willow, or she'd kill him. Fortunately, he ran his mouth about the Roblox game he was creating. Benjy was clever and far more strategic than Wes, so she bet his game was awesome.

He leaned forward and pointed. "Isn't that Willow's car getting towed?"

"Yeah. Let's give her a hand." Mika's heartbeat quickened. After her parents' accident, she couldn't take it if Willow was hurt. As her aunt parked, Willow came into sight and waved. Thank God, she was okay.

"Infamous Willow," Benjy said.

Mika gave him a look, hoping it would shut him up. When they got out, she grabbed his arm and whispered, "Don't you fucking dare."

"I won't."

But his shit-eating grin unnerved her.

"Hi, Mika." Willow smiled. "Hi, Benjy and Ms. Hayden."

"Hey. What's wrong with your car?" Mika asked.

"I don't know. Steam came rushing out of the hood." Willow pointed to the tow truck driver. He thinks it's some sort of coolant leak."

"The car likely needs a new hose, which isn't too bad. They'll check it out in the garage and give you a call." The tow truck driver handed Willow's insurance card back. "Are you catching a ride with your friends?"

"I can give you a ride," Aunt Val said.

"That'd be great." Willow beamed and slid into the back seat.

"Can Willow have dinner with us?"

Aunt Val checked for traffic, then pulled into the road. "Sure, they can both stay, but we're not eating until seven thirty. You can have a snack beforehand."

"Benjy's got too much homework," Mika blurted out, then glanced at him. He gave her a death look followed by a smirk.

"Thanks. I'll text my mom," Willow said.

Mika's phone vibrated after dropping Benjy off.

Wake up stupid. She's got serious rizz and looks at you like a meal.

Mika's mouth went dry, and she slipped her phone back in her pocket. She thought Willow was just being nice, but maybe there really was more there.

"Mom said yes." Willow squeezed Mika's shoulder.

Her touch electrified Mika. "Great. Hey, we have a ping pong table in the basement. Want to play?" Mika wanted to smack her forehead. Ping pong was so romantic. *Not.* Her mind went to the sofa. "We can watch some Netflix after."

"Sounds fun."

At home, Mika walked downstairs on wobbly legs, hoping Benjy was right.

"I like your house, and the woods are pretty."

"Thanks." Mika served the ball, and they hit it back and forth in silence for several minutes. Suddenly, Willow smashed it, and the ball whizzed by Mika.

"Forgot to tell you. My cousin's a state champion in Vermont. He taught me a few moves." Willow grinned. She stretched out both arms and leaned over the table. Her loose shirt hung low and away from her chest.

Mika drew in a breath at the sight of Willow's creamy skin meeting her low-cut bra. She didn't want to look away. "Um." She picked up the ball. "I'm getting along much better with Aunt Val."

"Good." Willow smiled.

"There's still one thing I don't get."

"What?"

Mika put down the ball and paddle. "In her bio on the Boston website, she said the research was rewarding and finding a cure for cancer was a lifelong goal. My mom told me their grandmother had died of breast cancer, and Aunt Val was the closest to her. So why would she give it all up to be my guardian when Aunt Pauline is only an hour away? I mean, I'm glad I don't have to move, but I still don't get it."

"You should relax and stop worrying. Your aunt seems nice. Maybe a little crazy since she agreed to take on a tough case like you."

Mika looked up.

"I'm kidding. Relax." Willow winked.

Mika's heart fluttered. It wasn't the first time Willow winked at her. Did she do it to everyone or did it mean something? Mika laced her fingers behind her neck. "Yeah, I figured you were joking."

"Good... I like your abs." Willow glanced down and stared at her stomach for a second.

Mika had forgotten her T-shirt exposed an inch of skin. A lot more probably showed with her arms raised. And Willow liked what she saw. Mika smiled.

"Hey, show me your bedroom." Willow headed toward the stairs.

"Okay. But, ah..." Mika rubbed the back of her neck. "It's a little messy."

"I don't care."

Panic rose with each step. Mika couldn't remember if she'd taken the pile of dirty clothes to the laundry room. Forget the damn clothes. Willow was going to see all her posters of women. She hesitated at the door, but it was too late now. She took a breath and swung the door open.

Willow walked around her room, taking every detail in, and for a few seconds, Mika thought she would die.

"I like your posters."

"Thanks." Mika swallowed. One wall had posters of her favorite musicians: Taylor Swift, SZA, Billie Eilish, and P!nk. Another wall had sports posters. One showed Greg Louganis in the dive of death, a reverse three-and-a-half somersault in the tuck position. The others were of the Buffalo Sabres, Megan Rapinoe, and Erica Sullivan. Erica was in the pool and smiling up at the leaderboard, realizing she'd won the Olympic silver medal in the 1500 meter freestyle. Being a swimmer, Willow would probably know that Erica was the first openly gay Olympic swimmer.

Mika ran her hand through her hair. There was no way Willow wouldn't see what all her posters meant. But she didn't comment and turned to the other wall.

"Not many people with Hubble Space Telescope photos in their room. They're beautiful."

Willow traced the outline of a giant red nebula, then touched the picture of Sally Ride, America's first woman in space. Sally had inspired Mika in science and life. Mika had a scrapbook of women in science, several pages of which were dedicated to Sally.

"Women science geeks. Gotta love 'em." Willow ran her fingertips down Mika's arm.

The touch soared to Mika's core, and she gazed into Willow's eyes. That *was* a flirt. She should just kiss Willow, like Jenn said. But what if she screwed it up?

"Time for dinner, girls," Aunt Val yelled up the stairs.

"I'm hungry." Mika practically ran out of the room. *Chicken.*

When she got to the dining room table, it was set for four. Two vases filled with roses were at each end. Mika looked up as Aunt Val carried dishes from the kitchen to the table. The woman from the coffeehouse was helping her. Was her aunt finally getting some?

"This is Brie Owens," Aunt Val said. "This is my niece, Mika, and her friend Willow."

"It's nice to finally meet you, Mika. I've heard good things about you." Brie thrust out her hand. "Your aunt says you're a swimmer. I used to swim in high school until I broke my leg my sophomore year."

"Hi." Mika shook her hand. "How'd you break your leg?"

"Stupidity. I was running on ice to catch up with my twin sister, Dani." Brie turned to Willow. "Hello."

"Hi," Willow said.

"Brie's an accountant."

"The one doing your taxes." Mika couldn't shake off her huge grin. She bet Brie was doing a whole lot more than taxes for her aunt. It was early January when Mika had seen them at the coffeehouse. And last month, her aunt said she'd introduce a girlfriend if she got serious. Way to go, Aunt Val.

"Let's eat." Aunt Val smiled slightly and winked at Mika.

Mika winked back, and her aunt's smile widened.

During the meal, Willow talked about her trip to Germany with her mom and grandparents last year. Aunt Val had traveled to some of the same places, and they talked like old friends. As they finished their meal, Brie told them about seeing the northern lights in Iceland a few years ago.

Everyone was getting along great, and Brie and Aunt Val seemed really into each other. Mika was happy for her. She missed talking with her parents and hearing them laugh. Iliana said the sadness would never go away, but it would lessen over time. Mika still didn't understand how she could be happy and sad at the same time.

"I'm going to grab the cupcakes Mrs. V dropped off yesterday. I'll be right back." Mika ran into the kitchen. She stopped for a moment and looked around. There were so many memories in her mom's favorite part of the house. They had the most fun baking. She sucked in a breath. *Get your shit together.* When she returned, she looked at Brie. "Did you know that Aunt Val turned forty-five on Valentine's Day?"

"You could have skipped the age part, smarty pants." Aunt Val took a cupcake and passed the platter.

Mika huffed. "You shouldn't worry about age unless Brie's a lot younger and doesn't want to date an older woman."

Her aunt raised her eyebrow, then smiled broadly. "Don't ever give up science for comedy."

"Ms. Hayden, you're not old, and you and Ms. Owens make a lovely couple." Willow gave Mika a sideways glance and a small kick under the table before taking a bite of her cupcake.

"Sorry," Mika said.

"I don't mind." Brie placed her hand on top of Aunt Val's.

Mika studied her aunt's face and suppressed a grin at her blushing.

Aunt Val cleared her throat. "And speaking of birthdays, Mika's seventeen at the end of June. Willow, maybe you could help me plan a party."

"I'd love to."

Willow looked at Mika. "Everyone talked about travel destinations but you. Where do you want to go?"

"Space." *Did I just say that?* "Um, I'd like to major in physics. I can't decide between being an astrophysicist or an aerospace engineer, but I'd like to apply to NASA." Mika gulped down some water. Her brain scrambled every time Willow was anywhere near her.

"If your grades in math and science are any indication, then you'll have no trouble getting into any college of your choice." Aunt Val smiled.

"I hope we go to Mars in my lifetime. Maybe you'll work in that program," Willow said.

"Yeah, that'd be cool. Traveling outside our solar system is my ultimate dream." Mika crammed a large piece into her mouth because her current ultimate dream was to kiss Willow and be her girlfriend. She had to get the guts up to tell Willow how she felt.

Each day her feelings for Willow were exploding like a supernova. Now that Willow was going to CUNY, Mika's desire to graduate high school early to go to Columbia University was stronger than ever. She didn't want to risk Willow moving to New York without her and possibly losing her to someone else. Where was the damn letter from Columbia? They hadn't turned her down or accepted her. It didn't matter. She was done with high school. One way or another she was leaving this town in late summer for New York City, a town with tons of different people and lots of gays.

Would Aunt Val understand? Or would she be like her mom and think that Mika wasn't ready and needed a fourth year of high school? Mika couldn't take the chance. She'd keep her plans a secret until the last minute.

Chapter Twenty

April

MIKA SAT QUIETLY IN the car while Aunt Val drove her to Binghamton for Mika to spend the night with Jenn before the charity invitational swim meet.

Aunt Val didn't seem to mind dropping her off and returning the next day for the meet, and Mika guessed that it'd mean she could have Brie stay overnight. She was sure they were already sleeping together; it was written all over her aunt's face with every smile and touch of their hands. Mika liked Brie and was happy for them. Now she just needed the same thing to happen for her and Willow. She'd invited Willow to watch her swim, and she'd said yes. Now she couldn't wait to tell Jenn.

Mika chewed the bottom of her lip. Didn't all gay people have gaydar? Why couldn't she tell if Willow was straight or not? Maybe it was something that developed over time. She hopped out of the car when Jenn came out to greet them, grabbed her bag and said goodbye to Aunt Val, then raced upstairs to Jenn's room.

Jenn didn't seem her usual self. "Why the look?"

"I called the genealogy company because the results were supposed to be completed way before now," Jenn said.

"What did they say?" She rubbed her neck.

Jenn pulled out another DNA test kit from her desk. "They can't find your sample. You have to retake it. They also said it could take longer because Mother's Day, Memorial Day, and Father's Day are coming up."

"This is bullshit. Maybe it's fate, and I'm not supposed to know anything." Mika flopped back on Jenn's bed and stared at the ceiling.

"This time, the return label is certified mail. Don't be afraid."

"I'm not."

"Yes, you are. Why else wouldn't you take it? It was your idea."

Mika grabbed the kit out of Jenn's hand. She opened it, swabbed her cheeks, and put the Q-tip into the test tubes. "Here."

Jenn placed it in the box and sealed it with the return label. "I'll take it to the Post Office after school."

Mika grinned. "Willow's coming tomorrow."

"You lucky dog." Jenn smiled back. "And I finally get to meet her."

"Please don't say anything."

"Lighten up. I'm not stupid." Jenn slung her arm around Mika. "Look, I'm on your side. Tomorrow, it will be nice to meet your *friend*. Now let's watch a movie."

Jenn laid on the bed with her Mac and two wireless headphones. She motioned for Mika to join her.

"This makes no sense. Why don't we go to your theater room?" Mika asked. "You have a freaking ninety-eight-inch TV."

"Trust me. We don't need any interruptions."

Mika took the headphones and laid down. It didn't take long for her to realize that the movie, *Imagine Me & You*, was a lesbian flick. She sat up and paused it. "Is the door locked?"

Jenn laughed. "Yes, silly. Lay back and enjoy. The reviews were great. It's an old movie, but it's supposed to be a sweet happily-ever-after."

Watching her first lesbian movie with her straight cousin wasn't how she'd imagined it going. If there were any sex scenes, Mika would die.

"Relax. You're safe with me." Jenn pushed her down and restarted the movie.

The film didn't disappoint. The chemistry between the two women was off the charts. Mika had never been bothered when a movie showed a man and woman kissing, but this set Mika's body on fire. In the final scene, Mika silently cheered Rachel on as she chased down Luce for a passionate kiss and their happy ending.

"Thanks, cuz." Mika smiled.

"I knew you'd like it."

"It hit home. I mean how Rachel didn't have a clue until she met Luce." Mika looked at Jenn. "I've had feelings for girls for some time, but it wasn't until I became close to Willow that everything intensified. I really like her, Jenn."

"You'll find the right time to say something. She'll be lucky to have you."

"Thanks. I need to get some rest now." Mika moved to the trundle bed and closed her eyes. She fell asleep thinking about Willow's smile, her laugh, and what it'd be like to kiss her.

The alarm went off early, and Mika hopped out of bed and rushed to get ready. Jenn took way too long to put on makeup and fix her hair. They all piled into Aunt Pauline's SUV five minutes behind schedule.

"I'm sleepy. How do you feel?" Jenn asked.

"Ready to kick ass and show everyone what I can do." Mika grinned. "Oh, sorry for the curse word, Aunt Pauline." But Mika could see her smile slightly when she glanced back through the review mirror.

An hour later, it was showtime. Mika wanted to do her best to impress Willow. After entering the swim deck, she looked up to the stands. Willow sat with Jenn and Carla. Her aunts and Brie sat behind them. They waved back, and Willow's gigantic smile pumped up Mika's confidence. Aunt Pauline looked uncomfortable, but Mika was proud of Aunt Val for bringing Brie. Mika looked back at the pool and focused on her plan of attack.

Today's rules were simple. When a swimmer won an event, a portion of the overall pot would be donated to a charity of their choosing. Mika hoped to win for the Cancer Resource Center of the Finger Lakes. Each swimmer was only allowed to do one event, so Mika signed up for the 200-yard individual medley because the donation money was double.

Although Mika could swim all four strokes and probably beat most of the swimmers here, she hated the breaststroke. And she often didn't swim the medley during the high school season because Ashley Devins and Carrie Tucker swam it. They enjoyed the sport of verbally slamming anyone that didn't meet their standard.

Time to forget them and focus.

"Start your warmups," the club's coach said. "And good luck."

The swimmers around her were from different clubs, and she briefly wondered how good they were. *Relax.* She visualized her race.

"Oh my, it's Mental Mika."

Shit, Ashley was to her left.

"You'll smoke her. You always do."

And Carrie was to her right. How had she missed them when she stepped behind the starter's block? Mika's muscles knotted. *Focus.* She closed her eyes while stretching her arms and said a little prayer to her parents. God, she missed them so much. But it was getting a tiny bit easier each day with Willow by her side.

"What are you doing here anyway? Aren't you a little below the league?" Carrie asked.

Mika gritted her teeth and didn't reply.

"Mishap Mika is pretending. And she's doing the medley. What a joke." Ashley threw her towel and hit Mika across the face. "Oops. Sorry, I was aiming for the bench."

So much for laidback and fun, dammit. If she had to swim against these two witches, she'd give it her all and not hold back. She dropped her towel on the nearby bench, returned to the pool, and splashed water on herself. *Get out smooth. Establish a strong tempo. Maintain breathing pattern. Ignore the others.*

"Swimmers, take your mark."

The horn blew, and she came off strong. Too fast, and she could tire quickly. Fuck it. She owned the butterfly and backstroke and was going to prove it. Her body sliced through the water like it had a mind of its own. The crossover turn was coming up, followed by the dreaded breaststroke. *Timing.* Her turn felt perfect, but fatigue crept into her muscles midway through, and her legs began to feel like sandbags. *Fuck Ashley and Carrie.* She pushed harder, concentrating on the turn into the freestyle and the last fifty. Her body burned, and her back felt like a rubber band about to snap, but she pushed harder. She reached the wall, glad it was over.

Mika paid no attention to the roar of the crowd, and she didn't look at the leaderboard. She probably took third or fourth since this wasn't her usual event. She hung off the starting block and stretched her arms with her head down, gasping for air. Eternity seemed to pass, then the girls from the club hoisted her out of the water, congratulating her. *First? Way ahead of everyone else? Really?*

Ashley glared and didn't say a word. Too bad little Ashley and Carrie got knocked off their pedestal.

"Beautiful." The club coach threw a towel around Mika's shoulders and led her to the side. "How do you feel?"

"Good."

He laughed. "I wish it was regular season, and you were on my swim team. Want to move to Binghamton?"

"Nope." Why was he acting so thrilled? Okay, so she took first, but it was just a charity race.

"Mika, this was for fun, but you crushed it. I've never seen you swim this fast before. Your time at 1:58:02 is better than most high school records. Shave a few more seconds off, and you'll capture the state record."

"Really?"

"Yes." He slapped her on the back. "Go celebrate with your family."

Aunt Val embraced her, but Aunt Pauline didn't want to get wet. Jenn congratulated her, then wandered off to chat with some of the male swimmers.

"Wow. You swam like you were in the Olympics," Carla said and high-fived her.

Willow wrapped her arms around Mika. "You were blazing hot."

"Thanks." Butterflies fluttered in Mika's stomach. She didn't want to let go.

"I'll join you in the locker room." Willow laced her arm in Mika's.

Mika was on a high, then she realized Willow would see her naked. "Ah, you don't have to. I'll get dressed fast."

"With the trash queens around, you need some company."

"Okay." Mika nodded reluctantly. She'd specifically selected a locker away from the main crowd.

Willow looked over the pictures pinned to the giant corkboard while Mika showered and dressed. She returned when Mika was putting on her socks and shoes.

"You ready, winner?"

They were words she could get used to. She smiled, picked up her bag and turned toward Willow. Her smile fell when Ashley and Carrie rounded the corner.

Carrie tapped Willow's shoulder. "I don't know what you see in her."

"Really, Willow. Why do you hang out with her?" Ashley asked.

"Unlike you, she's talented and kind. You're the ones I don't want to hang out with," Willow said.

"She's like a dumb mute. Barely talks to anyone except her baby video game buddies. But now she talks to you. Why?" Carrie raised her eyebrow.

"Leave her alone." Mika pulled Willow back and stuck her finger in Carrie's face. She crossed over the bench and got in Ashley's face. "You're such a fucking fake princess. All you do is put others down just to get a high."

"What're you going to do? Hit me? Guys aren't supposed to hit girls, you know?" Ashley pushed her and laughed.

Carrie stepped toward Mika. "She's female. I've seen enough

of her naked, but..." She rubbed her lip like she was thinking hard. Then she looked Mika in the eye. "Yeah. I bet a hundred dollars that she's trans."

Mika balled her hands into fists and stepped forward until she was practically nose-to-nose with Carrie.

"You two are full of shit." Willow pulled Mika away.

"Willow, the library is one thing, but you're giving her rides home and eating lunch with her once or twice a week." Ashley sneered. "She's a freak and a queer. People are going to think you are too." She narrowed her eyes. "Maybe you are."

Willow shrugged. "So what if I am? Or maybe I'm trans." She snapped her fingers. "I guess you haven't seen the signs around town. Ithaca is an LGBTQ+ friendly community."

Fear took over Mika as several other girls from the club had gathered around. Damn, this shit would reach Aunt Pauline and others in no time.

"Mika's not a freak, and who cares if she doesn't fit your teeny tiny view of the world? You two are dumbasses. Move along and take your shit elsewhere." Willow pointed to the door.

Ashley laughed. "Jeans and T-shirts all the time. No makeup. The only thing she's good at is the butterfly." She turned toward Mika. "Do you use those strong arms to pull your girlfriend's pussy to your mouth?"

"Fuck off, Ashley. You're both jealous because I beat the crap out of your pathetic records." Mika's heart pounded. The only thing keeping her from hitting them was Willow holding her back.

"A friend of Misfit Mega-lezzy Mika is no friend of mine. Come on, Carrie."

They left, but the other girls gawked briefly before dispersing.

"I'm sorry, Willow." Mika dropped her head.

"Don't apologize. They're the assholes."

Mika looked up. "Yeah, but I should have said and done more to protect you." Tears filled her eyes. When Willow reached out and gently wiped them away with her thumbs, Mika swallowed hard. "Thank you."

"Don't beat up on yourself. I'm no delicate flower; I can protect myself with words." Willow held up her arm and flexed her bicep. "But my muscles aren't as big as your beautiful ones." She gestured toward the door. "Let's go. Your aunts will be wondering what's held us up."

Mika's mind raced between feeling good over Willow's compliment and fear. After tonight, Ashley and Carrie would talk even more smack at school. Mika would summon the strength and take it, but it broke her heart that the evil bitches now had Willow in their sights. She swore that she'd come down on them if they went after Willow. Okay, she could handle this, but what was she going to do about her feelings? She wanted more than an ally. She wanted Willow to be her girlfriend. *Dammit, find the courage.*

Chapter Twenty-One

Mika rolled over and opened her eyes. Fuck her morning exercises. She curled up on her side but couldn't get back to sleep. Willow's text right before bed had rolled over and over in her mind, and she hadn't slept for shit.

Sorry it's late, Mika. Can you get a ride tomorrow morning? I need to leave early.

Had Willow changed her mind about hanging around her? Aunt Val knocked on the door lightly, but Mika's head hurt. Hell, everything hurt.

"Mika, are you up? School starts in thirty minutes."

"Yeah." She swung her legs over the side of the bed and hung her head.

"Are you sick?"

"No." She squeezed her eyes shut for a second and wiped her watery eyes with her shirt.

"Okay. Willow should be here soon."

Fuck. Fuck. Fuck. "She's not coming today."

"You'll never make it. Today's an easy day, I'll push back my meeting and drive you."

"Okay, thanks." Mika rushed to get ready. She flung open her closet and just grabbed something. For once, she didn't care that none of it would match. After washing her face and brushing her teeth, she headed downstairs. Her feet pounded on the hardwood as always, but the noise sounded extra loud in her brain. That's what she deserved for staying up most of the night thinking about the evil bitches and Willow.

Aunt Val came out of the kitchen with her coat on and carrying a bag and travel mug. "I made you hard-boiled eggs and toast. Since you're running late, I also did a half hot chocolate and half coffee."

"Thanks." Mika slipped on her coat. "Oh, I need my medicine."

"There's a pill box with your Zoloft in the bag."

"I need some Advil too." She hurried to the downstairs medicine cabinet and swallowed two tablets. They'd managed to get over most of their differences, and Mika didn't want Aunt Val to baby her. Her aunt knew her pills were for anxiety, but did she know the doctor had categorized her as high-functioning and able to hide her symptoms? She pushed down her sadness and headed back. "Sorry you had to shift your morning meeting."

"It's fine. Are you sure you're okay? Is something going on?

"Just tired and woke with a tension headache. No big deal."

Mika ate her breakfast on the way. Aunt Val glanced over multiple times but didn't say anything.

Her aunt pulled up to the drop off line. "I'll listen without judgment any time you want to talk."

"Thanks, again." Mika got out of the car.

"Call if you need a ride home."

Mika shut the door and walked toward school. Her legs felt heavy, and her head hurt more from the noise all around. She ignored the taunts from a few shitheads. Her headache settled down by the end of first period, but she had trouble concentrating. What would she say to Willow? Mika wanted to see her, but would she come to the library as usual? Sure she would. Willow was a good person. Perhaps that hurt the most because if Willow didn't want to be around her, she'd tell Mika to her face and not ghost her.

A classmate tapped his fingers on Mika's desk. When she looked up, the entire class was staring at her.

"That's the third time I asked you a question." Mr. Burns opened the classroom door and motioned for her to step outside. After the door shut, he whispered, "You can daydream here and there and still get an A, but you're completely checked out today."

"Sorry," Mika mumbled, ashamed to look at him.

"Your library time starts in fifteen minutes." He took a pad out of his pocket, unclipped the pen from his shirt, and scribbled on it. "Here's a hall pass. Go early, but I want your full attention the next time."

"Yes, sir."

On the way, she hoped there wouldn't be much shelving. Luck wasn't on her side. The cart was full. "Hey, Mrs. Simmons. Mr. Burns let me go early." She handed her the pass then jammed her hand in her pocket. "I'll get some shelving done, but this English test is coming up. Could Willow and I have extra time for study?" She hated lying to Mrs. Simmons, who was one of the nicest adults in the school. "You know I help her with math, and she helps me with English."

"Go on. The books can wait. Your classes are more important."

"Thanks." Mika pointed to the study room in the far corner. "Can we study there? It's less distracting."

Mrs. Simmons nodded. "I'll tell Willow when she arrives."

The study rooms had no doors and big windows, so the librarian and teachers could see in and check on students. She'd have to be careful and talk quietly. Mrs. Simmons was cool, but Mika didn't know her personal views; she could be conservative like Mika's grandparents.

She propped her English book up, pretending to study. Instead, her mind raced on what to say, or whether to say anything at all.

Willow dropped her book bag on the desk and sat beside her. "Mrs. Simmons said you were in here studying for an English test. I thought you didn't have anything until next month."

Mika glanced around the library. "I don't have a test. I wanted to talk to you," she whispered.

"It must be important if you lied to Mrs. Simmons."

Mika crossed her arms.

"What's wrong? If this is about me not picking you up this morning, I'm sorry. Mom forgot to tell me she had to leave her car at the shop for repairs. She asked me to drive her to work." Willow sighed. "She goes to the farthest auto shop south of town on Elmira Road."

A wave of heat and relief rushed through Mika as she worked out the logistics, and she rested her forearms on the table with her fingers laced together. "Sorry, it must have taken you an hour."

"An hour and ten minutes, not including breakfast and getting ready."

Mika was an idiot. She was a math and science nerd—nothing more. "Why are you my friend?" That wasn't what she had practiced, but it popped out anyway.

"Huh?" Willow wrinkled her forehead.

"Seriously. Why do you hang with me?"

Willow sat up straight. "Don't let the stupid stuff they said get to you."

"I'm... I don't—"

"Fuck those jerks." Willow pulled a string on her book bag, then looked at Mika. "I meant every word I said."

Willow's words meant everything to Mika, but there was one thing she hadn't said.

"Do you think I'm a lesbian?" Mika held her breath.

"It doesn't matter. Labels are bullshit." Willow glanced at her fingernails, then held her hands up to Mika. "Do you like my new colors?"

Mika hadn't noticed them until now. On Willow's right hand, the nails were different shades of red and pink, while the ones on her left hand were different shades of blue and green.

"The point, Mika, is I like my nails even if no one else does. I make my own decisions. Believe in yourself and fuck them. They're extra this past year, and that's bad, but you've got to ignore them." Willow smiled. "Let's open some books before you get caught in a lie."

"Do you want to come to my house for tutoring tomorrow night?" Mika bounced her leg up and down under the table, unable to stop.

"I'll check with Mom, but it sounds good."

Studying. Yep, that's all we'll do. But Mika had to find the courage to ask Willow if she could kiss her. Oh, how she wanted to so badly. But so far, she'd fucked up the courage to come out.

"Something else is going on in that big brain of yours. What is it?" Willow pushed her books aside.

Mika slumped down in the chair. "I get along great with my cousin, Jenn. One day she called me a lovable nerd. She didn't mean it in a bad way, but I'm too different for most people. Probably too different for you."

"Mika, don't slam yourself. I like you *because* you're different."

"I worry too much."

Willow laughed. "Yeah, you do." She put her hand on Mika's knee to stop her bouncing.

The touch ran through Mika like a live electrical wire, and excitement flooded her body.

"Don't define yourself by the shit others throw at you. Look at all the great things about you. You care about other people's feelings. You're way more mature than half the clowns out there. You work hard to pull A grades. You help others. I'd probably fail math if you didn't help me. And you smoke the bullies. They don't come close to your strong and fit body." Willow squeezed Mika's knee before removing her hand.

Mika needed to say it. Why couldn't she? *Stop being scared. Just say it.* She took a deep breath. "I'm gay. And I'm not trans. I think it's great if someone is, but I'm not. I'm okay being a girl; I just don't fit the mold." Mika fidgeted with her fingers, then cracked her knuckles. "I don't hate my body, except for my fucking period. It's just that I think people wouldn't throw shade if I looked more like the average girl. But I like my muscles."

"I hate my period too—I think all women do. And there's *nothing* wrong with your body. You should wear tighter clothes to show off your muscles. I like them. And remember what I said, labels are bullshit."

Mika's throat was so dry that it was difficult to swallow. "And I like you."

Willow rested her hand on Mika's forearm. She looked up into Willow's eyes, hoping it was more than a friendly touch.

"How many times do I have to mention your muscles before you get the hint?" She smiled. "I've never dated a girl, but I like you too."

She likes me! Say something. "Um, do you want to go out on a date? Like the movies. Or we could do something else if that's too public."

"I'm not going to hide. Fuck it if someone sees us."

"I'm supposed to visit my cousins this weekend. You could come early for tutoring and stay for dinner. Then we can talk about what movie to see or where to go and when."

"I'd love to." Willow grasped Mika's hand. "I've never seen you so nervous." She rubbed the back of Mika's hand with her thumb. "When you cracked your knuckles, I was scared you were going to break one of your fingers." Her smile grew wider. "Your skin is soft for someone who does lots of sports."

"Your skin is too. I like your wavy hair. Mine's straight and—"

"Cute as it falls around your gorgeous face." Willow let go of Mika's hand and picked her book up. She smiled once more over the top, then she put on a serious face. "Okay. Homework and study now."

Mika wanted to jump up and shout out, *Willow's so gorgeous, and she likes me.* If it wasn't for the glass windows, she'd ask to kiss Willow right now, but she had to wait until their tutoring session. God, tutoring night couldn't come soon enough.

Chapter Twenty-Two

NOW THAT SHE KNEW Willow liked her too, Mika didn't care when others pointed and threw shade. Her afternoon whizzed by, and she hustled home to text Jenn. When she walked in, she almost ran into Aunt Val.

"Hi, Mika. Can I please talk to you for a second?"

Not good. It usually meant trouble. Mika plopped down on the sofa. But her act of trying to look casual didn't do a thing for her nerves. Her stomach sank, and her pulse shot through the roof. "What's up?"

Aunt Val pushed aside the magazines and TV remote to sit on the coffee table in front of Mika. She placed her elbows on her knees and leaned close to Mika. "You can't go to your cousins this weekend."

Damn, word from Binghamton traveled fast. Aunt Pauline probably chewed Aunt Val's ass out. Mika swallowed. *Play it cool.* "Why?"

"Pauline said a couple of bullies confronted you in the locker room after the charity swim."

"I'm sure she had plenty to say about that." Mika narrowed her eyes. "She's judgmental and was probably on the side of the bullies. She and my Lavigne grandparents live in the past."

"For the record, I was the one who told Pauline you weren't coming over this weekend because she jumped to conclusions. I'm sorry this happened to you. I don't judge you by what you wear or who you hang out with."

Mika's chest rose and fell with anger. "And let me guess. She blamed you."

Aunt Val nodded. "You're a young adult. It's none of her or anyone else's business who your friends are or who you date. My only concern is your happiness and safety."

"Thanks." Mika took her phone out. "Gotta go. Jenn wanted to talk about something tonight. I guess this is it." That was a lie. Mika wanted to talk to her. "And she's not like her mom. We text all the time. We're like sisters." So why hadn't Jenn texted her already to warn her about this?

"If things get out of hand or you want to talk, I'll always listen."

"Thanks, but I can handle it." Mika stood.

"I'm sure you're quite capable. But please, if it gets violent, please tell me. Okay?"

"Will do." Mika took the stairs two at a time. After closing her bedroom door, she went into her bathroom for extra privacy and sat on the toilet, bouncing her legs up and down. The first call to Jenn went to voicemail.

I need to talk. Pick up.

She bounced her leg faster. She couldn't remember if she'd taken her anxiety meds this morning. Fuck, today at school had been too quiet. Ashley and Carrie were probably gathering their gang and would attack tomorrow. Mika called again, still no answer. A few seconds later, her phone vibrated.

"Hey, cuz. What's happening? Just so you know, Carla wants you to show her photog stuff Saturday," Jenn said.

"I won't be there."

"Why?"

Mika bunched her fist around her hair and took a few steady, deep breaths. "In the locker room last Saturday—" Mika tried to stop her tic, but it was as if her leg had a mind of its own. At this rate, she'd punch a hole in the floor.

"What about the locker room? And what does it have to do with this weekend?"

"Two girls from my high school were swimming on Saturday. They accused me of being a lesbian in the locker room. Your mom heard the story, and she blames Aunt Val."

"Fuck, that's cruel. Mom acted normal afterward and never said a word. I'll say something to—"

"No. Don't confront your mom. Just do your thing."

"Which is?"

"Spy on her. Let me know if she's talking smack to any of her friends or with the grands."

"Got it. Glad you appreciate my skills, cuz. Now don't let all this shit get you down."

Mika could almost see Jenn polishing her nails on her shirt. "Ah, I told Willow that I liked her, and she likes me too."

"Yes!" Jenn whooped loudly over the phone. "I like Willow. Let me know if you need any dating advice."

"Thanks. Love you."

"Love you too, cuz. And kiss Willow if you haven't already." Jenn laughed and hung up.

Next Mika called Willow and told her what'd gone down.

"Don't let it get to you," Willow said.

"Yeah." But Willow had no idea how bad these things turned her upside down, made her sick to her stomach, and twisted her nerves to the point of pain. "I'm worried about what Ashley and Carrie will do next." She clenched her phone tight.

"Mika, I have your back. I don't care what they say. You know you're five times better than them. I wish I could hug you now and make you believe it."

Mika's anxiety lessened at the thought of another Willow super hug.

"Hey, I have to go. Call me later tonight if you can. Bye."

"Bye." Mika didn't move. Was this all real? Her phone pinged.

Just so you don't forget, you're the bomb. You'll go on to do bigger and better things while those jerks'll be stuck with high school reunions being the highlight of their life. I have tons of homework. Later. XO

You're an amazing artist and kind. XO Mika's thumb hoovered over the send button, then she backspaced and typed, *So you really like my muscles?* She sent it without thinking, then nerves kicked in until her phone lit up.

Yes. And your abs. Mika, you're beautiful. Or do you prefer handsome?

She grinned. *Either. I can't wait to see you again. You're gorgeous. I love your smile, and whatever perfume you wear is intoxicating.* Her center throbbed. *And I want to kiss you so bad.* She erased the kiss comment but sent the rest. After several long seconds, there weren't any fucking bouncing dots showing Willow's response. That crappy sinking feeling kicked in, then the dots appeared. She swallowed waiting for Willow's answer.

A blushing emoji appeared. *Looking forward to seeing you soon. Now, I really have tons of homework. Bye. XO*

Bye. XO Mika blared Taylor Swift's "Cardigan" and danced around the room, imagining Willow in her arms.

After a few more songs, she headed back downstairs. This time, she stopped and studied the family pictures on the wall before continuing. Aunt Val didn't even look up when she came into the living room. "You work too much. I thought you said you're only part-time." She sat across from her in the soft swivel-rocker and stuffed her hands under her butt.

"I work around twenty-five hours a week." Her aunt put her laptop and reading glasses off to the side. "It might help if you talked about the bullies more. If not to me, then to Iliana."

"I was upset and hurt that Aunt Pauline said shit about me, but I'm okay. Tell me some positive stuff, something about the family. You know, things you and Mom liked to do. She told me a few things, but I'd like to hear about when you guys were kids." Her eyes watered with a few tears but nothing like the tons she'd cried in the past. "I miss them so much. My therapist said talking about good memories would help me. Can we try it?"

"Grief's a heavy cloak that doesn't shake easily, so good memories do help."

"You sound like a poet."

"No one's ever accused me of that." Aunt Val smiled. "My favorite memories were of summer camping in a tent. We all loved it, except for Mom. She'd hike with us but preferred to relax and read or knit. And she hated fishing." Her aunt chuckled. "While she stayed behind, we'd go with Dad. He fished, and we'd run along the trails playing hide and seek and getting dirty. Okay, I'd get dirty, and your mom only a little. Dad let us swim to wash off the dirt. We searched for wildflowers, and Dad would tell us the names of the ones we picked. And he kept a pair of binoculars handy. Looking at creatures from afar was like magic."

"Mom loved flowers too. She always pointed them and the birds out on walks through the park or hikes in the forest. She dragged me to Cornell Botanic Gardens all the time."

"You and I should visit sometime. I have a few favorites: the vivid blues of the chicory roots, the yellows of St. John's Wort, and the orange daylilies."

"I like flowers and birds, mainly to photograph. Sorry, but I'm not too deep in it." For the past four months, Mika had closed down her ears and mind whenever Aunt Val wanted to talk about her parents. It still hurt now, but it felt good at the same time. And although her aunt teared up, her face glowed, so maybe this was helping her too. "What else?"

"More magic happened after dinner when we'd stay up past nightfall. Dad would take us to catch fireflies. Then we'd sit by the fire making s'mores while Mom knitted. Those trips were our slice of heaven." Aunt Val grabbed a tissue and handed the box to Mika.

"How'd Grandma see?"

"She had a headlamp to focus light on her work. But times changed, and your mom eventually joined the 'hate tent-camping' club. That's when Mom moved our summer vacation to a bed and breakfast. Your mom loved it. She was almost a teenager and maturing fast. For her, swimming in a pool and showing off in front of boys was way better than playing in the woods and swimming in the lake."

Mika sat up straighter. "She had an interest in guys that young? How old were you?"

"I was ten, and she was almost thirteen. Your mom blossomed fast, but I was paranoid about the changes that I'd seen her go through. Just the thought of having a period horrified me. And I refused to carry a purse. I was the kid with the fanny pack."

"Did she have a boyfriend?"

Aunt Val chuckled. "God, no. Mom would have killed her. Good Catholic girls waited until sixteen to properly date. And by proper, I mean the first date was inviting the boy for dinner to be scrutinized by our parents."

"Sounds like she had a wild streak." Mika had never seen her mom act any way other than polished and polite.

"She broke a rule on occasion. One of her first dinner dates volunteered to help Dad with the yard. Mom had gone on an errand, and I went looking for Hannah. I found them in the shed kissing. He ran back to Dad with the tools, and your mom threatened to kill me if I told."

"You were only three years apart. But it sounds like you guys weren't close."

Her aunt's face turned blank. "She never really came out and said it, but I think I was an embarrassment to her. And in high school, she was a senior and I was a freshman with a big secret."

Mika bolted upright. "You knew you were gay back then?"

"Your mom was the girly girl—the cheerleader with the right makeup and proper dress. I hated dressing up. And while she flirted and dated guys, I had a massive crush on just one girl. We were studying at my house one day, and I kissed her." Aunt Val took in a deep breath and let it out. "Your mom walked in, and my new girlfriend dashed out in a flash. I never got another kiss from her, and I didn't date again until Andi in my senior year of high school."

"Mom ratted you out? I can't believe she'd be so mean."

"No. I told her it was just practice. She crossed her arms, huffed, and left me shaking in fear, but she never mentioned it. She was a great sister." Aunt Val smiled through more tears.

For a moment, Mika considered telling her aunt about Willow, but adult advice had a way of turning into instructions. Nope. It was best to stick with fun stories. "What about travels? Mom never told me much about when you were adults, except for Toronto."

"Oh, what'd she say?"

"Not much. She said that you forced her to do an outdoor activity for every museum and tourist event she picked out. She said that one hike was easy and pretty, but that she almost killed you when you made her camp in a tent for two days."

"No one ever forced your mom to do anything." Aunt Val laughed and crossed her leg, swinging it back and forth. "I took her to Sibbald Point Provincial Park. She wasn't happy when I took the tent out of the back, but she enjoyed herself. We shared wine and laughed around the campfire and didn't go to bed until after midnight."

She'd gotten her aunt to open up some, and it felt like they were finally bonding. "Can we go camping sometime?"

"Sure."

"I wanted to ask about Dad. He said something about Canada too. They met you at Niagara Falls on the Canadian side once, but Mom didn't seem happy about that story for some reason, and Dad dropped the subject. Did something happen in Canada?" Mika held her breath when Aunt Val looked like a deer in a hunter's spotlight.

She looked down at the floor. "I was having problems with my girlfriend and wasn't out yet."

The stories had helped, but now Mika felt like an ass for turning things sour. She wanted to know things, and it still bothered her that Aunt Val was a mystery. "Dad once told me you two went to a Red Sox game when he had a conference in Boston. It was right before you moved to Berlin. I asked him why we never visited you in Europe. He said you invited us, but Mom was afraid to fly over the Atlantic. That made no sense to me. She didn't have a problem when we flew to Hawaii. Were you two still fighting?"

"Honestly, I was so busy that I don't remember our minor disagreements. I should start dinner." Aunt Val stood and walked toward the kitchen.

"Again, I'm sorry for the mean and stupid things I've said."

Her aunt turned around. "Forget about it. I think there's a rule in the teenage book, 'Thou shall give hell to all adults.'"

"Especially aunts." Tears ran down Mika's cheek. "I miss them so much."

"I do too. It's going to take time."

Mika hugged her then slowly climbed the stairs. Watching sports with her dad had been so much fun, especially going to hockey games and eating tons of popcorn. They usually went to Buffalo whenever the Sabres played the Toronto Maple Leafs. Mika swallowed. They'd gone to their last game together early November last year. Dad had treated her to a matchup in Toronto. Their team got beat up, but it was great.

As Mika sat at her desk and opened her book, she remembered the weird passport situation. Anyone sixteen or older had to have a one, and Dad controlled hers. At the checkpoint, she thought the guard scrutinized three passports. When the guard handed them back, Mika thought the top one was darker blue with a different gold emblem. Dad quickly stuffed them in his pocket and drove away. When Mika said something, he glanced at the traffic around them and made some excuse about the sun reflecting at a strange angle. She'd dropped the subject but thought for sure it hadn't been an optical illusion.

Mika slammed her book and opened her laptop. She googled Canadian and US passports. *U.S./Canada dual citizens are advised to carry both valid passports (U.S. and Canada) when traveling to/ from the United States.* When she compared photos of the passports, her heart jumped into her throat. The Canadian one was darker blue with a lot more gold on front. Why would her dad lie to her? No, he won't. Maybe she didn't see things correctly.

Chapter Twenty-Three

MIKA CAME DOWNSTAIRS WITH a text book, glancing at the door every now and then for Willow. Everything was finally turning in her life, and she couldn't wait to share it with her. Her phone chimed with a text from Willow.

I'm running fifteen minutes late.

No problem. See you soon. Mika slipped her phone back into her pocket just as Aunt Val turned the TV off.

"How's school been this week?"

"Good."

"I ran into Mrs. Parker at Wegman's. It was her day off. She says that Willow is doing so much better in math now that you're tutoring her."

"Yeah." So Willow's mom and Aunt Val were friends now. *Great.* It made her uneasy that her aunt was now friends with her girlfriend's mom. *Girlfriend.* She hadn't kissed Willow yet but just thinking about her as a girlfriend made Mika's heart flutter.

"Anything else happening?"

How many times does Aunt Val have to ask me these questions? It seemed like a lot lately. "Nope." Mika tossed her book aside when there was knocking on the door. "That'll be Willow. We have to study." Mika hurried over. When she opened the door, her mouth went dry. Willow looked amazing in tight leggings, a short skirt, and a tight-fitting sweater.

"Hi."

"Hi. I like your outfit."

"Thanks. Can I come in, please?"

"Oh, yeah. Sorry." Mika stepped back. *She likes me and my*

muscles. Mika hadn't stopped thinking about those words since yesterday, and she wanted to get upstairs as fast as possible. But she had to be considerate. She hung up Willow's coat. "Would you like a drink? We have ginger ale, white grape juice, water, and Sprite."

Willow lightly squeezed her shoulder. "Ginger ale, please."

Damn, her touch felt so good. Willow followed her into the kitchen and the cats came prancing in, rubbing up against Mika's legs and begging for food.

"How long have you had them?"

Mika pointed to the tabby. "We've had Missy ten years, but the vet thinks she's twelve." She picked up Mr. Big. "This monster was a kitten when we got him at the pet store six years ago. But you grew even bigger, didn't you?" She cradled him and rubbed his belly. "He loves this. Missy will scratch the shit out of you if you do it to her." Mika put Mr. Big down. They used to wander through the house after the accident like they were looking for Mom and Dad, and she'd cry when they came to her. Now they were a gentle reminder of the good times with her parents.

"They're adorable." Willow bent down to pet them.

"It's good they're hungry because otherwise they wouldn't come near you. It takes them time to get used to strangers." Mika laughed. "They still don't come around Aunt Val unless she feeds them, but they seem to really like you."

Mika spooned wet food into the cat bowls and threw the empty can into the sink. She heard Aunt Val's sigh from the living room.

"Please rinse that and put it into the recycle bin. I'm getting tired of picking yucky cans out of the sink."

Willow bumped her shoulder. "Stop giving your aunt a hard time."

Mika was about to say something when Aunt Val rounded the corner.

"Sorry. Dinner might be a few minutes late. Mini crisis at work." She stopped to look at her phone when it chimed.

"We can wait. I heard your homemade enchiladas are dope," Willow said.

"Thanks." Aunt Val blinked.

Mika lightly punched her aunt on the arm. "Dope means good." She handed Willow her soda. "Let's go upstairs." As they passed by, Aunt Val pulled Mika in for a hug and kissed her cheek. It had taken Mika some time to accept her aunt and even longer to hug her back. It felt easy now, but it was Willow's hugs and kisses Mika wanted. And the last thing she wanted was for Aunt Val to find out about Willow or graduation. She'd probably question her to death or try to give advice. Mika would tell her eventually, but not now.

"Thanks for caring," Mika said into her aunt's ear. "We need to study."

"Keep the door open, please," her aunt said as they headed upstairs.

"No problem." Damn, did she suspect something? Upstairs, Mika softly shut her bedroom door.

"Your aunt said to keep it open."

"I'll tell her I forgot if she sees it." Mika grinned, then with two giant strides, she picked up the letter sitting on top of her dresser. "It came this afternoon." Her fingers brushed against Willow's when she handed her the envelope from Columbia University. Mika burst with excitement watching Willow's face light up tripled everything.

Willow unfolded the letter and grinned. "You got in. I bet your aunt's proud of you."

"Ah, she doesn't know," Mika whispered. "The mail usually comes around five p.m., and I've been trying to get to it before her."

"Why? I'm sure she'd be happy. She can drive to New York City to visit you. She might not see you much if you go to California. Even the economy plane tickets are getting expensive."

"Aunt Val doesn't know about any of my college acceptance letters." Mika tapped her fingers on her leg. "My mom tried to talk me out of graduating early. She thought I was too young or something. Dad was on the fence. Mom shelved the convo until after the holidays, but as you know..." Mika hung her head. She fought that sensation of wanting to throw up. Instead, she took a deep breath. "So I'm afraid she's going to try to stop me." She flexed her fingers to stop the random tapping.

"It's your decision, but she has to sign the high school admin papers for early graduation."

"I faked her signature."

"Huh?" Willow eyes widened. "She's going to be upset that you've kept it all secret. And you'd better hope Principal Harrington doesn't find out. She doesn't mess around."

"I know. I don't want to hurt her, but it's my life. This place is so crashy, and it's exhausting trying to block out the bullies. The work is vanilla, and I need the challenge."

"I get it but tell that to your aunt."

Mika was lost in the feeling of Willow's breasts pressed against her chest. She breathed in Willow's perfume and felt dizzy good.

Willow stepped back. "Your aunt will understand."

Fucking reality slam. "Yeah, she might understand about me needing more of a challenge, but I don't know what my mom told her. I've got the credits, and I'm leaving."

Willow sighed. "Okay, but think about telling her soon."

Mika nodded.

"It'll be nice having you a subway ride away. Now, let's study before you screw up your grades."

They flopped onto Mika's bed. Willow sat at the end with her back propped up against the wall. She stretched out her legs, put her math book across her lap and opened her notebook.

"Let me try to do these equations on my own. Then you can check me."

"Okay." Mika put her soda on the nightstand and settled on her belly with her feet tapping against the headboard. She looked at her homework while stealing glances at Willow's beautiful face. When Willow sipped her drink, Mika wished her lips were on her

instead of that can. The thought caused Mika's pulse to pound...
everywhere. She shut her book and sat up. "Chemistry is more
interesting now than math. Some aspects of astrophysics are
related to chemistry or geology." When Willow glanced at her
sideways, Mika swallowed. "There's so much going on in New
York. All kinds of sports, concerts...tons we could do when we're
not busy with classes. And they have great parks—"

"You're doing it again." Willow grinned.

"What?"

Willow tossed her text book aside. "You rattle things off fast
when you're nervous. Why do I make you nervous?" She brushed
the hair from Mika's forehead.

Right now, the impression left by Willow's fingertips was the
distraction. And she was so close that Mika had to kiss her. But
what if she screwed it up? "I have to go to the bathroom." Mika
jumped up and left the room. In the hallway, she saw Aunt Val at
the bottom step, looking up.

"Hey, I'm sorry. An email popped in at the last minute. I should
be done in about fifteen minutes. Do you mind having the leftover
vegetable soup?"

"Sounds good to me," Willow yelled out.

"Yeah, sure." Mika slipped into the bathroom. She took a deep
breath and tried to control things, but anxiety and excitement were
fighting it out in her stomach while her brain checked out. She
thought it'd be less scary after coming out to Willow, but it wasn't.
She hurried back just as Mr. Big tried to squeeze in. "No, boy." She
shut the door to stop him.

Willow glanced up and grinned. "Why didn't you use the en-
suite? Or is your hall bathroom better?"

"Ah...I was out of Advil." Mika rubbed and rotated her shoulder
as if that'd explain it away.

"Swim season's over. Did you hurt yourself in the weight room?"

"No." Mika curled up on the bed. When Willow laid down
behind her in a spooning position, Mika's body came to life in a

new, exciting way. Willow's breasts felt so soft up against her back. Everything tingled, especially between her legs. She'd never felt this intensity before. When Willow wrapped an arm around her and pressed tighter against her, it was all Mika could do not to moan out loud.

"You've been through a lot, but you've got your aunt, your gaming friends, and me. There are plenty of people that love you."

Mika swallowed and turned toward Willow. God, she had the most beautiful eyes. Mika couldn't see the freckles that dotted Willow's nose because she was wearing makeup, but she knew every last beautiful one was there. "When you're this affectionate, every pulse in my body feels like it's jumping out of my skin." She stared into Willow's eyes. "Can I kiss you?"

Willow nodded.

The low humming in the background of Mika's body instantly exploded as they kissed for several heavenly seconds. When Willow pulled away, it was like Mika stopped breathing. "Did I do something wrong?'

Willow smiled shyly. "Nope."

Mika gently kissed her again. When Willow pushed her tongue into Mika's mouth, everything else but Willow ceased to exist. Mika couldn't get enough. She slid her fingertips under Willow's shirt and rested her hand on the small of her back, pressing their bodies together. Willow trailed her fingertips down Mika's neck and caressed her collarbone.

When they broke off, shooting stars and fireworks exploded in her head. Oh. My. God. Willow had ignited a bonfire, and Mika never wanted it to end. She ran her tongue over her lips to taste Willow's sweetness. "I've, ah, never kissed anyone before." Worry shot through Mika when Willow's eyes grew wide.

"I never would've guessed. I've kissed guys before, but yours is the very best." Willow tapped her fingertip on Mika's lower lip and grinned. "But maybe we should practice more."

Willow kissed her with an intensity that melted all of Mika's fears. When Willow glided her fingertips under Mika's shirt and up to her rib cage, stopping short of touching her breasts, Mika could've rocketed into space. Again, they broke off breathless. They lay side by side holding hands.

"I want to be your girlfriend." The words tumbled out of Mika's mouth like her damn voice box and brain lived on different planets. They hadn't had their first official date yet. Maybe this was too soon, but Mika was ready. *Please say yes.*

"I'm yours." Willow ran her fingers through Mika's hair. "But we have to open that door and study because it's your aunt's rule. I'm sure we can figure out ways to do other stuff another time."

Other stuff? Oh, yeah! "You're right. But one more kiss now, please."

When Willow pressed her lips against hers, Mika's head went spinning into the outer stratosphere. Several minutes of kissing passed, and Mika could feel wetness pooling between her legs. Willow pulled back and motioned to the door, Mika jumped up and cracked it open. She stood at the threshold for several seconds, gazing at Willow.

"What?" Willow laughed.

Gorgeous, fun, bright, generous—so many feelings consumed Mika. "You're my girlfriend. No joke?"

"Yes. Let's study."

Mika ran full force and pounced on the bed, jumping up and down like it was a trampoline. Willow picked up a spiral notebook and swatted her gently. Her laugh melted Mika's insides. She hadn't felt this happy in a long time.

Fuck high school. She and Willow would graduate together, and they'd move on to college in New York City. Nothing could stop her now.

Chapter Twenty-Four

May

As Mika loaded books on the cart to shelve, a group of guys that were friends with Ashley Devins came into the library, talking loudly.

"It's a quiet zone," she whispered.

"Right," one guy said. He grinned and the rest of the group laughed.

Mrs. Simmons was on some conference call in the back of her office, so Mika didn't have any support. She flinched when Ashley came in and sat down with them.

Ashley sneered. "What are you looking at, Manly Mika?"

Fuck off, bitch. God, Mika wanted to say those words. She balled her hands into fists but turned away. Starting a fight and possibly getting thrown into detention with the rest of the Neanderthals wasn't the answer.

She pushed the cart into the corner farthest away from the group and began slowly shelving. Her anger built with every book. When she jammed one into place, several others fell to the floor in a heap. She kicked one of them then rested her head on a nearby concrete pillar and took several deep breaths. Things would be better once she got out of here. Her dream of living in New York with Willow couldn't come fast enough.

"Hey, gorgeous. I never figured you out for a book hater." Willow picked up the book Mika had kicked.

"Sorry, tough day. But you're here now. I thought you weren't coming in today. Is everything okay with your scholarship?"

"The guidance counselor didn't take long. She told me everything was on track for CUNY now that my math grade has gone from a C minus to a B, thanks to you." Willow wrapped her arms around Mika's neck and inched forward to kiss her.

Mika stepped back. "The assholes are in the library."

"They left. There are only a few freshmen at the tables and in the study rooms. Besides, I don't care if anyone sees us. Do you?"

"I wouldn't like the extra jeers, but you're worth it." Mika placed her hands on Willow's waist and pulled her forward. The contact ignited her body, sending tingles all over. She loved the feel of Willow's skin. Stars danced behind her eyelids when Willow's tender lips met hers, and the rest of the world disappeared. When Willow pulled away, Mika ran her fingers through Willow's hair and gazed into the most beautiful face in the world. "That was an amazing kiss. I'm so lucky."

"There's just one problem," Willow said.

"What?"

"I'd love to kiss you all day, but we have to shelve." Willow smiled.

"The cart's only a quarter full."

"Yes, but the jerks pulled two tables together and left a mountain of books in the shape of a pyramid." Willow ran her finger down Mika's cheek. "We'd better get busy."

Mika held onto her hands and took a deep breath. "Will you go on a date with me?"

Willow laughed. "I've been on several dates with you."

"Yeah, I don't mean joining Benjy for burgers or the movies. I want to dress up and take you to a nice place. Well, you'd have to drive."

"How about Friday? Then you can still play online games with your buddies Saturday night."

"But I'm supposed to tutor you at your house." Mika blinked.

"You can spend the night." Willow tapped her finger on Mika's chest. "Tell your aunt that I'm picking you up. Bring your extra *date clothes* in your overnight bag, and you can change at my house.

Mom's going to a friend's and won't be back until around eleven. So we can make out after our date. And Mom will never know." Willow gave Mika a quick kiss then grabbed the cart. She walked away laughing with an exaggerated sway in her hips.

Mika couldn't move a muscle. Willow was fire and dating her made Mika feel good again. She still hurt but no longer cried herself to sleep, and the bright future she dreamed about was within reach. But was Willow afraid of her mom finding out? Hell, she was keeping everything a secret from Aunt Val. She just couldn't take the chance of her aunt making her stay in high school. Another year in this dungeon without Willow would kill her. Nope. She'd probably be in jail for beating up one of the bullies if Willow wasn't around. Her future was the city with Willow.

"Let's get busy. I'm not kidding when I said they left a mountain of books," Willow whispered.

The rest of the week was peppered with more stolen kisses. Friday finally arrived, and Mika's mix of emotions was kind of like everything else in her life: a roller coaster ride. But for now, excitement was winning over panic that something would go wrong.

She changed in Willow's guest bathroom and looked in the mirror. Her black slacks, white button-down shirt with a black and navy striped skinny tie were simple, but she liked it that way. She gave Willow extra time, then grabbed her bag and made her way down the hall and tapped lightly on the door.

"Come in."

The door creaked as Mika opened it slowly. *Oh. My. God.* Willow's makeup made her look like a super model. Her dark blue, long-sleeve dress had sequins on half of the upper part. The dress fell below Willow's knees, but the top part showed off her cleavage. Mika's pulse pounded in her ears.

"Is something wrong?" Willow asked. "You're staring at me."

"You're so damn beautiful. You look like a Hollywood star." Mika glanced down at herself. "I didn't bring anything else."

"You look great." Willow straightened Mika's tie then kissed her. "Where are we going, handsome?"

"The Inn Restaurant in Trumansburg."

Willow's mouth gaped. "That's expensive."

"You're worth it, especially since it's our official first date."

"Thank you."

"It's a half an hour from town. Someone who knows your mom might see us. Is that okay?"

"Yes. I don't give a fuck what other people think. I can handle it, and I don't know how Mom will react, but she won't go nuts or anything. The worst that can happen is she won't let you sleep in my room during sleepovers, which is a good reason *not* to tell her." Willow tugged on Mika's arm. "Now, stop worrying. Wrap your arms around me and kiss me."

Just hearing those words put Mika on a high. And when they kissed, it was the best. They held hands most of the way to the restaurant. Then her nerves hit when they arrived. Everyone here was way older, and there was no hiding she and Willow were a couple.

"Remember what I said," Willow whispered.

Mika's confidence rose when Willow slipped her arm through hers. Although some people in the dining room looked surprised, plenty more smiled as the host took them to their table. Mika had always hated the box most people wanted females to crawl into. She believed that everyone should be allowed to be free, wear pants or a dress, and love who they wanted. But it was still scary as hell when bullies said things or posted crap online.

"Tonight's going to be fabulous." Willow smiled.

The host led them to a table for two next to a large window and away from other guests. Mika was happy for the privacy, at least for now, and shook off any remaining doubts. She pulled the chair out for Willow.

"Thank you," Willow said.

"I bet prom will be spectacular, but it's hard to beat the way you're shining tonight," the host said and smiled at them.

"Ah, yeah." Mika sat next to Willow. He handed them menus and described tonight's specials. Mika watched him leave then turned to Willow. "I never thought about prom. Did you go last year?"

"The dancing was good, but I left early." Willow frowned. "Levi surprised me in the hallway when I left the bathroom. He grabbed my breast and tried to force his tongue down my throat. He wouldn't stop when I said no, so I kicked him. Then I left."

"If he'd been gentle, would you have kissed him back? And have you ever, you know, with a guy?" Mika couldn't erase the hurt she saw in Willow's face. "Sorry. I'm an ass."

Willow put her hand over Mika's. "I've never gone all the way. Look, I think tonight makes it official. I'm your girlfriend. So forget what came before. I'm not interested in anyone but you."

Mika put her other hand on top and rubbed the back of Willow's.

"So, Mika Lavigne, would you take me to prom?"

Mika swallowed. "I'm not a good dancer." She didn't really want to be in the spotlight for the bullies, and she worried about them bashing Willow. Sooner or later, someone was going to find out.

"Forget it. It's stupid anyway." Willow picked up her menu.

"No, I'd love to have you on my arm. When is it?" Mika pushed down on her knee that wanted to bounce a thousand times a minute.

"The Senior Prom is the Friday before graduation, and you're considered a senior since you're graduating early. So you've got plenty of time to get a tux or suit. I assume that's what you prefer."

"Okay." Mika didn't totally feel ready to be out in her hometown, but she'd taken a big leap with Willow. With prom a month away, she'd have time to build her courage.

A woman walked up to their table. "Good evening. I'm Julia, and I'll be your main waiter tonight. Do you ladies need more time?" She smiled.

Mika fumbled with the menu. "A few more minutes, please."

Willow's mouth popped open. "This place is too expensive. I'll just have a cup of soup." She folded up her menu.

"No. Have whatever you want. I'm buying. This is our first official first date and a celebration of me getting into Columbia." Mika glided her fingertips on top of Willow's hand. They stared into each other's eyes. "I have money that I saved from a few odd jobs last summer. And I have a good allowance. Please."

"Okay."

Julia returned and took their order and left.

After ordering, they talked about their dreams.

"We're going to be busy with studies, and I'm going to try to work part-time in the library. I want to see you as much as possible," Mika said.

"We can make the best of it. The shows are amazing, and same-sex couples hold hands and kiss in public all the time," Willow said.

Mika gazed at Willow, now inches away. "I want to kiss you now, but it feels kinda weird to do it here. It's hard to wait until we get back to your room."

"I'm counting on tons of kisses." Willow rubbed her knee against Mika's under the table.

"Tell me more about your art. When did you start painting?"

Willow's face glowed with a bright smile. "I fingerpainted on the living room wall when I was little. Mom bought me an easel and some supplies and explained this was the only place I could draw and paint, but she kept my living room masterpiece for a while before painting over it. My art is an extension of my imagination. Sometimes, like my bedroom murals, it's a feeling of wanting to get away and enjoy nature. But mostly, I think art is an emotional language to communicate with others. When did you become interested in studying about the universe?"

"I liked to lay out on the lawn in the summer and look at the stars. Dad would point out the constellations, and he started taking me to the observatory. I like science and discovering things. It's silent in space. And did you know there's over five-thousand exoplanets?

NASA's observing other possible ones."

"What's an exoplanet?"

"A planet that is outside our solar system and orbits a star. Some may support life."

"I love your gigantic smile." Willow brushed the back of her hand down Mika's cheek.

"Excuse me, ladies," the waiter said as he balanced dishes on his arms while Julia placed the food in front of them. "Please let us know if you need anything else to help make your night special. Enjoy."

The food was great, but they skipped dessert to get back to Willow's faster.

Willow drove through the dimly lit streets toward her house. At a stop sign, she put the car in park. "The street lamp's burned out here, and the moon perfectly lights your face. Kiss me."

As their lips met, the tingling in Mika's body amped up a thousand times and exploded when Willow touched her chest and pushed her tongue into Mika's mouth. She ran her fingers through Willow's hair and moaned softly.

She broke off breathless when headlights came up behind them.

"To be continued at my house." Willow grinned.

But before she could put her car into drive, the other car pulled ahead and blocked them.

Ashley's new boyfriend, Ted, was behind the wheel. Ashley and Carrie jumped out and pounded on the windows of Willow's car.

"Freak lezzies."

"Trans weirdo." Carrie pointed to Mika.

For a split second, Mika froze, stuck between wanting to hide and wanting to punch their lights out. She heard the car door slam and looked over at the driver's side. Willow now stood outside and in front the car.

"Get the fuck out of here. My girlfriend and I don't need dogs like you throwing shade," Willow yelled in Ashley's face.

Mika's heart pounded. *I have to protect her.* She hopped out. "Fuck off!" Carrie stepped back like she was afraid. "And leave my girlfriend alone." She jabbed her finger in Ashley's direction. A chill ran up Mika's spine as Ted got out of the car. He was the tallest and heaviest football defensive tackle in central New York, and he'd just transferred to their school this year. Mika didn't know what he'd do. She moved to Willow's side and slipped her arm around her waist. "Leave us alone," she said in a quieter voice. "We don't give a shit about what you do."

As Ted moved closer, Mika dropped her arm and walked toward him. "Take your girlfriend and leave. We haven't done anything to you. You attacked us."

He stared down at Mika. He was so close that Mika choked on his cologne. She swallowed. It'd only take one punch of his massive fist to knock her out. "Come on, man. This is going to end badly for everyone."

"Nice clothes."

What the fuck? Mika shifted her weight to her other foot. "Everyone should dress the way that makes them feel good, right?" The touch of Willow's arm through hers eased her fear.

"And she's sexy as hell," Willow said.

Ted stood there with his arms crossed.

"She walks around like a mute but checks out all the girls. You've seen her," Ashley said.

"I mind my own business." If it wasn't for Ted, she'd punch Ashley's lights out.

"Do something," Ashley smacked his bicep.

Ted shook his head. "You said she was harassing you. But you're the one throwing homophobic shit."

"She's a lezzie." Ashley flicked her hair back.

"And so is my older sister in college. I guess we're done here." He looked at Mika and Willow. "Have a nice evening."

"Your sister's gay?" Ashley asked.

"Get in the car before I leave you in the middle of the street."

Mika and Willow watched them pull away.

"Wow, I never expected that to turn out that way," Mika mumbled.

"Are you girls okay? I heard the screaming and thought that guy was going to hurt you. I can call the police." A woman stood on the sidewalk with no jacket and her arms wrapped around herself.

Fuck, a police report was the last thing Mika wanted. "No need. We were just leaving. Thanks for the support." She waved. "Let's get out of here," she whispered to Willow.

Willow drove carefully as usual. "You were strong."

"And you were fearless." Mika rubbed her arm.

After pulling into the driveway, Willow turned to Mika. "Don't let it spoil our evening. We have every right to kiss like any other couple."

"Tomorrow, everyone will know you're my girlfriend." Mika caressed the side of her face.

"Good. And now, chuck that shit. I want to make out with you."

"Your sexy girlfriend?" Mika grinned.

"Yeah, my sexy, handsome, sweet girlfriend." Willow hurried inside and slipped out of her heels. "Catch me if you can." She ran up the stairs.

"Oh, I will." Mika passed her and ran into the bedroom.

Willow slammed the door, tossed her shoes to the side, and pushed Mika onto the bed.

"You're gorgeous." Mika stared at her.

"Thanks. This dress was hell to get into." Willow turned and lifted her hair up. "Unzip me, please."

"Ah, sure." Mika couldn't believe things were moving this fast, but she wanted it. She tried to still her shaky hand, then took a breath as she unzipped the dress. She swallowed and ran her fingertips down Willow's spine. Her silky skin was beautiful, and Mika wanted to see a lot more.

"Feels good." Willow turned and lowered her dress.

Willow standing in front of her in nothing but her underwear took Mika's breath away. She wanted to devour her slowly, enjoy the rush of feeling her for the first time. She stepped forward and traced her fingertips down Willow's face, neck, and collarbone but stopped at Willow's breasts. "Can I?"

"I like how you ask permission instead of taking me for granted."

She gently cupped Willow's breast, rubbing her nipple through the bra. The moan from Willow put Mika on a bigger high. Her hands skimmed down Willow's back to her ass.

"Girls, I'm home early."

They jumped apart.

"Quick! Get into your pajamas," Willow said. She picked up her dress, ran over to the closet, and tossed it in. She pulled on an oversize night shirt. "Move, Mika."

Mika took off the tie and toed off her shoes. She picked up her bag but froze as she heard Mrs. Parker's footsteps approaching.

The door creaked open. "Hi, girls. Why was the bedroom door closed?"

"Ah, it's my fault," Mika said. "I um, went to the guest bathroom and closed it by habit when I came back."

Mrs. Parker scrunched her eyebrows. "Aren't you spending the night? You look like you're going out on the town."

Goosebumps raised on every inch of Mika's skin. "I wanted to run out for munchies. Can't do that in my pajamas." She laughed and glanced at Willow who was wide-eyed. *Shit.* Like that dumbass statement was going to fly with why she wasn't wearing her jeans. "I was going to order from this fancy restaurant that has great food but a dress code. Then we were going to start a fire and watch a movie on the downstairs TV." The words that spilled out of her big mouth sounded somewhat normal, but her insides were twisting.

"What new restaurant?" Mrs. Parker asked.

"I told her not to call for takeout because we had Buffalo wings in the freezer. And I didn't want to drive this late at night," Willow said.

"It's late to be eating spicy food too." Willow's mom shook her head. "Never mind. You teenagers eat at weird hours. Want me to fix your wings?"

"No. I grabbed a bag of chips instead." Willow pointed to the Fritos on her dresser.

"Okay. See you downstairs." Willow's mom left, and Mika fell face first on the bed.

"I can't believe Mom bought that one." Willow laughed. She smacked Mika's butt and kissed her. "Get dressed for bed. I'll meet you downstairs."

The most beautiful girl in the world was her girlfriend. And if touching and kissing Willow sent Mika into the stratosphere, then what would sex do? Yeah, they'd almost gotten caught, but fear was soon replaced with a wonderful craving to have Willow.

Chapter Twenty-Five

WITH EACH PASSING DAY, Mika's brain was stuck on the next time she'd get to kiss and touch Willow. It was getting harder and harder to find a place to be together. They'd kissed behind the book shelves at the library. They'd lied about going out to dinner. Willow would sometimes drive them to an obscure location to make out.

The last time, their hot and heavy session was going fast. Mika had slipped her hand underneath Willow's shirt and caressed her from her bellybutton to her breasts. Willow's silky-smooth skin had put Mika's senses on overload. As Willow moaned for Mika to go further, another car pulled up nearby. She ducked down, and Willow drove them out fast. They needed privacy, and the only place for that was their homes. They had kissed at each other's house, but the night Willow's mom almost caught them was a close call. Mika didn't know what to do, but she'd think of something. She headed down the stairs to switch the laundry.

Aunt Val was sitting in the living room. "Dammit." She slammed her mug down and the coffee spilled. She stood and paced back and forth.

Mika jumped. Had Aunt Val found out about them? "Um, can I get you another cup of coffee?"

"No, thank you." Her aunt rubbed her forehead.

"What's wrong?" *Yep, I sound scared.*

"My company has a conference in Boston this weekend. The keynote speaker quit at the last minute. I'm the only person who knows the material, so headquarters asked me to go. I'll have to leave Friday, but I should be back late Sunday."

Crap. Her cousins weren't home this weekend, and she

doubted Aunt Val would let her stay home alone. The last thing Mika wanted was to sit in a conference room around a bunch of boring adults. At least, she wouldn't have to go to school Friday. She cleared her throat. "I won't be any trouble. But can I sit in the back where I can text and play games on my phone?"

Her aunt flung her head back and burst out laughing. "I wouldn't put you through that torture. I called Mrs. Parker. You're going to Willow's after school on Friday, then I'll pick you up from school Monday afternoon."

Mika wanted to jump in the air and scream. "That's cool." She thumbed over her shoulder. "I'll go upstairs and call Willow to talk about what food we watch and what movies to eat." Mika shook her head. "Ah, you know what I mean."

"Yes, I know. Get packing, crazy teen." Her aunt laughed again. "Wait, Mika." She motioned for her to come closer, then she wrapped her in an embrace. "I love you."

"I love you too, Aunt Val." Mika meant it, and it felt good to say it.

Aunt Val held her at arm's length and smiled wide. "Go on and make your plans. Have fun this weekend."

If Aunt Val knew what plans were already tumbling into Mika's brain, she'd stay home and lock Mika in her room.

Willow picked Mika up as usual for school, but they didn't go. They rode around until they were sure Aunt Val had left. They came back to Mika's, downloaded the sick forms, filled them out electronically and faked the signatures of Aunt Val and Willow's mom to each document, then emailed them to the school. It'd been a long time since either of them were sick. So they thought the school secretaries wouldn't check the signatures.

The excitement of their previous make-outs had been driven by the fear of getting caught, but now it was pure desire. Mika had dreamed about touching every part of Willow's body, and she'd watched several movies to get ready. Holding Willow's hand, Mika led her into the bedroom where she'd gotten up extra early to put on fresh sheets.

After kissing, Willow said, "Do you want to undress me or watch me get undressed?"

Mika sat on the bed. "Take off your clothes to your underwear. Then I'll do the rest." Her body hummed as Willow slowly removed her pants and top.

"What about your socks?" Mika teased.

"Silly." Willow pulled them off and tossed them over her head. Then she stepped forward and put her arms around Mika.

Mika's heart beat like a drum. She wrapped her arms around Willow's waist and kissed the swells of Willow's breasts. She lightly caressed Willow's back as she moved her fingers up. She looked up into Willow's eyes when she found the bra hooks. "Can I?"

Willow nodded.

Mika unfastened her bra, tossing it aside, and gazed at her. "Beautiful." She skimmed her hands over each breast and kissed each nipple. She moved her hands lower and slowly removed her panties.

"I want to see you too," Willow whispered, and she held her gaze on Mika.

Mika almost ripped her T-shirt off. Willow's face shone brightly with an adorable smile which gave Mika the courage to strip off her sports bra, jeans, and boxers. The room suddenly felt cold, but she liked the way Willow looked at her. "Let's get under the blanket." She climbed in next to Willow. Her nipples were hard even before her chest met Willow's. When their bodies pressed together, every inch of Mika's body tingled. She kissed Willow. After they parted from the long kiss, Mika said, "Tell me anytime if I do something wrong."

"You're so sweet."

Willow kissed her harder taking Mika to new heights. Mika broke away and moved down Willow's body. She gently kissed one nipple while gently stroking the other with her thumb. "Is this okay? Am I doing it right?"

"Feels good." Willow stroked her hand through Mika's hair.

Mika skimmed her fingertips down to Willow's bellybutton, drawing light circles. "So soft."

"More," Willow said.

"Can I go between your legs?"

"Yes."

Mika lightly caressed Willow's folds before touching and rubbing her clit. She was so wet, and the louder she moaned, the more Mika rubbed. She stopped kissing Willow's breast and looked up. They stared into one another's eyes.

"Don't stop."

Willow's breathing grew heavier, and her eyelids fluttered with each touch of Mika's fingers. Willow cried out her name and raised her body up off the bed, then came down again, breathing hard. She grasped Mika's hand. "Slower."

Mika felt Willow's body gradually relax, but she still had a hazy look in her eyes.

"Let me count to ten to catch my breath."

"Okay." Counting wasn't in any books Mika had read or any movies that she watched. "Did I, you know, make you come okay? Or should I have done something differently to make it last?"

Willow laughed. "You're so sweet, worrying about doing it better. Trust me, you were fantastic." She flipped Mika on her back and straddled her and kissed Mika hard, then more softly from her neck to her breasts.

Now Mika understood what people meant when they said a kiss took their breath away. Her moans were like an out of body experience. She touched her own breast as Willow stroked between her legs. She was like a wild river getting ready to burst through a dam.

Willow stopped and looked at her. "I want all of you."

What was she talkin— "Oh!" Mika threw her head back as Willow kissed her between her legs. When Willow took Mika's clit into her mouth, the beating of Mika's heart was like a runaway train going faster and faster. Time ceased to exist. Her body quivered, and her eyelashes fluttered as she rose to a high. It was so much more than she thought it would be.

Willow lay beside her with her hand on Mika's chest. It was the best night of Mika's life so far. Her body parts continued to tingle, and every molecule in her body swirled with the emotions of them finally being together. Today was lit and beautiful, but that just didn't come close to describing what they'd just done. If this was how their first time felt, then the next time would blow the roof off.

"What's going through your head?" Willow traced her fingertips over Mika's torso.

Mika gazed into her stunning face and smiled. "I...I feel so many wonderful things. Was it that way for you?"

Willow scooted up and kissed her. The fireworks exploded again when Willow placed her leg between Mika's, pressing against her clit.

"Does that answer your question?"

"Yes. You're beyond beautiful. I knew that way before we even kissed." Mika wanted to shout out that she loved her. But was it too soon? Tonight was fire. She needed to concentrate on the moment and didn't want to push Willow. Still, her doubts wouldn't go away. "But I really don't get why you chose me."

"You're joking, right?" Willow frowned.

Words didn't come, and she shook her head.

"Mika." Willow cupped her face. "Dump those insecurities, because you're spectacular. You're smart, caring, a blast to be around, and funny, and," Willow trailed her fingertips down Mika's chest again, stopping at her belly button, "I love your body. Your muscles, your face with piercing eyes. I've never seen such a rich mix of green and brown with specks of amber. I should paint you. Even your intelligence is a turn-on." Willow kissed her nose and smiled again. "Okay?"

Willow's dazzling smile held her in a daze. "Okay. And ditto for you, except I think you're perfect."

"I'm far from perfect." Willow laughed.

The delightful sound put another smile on Mika's face. "Well, I disagree." She kissed Willow. "Since I have to live on campus my first year, I'm going to apply for a single room. We could study together and have sex whenever we want without sneaking around."

"I like how you think, devil woman." Willow leaned up on her elbow. "There's something I have to ask though. If it wasn't for me, would you be going to California instead?"

"Cal Tech and UC Berkeley are tops for astrophysics. Maybe I'll go there for an advanced degree someday. But right now, I don't want to be three thousand miles away. I want the freedom to be away from home and close enough to come back for a visit. You make me happy, and your happiness matters to me. Just thinking about studying with you or going out for a meal and holding your hand excites me. We can do that together in New York."

They made love again, and Mika felt more comfortable as Willow told her what she liked. Today was like the world's biggest fireworks display, and Mika never wanted it to end.

"Mika?"

She froze for a second at Aunt Val's voice, then they both tumbled out of bed and ran around searching for their clothes.

"Shit, I left my backpack downstairs. You've got to get out of here," Mika said. She toppled over trying to pull on her jeans too fast.

"I'm not ashamed of us. Are you?"

The hurt in Willow's eyes crushed Mika. "No. But think. We skipped classes."

"Yeah, my mom would be mad about school too. How do I leave?"

"I'm thinking. Finish getting dressed."

"I'm not sure where my underwear is." Willow slipped her top on and looked around the room.

"Don't worry about it. I've got to get you out of here," Mika mumbled as she buttoned her shirt. It sounded like her aunt was still downstairs. When they'd gotten dressed, Mika cracked open the door and glanced into the hallway. "Clear." She led Willow to the second-floor study and opened the window.

"No way." Willow stood ramrod upright with her arms crossed.

"The pergola is only a couple feet down. Then there's a trellis in the middle. The vines aren't the type that cut. I've done it before. Then you leave through the back gate." She heard footsteps on the stairs. "Hurry."

Willow gave her a quick kiss and climbed out the window. She made it safely to the ground. Mika shut the window and grabbed a book off the shelf. She ran into Aunt Val near her bedroom door. "Did your conference in Boston get canceled?" Although her insides churned chaotically, Mika hoped she sounded calm.

"I got the word before getting to Albany and turned around. Four freaking hours wasted. Why aren't you in school?"

"I'm way ahead, so they gave me this research paper to work on." Unlike the other little white lies, this seemed wrong, and from the looks of it, Aunt Val wasn't buying the story. "And you know my afternoon classes are easy for me." *Shit, I'm rambling.* "I can do chemistry and math in my sleep, and I'm pretty fit, so gym's no big deal."

"Why didn't you mention that before? And I thought you had a test coming up."

"Yeah, must have slipped my mind because I was studying so much for the test. But I'm up to speed." Heat flared up her neck. She had to end this conversation. She pointed to her bedroom. "I need to sit at my desk and write some notes."

"What were you doing in the study?" Aunt Val followed her to her bedroom. "You don't like going in there."

"Yeah, it's tough." Mika held up the book. "Just getting this for research."

Aunt Val smiled. "Looks like you picked a good book."

Shit, what had she picked up?

"How To Annihilate a Narcissist: In The Family Court?

Interesting topic." Aunt Val glanced at Mika's messy bed.

Mika's heart hammered against her ribs, and she couldn't get her mouth and brain to coordinate a response. If she didn't have a stroke, she was definitely dead when Aunt Val finally blew up.

Aunt Val placed one hand on her hip and the other against the door jam. "Your shirt is buttoned crooked, and you usually make your bed." She tapped the wood with her index finger, continuing to stare Mika down.

Think. "The cats came up and got under the covers. I shooed them out, then I relaxed and took a nap. I don't know about my shirt; I guess I did it on auto." She clenched the book to her chest. "And I was writing a paper comparing novels and non-fiction." She swallowed. "For English. That's what I needed to work on."

"The school library would be a better place to research and write your paper." Her aunt picked up Willow's socks from the floor and inspected them. "Tropical fish. Pretty."

Oh, boy, Mika was dead now. She always wore plain socks, and Aunt Val knew it. The room tilted when Aunt Val picked up Willow's bra.

"Planning on growing into this?"

Mika opened her mouth, but no words came out.

"And did you forget Willow's car is parked out front?" Aunt Val tossed the bra to the side. "Where is she?"

They both turned at the loud banging on the back door. Mika gripped the railing as she followed Aunt Val downstairs.

Her aunt waved at Willow before opening the door. "Hello. Isn't it fun playing in the wet backyard? All that rain we had is good for the garden." Aunt Val didn't move to let Willow inside.

"May I come in, please?" Willow asked.

"Sorry you couldn't get out the back gate. I put a lock on it since I read about recent break-ins across town." Aunt Val stepped back. "Your socks and bra are upstairs. Please finish dressing while I call your mother."

"Please don't do that, Ms. Hayden."

Mika was too terrified to speak when Aunt Val's stern look fell upon her.

Her aunt turned back to Willow. "I have nothing against you dating Mika, and I'm also aware teenagers have sex sooner or later." She crossed her arms. "But I won't lie to your mother. Hooking up at this house is the worst place. It could make hateful people gossip. Some might accuse me of influencing you two, or worse." Aunt Val bit her lower lip. After a few seconds, she sighed. "You have no idea what crap me and other women have been through. As sad as it is, plenty of haters love to distort the facts to prop up and push their view of morality."

"What are you going to do?" Mika asked.

"Mrs. Parker and I will need to discuss the matter. For now, get properly dressed and sit on the living room sofa. Bring down your phones and laptops. And I don't think you'll be spending the night at Willow's any time soon."

Mika felt lousy as Aunt Val's facial expression changed to a mixture of disappointment and sadness. "I didn't mean to hurt you. Willow's very important to me. She's more than a girlfriend."

"I feel the same way. I'm so sorry, Ms. Hayden," Willow said.

"I understand your feelings, but it'd be easier if Mika was seventeen," Aunt Val said. "Regardless, it wasn't the best idea to do it in this house." She sighed. "Let me talk to your mom. Then we'll all discuss it. In the meantime, tell me the truth. How did you skip school today? They didn't call me."

Mika lowered her head and quickly explained what they'd done. She expected Aunt Val to scream, but heavy silence filled the room like a smothering blanket pressed against her face. She looked up, and Aunt Val pointed toward the staircase. Mika took Willow's hand. She was petrified of what her aunt and Willow's mom were going to decide. She hadn't said the words, but she loved Willow.

Upstairs, Mika dressed quicker than Willow and headed downstairs to the sofa. Aunt Val was in the sunroom talking on her phone.

Mika picked up her phone and texted Jenn. *Aunt Val caught me and Willow.*

53X?

Yes.

8?

Mika scrunched her eyes, looking at Jenn's text. *Huh?*

8 is shorter than 69. u need a link to text abbrevs.

I still don't know what you're asking.

oral dummy

Mika's hand hesitated, but her cousin was the only one she could talk to.

Yes. Well, Willow did me.

Within seconds, her cell vibrated. Aunt Val was still in the sunroom with her back turned, so Mika answered. "Jenn, I can't talk now."

"Finally, you've lost your virginity. And what a way to go."

"Quiet," Mika whispered. She heard Willow coming downstairs. "Gotta go. Later." She hung up and slipped the phone into her pocket.

"I'm not ashamed of what we did." Willow sat down and laced their fingers together.

"Neither am I."

Aunt Val opened the sunroom sliding door and entered the living room. She cleared her throat and took a seat across from them. "Mrs. Parker will be here soon. Give me your electronics."

"But our homework is on the laptops," Willow said.

"Yeah." Mika's nerves quivered.

"Hand them over. Willow, I'll give yours to your mom when she arrives."

Mika wished she and Willow lived in a bubble and didn't have to deal with this. Mika was done with all this. She wanted to go to college and live with Willow, even if it meant they had to pay every cent themselves. Aunt Val and Mrs. Parker might ground them this time, but they couldn't keep them apart forever. Could they? Fear rose up in Mika. She'd die if they were forced apart.

Chapter Twenty-Six

Mika crossed her arms and stared at her aunt. "It's cold in the sunroom."

"Here, take the blankets." Aunt Val handed Mika the throws folded on the side of the sofa. "The thermostat is set at sixty. Turn it up, and it'll warm up fast. You'll be fine. I need you to sit where I can see you. Now, please," she said sharply.

Mika led the way, and Willow followed. Before shutting the door, Mika glared at her aunt.

"I don't care what she says. We didn't do anything wrong." Mika rubbed Willow's hand.

"We *did* skip school." Willow swallowed. "I've never lied to Mom before."

"Do you regret going all the way?" Mika held her breath.

"No."

The memory of Willow's soft, perfect lips all over her body made Mika shiver. "Me either."

Aunt Val tapped on the glass of the sliding doors between the sunroom and living room. "Study."

Mika took out her history book, and Willow took out a novel. They held hands as they read. Mika would fight anyone who tried to separate them.

"There's Mom," Willow said, her voice shaky.

Mika looked up to see her aunt greeting Mrs. Parker. Mika's bravery turned to mush, and she felt small. She wasn't afraid of Aunt Val, but she didn't know Mrs. Parker. What if Mrs. Parker had a hellish side and locked Willow away. She took a deep breath as Aunt Val waved for them to come into the living room.

Sitting in the middle of the sofa and holding hands with Willow should have chased away any doubts, but it felt like they were facing a prison parole board with Aunt Val and Mrs. Parker sitting across from them. Coffee and cookies were on the table between Aunt Val and Mrs. Parker, but Mika and Willow had nothing.

"We have some rules," Mrs. Parker said. "Willow, if you ever skip school again, you'll sorely regret it. For now, focus on school. You can only see one another on the weekends with an adult present. There are only five weeks left, so it's not going to kill you to have some time apart."

Mika clenched her jaw tight, and out of the corner of her eye, she saw Willow drop her head.

"But I need help to pass my math class," Willow said softly.

"Zoom."

"Look, we both know what first loves are like. But please slow down. We need to know you're safe." Aunt Val picked up her coffee and sipped it.

Mika scrunched her eyebrows. Her aunt was paranoid with keeping her safe. *What the fuck? Take a chill pill.* "I bet you and Andi had sex in high school."

"This discussion is about you and Willow," her aunt said.

"Honey." Mrs. Parker grasped her daughter's hand. "You're of legal age but Mika isn't. Fooling around in this house puts them in jeopardy."

"What are you talking about?" Willow asked. "It's not illegal for Ms. Hayden to be gay."

Mrs. Parker looked at Aunt Val. "You need to tell them about the threat."

"What threat?" Mika bolted upright.

"Aunt Pauline threatened to go to court and remove you from my care. She thinks that my gayness is a bad influence on you." Aunt Val rubbed her temple.

"Can she do that?"

"There's no need to worry. She doesn't stand a chance in New

York courts, but she could make life hell if she finds out about you and Willow." Aunt Val bit into a cookie like she was taking a bite of Aunt Pauline.

"I'm sorry she has it out for you. You're like Mom and Dad. You care about me."

"Thank you, sweetie. But please don't ever fake my signature again, or you'll see my mean streak." Aunt Val leaned back in her chair and crossed her legs. "And don't worry about Pauline. She thinks her money can buy anything, but she's wrong. It'd be a shame if things went south now that she's being a bit nicer."

"Nice. Yeah, right." Mika grumbled. "Sometimes she reminds me of a boa constrictor waiting to squeeze the life out their prey." When Willow and Mrs. Parker looked at her, Mika swallowed. Maybe she shouldn't have said that.

Mrs. Parker cleared her throat. "I hate to mention this. But since Willow is eighteen and Mika is underage, Pauline might accuse my daughter of statutory rape."

"Huh?" Willow mumbled.

"Willow didn't rape me. It was my decision. Why would Aunt Pauline do that?" Mika rested her hand on Willow's thigh.

"Every state is different, but under New York law, an individual has to be seventeen or older to legally consent to sex. Mika, since you're still sixteen, my daughter could be prosecuted for breaking the law."

"A judge would likely throw it out since you're close in age. But still: school's what's important, and your birthday's not far away." Aunt Val's stare lingered on Mika.

Yeah, like some magic pinky swear. Aunt Val couldn't be that dumb. She and Willow would find some way.

"I agree," Mrs. Parker said. "I don't want you to date until after graduation."

"This is bullshit." Willow straightened her posture.

"Watch your language, please."

"Mom, teens date all the time. Couples even kiss in the school hallways. We shouldn't be treated differently than a hetero couple. Most of our generation doesn't care except for a few jerks. Screw them. I'm not going to hide who I am."

Aunt Val sighed. "I understand, and it's not fair that people treat you or me differently. I'm worried about Pauline causing problems, and I don't want to see either one of you get harassed. Speaking of bullies, how's that been?"

"It's nothing. We can handle it," Mika said.

"Ashley's one of the girls who bullied Mika at Jenn's pool. I'm sick of their shit," Willow said. "We were in the car the other day. They stopped us and called us names. I said I was Mika's girlfriend then told them to fuck off. It felt so good to speak my truth." Willow grinned.

"I know you're upset, but please watch your language." Willow's mom gave her a stern look, but Willow continued to grin.

Mika was lucky to have her. She was brave and didn't hesitate to defend their relationship. Ashley and crew had only dropped a few nasty names since, but they hadn't given up totally.

"Honey. You've never mentioned bullies before."

"Mom, we can handle it," Willow said. "And I want to clarify something about dating. I've asked Mika to the prom, and we're not backing out. We want to show everyone that we're not afraid."

Aunt Val and Mrs. Parker exchanged a glance while silence hung in the air.

"By prom, Mika will be close to seventeen—"

"It'll only be ten days," Mika said.

Aunt Val raised her eyebrow. "I can't imagine Pauline creating trouble around her birthday. I'm okay with them attending the prom, but are you?"

Mrs. Parker nodded and looked at her daughter. "I guess you'd better start looking for a dress."

"Thanks, Mom." Willow kissed Mika's cheek.

"Willow, you and I will talk more later about the bullies. Right now, let's talk more about safe sex." Mrs. Parker dunked a cookie in her coffee.

Oh, not that topic. Mika felt like her eyes were going to pop out of her head as she silently pleaded for Aunt Val not to talk about *specifics.*

"Look, I'm no fool," her aunt said. "If you do anything, don't sneak off and make out in the back of a car in the woods. Some nut could hurt you. Intimacy shouldn't be taken lightly."

Mrs. Parker cleared her throat. "Did you take precautions today?"

Mika could feel the heat creeping up her neck. She looked at Aunt Val, who seemed relaxed sipping her coffee.

"You should use a latex glove with lubricant during vaginal penetration. And a piece of plastic wrap for oral sex," Mrs. Parker said.

Aunt Val coughed and put down her coffee cup.

OH MY GOD. Mika just wanted to disappear. Out of all the things she thought Mrs. Parker would say, that wasn't one of them. She looked at Willow. Her reaction was the opposite. Fire shone in Willow's eyes. Mika had never seen Willow angry.

"Mother, plastic wrap is bullshit. There's zilch of a chance of us getting an STD if that's your point. My disastrous, short-term thing with that asshole jock ended over six months ago. I never had sex with him or went near his penis, and I hated kissing him. Mika and I are healthy, and we're not dating anyone else. You will not dictate how and when I have sex with her."

Mrs. Parker rolled her eyes, and Val's mouth hung open.

Mika's temperature zoomed, and she felt like her face was on fire.

"I think that covers the bases for now." Aunt Val shot up out of her chair. "We should all think about this and talk another time after we've cooled down. Why don't you girls go to the kitchen and look through the take-out menus for dinner tonight?"

Mika trudged off holding Willow's hand.

"Sorry if I surprised you by admitting how far we'd gone."

Willow brushed the hair from Mika's eyes. "I'm not ashamed of us."

"Neither am I, but it isn't long until school ends. Aunt Pauline is a wild card. If she finds out about any of this, she'll drop her nice persona and arm herself with a sledgehammer and a machine gun."

"Sorry to say, but she sounds like a total bitch."

"She's usually nice, but when she's nasty, she can take it to the max. No need to worry. I don't think she'd ever hurt me, but she'd go after Aunt Val."

Willow pulled her into her arms, and warmth flooded Mika's body as they pressed tighter together. But it was more than physical. Willow had stuck up for them and didn't back down from her mom's harsh lecture. Willow was her girlfriend, and they had an emotional connection. That would only grow stronger when they'd move to New York.

Chapter Twenty-Seven

MIKA WALKED AROUND ILIANA'S office, looking at the paintings again.

"Which one is your favorite?" Iliana asked.

"This one." Mika pointed.

"Vincent van Gogh's *The Starry Night*. What attracts you to the painting?"

"It's sad but beautiful at the same time. Kind of like my life."

"Meaning?"

"Things are going well now, and the sadness no longer eats me alive." Mika looked back at the painting.

"Do you paint?"

"Not really. I took one class for fun."

"Come sit."

Mika sat in the middle of the sofa as usual with Iliana across from her.

"You mentioned that you feel well enough to stop therapy. Your aunt will want to know my opinion."

Mika nodded.

"You've come a long way in five months, but let's talk about it more at the end of the session."

"I can only come for a couple more months anyway. I'm graduating early this year and going to Columbia University in the fall."

"That's wonderful. How do you feel about taking such a big leap?"

"I'm not nervous about college. I haven't told Aunt Val yet." Mika rested her arm across the back of the sofa. "It's just I'm so tired of high school. I'm ready to get out. She controls my college fund, but

I know there's enough in it."

"How do you think your aunt will react?"

Mika cleared her throat. "She's kind of upset with me at the moment. She caught me the other day after having sex. At first, she didn't want me dating until I turn seventeen, which is stupid, but she caved for us going to the prom. Sometimes she treats me like I'm too young. Hell, there are a lot of teen couples that have sex."

"Mika, having sex is a normal part of development. Are you too young? Your view and your aunt's may differ. She might be concerned about your heart getting broken, STDs, or an unwanted pregnancy."

Mika sighed then rested her ankle over her knee, bouncing her foot up and down. "I'm gay, and so is Aunt Val. Are you homophobic?"

"No."

"My grandparents are. The ones in Wyoming and the ones that died. Aunt Pauline too."

"I'm sorry to hear that. It must be heartbreaking knowing the ones you love are unaccepting."

This was the first time Mika had told anyone outright. It felt a little scary to finally say the words, but at the same time, it felt good. She was tired of hiding, and she needed to be brave like Willow. "So you're cool with it."

"Of course." Iliana took off her glasses. "Sadly, there are some therapists in our country that align with the ultra-religious right, but I personally question their ethics. So tell me about your girl." She smiled.

Mika relaxed. "Her name's Willow, and she's going to CUNY in the fall to study art. She mainly paints portraits and landscapes. She's kind and beautiful." Mika smiled widely. "I had a massive crush on her for the longest time. We really got to know each other working in the library. Then we kissed. It was beyond phenomenal. Then things just happened."

"Congratulations. She sounds nice. And besides smiling, you're not bouncing your foot or leg."

"I'm not nervous. I think there'll be more freedom to be us in New York," Mika said. "Sure, there are bigots everywhere, but I don't think I'll have college students bullying me because I'm too math geeky with a less girly frame." She shook her head. "I don't understand the cliques and why they think everyone has to fit in and like the same things and dress the same way. Jeans and a T-shirt are comfortable, and I can't stand dresses." She looked up and grinned. "Not on me, but they're pretty on my girlfriend." The heat of a blush rushed up her neck as she thought back on the times Iliana wore a dress. Mika cracked her knuckles. "I'm happy with my girlfriend, but is it normal to, you know, look and appreciate other girls? I mean, I don't say anything. If I do, it's, 'That's a nice outfit' or 'I like the color.' You know, just compliments. But is it normal to think more in your head?" She had to be red by now. Good thing Iliana wasn't wearing a dress. After that day when Mika had stared a little too long, she'd noticed Iliana's dresses were longer.

"Yes, Mika. It's normal. But there's a difference between an admiring glance and staring."

"Yes. I understand."

"Now, tell me about your plans for New York. It must be exciting to move there with your girlfriend."

Mika smiled wide. She went on and on.

Iliana stopped her with minutes left in their session. "You're going to have to think about how you're going to tell your aunt."

"Yeah, I need money released for tuition and housing."

Iliana held her hand up. "No, Mika. That's not what I mean."

Mika hung her head. "I'll upset her."

"She'll miss you, and it will likely make her sad, yes."

Mika swallowed, and her eyes teared up. "And I'm going to miss her. I've gotten to like her a lot." She smiled. "But it's the right thing for me. I want to be with people that want to learn and have goals. Ithaca's a great town minus about ten people. I love it here. I mean..." She closed her eyes for a second. "I want to see other places and do other things. There's so much more out there."

"Tell her that but just think over your words carefully before you do."

Mika nodded.

"Now about sessions. How about monthly? That would put us around the beginning of June well before graduation."

"How about after graduation and after my birthday?"

"In July? You're really trying to get out of therapy, aren't you?" Iliana crossed her arms and grinned.

After booking the next session, Mika walked to the Commons to meet Willow for lunch. She couldn't wait to tell her how well the session went. Mika had finally said the words, *I'm gay*, and the world hadn't imploded. Better than that, she felt totally free for the first time in her life. Now she just had to get free of high school, and her life with Willow would be perfect.

Chapter Twenty-Eight

MIKA WALKED DOWN THE hall and saw a group of students standing around her locker. Some quietly pointed while others laughed. She clenched her hands tight. What had the fuckers done now? The closer she got, the more her stomach twisted into a knot. "Excuse me. I need to get through."

A hush fell over the group, and they parted, then a few began snickering. Straight ahead was a giant dildo taped to the outside of Mika's locker. Spray painted below were the words, *Buy your own harness.*

"I hear you're trans and want the docs to sew one on you. Freak." Jackson Thornton shoved her.

They'd made her life hell, and she'd ignored them most of the time, but this was too much.

"You wanna feel a real big hard cock." He grabbed himself and turned to the crowd, laughing.

Mika tensed every muscle in her body. *One more word, and you're going down, fucker.*

He leaned up against the lockers, staring at Mika. "I bet Willow loves a big hard cock."

Mika kicked him in the balls, then punched his face as he bent over to cup his junk. "Fucking asshole."

"Cunt." Jackson rose and threw a punch.

Mika ducked. Using Jackson's momentum, she shoved him face first into the lockers and twisted his arm behind his back.

"Stop it! Now!" Mr. Howard pulled them apart.

"The bitch assaulted me," Jackson squealed.

"And you assault me every day with your sneers and words."

Mika hoped he hurt all week long.

"Enough. Everyone step back." Mr. Howard pulled out his phone and took a picture of the lockers before unclipping his walkie talkie from his belt. "Janitorial services needed at locker 1213. Vandalism with spray paint." He looked at Jackson then Mika. "Come with me."

Jackson deserved exactly what she'd given him; it'd been coming for a long time. But being sent to the principal, Mrs. Harrington, for disciplinary action made Mika feel nauseous. She prayed it didn't affect her early graduation.

When they got to the office, Mrs. Harrington talked to Jackson first, and she took forever. Mika bounced her leg up and down.

Jackson came out frowning and sat in a chair across from her.

"Come in, Mika." Mrs. Harrington gestured to her office. "Before I discuss disciplinary action, I want to listen to your side of the story. And I want to hear about anything else that might be relevant to your actions today."

Mika glossed over a few things but generally laid out the facts. Mrs. Harrington listened and didn't interrupt her.

"You're a wonderful student: polite and, up until now, you've never been in any disputes. I'm sure the bullying must've been deeply troubling and hurtful, but you should have immediately come to my office."

"Yeah, violence isn't a solution, but I can't let him or the others walk all over me."

Mrs. Harrington slid a tissue box in front of her.

I'm not going to cry. I'm mad as fuck. Mika slumped in the chair and looked out the window.

"How long has this been going on? Who are the others?"

Mika clenched her jaw so tight it hurt, but she wouldn't look at Mrs. Harrington. "I don't know when it started. I was an outcast way before high school."

Someone knocked on the door, and Mika was happy for the interruption. Now she just needed to think about what to say to get

Mrs. Harrington to stop asking questions.

"Come in."

The secretary poked her head inside. "Mr. Thornton is here. I told him you'd want to talk with him, but he has to get back to work and insists on a later appointment."

"Schedule it, please. He's also welcome to call me after four today." When the secretary left, she glanced back to Mika. "Shutting down won't help," she said softly. "Did the bullying get worse when you moved into high school?"

"Yes."

"Do you know of anyone else being bullied by the same people?" Mrs. Harrington steepled her fingers and waited.

Mika couldn't take Mrs. Harrington's prolonged silence, and it became clear she would probably wait an eternity for an answer. Her insides began to quiver. But hell, the whole school probably knew by now that Willow was her girlfriend.

"You mean like my girlfriend?" Mika swallowed.

Mrs. Harrington nodded.

"Yes, but nothing this horrible has happened before." Mika lowered her gaze, and tears burned at the back of her eyes. "We haven't been dating that long. This will probably scare her away." Mika snatched a tissue as the tears fell.

"My door is always open for anyone to come to see me anytime, and the counselor is also available. It's better to talk before things blow up like this." Mrs. Harrington sighed. "You've been through so much, Mika. Your aunt says you're still seeing a therapist, and that's good. You need to open up about this to her."

"You called my aunt?"

"We've talked a couple of times. She's concerned about you." Mrs. Harrington tapped her long fingernails on the desk. "Listen to me. I can't let you go scot-free. You're suspended for two days beginning today."

"But I have a chemistry quiz today." None of this was her fault. Wasn't the rest of the day fair enough?

"You'll take it another day. Jackson gets five days because of his continued bad behavior. I do not tolerate bullies. I'll be discussing the situation with the staff, and then I'll address the entire school."

"That'll put me in the spotlight and make them hate me more." Mika grabbed more tissues and hid her face.

Mrs. Harrington took a deep breath. "If I don't talk to the student body, this can happen again to you or someone else. The students have to know that any form of bullying and abuse is not tolerated. Mika, there's nothing wrong with you. You're the victim. However, I would have preferred that you hadn't tried to solve it with kicking and punching."

There were voices outside the office and then another tap on the door.

"Ms. Hayden is here," the secretary said.

Mika bit her lip to where it almost bled. How would Aunt Val react?

Her aunt walked in looking totally confused. Then she hugged Mika. "Are you okay?" she asked softly.

"Yeah."

Mika sat in silence while Mrs. Harrington filled Aunt Val in on what had happened. Just hearing the facts made her want to vomit.

"Ms. Hayden, as I mentioned before, Mika is an exceptional student. There's not much time left before graduation. And while she's not the instigator in this situation, the Thorntons could demand action."

Aunt Val sighed and turned to Mika. "They could press charges since you hit him first– Wait a minute." She scrunched her eyebrows together. "Principal Harrington, what do you mean, since graduation is so close?"

Mrs. Harrington stared hard at Mika. "Your aunt's signature is on the paperwork, but she doesn't know? I fail to see how that's possible. Now would be the time to explain yourself, Mika."

Mika cleared her throat. "I've always taken extra classes during the regular and summer semesters. I have so many credits that I didn't even need this semester. I *have* to graduate this year. This place is killing me."

"The ceremony's next month. You haven't even gotten—"

"I started applying last year. I don't want to be here longer than I have to."

"Ms. Hayden, I had no idea she faked your signature, but I'll allow it if you approve. Mika, I'm disappointed in you for keeping your aunt in the dark. Now you should give your aunt a fast recap on your college plans."

"UC at Berkeley, Cal Tech, and Columbia have accepted me, and I want to attend Columbia." With such impressive schools accepting her, Aunt Val shouldn't be too mad, but she also didn't look happy.

"What a coincidence since a friend told me their daughter had received a scholarship to study at CUNY," Aunt Val said.

Mika squirmed under Aunt Val's glare, but then her look softened, and Mika could have sworn she saw a glint of sadness in her eyes.

"I'm not going to stand in the way of your graduation, but we need to talk about your college plans pronto." Aunt Val turned back to the principal. "Are we through, Mrs. Harrington?"

"Yes."

When they left the principal's office, Mika expected the worst but got silence. She hurried to keep up with Aunt Val as she marched to the exit. They had to pass by the library and its wall of windows. A few students gawked at them when they walked by.

They got back to the car, and her aunt pushed back against the headrest. "I know you're hurting, but you should have used words instead of fists."

"I know."

"Everyone's human, I know that." Aunt Val raised her eyebrow. "If this happens again, try to use words and report the little cowards."

Mika nodded.

Aunt Val drove away, but instead of driving home, she drove

them to Java Heaven's new drive-thru. "Want anything?"

"Can I get a strawberry or blueberry muffin and a mocha latte?"

"Sure." Her aunt smiled and rubbed Mika's arm.

Mika devoured the muffin as Aunt Val drove north to Trumansburg, then turned west. "Where are we going?"

"The Finger Lakes National Forest. We can blow off some steam with an easy hike."

Was she nuts? There were plenty of trails closer to home. "It's supposed to rain, and I don't have any gear with me."

"I put raincoats, an extra sweater, and boots in the back," Aunt Val said.

So she wasn't too mad. Mika had thought that she'd be home scrubbing all the tile floors by now, so if hiking was her punishment, she'd take it. It started to rain as they layered up.

After several minutes of walking in silence, her aunt pointed to the trees towering over them. "The maples and willows are blooming, but it'll be a while before their canopy fills out. That means plenty of sunshine warming the forest floor. Keep your eyes open for early spring wildflowers."

"Spring Beauties are over there," Mika said and pointed to the pale pink striped flowers spread out almost like a blanket of snow.

"Good eye."

"Mom loved them." Mika stopped and gritted her teeth, but a few tears gathered in her eyes.

"I miss her too." Her aunt put her arm around Mika's shoulder.

The hurt came roaring back, and Mika fell into her arms.

"I didn't mean to make you sad, sweetie."

Mika released Aunt Val and rubbed her eyes. "It's getting better. But sometimes I feel guilty when I'm happy and having fun."

"That's normal."

"Do you know more wildflowers? Mom was always good with their names." Mika looked down the hiking trail.

"Yes. We learned during our camping times. Want to continue?"

Mika nodded. Along the way, Aunt Val showed her what

bloodroot, trout lily, and toothwort looked like.

Her aunt tugged on Mika's sleeve. "Look over here. I love this one. It's hepatica."

The petals were a deep blue, almost purple. Mika got to her knees to smell their fresh, delicate scent. *That's exactly how Willow smells.*

"When I was a kid, we used to camp in a different region of the Finger Lakes. There are so many wonderful parks nearby, but I wanted to bring you here because your mom brought me here my first time. Is it okay to tell you the story?"

"Yes." She wanted to know everything Aunt Val could tell her about her mom.

"I was a high school sophomore, and she was a freshman in college. I was jealous because I still had two more weeks of school, and she was already done. Anyway, one of the mean girls in school caught me looking at a female student and called me a sick lezzy. She'd been saying crap all year, and I'd had enough. I punched her in the face and broke her nose."

Mika's mouth popped open. *That* was unexpected.

Her aunt smiled. "See, I told you we're all human. Anyway, Mom got the call that I was suspended for a week. She was working at the bakery and couldn't pick me up. Dad was working the night shift and was sleeping. So your mom came, and the two of us sat down with the principal. He told her what had happened, but your mom had been his favorite pupil before he became the principal, and she'd never been in trouble. That helped as she sweetly convinced him not to tell Mom and Dad what I'd been called. Then to my surprise, she brought me here. I had a few hours of peace before going home to face Mom."

"She protected you."

"Yes, she did."

"She must have given you the 'I'm the older sister talk.' What did she say?"

"Yeah, she always pulled the older sister's superiority card." Aunt

Val gazed off, as if reminiscing, then she put her hand on Mika's shoulder. "Your mom asked me if I was a lesbian. I was scared shitless and said maybe." She slipped her arm around Mika. "She put her arm around me and said 'I love you no matter what, but if you ever come out, don't tell Mom and Dad because they'll freak. And wait until you've moved out of the house, because I'm afraid they might kick you out.'" She kissed Mika's cheek. "We didn't talk about it the rest of the day as we walked the trail, identifying beautiful wildflowers. It was a spectacular afternoon until I got home. I had to clean a different room of the house for two hours every day of my suspension, and I couldn't go anywhere for a month. Thankfully, Mom and Dad never found out that I was queer until I messed up with Andi."

Mika was too choked up to say anything.

"I love you, Mika, and I'll always accept you for who you are. As for today, I won't punish you, but it would be nice if you helped out a little more around the house."

"I will. Thank you for everything." Mika squeezed tears from her eyes, and Aunt Val rocked her in her arms. "Even through all the shitty stuff that's happened, I know I'm lucky to have you. I'm sorry I kept things from you and that I faked your signature. I promise never to do anything like that again."

"Thank you. And I won't stop you from early graduation if that's what you really want," her aunt said. "But I'm going to miss you so much." She smiled and tears filled her eyes.

Aunt Val's tears came on so strong that Mika didn't know what to make of them. She seemed more upset than she ever had before. "New York is a lot closer than California."

"True. So I can visit you plenty." Her aunt wiped her face and took Mika's hand. "Let's find more wildflowers, then have lunch at Glenwood Pines. It has a beautiful view of the lake."

They walked along in silence for a few minutes, but Mika stopped when more tears clouded her eyes. "Thank you for telling me stories about my mom. Got any about my dad?" Mika asked, her voice shaking slightly.

"Both your parents were very proud of you. Your father didn't like work travel because he hated being away from you and your mom. He was a good man, Mika."

Mika fell back into her arms. "I love you, Aunt Val."

"I love you too...so, so much."

They cried together for several minutes. While it felt freeing to talk about things, it also seemed a little strange. Mika felt like she was comforting Aunt Val rather than the other way around. But at the same time, it felt so good. She guessed that was what happened when people really loved each other. God, how could she have been so blind to not see how much her aunt was hurting? She'd never hurt Aunt Val again.

Chapter Twenty-Nine

June 19

Mika took her time leaving the school building. She sat on the edge of a concrete wall at the school pickup zone. It was a warm sunny day and the last day of school for seniors. She and Willow graduated on Sunday. *Good riddance, high school.* But the best part would be Senior Prom tomorrow. Mika wasn't good at dancing but was so freaking happy because Willow was going as her girlfriend for all the world to see.

Willow had already left because her final dress fitting was right after school, so Mika waited for Aunt Val. They were going to pick up her tux, then swing by the florist to get the corsage Mika had ordered for Willow. She laughed. She didn't know why, but her aunt seemed super nervous. But this would be freedom at last. Sure, she'd miss Benjy, but she was ready to move on.

Her phone rang. "Hello."

"Hello, dear. I bet you're excited for graduation," Grandmother Lavigne said.

"I am." Mika had told them about Columbia but not one word about Willow and prom.

"I'm sorry we couldn't make it. It's been so hard since your grandfather fell."

"What?" Mika jumped down from the wall.

"It's not too bad. His hip's a little sore, and he's limping, but it could be a lot worse."

Mika didn't like her grands' politics, but she didn't want anything bad to happen to them. "I'm sorry. Can I talk to him?"

"He's taking a nap now. Mika, dear, he's eighty and still tries to do things like he's forty. I'm surprised he didn't get hurt before now."

Sadness settled in Mika's chest when she heard her grandmother sniffle. Shit, Grandfather had to be okay. She couldn't lose him six months after she'd lost her parents.

"This last trip was hard on him, and the doctor says his arthritis is getting worse. He checks on the horses every day with the ranch hands. I'm worried about him, dear," she said.

"Me too." Mika tried to keep her voice calm. "I'm glad Jenn, Carla, and Aunt Pauline are coming to visit you next week. That should cheer him up." She jammed her hand in her pocket. Grandfather's personality was different than Dad's, but in vintage photos, he and Dad looked like twins. And everyone always mentioned how Mika, Dad, and her grandfather had the same hazel eyes.

"Dear, I know it's last minute, but could you please come out with them? I don't know how much time he has. Surprising him would cheer him up. You know we miss your dad terribly."

Mika could tell her grandmother was crying, and her heart ripped to pieces. She'd wanted to celebrate her birthday with Willow, Aunt Val, and her friends, but losing her grandfather would be like losing Dad all over again. She rubbed her eyes and pinched the bridge of her nose. "Okay. I'm sure Grandfather will be fine, and I'd love to ride horses with my cousins."

"Wonderful. Bye, dear."

Her grandmother sounded so happy when she hung up. It'd be a disappointment to Aunt Val, but hopefully she'd understand. Mika called Jenn. There was a pause after she told Jenn the gist of their grandmother's call.

"Really? Wow, we're going to have a blast. But I didn't know Grandfather fell," Jenn said.

"Maybe your mom didn't want to say anything to worry you."

"Maybe. What about your birthday and your girlfriend?"

Mika drew a deep breath and blew it out. "She's supportive and will understand. We've got prom in two days. I'm more worried about Aunt Val's reaction."

"Speaking of reactions. Mom hasn't said anything to me about your prom," Jenn said.

"Why would she?"

"There's an article in the IHS Tattler about prom and who's been nominated for prom King and Queen. Someone nominated you and Willow. They didn't call you a lesbian couple, but it's not too difficult to guess. Mom printed it off and left it on the kitchen island. Mom looking at your high school newspaper's website is weird."

Mika rubbed her forehead. "No one talked to me about it, so I didn't know about the article. Let me know if she says anything."

"Will do. Hey, but wouldn't it be cool if you guys did win?"

"Unlikely." Mika squeezed her eyes shut for a second and took a deep breath. "Jenn, I love her."

"Listen, cuz. You're headed to the city with her, and your life's going to be fantastic. So, if you hear a little bitching, ignore it. And you know Mom's going to bitch out your aunt."

"Do you think your mom will tell the grands?"

"Nah, it'd give them a fucking heart attack." Jenn laughed. "Chill. We're going to have fun in Wyoming. And if they say anything, it'll probably be, 'Are you confused, Mika?'" Jenn mimicked their grandfather's tone. "'Maybe you need to attend church more.' Oh shit, I'm going to die if they force us to go to the Catholic Church on vacation."

Mika wanted to laugh but couldn't.

"Lavigne!"

She turned at the sound of Benjy's yelling. "I have to go. Benjy's heading this way, and Aunt Val will be here soon. Bye, cuz."

"Bye. See you soon."

Benjy was the best friend anyone could have, and she'd felt like an ass for canceling on him a lot. But Willow meant everything to her.

"How's it going?" Mika sat up on the wall again.

"I'm bummed. You're graduating this weekend, and I'm not.

It's like time disappeared, and...you'll be gone." He shrugged his shoulders. "I get that Willow's important, but I'm your best friend. It's like you disappeared. You never tell me things anymore, and you rarely text." He blinked.

Fuck. Were those tears in his eyes? "I'm sorry, dude. I'll try harder to keep in touch. So, whatcha been up to? Are you helping your dad at his store and making awesome wood shit?"

Benjy jumped up on the wall and sat beside her, dangling his long legs back and forth. "Yeah, I start in the shop next week. I like making things with my hands, but I don't want to make the average furniture like Dad. I mean, his pieces are lit, but if I choose that career, I want to design fancy modern shit." He grinned. "Dad's going to let me try. You got any special plans for the summer?"

"My grandmother just called. Grandfather fell, but he's okay. I'm flying to Wyoming with my cousins to surprise him."

"Lit. I've never been out West. When do you leave?"

Mika rolled her shoulders to relieve some of the tension that had been building since she'd agreed to go on the trip. Pulling this off was going to upset a lot of people. Shit, besides her birthday, she'd also miss the Fourth of July. "We leave on Tuesday for two weeks."

Benjy stared at her. His mouth hung open, and his eyes bugged out of his head. "Shit. Your aunt's not going to be happy."

"Yeah, she doesn't get along with them."

"Mika, think. It's your birthday week."

"I know. But Grandfather's not doing well. We can celebrate another time. I'm sure it'll just be a cake and dinner with Aunt Val, Brie, Willow, and her mom, and you and your family."

"Oh, fuck, this is not good." He shook his head. "I've been hiding it from you, but your aunt asked me and Willow to help plan a surprise party for you. Wes and Tiana are coming, and some of our online gaming buddies from Dryden and Cortland."

"What?" A sinking feeling threatened to overwhelm her.

"And you'll miss the Fourth of July. And think how sad Willow's going to be."

"I know, but we'll be together in college soon."

"She was going to take you to see the fireworks at the Inn at Taughannock Falls. She wanted to go back there because it was the place of your first proper date."

Mika found it hard to breathe. They sat in silence for a minute as a few people walked by. "I just couldn't say no to Grandmother. She choked up a couple of times and sounded like she was crying. I got the feeling that Grandfather's fall was a lot worse than she said." Mika swallowed. "I also remember overhearing him telling someone at the funeral that his body couldn't take many more plane rides." She wiped her eyes with her shirt and sniffled. "We last went out there as a family three years ago at the end of school. I love you guys and Aunt Val, but I miss my parents so much. I want to go and ride my dad's favorite horse. When I look into Grandfather's face, I see his old, weathered skin, but I also see my dad."

"I get it that you miss them. But be prepared to make a big ass apology." He smacked her thigh hard.

There was nothing she could do. The Wyoming trip would upset Aunt Val, but if she didn't go, her grandparents would be upset. If Grandfather hadn't got hurt, she probably would have stayed at home. She didn't know how, but she'd make it up to Aunt Val and Willow after.

"Other than your texts, which only take a nanosecond to read, what's been going on?" He crossed his arms. "You and Willow must be hooking up a lot."

"Shut up." Mika pushed his shoulder gently, trying to hide a smile.

"Hey, I don't talk shit. I'm only telling you that there's a lot of talk going around. And some of it is good." He uncrossed his arms. "Did you know Tiana stood up for you against Carrie Tucker?"

"Really?"

"Yeah. Carrie was talking shit. Tiana pushed her, got in her face, and told her to shut the fuck up. She asked Carrie if she was jealous because you two are such a cute couple. The best thing was the crowd around them cheered Tiana on. Somebody yelled that it was about time someone stood up to her and Ashley." He grinned.

"That's cool."

"Yep, that happened two days ago, but you're too wrapped up in gooey, lovey-doveyness with Willow to notice."

Mika rolled her eyes. She did feel guilty for neglecting her friends. Most of her spare time had been eaten up by school and Willow.

He put his arm over her shoulders. "Forget them anyway. Think about going to college and leaving all that shit behind. And most of all, think about me."

"Thanks, but I belong to Willow. Please remove your arm."

He laughed. "And Wes and Tiana are finally together. Wes was nervous about meeting Tiana's family last Sunday. Her older brother came home for dinner with their grandmother. Guess what he said?" Benjy waited several long seconds.

"Come on. Tell me."

"'I don't care that he's white, but don't you think his hair is a bit too red?' Then he laughed. Tiana chewed him out, then her grandmother smacked her cane on the table. Everyone stopped talking and looked at the old lady. She looked at Wes. 'I like your wavy red hair. Very stylish. young man. Now, sit your bones down and tell me a little about yourself.'

"Wow. That's dope. What about you?"

"I met a cute blond called Tricia. She lives in Trumansburg. We've been on a couple of dates. So, you're not the only one sneaking around." He blushed. "And I'm going to her prom. It's the same date as yours. Willow said you were going. You haven't chickened out, have you?"

"No way, man. I'm going in a tux. Hey, it's great to hear you're dating someone. Listen, dude, I'm sorry. You've been my best friend for so long, and I've been an ass. I've been caught up with Willow..." She looked him in the eye. "I'm... She means so much to me." Heat began creeping up from her neck to the top of her hairline. "And yeah, we've been intimate. It's been mind-blowing magical."

"You've got that look like she's the one. I'm happy for you."

Aunt Val pulled up in her dad's Mustang.

"See you at my graduation party. And bring Tricia if she's available."

"Ready to take a lake drive before we get your tux?" Aunt Val dangled the key fob in the air.

"Oh, yeah." Mika grabbed the fob. She'd finally gotten her junior driver's license, but she still couldn't drive by herself until she turned eighteen because of the state law. And it sucked that she couldn't take the Mustang to college. But there was no need for a car in New York since they could go anywhere on the subway.

"I have good news for your birthday next week," her aunt said. "I bought four tickets for *Rent* at Binghamton University's Anderson Center. It's the day after your birthday. You can take Willow and whomever you like. Afterward, I can drop you off at your cousins for a visit."

Mika's mom was going to take her to that show when it was playing on Broadway. For whatever reason, they never made it. Did Aunt Val know about that time? It didn't matter. Mika was going to miss it again, and this time, it was her fault. "Um, about next week. Plans have changed." She checked for traffic, then turned onto East Shore Drive.

"What do you mean?"

Mika cleared her throat. "Grandfather fell, and my grandmother thinks it'll cheer him up if I visit with Aunt Pauline and my cousins." She left out that she'd already said yes. The silence that followed was like walking on a frozen pond and not knowing when the ice would crack.

"Please pull over."

Mika trembled inside, then put on the turn signal and parked. But Aunt Val didn't say anything until Mika looked at her.

"When did you find out about this?" her aunt asked softly.

Mika was thanking her lucky stars that Aunt Val didn't rip off her head. Yet. "Grandmother called about twenty minutes ago."

Aunt Val pressed her lips together tightly, then she cleared her throat. "I'm sorry to hear about your grandfather. How bad is it?"

"Grandmother said he's limping around, but she sounded like she was crying." Mika shifted in her seat. "They go Tuesday."

"That soon?" Aunt Val pinched the bridge of her nose. "Well, at least it's not the day after graduation. Or are our Monday spa plans canceled?"

Mika was so preoccupied with graduation and the after-party that she'd forgotten. The spa wasn't her thing, but Willow wanted to go. "I'm still up for the spa. And I'm sorry about the *Rent* tickets."

"They won't go to waste. I'll ask Mrs. Parker and Willow. Brie might be able to go too." Aunt Val cupped Mika's face. "But I was looking forward to spending time with you on your birthday, even though I would've had to share you with Willow."

"Can I please go?" Mika felt like shit, but she had to tell her everything. "It's for two weeks."

"What the fuck?" Her aunt furrowed her eyebrows.

Mika swallowed. Aunt Val cursed occasionally, but Mika had never heard her say the f-bomb.

"Sorry for the language. I'm not mad at you, and I want you to spend time with your dad's family. I'm sure with their money they could have made the trip after your birthday. And frankly, I'm not comfortable with you going out there since they're so homophobic."

Mika gripped the steering wheel. Aunt Val was probably right. She hated to think how they'd react when she came out.

"I'll be with my cousins and Aunt Pauline. The grands are homophobic, but they don't know about Willow." She sighed and bit back her tears. "And honestly, I'd like to ride Dad's old horse. He had a favorite splash white American Saddlebred."

"I have no idea what kind of horse that is." Her aunt chuckled lightly. "You can go, and we'll celebrate your birthday another time." She brushed Mika's hair back. "Be careful. I know you trust Jenn, but don't say anything about Willow, especially about her being your girlfriend. The less they know, the better."

Mika wasn't about to tell her that Jenn had known for months. She'd never stab her in the back. "Thanks, Aunt Val. There's a lot of Dad around the ranch: pictures, the horses, and his old bedroom. He loved Wyoming, but when he came out to visit Aunt Pauline and her then-husband, he decided to go to college here. Then he met Mom, and of course made history." Mika pointed to herself.

"You are a piece of magnificent history." Aunt Val's smile was bittersweet. "I understand. Go and have fun. I'll rearrange the party."

Mika released her seat belt and hugged her. "Riding under the stars is the best. Maybe you should come too and try to mend your differences." Mika laughed when Aunt Val crossed her eyes and made a funny shape with her mouth.

"Your dad and I got along wonderfully, but his family can't stand me. Have you told Willow?"

"Not yet."

"You should tell her in person."

"You're right. Thanks." Not hugging Willow for two weeks was a drawback, and not having sex with her anytime soon was the biggest bummer. Mika could feel the heat from a blush crawling up her neck and spreading over her face. She turned away. God, she swore her aunt could read her mind.

"Now, Ms. Chauffeur. Take me for a spin by the lake. The tailor doesn't close until six. Has Willow talked about her dress?"

"She wants to surprise me." Mika drove away carefully. Just the mention of Willow sent warm tingles throughout her body. Thinking about how beautiful she was going to look on Friday night intensified those tingles, especially between her legs. Damn, if they weren't chaperoned every second, Mika would love to slowly take off Willow's dress at the end of the night.

Chapter Thirty

Prom, June 20

MIKA STOOD IN FRONT of the full-length mirror, frustrated that she couldn't get the damn bow tie to work. "You hired a spy." She faked a stern look.

"Of course." Her aunt winked. "No. Brie's cousin is not going to spy on you. He gave me a good price on the limo."

There'd be little time to make out tonight, but Mika prayed the interior window separating the cabin from the driver was dark.

"Let me help." Aunt Val somehow got the black and white striped bow tie perfectly adjusted. "I think you look great." She put her hand on Mika's shoulder and moved to the side.

For once, Mika was happy with how she looked. "Thanks."

"Ready to go pick up your girl?"

Mika grinned. "Definitely. Thank you for everything. You're the best."

Her aunt smiled and wiped away some tears. "I'll get the corsages." She pulled the white rose out of the refrigerator and pinned it to Mika's lapel. Then handed her a container with the double pink roses for Willow and kissed Mika's cheek.

Roses were a popular choice for corsages, and her mom's favorite flower. Tonight was about fun and happiness. "I think Mom and Dad would've really liked Willow."

"I think so too."

Mika walked out into the blazing sun. A heatwave was baking most of the country, but just thinking of Willow raised Mika's temperature. The limo driver opened the door for her. It was more luxurious than she had imagined. The one bench seat could easily fit four. He also explained how the ceiling panel changed color and could be timed to music or display other patterns.

"Cool."

"There's water and soft drinks in the mini fridge but no liquor," he said.

She gave him a thumbs up and pointed to the window between the seating and his driver's seat.

"I really can't see much, so you'll have to press this button to talk to me." He cleared his throat. "This is the senior prom. Shall I take the long way to the banquet hall?"

"Yes, please." Mika smiled as he shut the door. *And maybe a feel of Willow's breasts if it doesn't mess up her look.* She took a deep breath as the limo moved. Soon, she'd see beautiful Willow.

Mika's excitement built on the short drive to Willow's house. Her legs shook as she exited the limo. Fuck the bullies. Her confidence grew with each step to Willow's door.

Mrs. Parker opened the door. "Hi, Mika. Come in."

Time stood still as Willow descended the stairs. Her long hair was pinned up into a fabulous look that added to her already gorgeous face. She wore stilettos with a frilly navy-blue dress. The neckline was low, although Mika wished it was lower, and a sparkling necklace hung around her tender neck. Mika couldn't wait to run her fingers over Willow's neck, down her collarbone, and to her chest. It was ankle-length, but one side came up above her knee, making her legs look even more amazing and mouthwatering.

"You're above Gucci." Mika couldn't take her eyes off of her.

Willow turned her back to Mika. "Do you like my French braid knot bun? Mom did it."

"Your hair's amazing." And so was the low cut back showing off Willow's skin. Mika ran her fingers over Willow's shoulder blades, then lightly touched her shoulder. "This is for you." She held out the corsage then fastened the double rose around Willow's wrist and grinned. "Good thing I asked which one you wanted. There's no room on those spaghetti straps to pin it."

Willow ran her hand from Mika's shoulder down to her hand and gently squeezed Mika's fingers. "You look fabulous."

In the backseat of the limo, Willow crossed her legs, and her dress hiked up higher. "Do you like my dress?"

"Yep, you make it vibe, and you're going to make the other girls jealous." Mika ran her fingertips up Willow's leg. She moved her hand under Willow's dress and kissed her neck as she caressed her inner thigh. "Can you lower the dress straps?"

"A little. I don't want to mess it up."

It was a turn-on with just the one side down a little further. Mika enjoyed Willow's moan as she kissed and sucked the swell of Willow's breasts and rubbed her clit through her panties.

"I'm..." Willow bunched up Mika's hair in her hands. "Oh, my God. I've never come that fast."

"Guess I did a good job." Mika smiled.

Willow repositioned her dress, and they drank a soda.

The limo stopped about ten minutes later, and the driver tapped on the window. "You have to unlock the door."

Mika popped the lock, and he held the door open for them. She held out her arm and guided Willow inside. There was a line as every couple posed for photos. Ashley Devins was ahead of them. She turned and stared for a second, then she flicked her hair back but didn't say a word.

"Hey, you two look marvelous." Tiana walked up to them and gave them an air kiss.

As she and Willow talked dresses, Mika shook Wes' hand. "How's it going?"

"Great." He smiled wide at Mika. "I had a crush on you earlier this year, but I'm glad you turned out gay because I'm really into Tiana. She's sweet and we have fun."

"Good." Mika bounced on her toes, not knowing what else to say to him.

"Is Benjy coming?" Wes asked.

"No. He's at his girlfriend's prom."

They waited their turn for pictures, and Mika's pulse ticked up as she watched couples before them pose.

"He's going to click the shutter really fast," the assistant said to Mika and Willow. "So don't worry about your eyes being shut or anything. You'll have multiple shots to do a couple of poses. In a few days, you can buy the images online. Your turn."

In the first pose, Mika stood behind Willow with her hands on Willow's waist.

"Good. Now, half turn toward me," the photographer said.

Mika kept one arm around Willow's lower back.

"Miss, ah, the one in the dress, put your arm around your date's back. Then one hand on the shoulder. Smile at each other."

Mika briefly saw Ashley's gang looking at them. Mika wasn't hiding any more. As the photographer clicked away, she kissed Willow. Not a quick kiss. This was a full-on French kiss. Instead of jeers, there was loud applause and whistling.

"Now that's the way to begin the night," someone shouted.

Mika pulled away and smiled at Willow, who looked like she'd taken a happy pill.

"You have one more pose. What would you like?"

Willow grasped Mika's right hand. "Keep your hand on my back. Don't let me fall." She leaned back and kicked out the one leg showing off her beautiful skin and stiletto.

As the cheers from the crowd grew louder, Mika kissed her again.

"I got it, ladies." The photographer handed them a card. "Great job."

When they entered the dance area, the bullies had moved on.

The night was magical. Somehow, Mika didn't step on Willow's toes. The slow songs were the best, and they kissed several more times.

"And now for the crowning of Prom King and Queen," Mrs.

Harrington said over the microphone.

"First, the runner-up couple." She ripped open the envelope. "Mika Lavigne and Willow Parker."

Mika was shocked at first, but then Willow jumped up and down, smiling. Everyone around her was clapping. When Willow hugged her, Mika couldn't help but be sucked into the excitement. She walked onto the stage, proud to be holding Willow's hand. Oh, shit Ashley and her umpteenth boyfriend were also in the running.

"And the King and Queen are..." Mrs. Harrington looked around the room. "Aaron Williams and Debbie West."

Mika breathed a sigh of relief that she didn't have to share the stage with Ashley. The congratulations and photos that followed were a whirlwind. As both couples stood together for the last photo, the crowd shouted, "Kiss, kiss, kiss." The photographer clicked away as the couples kissed, and there was a roar in the room. The rest of the night breezed past with Mika on top of the world.

It was well after midnight when she walked Willow to her door. Mrs. Parker said hello and left them alone in the living room.

"Now graduation and the after-party, then Wyoming. Again, I'm sorry about the last-minute changes. Do you forgive me?"

"Hey, that's three more days together, and I intend to make them count." Willow ran her fingertips down Mika's cheek. "Good night."

"Good night." Mika kissed Willow once more. She couldn't get enough of her soft lips.

Mika stretched out in the limo. The ride home was lonely without her. After Wyoming, they'd have a fun summer then move on to the city together. Willow loved her, and that's all that mattered.

Chapter Thirty-One

June 23

DURING THE GRADUATION CEREMONY, Mika turned and glanced back at Willow from time to time. Her smile made Mika feel like everything was all right and all her worries had left her body. When it was all over, they took pictures together, holding their diplomas.

"I'm so proud of you." Aunt Val smiled and hugged Mika tight. "Are you ready to party?"

"Yeah! I'm driving. Willow's in front with me, and you guys are in the back." Mika held out her hand. "Keys, please."

"I'll drive since you're so excited."

Mrs. Parker cleared her throat. "I second that decision, and Brie can sit up front with Val. I'll sit between you girls so you don't get too lovey dovey."

"Mom!" Willow narrowed her eyes.

"Just kidding. You can sit together." Mrs. Parker chuckled.

Mika kissed Willow, no longer caring who saw.

"Hmm. That's what I like." Willow grinned and smacked Mika on the butt with her diploma.

Mika turned to Aunt Val. "If I can't drive, then you have to turn up the music so we can sing and dance."

Her aunt rolled her eyes and pointed to the car. "Let's go. Benjy and his parents left right away for the house, and Pauline and your cousins should be arriving any minute."

Jenn had graduated the same night as Mika's prom. But Mika really didn't want Aunt Pauline attending her graduation, so she'd told a little white lie that tickets were limited. Instead, she'd given the extra tickets to Benjy and his family.

At home, the basement was decked out in party streamers and glitter paper, and Benjy was blowing up balloons. "Congrats." He hugged her and Willow.

"We are so proud of you," Mrs. V said. Her husband smiled and nodded.

"Thanks, Mrs. & Mr. V." Mika hugged Benjy's parents.

As more people flowed in, the chatter grew louder and louder, and someone turned the stereo up. They danced until Mika's feet hurt, then Willow pulled her off to the side.

"You don't have to do that," Willow said to Brie, Mrs. V, and her mom, who were gathering up dirty dishes. "Mika and I can take them upstairs." She motioned to the mountain of dishes.

Mika grinned and gave a mock salute.

"That's right. Your girlfriend's in charge." Jenn clapped Mika on the back. "I'll help too."

Mika walked up the stairs first, balancing dishes on her arms. She stopped when she entered the kitchen, and Willow and Jenn almost ran into her.

"For Christ's sake." Aunt Val threw the sponge into the sink like a baseball pro, and soapy water flew high into the air. She turned on Aunt Pauline. "We have plans for tomorrow, and they're flying out of Syracuse on Tuesday morning at ten a.m. Pick her up then."

"But that'll add an extra hour to the trip." Aunt Pauline crossed her arms.

They looked like they were about to tear each other's throats out.

"Mom, it's not a big deal," Jenn said. "Maybe Mika can spend Monday night with us, or Carla and I can sleep over here."

"No!" her aunts said in unison.

Jenn and Carla hadn't slept over once since Aunt Val had become Mika's guardian.

Aunt Val softened her stance. "I'm sorry I raised my voice. Mika needs to stay here because we have plans for tomorrow."

She leaned against the sink. "Girls, please put the dishes down and return to your party. We need some privacy to discuss this."

Mika dumped the dishes less gracefully than Jenn and Willow.

Halfway down the stairs, Jenn whispered, "Mom thinks that Aunt Val's and your lesbianism will magically rub off on me."

"Drop it," Mika whispered.

The party wrapped up around eleven, and Willow and her mom were the last to leave.

"See you tomorrow," Mika said.

Mika floated on a cloud when Willow pulled her in by her shirt and kissed her goodnight.

Aunt Val closed the door. "You've been brave kissing your girlfriend in public. I hope that Jenn and Carla don't say anything to their mom."

"They won't. And it's getting late." Mika looked at Brie. "You should spend the night."

Her aunt tilted her head. "Goodnight, Mika. See you in the morning."

Mika laughed and ran up to her bedroom. Wyoming was going to be lit. She'd miss Willow, but Mika would be seventeen when she returned, and she'd be able to have Willow in her arms legally. Her phone chimed, and she smiled at Willow's picture. "Hi, beautiful. Miss me already?"

"Yep. I checked my email and wanted to tell you the good news. I snagged a work-study position." Willow bounced up and down on her bed.

"That's great."

They talked for another hour, dreaming of their planned life together before saying goodnight. Seeing each other between their college hours and Willow's job would be a balancing act, but that didn't bother Mika. She just knew it was going to work out. Willow was her girlfriend, and Mika would do what it took to keep them together. She loved Willow.

Chapter Thirty-Two

June 24

MIKA WOKE UP, SHOWERED, and dressed quickly. She bumped into Aunt Val coming out of her room. "Sorry. Ready to go to the spa?"

"Funny how you never liked that idea until Willow and her mom proposed the trip."

Mika nodded. And if she was lucky, she and Willow would be in the same room for a massage, and she'd catch a glimpse of Willow's naked body.

"Let's eat breakfast." Aunt Val motioned toward the stairs. "After you, Romeo."

Traffic wasn't bad, so they arrived about ten minutes early.

Willow's mom opened the front door. "Good morning. You both look chipper. I have no idea what's taking Willow so long. Mika, go up and check on her."

"Sure thing." Mika took the steps two at a time. She tapped on Willow's bedroom door then opened it a crack. "Can I come in?"

"Yes."

"You're still in bed?" Mika sat on the edge.

"It's early." Willow intertwined their fingers. "God, this weekend was fun. You were so handsome. Lay down with me, my king. We've got time." Willow yawned.

Mika crawled in and spooned against Willow's back. She could smell the scent of Willow's shampoo. She gently brushed her hand along Willow's forearm to her fingers. Her skin was so soft. She nuzzled her face against Willow's neck.

"You'd better stop, or I might hold you captive in bed." Willow laced their fingers together.

"Mm, I like that idea, but we have plans today, and it's getting late."

Willow stretched for her phone. "Shit." She jumped out of bed. "My alarm didn't go off. Pick out my clothes while I shower."

"Ah, okay." Mika almost laughed as Willow frantically ran out of the room. She couldn't believe Willow, who set alarms for everything, had overslept. Mika set out some clothes for her and went downstairs to wait.

The spa was better than Mika had expected. At lunch, Mrs. Parker asked her about the trip. Mika talked about the fun things she'd be doing with her cousins and warned everyone that the cell phone service was unreliable on the ranch and trails. Aunt Val's smile dropped. She was clearly still pissed at Aunt Pauline.

"So." Mika clapped her hands and grinned widely. "I can't wait until we go to New York."

"It's going to be fantastic checking out our dorms," Willow said.

"Girls, you have to be realistic." Mrs. Parker fidgeted with her napkin. "You'll see each other, but your priorities have to be college and work."

"I know you're both worried that this," she pointed between herself and Mika, "is just a passing phase. But it's not. Thank you for having faith in us and giving us a chance. We'll both work hard to make it, we promise."

"Here's to your success in school and with your relationship." Aunt Val held up her wine spritzer, and everyone clinked their glasses.

When it was time to leave, Willow and Mika held hands and followed behind.

"Enjoy Wyoming. I'll miss you terribly, but I'll save up tons of kisses for you." Willow hugged Mika fiercely.

"I love you," she whispered in Willow's ear.

Willow pushed back and looked into Mika's face.

Was it shock? Did she not feel the same way? Mika's heart

sank. What the hell was she thinking? She should've said it last night when they were alone. Now, everyone was a witness to this awkward moment. Mika's chest hurt, and she couldn't breathe.

"Interesting timing." Willow smiled and brushed the hair out of Mika's eyes, then she lightly kissed her. "I love you too. Next time, tell me when we're alone so I can *show* you my love."

Hot damn, the rush of energy and happy tingling through Mika's body was like a supernova explosion. Willow was hers. It couldn't get any better. Everything was perfect. "Would it be too much for me to yell and scream it?"

"Don't you dare."

Aunt Val cleared her voice. "Ahem, we're standing right here."

"See you soon." Willow parted from her slowly.

Mika watched Willow leave before getting behind the wheel of the Mustang.

Her aunt slid into the passenger seat and handed the keys to Mika. "Sweetie, sharing all the fun and excitement of college with Willow will be a big adventure." She held up a finger. "Just remember that your education comes first."

"Stop worrying. We'll be okay." Mika drove home carefully with a smile on her lips. The feeling of hearing Willow say *I love you* was like a thousand birthday presents all at once. She parked the car.

"Good job driving." Aunt Val smiled.

"Thanks."

"By the way, you need to pack up any last-minute things. I've agreed to let Pauline pick you up at five."

"Sorry that she wore you down. I love you, Aunt Val. Thanks again for everything."

"You're welcome, and I love you, too." Her aunt turned away.

"Hey, wait. Are you crying?"

"Yes." Aunt Val wiped her eyes with the back of her hand.

"Why?"

"You've grown up quickly. I've just gotten to know you, and we'll only have July and part of August when you come back."

Mika pulled her into a bear hug. Aunt Val kissed her cheek and held on tight. They didn't speak for several seconds. Aunt Val would never take the place of her parents, but her love was the real deal. She cared.

"I understand with your grandparents getting older. We can celebrate your birthday when you come back. Go have fun riding horses." Her aunt smiled then turned toward the living room. "I need to work on a report while you finish packing. Come downstairs if you need anything."

"I will. And I'll send you some pictures."

Mika practically ran upstairs. This was going to be the best summer yet, and these two weeks would fly by. Willow loved her, and she'd be back in her arms again soon. She shoved her bedroom door open and glanced around. Good thing Willow didn't judge her by her clutter. All she had left was to toss her toiletry bag into her suitcase. With a couple of hours to kill, she went to work cleaning.

She stuffed some old clothes into a bag for charity, then straightened up her desk. Her phone chimed, and she glanced at the message from Jenn.

hey carla said something about sci-fi stories. creepy. she's geeky like u.

We were talking about Shades of the Stars (Legend of the Dreamer) anthology. I'll grab it.

whatever. i hope u don't stick ur nose in books for the whole trip.

Nope.

k. can't wait until u get here. GOT BIG NEWS!!!!

Mika sent a thumbs-up emoji.

Since Mika had become an avid eBook reader, she hadn't touched a paperback for a long time. Two weeks ago, she boxed up all her paperbacks. Aunt Val suggested putting the box in her parents' old library. It still felt weird to go there, so she asked her aunt to do it. Now she'd have to go in there and search for the sci-fi anthology.

The box was near the desk, and she began searching for the book when she saw an iPhone on the floor between the desk and the wall. She froze and couldn't breathe for a second. It was her mom's phone. Her hand shook as she picked it up. After finding a charger in one of the drawers, she sat waiting and dreading what she might see. The screen lit up, and her whole body quivered. A pain ripped through her, and tears clouded her eyes at the sight of the phone's wallpaper image of her and her smiling parents.

She couldn't breathe for several seconds, then she tossed the phone on the desk and ran to the bathroom. Hoping to wash away the nightmare, she splashed water on her face, but it didn't stop the pain. This wasn't fair. Every time she healed a tiny bit, a memory popped into her head, or she'd see an object related to her parents, and it'd drag her backward. When was it going to end?

She slowly walked back to the desk and stared at the phone for several minutes. Her mom always took tons of pictures with her phone. Mika wanted to see them and hear her parents' voices. She picked it up like it was fragile and tapped the screen. The passcode screen appeared. Mom had told her the passcode, but what was it? Mika tried everyone's birthdate, but it didn't work. Next, she typed in her parents' anniversary date, and the phone unlocked.

Her hand shook as she tapped the photo icon and scrolled through the images. Tears fell, and she wiped them away with her shirtsleeve. She opened voicemail next and saw one from her dad back in September. She smiled and cried at the same time. Finally, she got the guts up to listen to it.

"Hi, my darling sweetheart. New York isn't much fun without sharing it with you two. I'm working late and miss sitting beside you, cheering Mika on at her swim meet. I called Val and chewed her out about not visiting."

Mika paused the voicemail. It felt so good to hear his voice. He was always upfront with the truth, and she could imagine him talking to Aunt Val. She pressed play to hear the rest of the message.

"She convinced me that her work was taking up all her free time. Also, she said the Boston Lab is in more trouble than she imagined when she agreed to take over. Look, darling, I don't want to argue with you. Think about this, and we can talk tomorrow. Val's in the States now, and Mika's a bright young teenager. She loves you and would never turn against us."

Huh? What was her dad talking about?

"I think you and Val are scared shitless, and you're both afraid of your parents. And I don't blame Val for her feelings. She sacrificed a lot. Please talk to her. The letters may have worked in the past, but there's no excuse for not talking now. Think about it. I love you, my darling."

Mika's breathing stilled. What was this about? She glanced at the phone log. Conversations between Mom and Aunt Val popped up shortly after her dad's voicemail. Then during the last week of her parents' lives, her mom had four conversations with Aunt Val that lasted between twenty minutes and an hour. Whatever her dad was referring to, it certainly lit their fire. If they'd talked that much, maybe they'd also texted.

Mika tapped the message icon. Aunt Val's name was pinned to the top. She skimmed her mom and Aunt Val's first text chat about their parents. Jesus, it was like reading *The Lord of the Rings*. Mika scrolled further, and the texts became shorter. She finally saw one with her name on it.

Nov 8 at 6:45 PM

Mika will be seventeen soon. Come home, please. I was wrong. Andrew wants to tell her. You live in Boston. Stop the bullshit excuses.

Wow, her mom only cursed when she was really upset.

What do you want from me?

She's mature for her age. And maybe my decision to tell her at eighteen wasn't the best.

You should have told her years ago.

What's done is done. She deserves to know you. Please visit us.

Mika's body shivered, and the pit of her stomach hurt. She grabbed a throw folded up in the corner chair and wrapped it around herself. Despite her hands trembling, she began reading again.

<u>*Nov 12 at 5:28 PM*</u>

Please come home for Thanksgiving.

Why? You know Mom and Dad won't come over if I'm there.

Val, I'm sorry about what I said on the phone the other night. And I'm sorry for cursing.

Apology accepted.

If you come home, I'll make sure Mika is here and not running around with her cousins.

I'll try, but no guarantees.

Thanks. I love you, sis.

Mika blinked. Why didn't Aunt Val respond with love?

<u>*Nov 20 at 7:30 PM*</u>

Sorry, Hannah, I can't make it for Thanksgiving.

Why?

Major project deadline.

I'm sorry I only communicated through letters for so long. If you can't make it for Thanksgiving, please come home at Christmas.

I'll look at my calendar tomorrow.

I'm looking forward to hugging you. I'll call tomorrow. It'd be good to hear your voice.

Mika remembered her grandparents diving into cultural and political issues. Oh, that would have been one hell of a fireworks show if Aunt Val had been there. She skimmed over a couple more then stopped again.

<u>*Dec 10 at 10:47 AM*</u>

I'm sorry, Han. I have to attend an official Christmas Eve function. It'll be late afternoon on Christmas Day, maybe early evening before I make it.

You're the goddamn director. Send your deputy. Or is this

another fucking excuse?

Mika reread the line. Her mom said fuck. Mika had never heard her say that.

I'm sorry. That's the best I can do.

We want to see you, Val. Why don't you want to see Mika?

You always send me pictures.

Goddammit. That's not the same, and you know it.

Dec 10 at 2:47 PM

Come on, Val. Text back or answer my call, please. I'm sorry for cursing. I'm frustrated that you're avoiding us. Why?

Dec 10 at 6:55 PM

Val, please respond. You need to get to know Mika. God, there are things she does that remind me of Andrew, but she's got your science brain, and she looks exactly like you did at that age.

This was all sounding really fucking weird. Mika realized she had dark straight hair and darker skin like Aunt Val. Sometimes people pointed that out, but why was her mom comparing them? Mika took a deep breath and forced her eyes back to the text.

I never expected that making you and Andrew happy would rip my heart out. After all these years, I can't shake the memory of holding her for the first time. A child's birth is never forgotten, especially when they arrive too damn early in the back car seat.

Mika jumped up so fast that the chair fell over. She squeezed her eyes tight and rapidly tapped her fingertips on both legs. *Breathe. In, one, two, three. Out, one, two, three.* She ran to her room, slammed the door, and collapsed onto the bed. She didn't move until the pillowcase was wet from tears. Like a zombie, she hauled her depleted body up, showered, and dressed. She needed a distraction and put in her earbuds to listen to Taylor Swift, but nothing would erase what she'd just read. "Fuck." She bolted upright, threw off her earbuds and paced.

Why had her mom said she knew nothing about her birth mother? And why did Aunt Val give her up? Could she not take care of her? Was she so busy with work that she didn't have the time? Or was it because Aunt Val didn't want her? But it didn't sound that way.

"Mika, Pauline called. She'll be here in five minutes," Aunt Val yelled from the foyer.

Stay calm. "I'll be down soon."

Mika was happy to be going to Wyoming because there was no way she could stay in Ithaca without strangling Aunt Val for the truth. She balled her hands into fists. She was so fucking mad that everyone had kept the truth from her.

Chapter Thirty-Three

MIKA RUSHED TO THE bathroom and splashed water several times on her face, trying to hide the traces of tears. *Breathe.* She yanked her phone out of her pocket and called Willow. "I gotta talk to you. I don't have much time." She sat on the toilet and hung her head.

"What's wrong? You sound—"

"Yeah, I've been crying. Aunt Val isn't my aunt. She's my mom. My birth mom. I found my mom's old phone. I listened to voice mail and read lots of text messages." Mika took a deep breath and squeezed her eyes shut. Her body shook from the overload of emotions like a boat in a hurricane.

"Oh, Mika. I can't imagine what you're—"

"Feeling? Fucking mad as hell. They lied to me. All of them." Mika fought not to bounce her leg, but she couldn't stop her anxiety tic. "After the accident, she should have had the fucking courage to tell me the truth."

"Getting mad won't solve anything. Go talk to her and get the whole story," Willow said softly.

"No way." Mika stood and paced. "I'm so mad, I think I'd rip her head off. And Aunt Pauline is supposed to be here anytime."

"Think it over. You just went through the death of your parents, who also didn't tell you the truth. Your aunt comes in, and I bet she didn't want to hurt you more. I'm sure you would have pushed her away if she'd told you early on. Now you know her a little. And the person I see is a person that loves you. Did she have problems with her sister? Yeah, it sounds like it from what little you told me. She's hurting too, and probably feels like shit for not working it out with your mom. But she's trying now. I think she wants the best for you."

Mika grabbed some tissues and slid down the door. "I kind of get what you're saying. I just feel betrayed. I'm not a little baby." She wiped her eyes and blew her nose.

"Look, you told me both sets of grandparents said anti-gay things. Maybe they talked your aunt into giving you up."

"Yeah. Wouldn't that be awesome to introduce you as my girlfriend and see my grands' faces." Mika laughed bitterly.

Willow sighed. "You do know that's *not* a good idea. So work hard not to let it slip out of your mouth on the trip. Let's get into college and do it later if you still want to tell them."

"Yeah, you're right." Mika stood and looked in the mirror. God, her red puffy eyes made her look like something out of a horror film.

"Are you still wanting to rip your aunt's head off?"

"Not so much. Thanks."

"Can you see there's probably some deeper shit that she might be going through?"

"Yeah. Are you sure you want to be a painter and not a shrink?" Mika rested the phone on her shoulder while she ran water over a washcloth.

"Yes. And sometime, I want to paint you in the nude."

Mika smiled at Willow exaggerating her already sexy voice. "Oh, yeah? I have to go. I love you."

"Love you too."

Mika wiped her face with the cold cloth, but it did little to improve her looks. As she stepped out of the bathroom, she heard tapping on the door, and hoped it was Jenn.

"Pauline's a few minutes away and wants you to come downstairs," Aunt Val said through the door. "She and I had an argument over the phone, and she doesn't want your cousins coming inside. Do you need help?"

"No." Oh, that was convenient. If Aunt Val could argue with Aunt Pauline, then Mika could make up a story about arguing with Jenn. Mika put her ear against the door and listened for her aunt to go downstairs. When the driveway alarm went off, followed by Aunt Pauline's SUV horn, she picked up her suitcase and ran down the stairs.

"Have you been crying? Are you okay?"

Although Mika had kept her head low, Aunt Val still noticed. Time for the lie. "Just a strange text from Jenn. It upset me, but I'm okay now." Mika couldn't let her aunt see Jenn, or she'd see right through the lie.

"Here." Aunt Val held out some money.

Mika shrugged. "Grandfather Lavigne's loaded. And I'll be spending all my time on the ranch."

"That's not the point. I want to contribute. And I bet that taking money from your grandparents comes with strings."

"Thanks." Mika grabbed the cash and stuffed it in her pocket. She flew out the door and tossed her bag in the SUV. Whatever the reason Aunt Val gave her up, Mika didn't have to act like an ass. She looked back. Confusion and hurt were written all over her aunt's face. Mika jogged over and hugged her, and with each second, Mika squeezed tighter and almost broke. Instead, she held back the tears and mumbled, "I'll see you in two weeks."

"Are you having second thoughts?" Aunt Val asked softly.

"No. Like I said, Jenn and I had a stupid text fight. We'll work it out." Mika let go.

"Okay. Love you. Have a great trip."

That almost did Mika in. She couldn't look Aunt Val in the eyes and hurried back to the SUV. She hopped inside and waved without looking.

They barely reached the block's end when Jenn gave her a look. "You've been crying? Did you argue with your aunt?" she whispered.

Time for lie number two. "Yeah. Don't worry. It'll be better in Wyoming." Mika scrunched down in the seat. Fortunately, Jenn didn't say another word all the way to Binghamton which was unusual.

"Mom. I have this project that I have to finish tonight. I need Mika's help. Could you please keep Carla busy so she doesn't bug us?" Jenn blurted out when they pulled up to her house.

"Go on. Carla can help me with dinner."

"She means having Carla pick out restaurant delivery. And when your aunt called the other day, I heard Mom pathetically trying to act innocent. Knowing Mom, she probably wanted to piss her off by telling everyone at the last minute," Jenn said under her breath as they made their way upstairs. "Oh, Grandmother said there was a surprise. I wonder what that is?" Jenn locked her bedroom door and placed the chair under the door handle.

"Why are you barricading us in?"

"We have to be alone; I have earth shattering news. Your DNA results came in." Jenn rushed to the desk and typed furiously. "I glanced at your matches." She looked at Mika wide-eyed. "Sit. I'm worried you'll faint when you see this."

Mika plopped down in the chair next to Jenn. She didn't know how much more she could take today, but when Jenn hit the button and pointed, Mika scooted closer in for a better look. There was a small picture of her dad. The text below read, Andrew S. Lavigne, Father. 3,528 centimorgans, 50% shared DNA. That couldn't be fucking real. Next was a small pink graphic of a female outline with the letter B in the center. The text below read, Blue28, Mother. 3,587 centimorgans, 50% shared DNA. The room spun faster with each beat of Mika's heart. She slumped over with her head between knees.

Jenn squeezed her shoulder. "Mika, your dad is your bio dad."

"Why didn't he tell me?" Tears filled her eyes, but at the same time, she was mad as hell. Mika stood and swiped her hand across Jenn's desk, scattering books and papers all over the floor.

"What the fuck's wrong with you? That's my stuff. Calm down and pick it up."

"Sorry."

"Your dad was a great guy. And now you know he was your

real dad. Jeez, I thought you'd be happy. Not go ballistic wacko. And why are you crying? You know, I'm beginning to think you're a little bipolar. Maybe you should talk to your therapist."

"Shut up. I don't need your fucking opinion." Mika laced her hands behind her head and paced back and forth. "I'm sorry. I didn't mean that. It's just..." She put her hand over her mouth to hold back her emotions, but her tears fell. She was nothing but a helpless mess.

"Something else is going on. You were already being weird when we picked you up. Tell me," Jenn said calmly.

Mika ripped out some tissues from a nearby box and blew her nose. She usually shared everything with Jenn, but she couldn't talk this time. She wanted to run to Willow, but that was impossible. And for the next fourteen days, she'd be lucky to sneak out a private conversation on her grandparents' home phone without someone hearing. No, she couldn't risk that. She had to put this all in the back of her mind until their trip was over.

"Mika, stop wearing a hole in my floor. Look, I get it. It hurts that your dad withheld the truth, but don't you want to find out the whole story?"

"What info is there about this Blue28 woman?" Mika waved her finger at the screen. What the fuck had Aunt Val posted?

"None. She has no tree or bio, but you can email her. Your communication goes through the company, so you never know each other's real email unless you give it out." Jenn typed some more. "Sit down. I wrote an email for you."

"What?" Mika shouted.

"Relax. I didn't send it. Just cool off, sit down, and read it. See if you like it." Jenn guided Mika to the desk seat. "Oh, I used proper capitalization and ran a grammar check."

Mika figured she might as well read it. And she didn't need Jenn poking her for more info. She sighed and began. Jenn had written a question about genetically inherited medical conditions that Mika thought was good. And the paragraph asking whether she had any siblings was spot on; whether she had any had always intrigued Mika, but now it didn't matter. She was an only child unless Aunt Val had other love children. A bitter laugh escaped her lips at the thought.

"Hey, you don't have to send it."

Her parents were dead, and only Aunt Val had any answers. The letter would likely put her aunt on edge and give Mika an advantage. Then she could confront her once she got home. Mika added a few sentences. "Send it. And then I don't want to talk about it anymore. Not one word."

"I'm not sure what bug crawled up your ass, but okay."

"Sorry." Mika rubbed her hair. "It's just a lot with everything that's gone on." She doubted she'd sleep much tonight, and tomorrow would be rough. Her mind began to spin out of control again. How did Aunt Val hide a pregnancy? And how much did Aunt Pauline and her grandparents know? Had Aunt Val been bi at one time? How could everybody keep this information from her?

Fuck 'em all. Mika would worry about it after the trip. She'd ride horses until her ass fell off and stay up every night until they were zombies. Jenn liked to sneak booze, and this time, Mika would have more than one taste of rum and Coke. The Lavigne house was so big that her grandparents wouldn't catch them. And Mika wouldn't play nice. She'd warn Carla not to tell on them. But Jenn was right; she did have to calm down and shove all this shit aside.

Chapter Thirty-Four

June 25

MIKA WAS HAPPY TO finally be in Wyoming. The trip from Syracuse to Sheridan County Airport was a hassle. They had to fly to Denver and spend the night before going on to Wyoming. But Aunt Pauline pulled out at the last minute, leaving Jenn and Mika responsible for Carla. Then at the counter, they found out their flight had been cancelled, and the only one available wasn't direct.

"I'm so happy to be off that plane. It was so damn cramped," Jenn said as she walked off the staircase onto the tarmac.

Mika squinted into the summer Wyoming sun. "At least the grands sprang for business class to Denver. The lounge restaurant and game room were lit."

"Yeah, I liked them, and the hotel at the airport was nice," Carla said.

Jenn stopped in her tracks and glared at her sister before looking at Mika. "Going from Syracuse to Denver via Orlando is not my idea of fun. Yesterday was horrid after nearly nine hours—" She held up her finger. "Correction, nearly twelve hours after driving to the airport, going through security, the layover, and taking a fucking shuttle to the hotel. Then today, we had to arrive at the airport two hours before a fucking one hour and fifty-minute plane ride. Yee-haw, what fun." She looked at her sister again. "Don't say another word."

"Cool down. The cancellation wasn't the grands' fault."

"Mika's right. Look, the grands are ancient and could die any minute. Let's have fun. Stop being..." Carla shifted on her feet, "a grump."

Jenn threw her head back. "I hate it when my little sister is right." She put on a fake smile and marched toward the small terminal building.

Inside, Mika spotted her grandparents waving from behind the small security area. Carla ran to them.

"Sorry, Mika. I know our grands spent a lot of money for our vacation. I'm just tired from watching over Carla and having to share a bed with her. It is good to see them."

"I get it. I never expected your mom to drop us at the counter and leave." And Mika would bet a hundred that Aunt Pauline never told Aunt Val. She and Jenn went through the gate and hugged the grands. The tension melted and everyone acted like they hadn't seen each other for a century.

"Glad you could come, Michaela." Her grandfather tussled her hair like she was a little girl.

"You're looking better. No limp," she said, thinking he was walking around fine.

"Ah, your grandmother babies me too much. She had me back to full health in no time."

Her grandmother fidgeted with her hands. "He's a tough one. Come on, girls. We've got a lot to do today."

A new ranch hand was waiting outside and loaded their luggage while her cousins settled into the Jeep Grand Cherokee.

"What's your name?" Mika asked the ranch hand.

"Johnny." He smiled.

"Come on, Michaela." Grandfather held the door open for her.

Mika ignored his call. "Thanks, Johnny." It bothered her that the grands never introduced their hired help. They almost acted like they were robots and not people. She wondered if they'd always been this way, or if their wealth had gone to their head. She joined her cousins in the third row. Johnny drove and the grands rode in the middle seats.

"Look at the middle entertainment system." Grandfather

gushed like a little kid as he played with the display screen.

He was in good spirits and tortured them with old Hank Williams country music. Carla giggled and tried to sing along while Jenn put in her earbuds and tuned everyone out. Mika didn't mind the different music as long as it was temporary. She gazed out the window as they left the airport. There wasn't much greenery here except for irrigated crop circles. The pine trees she saw were small.

An hour and a half later, they got to the gates of the Lavigne Ranch, and the land turned greener because it was built along a creek that flowed from the mountains in the national forest.

Everyone hopped out and Johnny unloaded the luggage at the steps of the gigantic six-bedroom house.

"Mika, get back in," Grandfather said as he slid behind the wheel.

She looked at Jenn, who shrugged.

"They've got business, girls. Let's settle in," Grandmother said and went inside.

"Where are we going?" Mika sat beside him up front.

"I bought another horse that looks like your dad's favorite. I thought it'd make you a nice graduation gift."

"We don't have a trailer."

"Oh, well, they sold me one." He spit out the window and took off.

Shit, he wouldn't have any tread left if he kept driving this fast down his road. "How far's the other ranch?"

"Over an hour. It'll be fun, just you and me." He tuned SiriusXM to country music. "All this satellite stuff is amazing. Without it, we wouldn't be able to get a phone and TV shows into the house. But things blank out here and there when storms hit."

He took a corner fast, throwing her to the right. "Whoa." She was honored that he trusted her to help with the horse and trailer, but she wasn't that comfortable with his driving. "I passed my junior driver's class. Why don't you pull over and let me show off my skills."

"I've got it. You sit back and relax." He half-smiled at her then sang along with the radio.

She settled down when he let her plug in her iPhone. She played Taylor's early songs, thinking he'd like the country sound.

"This is good. Who is she?"

"Taylor Swift."

"Never heard of her."

"She's a mega-star." Mika gripped the door arm rest as he took another fast turn. "Hey, what's the rush? Slow down."

"I know these backroads." He waved his hand in the air but eased off the gas.

She breathed a sigh of relief and closed her eyes, not to nap but to calm herself from his driving. The second song was "London Boy." Grandfather must have hit shuffle. She glanced at him. "This is one of my favorites, but I don't know if you'll like her later songs."

"I like the rhythm. You know I can be a little modern too."

Towards the end, she closed her eyes again because the scenery had become boring. She wanted to ride horses, not go on some long road trip to buy one. Why couldn't he send Johnny for the horse? Then "You Need to Calm Down" came on. She swallowed, hoping he wouldn't catch the subtle gay reference without the video. She tapped rapidly on the side of her thigh where he couldn't see. Then the line hit, and he turned off the music.

She turned on "Fast Car" with Tracy Chapman and Luke Combs. "Hey, this is a great song from the Grammies that I think you'll like."

He hit the off button hard and frowned at her. "Now, I remember that Swift woman's song and her video. Promoting gay as normal is sickening."

"Keep your eyes on driving," she yelled as the Jeep's right wheels ran off the road. "I don't watch her videos. I like that song for the bass and melody." She unplugged her iPhone, hoping the lie would hold. "You can listen to more country." When he turned the radio to some sort of conservative talk show, she put in some earbuds and shuffled her playlist.

After what seemed like eternity, she sat up. "Aren't we there by now?"

"Nope."

Her mouth gaped at the museum sign. "That's Buffalo Bill's Museum." *What the fuck?* They couldn't be in Cody. That town was near Montana.

"We don't have time to stop."

She checked the time on her phone. "We've been on the road for almost two hours. Where are we going?"

"We have friends in Cody. Not to worry."

This was all so weird. "Are we staying with the horse and going back in the morning?"

He hesitated. "Yep, that's the plan."

This was nuts. There had to be ranches closer to her grandfather that sold horses. And why was he acting so cold? She glanced at her phone again. Great, no cell service. Her leg bounced up and down as he drove farther west into the Absaroka Range and turned north onto a gravel road. A big sign read, *Broken Horse Camp. No Trespassing.* She sighed; at least they'd arrived safely. After they hitched the trailer and got the horse, she was going to insist on driving back to a hotel in Cody. She'd be damned if she was going to stay with strangers. And her suitcase was back at the ranch.

"The barn's down there." She pointed to a few horses eating hay outside.

"We have to go up here to check in." He drove into a parking lot, past several buildings that looked more like a school than a ranch and parked behind one. "Come on."

"Check in?" She followed him as he walked toward two small buildings with no windows. "Where's the office?"

He didn't answer. An old woman and two men exited one of the buildings and headed straight for them. They looked like some religious order. "Hi. My grandfather said he's buying an American Saddlebred."

The two men grabbed her.

"What are you doing? Grandfather?" She looked at him, but he wouldn't look at her.

"It's for the best. I read the article about you and that girl going to prom. Then we saw your picture kissing her. You're not like that. They can help you find God again." He turned and walked away.

Her heart shattered in a million pieces. He'd planned this? "Stop. Grandfather, please don't do this." She fought the men, but they were too strong.

They shoved her into one of the windowless rooms where two women were waiting next to a shower stall. The old woman shut and locked the door once the men left.

"Strip. We need to search you before the shower. We'll give you new clothes afterward," the old woman said.

"No. You can't do this to me." Mika crossed her arms when the old woman pulled a whip out of a holster on her belt.

"Dare to call my bluff?"

"Fuck you."

The woman cracked it hard against Mika's side. She cringed. Never in a million years would she have thought the old woman had enough strength to hit her that hard.

"You will not use profanity. We work on a point system here. You start with zero and go home when you acquire a hundred points. Completing chores, attending classes, and doing exactly what you're told gains you points. The more you disobey, the more points you lose. Every swear word is minus ten points. Punishment for acting out is at my discretion. You're to address me as Mother Abigail. Now strip."

Mika's skin just above her elbow was red and swelling where the whip had hit her. She could even feel it underneath her T-shirt in the back.

The woman coiled the whip.

"Okay." Mika pulled off her clothes and stood in her underwear.

"You will be polite and finish every sentence with 'Mother

Abigail.' Everything off. We have to be thorough."

Fuck, they were really going to body cavity search her. She took off her underwear and squeezed her eyes tight when they began their search.

The men returned as she pulled the new shirt over her head. Humiliated, she followed behind Abigail the Bitch as instructed. "That's our church, the cafeteria, and main classroom, the admin building…"

Mika had a mental map in her head. As she scanned around, she didn't notice a fence. She was going to escape as soon as possible.

"And these buildings are for isolation."

"I assume that's when I disobey."

The old woman stopped and stared at her. *Now what'd I do wrong?*

"The correct response should have been, 'I assume that's when I disobey, Mother Abigail.'"

The old bitch opened one door, and the men forced Mika inside. There was nothing but a desk and a Bible.

"You will sit in here until I say so. When I come back, you must confess your sinful lust and pray with us to heal you."

At least the bitch didn't hit her with the whip again.

"Don't try me, child."

Minutes turned to hours. It had to be the middle of the night, and Mika was hungry. She wanted to sleep, so she stood on the chair to unscrew the lightbulb, but it was too hot and almost burned her hand. More time passed, and her belly ached. How could her grandparents do this to her? She had to find a way to escape, or she'd die in here.

Chapter Thirty-Five

Early July

"WHAT WERE YOU THINKING, child? You could have gotten lost and wandered for miles. It's cold at night without a coat. A bear might have eaten you before we found you," the old bitch said.

Mika stared at the floor. *Being eaten is better than being here.* Tears formed in her eyes. Since she'd been forced into this place, she'd tried to run away twice, but they'd found her and locked her in one of those tiny, windowless rooms with a chair and a Bible. The last time she was in here, she broke the light bulb with her shoe. They stripped her and hit her ass with the whip. Now the light bulb had chicken wire wrapped around it. She couldn't sleep even if there was no light because they returned almost every hour or so, preaching religion and demanding she confess her sins. The only way she could tell night from day was by the temperature. Although they'd left her a blanket and her coat, she shivered, more out of fear than cold, but she wasn't going to let them beat her down.

"What day is it, Mother Abigail?" It felt like she'd been in here for months.

"Where are your manners?"

"Please."

"July the sixth," the old bitch said.

Happy fucking belated birthday to me. Mika jumped when the door opened and slammed. Two younger women came inside. At first, they stood next to Mother Abigail, then they circled around Mika.

"Michaela, it's unnatural to act on your attraction to the same sex," one yelled.

Fuck her ignorant grandparents for buying the bullshit this camp pushed. Mika would never trust them and never speak to them again.

The woman slapped her hand on the desk. "Are you listening to me?"

Mika turned toward the talking head. She couldn't remember their names, except the old bitch, fucking Mother Abigail. It didn't matter. They could all go to hell.

"You're wasting your breath," the old bitch said and left.

The two younger women stayed.

"Stop scowling at me. Look at me with respect. Michaela, you have to let God into your heart and mind. He can transform you."

Mika scoffed. "I believe in God being love, and this isn't love. Leave me alone."

The other one opened the door wide, and the men came in. Mika silently groaned when she saw Harvey. He hit the hardest, and he came at her with a look.

Harvey grabbed her and body-slammed her to the ground. Then he forced her face down while the other one pulled down her clothes.

"Hold her," Harvey snarled. He whacked her five times with the whip, then shoved her back into the chair. He pointed his finger in her face. "Don't move, except to open the Bible."

After the punishment, the two women began their preaching routine, stopping every now and then to tell her she was an abomination. When they finally left, Mika flipped the bird and pushed the Bible onto the floor. She'd get in trouble for that but didn't care. She put her head down on the desk and cried. Where was Aunt Val? Was anyone coming to rescue her?

"Time for prayer," the old bitch said as she entered with another woman. "What have you done to the Holy Gospel?" She picked it up, dusted it off, and returned it to the desk.

Although Mika tried to not let Mother Abigail upset her, she was terrifying. She reminded Mika of Aunt Lydia in the TV series *The Handmaid's Tale.*

"I'm waiting for an explanation."

"I'm sorry," Mika glanced up, "Mother Abigail. I accidentally knocked it off when I put my head on the desk. I'm very hungry, and I can't sleep or think. Please can I have some food, Mother Abigail?" Mika bowed her head, hoping that the apology would get her something.

The old woman sighed, and the other woman placed a bag and large insulated mug in front of Mika. Without thinking, she gulped the warm liquid down. Chicken broth never tasted so good.

"Where is your gratitude?" the bitch asked.

Mika put the cup down. "Thank you, Mother Abigail."

"Say the mealtime prayer with us."

Mika mumbled along with the few words she remembered. Then she opened the bag to find an apple and a half peanut butter sandwich. It tasted amazing after nothing but small meals of dry granola cereal and water.

"Slower, child," the younger woman said.

After reading the Bible and giving their spin on it, they kept repeating that homosexuality was a choice and that she could change if she really wanted to. When Mika took the last bite and crumpled the bag, the women stopped reading and stared at her.

Mother Abigail swiftly crossed the room and got in her face. "Look at me."

Mika sat rigid.

"You could have a husband and beautiful children if you stopped dressing like a man and accepted God's gift of beauty."

Did the old bitch really think this crap would work?

"It's wrong to give into the Devil, child. Don't you want to be normal?"

"I am normal."

The old woman slapped her, then pointed to the corner. "Stand

and face the wall."

Fuck you all. Mika fought them, and they called for help. Two men came inside and forced her over to the corner of the room. Mika expected something bad, but they only slipped a super heavy backpack onto her shoulders.

"The rocks will remind you of the weight of your sins. Harvey will remain in the room," the old bitch said.

The door shut, and Harvey read the Bible out loud. Mika tried to stand tall, but her shoulders hurt after a while.

He stopped. "You're a clever one, but you won't succeed. Confess your sins."

"I'm normal. You guys are the ones that're sinful." Fear shot through Mika when she heard his footsteps coming slowly toward her.

"Why don't you like men?"

When she heard him unbuckle his belt and slide it off, she squeezed her eyes tight. Her pulse pounded, and her throat went dry. "Please don't," she cried.

Silence hung in the room. He moved closer so his breath was on her neck, and she assumed the worst. He laughed when she whimpered. But he stepped back and whacked her across the back of her legs three times. The dress they'd provided wasn't much protection, and her skin stung like hell. He left but returned minutes later to add more rocks to the pack. The tender skin wasn't as bad as the fear of what he'd do next. Thankfully, he only read the Bible again.

Despite wanting to stay strong, she couldn't stop the tears from falling. Hours passed, then someone else replaced Harvey.

"Please may I sit. I'm tired."

"No. You're disgusting." The woman continued the hellish ritual.

Every time Mika's knees buckled or she leaned against the wall, the woman would smack the back of her head. When Mika collapsed, they took the pack off, sat her in the chair, and gave her a little food. She slept a little, but when they woke her, she was drained. They pushed her into the corner. The backpack routine continued.

Mika stirred. She was on the floor and didn't remember falling this time.

The old bitch scowled above her. Then she kicked Mika. "Get up."

Mika rose and stumbled toward the chair. A man pushed her into it.

"Convince me that you will obey, or you'll remain standing for a few more hours. And Harvey might have to teach you an even more painful lesson."

The old bitch was so close to her that Mika had trouble focusing her eyes. But she'd be damned if she gave them any satisfaction. "I'm sorry, Mother Abigail." *And fuck you.*

"What else?"

"I won't try to escape again or resist, Mother Abigail." *And fuck you.* "Please may I have some water, Mother Abigail. I'm so thirsty."

They gave her the usual half cup, and she drank it in no time.

"And do you believe in Jesus Christ?"

"I put my faith in Jesus Christ, and he knows that my girlfriend Willow and I are not sinners."

"Ignorant child," the old bitch growled.

Harvey whacked her harder than before, and she stopped counting after ten hits. She clenched her teeth, trying hard not to cry out. They added more rocks to the pack before they left. After what seemed like forever, Mika slumped to the floor. She couldn't take much more.

She missed Willow and Aunt Val and just wanted to go home. Her aunt may not have told her the truth, but she did love her. Why else would she have given up her dream job to come to Ithaca to be Mika's guardian. Mika hoped she'd get out of here so she could tell Aunt Val how much she loved her. Tears ran down her face as she curled into a ball. *But will anyone come for me?*

Chapter Thirty-Six

Late July

MIKA STUMBLED TO HER feet with the pack of rocks when she heard the door open. Her muscles were weak, her stomach ached with hunger, and her throat was dry as the desert.

"Turn around." The old woman grabbed Mika's jaw and glared at her. "Are you going to cooperate? Are you ready to let God into your heart?"

"Please, let me have some food, and water, and sleep." She glanced at the man behind her. *And not with that creep.*

"Pray with me, Michaela, and promise the Lord you will try to be obedient and faithful." The woman released her. "Then you can sleep."

Mika had to face reality. The grands were too rich and powerful in Wyoming. They probably paid ridiculous money for this bullshit. Her only hope was to play the game and tell them what they wanted to hear. She nodded.

"Repeat after me. I am a sinner and pray to Jesus Christ to guide me into God's light..."

They gave her food and water. The plate and cup were dirty, but Mika would have eaten dog food. When they opened the door, it was dark. But there were lights in surrounding buildings. They led her to a building with a sign, Bunkhouse 4. The prayer woman took her inside, and the other girls stared at her, their eyes just peeking out from under the covers.

"Hi, Michaela. Your bed is above mine. I'm Sandy, the Bunkhouse 4 counselor."

Mika didn't trust anyone, especially Saccharin Sandy with her big-toothed smile. All she wanted was to sleep and forget these phonies, but Sandy led her to a wash basin.

"Here's your toiletry bag. Wash up for bed."

They'd taken Mika's phone, wallet, earbuds, and a pack of gum. Besides the awful clothing, she'd been issued a bag containing a toothbrush and hairbrush with a cross on the handle. She'd wanted to laugh when she first saw the items, but fear had kept her lips frozen. She did her business and crawled into bed, laying on her stomach.

When the light of dawn shined through the windows, the other girls rose. Four stalls were in the back, and the girls took turns relieving themselves and getting dressed behind the doors and out of sight from everyone. *God, that'd be a great place to kill myself. If only I had something to do the job.* She only half meant it. A piece of her desperately clung to the hope of a rescue.

"Michaela, get moving. Breakfast is the best part of the day," Sandy said cheerfully.

Mika eased down the ladder and stared out the window for a minute. What was she thinking, trying to escape? She didn't know where to run.

"Here's some clean clothes for you."

Oh, great, another dress, and of course, it had a cross over her heart. At least the socks felt softer than the last pair they'd given her. The woolen ones scratched her skin.

Mika was the sixth girl in the bunkhouse. A row of light jackets hung on hooks by the door with name tags taped above. Boots were on the floor below the jackets. It was like being back in kindergarten.

"These are yours," Sandy said.

Mika slipped on the oversized windbreaker, but the boots fit. They hustled along the walkway to a central building, and Mika was last. With each step, every part of her body hurt. Sandy stayed with her at the end of the line. Mika had been in Bunkhouse 3 previously. The counselor had been near the front of the line the last time Mika tried to escape. She'd bolted for freedom like she was in the Olympics. Her winning track legs carried her far away, but they'd called in help to find her.

"I hear it took some time for you to think logically. It will get better now that you've accepted Jesus Christ." Sandy put her arm through Mika's and pulled her along.

How Sandy could believe this was beyond Mika's ability to understand. The woman looked to be about twenty. She must've been brought up in a household full of this crap. Did she not know how the old counselors punished them?

As they entered the large hall, the smell of food caught Mika's attention. She was so hungry. The room's large windows let in plenty of light, even on a cloudy day like today. The tiny ones in the bunkhouse were restrictive; a skinny person would get stuck trying to squeeze through them. And there'd been no windows at all in the punishment room.

A clock chimed seven times, and the old bitch ordered them to line up for food like they were animals called to a feeding trough. Breakfast consisted of scrambled eggs, two slices of toast, apple juice, and water. They had to say a group morning prayer before eating. Mika couldn't remember it and mouthed along. Girls sat on one side of the room at picnic style wooden tables, and boys sat on the other side.

"No talking, and keep your eyeballs to yourself," one woman said.

"Do you know what day it is?" Mika whispered to the girl on her right.

The girl didn't answer.

"It's July twenty-fourth," the girl sitting across from them said.

Tears filled Mika's eyes. She'd been here a month and spent most of it in isolation.

"Quiet. You'll get in trouble with Mother Abigail," whispered another girl.

Mika jumped as a woman smacked a whip in the middle of the table.

"Eyes down. No talking." The woman rested the whip on Mika's shoulder. "I hear you're a troublemaker."

Mika did as she was told. *A month. I'm never getting out of here.* Her tears fell into the food as she pushed it around the plate. But she was so hungry, and she had to eat if she was going to try a third escape. It was better to die trying than to be a little lamb and take this garbage.

She'd only eaten half before they were all ordered to scrape their plates and sit back down for morning sermons. First, it was their version of Bible study, then how homosexuality was sinful. That was followed by a quick break and more religious teachings. Yada, yada, yada. Mika didn't want to focus on their crap, but she had to play the game until she could figure out how to successfully escape.

Lunch was a chicken salad sandwich, an apple, and water. After what she'd been through, it tasted damn good. They returned to the bunkhouse at one o'clock and were ordered to nap for a half hour, then they'd muck out the stalls. It was like they were being programmed. At the stables, Mika recognized some of the women that worked with Mother Abigail to torture her. She wanted to throw some horse shit on them. She shoveled away while thinking about another escape.

At three o'clock, they filed back to the central building. Mika's attention was more on the weather outside than on the speaker. The dark swirling clouds grew heavy. But she'd rather be out there in the coming storm than be locked up in here.

The old bitch smacked a wooden staff down in front of her. "Listen up, child."

Mika was so thankful when dinner rolled around. Salisbury steak with mushroom gravy, mashed potatoes, and salad. More sermons followed, then they were ordered back to the bunkhouse. While everyone else crawled into bed, Mika had to sit at a desk rehearsing the morning prayer where Sandy could see her.

"You have to memorize it. They'll give you three more chances, then it's back to isolation. It's not long. You can do it."

The next day was pretty much the same. It was mind-numbing. They had tortured her body, and now she had to put up with all this brainwashing bullshit. Would there be anything left of her brain? She'd eat to gain strength and try to escape. She got in trouble again for looking around, and they took away her breakfast.

"Here. Eat this," Mother Abigail said.

The bowl rattled as she dropped it in front of Mika. She lifted a spoonful of the soupy oatmeal to her mouth. It tasted sweet, but something wasn't right. The girl across from her shook her head slightly.

"Eat!"

Just as she finished, she heard the backfire of an engine and looked out the window. An old truck pulled up. The thing looked like it was ready to fall apart. The driver parked near the parking lot gate. The driver's door was painted with the words, Let's go, Sabres, and below them was their logo. Mika frowned. This place was a long way away from her favorite hockey team. A young couple dressed in black exited the truck.

"Eyes down before Mother Abigail sees you," Sandy whispered harshly.

She thinks I'm a dog. Come closer, and I'll bite you. As Mika lowered her head, her eyes seemed to move slower than her brain. Something was wrong.

"That must be the visiting minister, but he's early," the old bitch said.

When Mother Abigail and another camp counselor marched out to greet them, Mika looked back. The wind had picked up, and a refreshing draft blew into the stuffy room before they closed the door. The clouds were darker than yesterday. By the sound on the tin roof, it had begun raining.

Mika swallowed when the couple stepped into the center of the room. He had an oversized scarf with a cross.

"Here, Reverend Thomas." His assistant handed him a Bible.

"Thank you, Sister Allison." He cradled the Bible against his chest like a newborn baby and glanced around.

A chill rippled over Mika's skin as his gaze settled on her. A minister that loved hockey was creepy.

"This is Reverend Thomas. He's visiting today. Please be on your best behavior." The old bitch glared at Mika.

The minister stood close to Mika and started with the basics. It was more mainstream and not crazy like the camp counselors. After a good ten minutes, he still hadn't lectured them on the evilness of homosexuality. Maybe he'd skip it.

"The camp counselors are helping to save you from your same-sex attraction," the minister said.

Nope. Mika resisted rolling her eyes. She tried her best to tune him out, then became nervous when he walked toward her, stopping just a few feet away.

He glanced around. "One of my proudest moments was when I helped a family with twins. One was straight, and the other had wrongful desires." He stared down at Mika. "But Dani was delighted when her sister, Brie, was saved. Now, Brie is much happier and very close to our hearts."

Huh? Brie had a twin named Dani. *WTF?* A Buffalo Sabres fan who talked about Brie and her sister couldn't be a coincidence. Was this whole thing a dream?

He put his hand on Mika's shoulder then turned to Sandy. "Is this the one who tried to escape?"

"Yes. Her name's Michaela."

"Well, Michaela, gather up all the dishes. Allison and I will pray for you while you wash them. Hopefully, you can wash some sin away."

"But, Reverend, we pick a team that rotates dishwashing duty."

"I'm sorry, Ms. Sandy. Michaela needs extra prayers and guidance." He smiled. "It doesn't matter if she's here all day washing.

We'll pray over her."

The old woman stepped forward. "I think a little extra manual labor is a good idea. Keep your ears open to the Lord while you work, child."

Mika gathered the dishes on the cart. It was like a mountain, and she struggled to push it into the kitchen. Her legs felt wobbly. Maybe she'd heard wrong. Reverend Thomas and Sister Allison followed her. Sandy came in for a few minutes.

"Wash them well. If you don't, the elders will punish you," Sandy said.

Funny, Mika thought she had a look of sympathy on her face.

"We can handle her while you attend to the other lost souls." Reverend Thomas nodded, and Sandy left.

He moved behind Mika, opened the Bible, and began reading. Allison positioned herself in the door between the kitchen and dining room. Mika tried her best to wash the dishes, but she just wanted to sleep. Her muscles didn't match the commands from her brain. She squeezed her eyes tight and shook her head.

"Mika, are you okay?" he whispered.

He didn't call her Michaela or child. That was good. "I feel strange."

"They sometimes put sleep medicine in the food of 'troublemakers' to keep them quiet. Allison will help you gather up the trash bags. You'll take them outside. Then you're going to run to the large garage. The rain has slowed but watch your step. A woman named Dutch will help you escape."

Mika turned with her mouth open, but he began reading the Bible again and didn't look at her.

"Let's go." Allison tugged her along.

Mika's arms stretched like rubber bands as she carried the trash bags. Allison opened the back door, and Mika slipped through. The rain had slowed to a light drizzle and felt good on her skin.

"Run," Allison whispered.

Mika dropped the bags and ran as fast as her rubbery legs

could. The walkway to the garage was a pattern of uneven stones, and she almost tripped several times.

Then she heard Allison yell to someone, "She's right here, taking out the trash. I have my eye on her."

Mika ran harder, slipped, and face-planted on the walkway. It hurt like hell, but she pushed up and onward, running smack into a super tall woman.

"I'm Dutch, and I'm helping your aunt."

"I'm so tired," Mika murmured. Dutch put her arm around her, and they hurried along. A truck was on the other side of the garage, parked underneath a tree, and out of sight from the dining hall.

"What's that?" Mika pointed to the monster truck.

"It's a Ford F150 Raptor."

"How'd you get the thing up here without them noticing?"

"I brought food up yesterday, then removed a part so it wouldn't start."

Dutch picked her up and placed her in the passenger seat. Once Dutch was behind the wheel, they shot out like a rocket. As they approached the main road, Mika looked back. The camp counselors were running for their vehicles. Thomas and Allison pulled out first and left the old truck sideways, blocking the exit. Mika glanced at Dutch. "Will they catch us?"

"Don't worry. We'll get out of here soon." She rounded the corner and turned the truck off-road. "This is an old logging road that cuts over the mountain. We'll be long gone by the time they clear the roadblock."

"But how will Thomas and Allison escape?"

"On two ATVs we hid in a nearby tree line. The camp counselors will try the other ATVs in the garage, but I ripped out the battery cables." Dutch grinned.

Mika could hear the loud hum of the ATVs in the distance. "Why me? What about the others?"

"I'm a friend of Brie's. We hadn't been in touch for some time, but she knew I was involved in helping queer kids. I'm sorry about the other teens. If we try to rescue a teen placed there by a parent, then the parent can sue us for interfering with their child's religious education."

"That's bullshit."

"I know, but shutting the camp down takes a mountain of evidence. Count your blessings that your aunt is your legal guardian."

My aunt. That was bullshit too, but Aunt Val wasn't evil like these people. She curled up in the seat and fell asleep. When she woke, they were on a highway in a different truck. She barely remembered being switched but didn't care. She was out of that hell hole.

"Welcome back. You had a good sleep." Dutch smiled over at her. "There's water in the cup holder. You need to hydrate."

Mika chugged the entire bottle of water down with only one breath in between. Someone shoved a protein bar in her hand. She turned to see the reverend and his assistant in the back.

"Hi. I'm Tommy. You were sound asleep when we met up with Dutch and got the new truck. I'm glad you've been able to sleep."

"You sound and look less like a preacher now," Mika said.

He laughed. "I know how to play the role."

"And what about you?"

Allison took off her coat and rolled back the sleeve of her shirt to reveal a tattoo of two women kissing.

Mika smiled. "So this isn't a dream."

"No. We'll have you with your aunt and Brie in about thirty minutes."

When they pulled up to the cabin, Aunt Val and Brie came running out. "I'm so happy you're out of there. I love you so much." She gave Mika a giant bear hug.

"I'm happy to be the fuck away from that place," Mika grumbled.

Her aunt bit her lip. "In this case, cursing is highly appropriate. I'm sorry your grandparents blindsided me, but you're safe now."

"Hi, Brie."

"Hi, kiddo." Brie clapped her on the back.

Mika couldn't stop the tears clouding her eyes. Her dad had always called her kiddo, but there was no way Brie could've known that.

"Thanks, buddy." Brie clapped Dutch on the shoulder.

"You're welcome."

"Folks. We need to leave," Allison said. "Tommy, you're in front with me. And you three are in the back. Are you hungry, Mika?"

"Starving."

"There's a small cooler on the floorboard just for you. Let's roll." Allison slid in behind the wheel.

"Where are we going?" Mika asked.

"The best place in North America. My home country, Canada." Allison grinned.

"Oh." Mika lifted the lid to find two six-inch subs, potato salad, an apple, a giant chocolate chip cookie, and a bottle of water. She didn't waste any time. Fatigue set in after eating. When Aunt Val put her arm around her, Mika rested up against her. She was mad at her but happy at the same time. How could that be? Maybe Aunt Val felt guilty for lying all these years. The least Mika could do was give her a chance to tell her story. Mika snuggled further into her aunt's warm embrace. *She loves me. Give her a chance.*

Chapter Thirty-Seven

As THEY WENT FARTHER north, the land around them changed from mountains to rolling hills with prairie grass and farm land. Mika stared out the windows at the vast emptiness of it all. The excitement of escaping that hell hole and finding out that Aunt Val and Brie were behind her rescue lasted only minutes. The fear hadn't left. Whenever a car came up fast alongside them, weird goosebumps rippled over her skin like biting insects. She wanted to sleep, but she couldn't. What would they do if the police stopped them? They'd take her away for sure, and maybe put everyone else in jail.

"Sweetie, you're safe." Aunt Val put her hand on Mika's bouncing knee.

Mika hadn't realized she was doing it until her aunt touched her. "We must have driven for a couple of hours. How much longer?"

Tommy looked at the map info. "Four hours and twenty minutes to Allison's place."

"You should get some sleep." Her aunt rubbed Mika's shoulder.

"That feels good." Mika looked into Aunt Val's face. Why had she never seen the resemblance before?

"Rest your head in my lap," her aunt said.

"And your feet in mine. Foot massages are my specialty," Brie said.

Mika stretched out, but her muscles involuntarily tensed tighter. What if she had to run?

"Relax. I'll protect you," Aunt Val whispered.

Mika bolted upright. "I need to call Willow."

"I know it's hard, but you can't call until we're safe in Canada." Aunt Val held her hand. "She knows we're getting you out but not the details."

"That makes no sense. Why?" Mika's heartbeat shot up again.

"I didn't want to put her in the position of lying to the police if she was questioned. And I'm worried the phone call might be traced."

Mika laid back down and tried to regulate her breathing. To calm herself, she thought about good times with Willow and imagined summer trips together. Her muscles loosened, and she drifted off into sleep and into dreams. She was swimming with Willow under Buttermilk Falls. Strangely, no one else was around. But every time she reached out, she couldn't touch Willow. Then someone grabbed her shoulder. She turned and looked into the cold eyes of the old lady. *I tell you when you can sleep.* Mika opened her eyes and pushed up.

"You're okay." Her aunt wrapped her arms around her. "I was trying to wake you, but you were sleeping very deeply."

"Yeah." She could see the bright lights of the border post through the windshield. There were several lanes, each with a swing gate, a booth, and cameras. Her pulse skyrocketed again. After 9/11, everyone had to have a passport, and her parents had hers.

"Did you find my passport?" she asked.

"Yes. Don't worry."

"This place is huge," Mika said.

"The other posts close at five p.m. This is the only Alberta post open twenty-four hours. It's fine. They like Americans, and you're a kid," Tommy said.

Mika looked at Aunt Val. Her smile didn't look that convincing. She and Brie handed over the passports to Tommy. He opened two then twisted in his seat and stared at Mika then Aunt Val.

"She's a dual citizen?" he asked.

"Yes," Aunt Val said.

"I remember asking Dad about mine being a different color when we went to a Maple Leafs game in Toronto." The puzzle pieces came together as Mika remembered her aunt's first job was in Toronto. "I don't remember when I got the passport."

"Almost five years ago, your family took a trip to Cancún."

Allison glanced into the rearview mirror. "So her passport's almost expired." She had a hard look on her face.

"Relax." Tommy handed the passports to her.

Allison came to a halt in front of the border guard. "Good evening, sir."

"Good evening." He held out his hand. "Passports, please."

Mika felt queasy as he took freaking forever, then her stomach dropped when a border patrol truck parked sideways several yards in front of them. Another guard walked out of the building and motioned for Allison to drive forward.

The man gave the passports back. "Pull through the gate and stop next to the guard. Roll down all the windows."

"Yes, sir." Allison moved at a snail's pace. "I'm not sure if her dual citizenship is going to hurt us or help. You should have mentioned it to me."

"I didn't think it'd be a big deal." Aunt Val swallowed.

"Passports." The guard looked stern as he took them from Allison. He walked around the vehicle, glancing back and forth between each of them and their passports. "Miss, could you please face me and brush the hair from your eyes."

Mika's anxiety had crashed through her, making everything sound far away.

Her aunt gently nudged her. "Sweetie, he's talking to you."

Mika swiftly ran her fingers through her hair, hoping that he didn't see her hand trembling.

"What's your full name, date of birth, city of birth, and present hometown?" he asked.

"Michaela Lynn Lavigne. I turned seventeen on June 30." She didn't know her birth city. *Fake it.* "I was born outside of Toronto. And I currently live in Ithaca, New York."

"Happy birthday. How was your party?"

Her breathing plummeted and a coldness took over her body.

The same fear she'd had at camp hit her like a big Mac truck.

"Sweetie," Aunt Val whispered.

Mixed bag of fucking rocks that I'd like to shove down my grands' throats. "I was visiting my grandparents. It was okay. Their present wasn't what I expected." Bile rose in her throat, burning along the way.

"Can you tell me who you're traveling with?" he said.

"My guardian, Aunt Val Hayden." She pointed to her aunt but mentioned the others only by their first name.

"What wonderful things will you be doing on this trip?" the officer asked.

"We're visiting Banff National Park," Aunt Val said.

"I was asking the young lady, ma'am."

"Ah, well, I wanted to catch a Calgary Flames game, but these guys," Mika pointed up front, "wanted to hang with their buddy in the summer. So, we missed all the action. But Allison is going to be our personal tour guide for the parks."

"Missing hockey is a shame. The Calgary Flames are the best team in the world. Better than the Toronto Maple Leafs. I assume they're your favorite team?"

"No. Mine's the Buffalo Sabres. Besides being the closest to Ithaca, they've also won more games over the Leafs." Mika faked a smile because she didn't have a clue what she was supposed to say if he asked more detailed questions about Wyoming and their route into Canada.

The guard smiled slightly. "Young lady, I need you to step out."

The cool wind coming through the window felt like it had dropped a ton.

"Ma'am, open the door and let her out." His eyes bored into Aunt Val.

Mika glanced at his name above his badge. "Why, Officer Brown?"

"I need to ask you some questions inside, please."

Aunt Val got out and held the door open. As Mika walked

alongside of Officer Brown, her aunt followed.

He turned swiftly and held up his hand. "Not you, ma'am."

"Officer Brown, please let her go with me. She's my favorite aunt and," Mika didn't have to fake the tears, "I've lived with her since my parents died." She needed Aunt Val by her side. She couldn't shake the feeling that this might be the last time they saw each other if it all went wrong.

A border guard truck whipped in tight behind Allison's truck, pinning them in. When their lights began to flash, Mika clung to her aunt. "I've been through a ton of shit with this fucking religious camp that turned out to be pray away the gay. Only they stopped me from sleeping when I wouldn't comply. Then they..." Her throat closed, like someone had shoved cotton balls down it, and her eyes filled with tears.

"Oh, sweetie. Canada has banned conversion therapy. You're safe here."

"I'm sorry that you went through that experience, Michaela," Officer Brown said softly. "But I'm required to ask you some questions. Your aunt can see you from the window."

So she didn't have a choice. "Okay, but I like to be called Mika." She blinked to squeeze the tears out of her eyes and followed him into the post. Every second that passed felt like her life was draining away. She was no longer angry at Aunt Val for hiding the truth. All she wanted was to go home.

Officer Brown sat on the desk, swinging his leg. "Have a seat."

The wooden chair reminded her of every chair at the camp, solid and with no cushion. The glint of flashing lights coming from Montana caught her attention. It wouldn't be long before they took her away and arrested Aunt Val. Tears rolled down her cheeks. "Please don't do this," she whispered.

He looked in the direction of the lights. "Canada has a national law against conversion therapy. We won't turn you over, but your case is complicated. For starters, your passports expire in three weeks, and you're a minor. Another officer is communicating with headquarters now."

"I want to call Willow."

"Who's that?"

"My girlfriend."

He scooted another chair across the floor and sat close to Mika. "Maybe later. I'm sorry, but I have to ask these questions."

She wasn't going back to Wyoming, but why couldn't she talk to Willow? The weight hanging around Mika's shoulders grew heavier. "What are your questions?"

"Who put you in the camp? And are you traveling freely with Ms. Hayden?"

Anger rose up in her, and she clenched her fist. "My grands, and I never want to see them again. Aunt Val's my guardian. I want to be with her and go home to New York."

A female guard walked up to them. "Sir, Ms. Hayden insisted that I give you these documents."

"Thank you, Joyce." He looked at the first document. "Good. This proves that Ms. Hayden is your legal guardian." He looked at the next one. "And here's your Canadian birth—" He paused, scanning the paper.

"My certificate?" Mika wet her lips. "Is my dad, Andrew Lavigne listed as my father?"

Officer Brown smiled. "This should be all we need." He straightened the papers. "Now—"

"Please don't change the subject. Who's my birth mom? Hannah Lavigne or Val Hayden?" All of her tears must have dried up every drop of moisture in her body. Her lips, mouth, and throat were so dry that she thought they'd cracked.

His smile faltered. "It's your original birth certificate with Valerie Hayden listed as your mother." He handed Mika some tissues.

"Headquarters wants to talk with you, sir," Joyce said.

"Would you like a drink? We've got Coke, ginger ale, or Fanta," Officer Brown said.

"Ginger ale, please." Mika had heard it also calmed the stomach.

"Joyce, please get Mika a drink while I take the call."

"Yes, sir."

Officer Brown went into a closed office, but Mika could see him through a large window writing things down. The female guard returned with the soda. Mika sipped it slowly, and the ice-cold drink helped her throat. The guard went into the office. She wasn't there that long, but she smiled and nodded to Mika when she left. Mika stared down, concentrating on the soft swirls of the gray carpet.

"Oh, sweetie." Aunt Val rushed to her side.

That had to be a good sign. Mika put down the drink and hugged her aunt. She was afraid to speak at first. Then she realized she was holding her breath. "I love you, but when this is all over, I need you to tell me the truth."

"I love you too. I have a lot to tell you, but there's never been a good time," Aunt Val whispered. She turned to Officer Brown. "I couldn't leave her in that camp. There's nothing wrong with her, and you have a national law against conversion therapy. You can't turn her back over to them." Tears rolled down her cheeks.

He held up his hands. "Ms. Hayden, I can assure you that Canada will not mistreat your niece. We don't treat citizens like you do in some parts of the US."

"Can we go, please?" Mika asked.

"I'm afraid you have to be temporarily placed in our government's Child Protection Services until things are verified and worked out with the US authorities."

"That's not fair. You have the papers that Aunt Val's my guardian."

"Yes, but they have to be verified by headquarters. The important thing is you won't be returned to the camp. You and your aunt must remain in Canada until everything can be worked out. Now, tell me why you think the Buffalo Sabres are better than the Calgary Flames. Be careful, or I'll have to arrest you for disrespecting the country of your birth."

He joked around with her some more, but it didn't stop the rock tumbling around in her stomach, and neither did the ginger ale. She wanted to throw up.

"The escort is here. Mika, you'll ride with the officers in the lead truck. Ms. Hayden, you'll have some paperwork to complete and more questions to answer, but a lawyer will be present."

"How long?" Tears rolled down Mika's face.

"I honestly don't know. I wish you all the best." Officer Brown smiled.

The female guard walked them outside, and Mika sat inside the lead truck with another female guard.

"Hi, I'm Amy," the guard held out her hand.

"Mika." She didn't shake hands and turned her head away. Her whole body was off balance. Her muscles had turned to mush, and she could barely think. Aunt Val had done so much, and she'd organized the rescue. Mika loved her, but she wasn't... She slumped into the seat with her head back and closed her eyes. Everything had exploded, and there was no putting it all back in the box. She had nothing to hang on to but Aunt Val's promise that she'd finally hear the truth.

Chapter Thirty-Eight

MIKA PACED BACK AND forth inside the hospital room. Besides medical doctors, she'd had to see a psychiatrist. It had taken her a ton of time to get used to Iliana, and talking to someone new wasn't easy. Worse, no one would give her an answer about going home. She turned as the door creaked open. Doctor Thompson entered. "When is this lab rat experiment you're putting me through going to end?" She crossed her arms, more to keep them from trembling than to look angry. "It's been days."

"I'm sorry you feel that way. That was never our intent," the doctor said. She sat in the chair and motioned for Mika to sit.

"Sorry. I'm just...exhausted over all of this." Mika cracked her knuckles and sat.

"A thorough medical exam with blood tests and sessions to access your emotional state are routine. I'm sorry we had to ask about the details of the abuse." The doctor opened her chart. "We verified that you'd been on a low dose of Zoloft which was stopped abruptly during your stay in the camp."

"Yeah, the shrink said the side effects of coming to a screeching halt added to the fucked-up camp crap. I think I need it again." Mika tapped her fingers on top of her legs.

"We agree, but it has to be gradual."

Another woman entered the room.

"This is Deanna Campbell from Alberta's Child Protection Unit. She'll take you to our headquarters for a visit with your aunt."

"Hello, Mika."

She glanced down at Deanna's outstretched hand and shook it. "When can I go home?"

"That will be up to a judge. In the meantime, you'll go into temporary housing with other girls."

"Will there be more lab rat experiments?" Mika crossed her arms again.

"Yours is a better case than some: no drugs in the home and no father causing domestic assault, but there are some serious charges against your aunt."

"She's never done anything to me. Who says that she has?" Mika paced again.

"The Canadian government needs to protect you until we can get answers and resolve the issue. Now, let's go see your aunt." Deanna opened the door.

Going outside was bliss. A light breeze blew through the trees like a breath of freedom and going to see Aunt Val had to be a sign of hope. They got into a car and drove across the street. The building had giant white tiles with a few gray and red ones mixed in, but the front was entirely gray. It didn't look welcoming. If she was in charge, she'd fire the architect.

The interior wasn't much better, except for a few plants in the lobby. They walked down a long hallway, and Deanna opened an office door. Everything blanked out when she saw Aunt Val and Brie. She ran in and jumped into her aunt's arms. "I want to go home."

"I want to take you home, sweetie."

She lingered as her aunt stroked her hair, not caring that she probably looked like a baby. Whatever reason Aunt Val didn't keep her was insignificant now. She still wanted the truth, but Aunt Val clearly cared deeply for her.

Mika stepped back. "How's Willow?"

"She's holding up." Her aunt took a FedEx manilla envelope from her hand bag and handed it to Mika. "This arrived at our hotel yesterday. She sent it overnight."

Mika carefully opened it. The first thing that caught her eye was the stunning drawing of them kissing. It looked so life-like. Below,

Willow had written, *Remember, you're tough, and I love you. I'll see you soon. Willow.* "This is amazing." She showed it to Aunt Val and Brie. "Please thank her for me. I'm so lucky that she's mine." Mika wiped away her tears. "How's Benjy and everyone else?"

"They all miss you." Aunt Val rubbed her arm then squeezed her hand.

They talked for about twenty minutes. Her aunt mentioned Benjy was working for his dad this summer. But most of it was basic chat.

"If I can't go home now, do you know when?" She glanced around at the sofa and small table with two chairs. It wasn't a police cell, but it wasn't a five-star hotel either. And the child protection lady near the door made her feel like a prisoner.

"We're not sure," Aunt Val said.

Mika looked at Brie, figuring she wouldn't sugarcoat the answer. "How long? Tell me." But all Brie did was look back at her aunt.

"It could take a couple of months." Tears brimmed in her aunt's eyes.

"That makes no sense. You're my..." Mika stepped away and looked down at the floor, "guardian."

"I guess there's just more paperwork and interviews," Aunt Val said softly.

"I need to be home for Mom's birthday and college." Tears rolled down Mika's face. "I don't want to miss all that. Why is this happening? What aren't you telling me?"

Aunt Val took a deep breath. "Your grandparents have accused me of grooming you."

"Grooming me?" Anger boiled inside. "What the fuck? That's ridiculous. You haven't done anything like that. I was gay before my parents died; I just hadn't put it into words." Mika wiped away her tears with her T-shirt then stepped toward Deanna. "You're with child protection. Aunt Val hasn't abused me. She's never touched me sexually, and she didn't make me have a relationship with my girlfriend."

"Sweetie, please stop yelling." Her aunt placed her hand lightly on Mika's shoulder.

"I'm sorry, Mika," Deanna said. "That's not my job to assess. I'm only transporting you for this visit and then on to temporary housing." She looked at her watch. "We need to move on. You'll have another visit soon."

"What? I get to see them for thirty minutes in this drab room, and you call that a visit? I'm not going anywhere without Aunt Val and Brie." Mika wrapped her arm around her aunt's neck, grabbed Brie's hand, and tugged her toward them.

Brie pulled them together in a group hug. "You have to go. The lawyer's on the case, and I'll help your aunt. The important thing is the Canadian government has promised they won't send you back to Wyoming."

"What's the worst-case scenario?"

Aunt Val touched her forehead to Mika's. "You could remain under Canadian care until you turn eighteen."

"No!"

"Sweetie." Her aunt threw her arms around her neck. "I promise we're fighting this hard, and we'll win. It takes time."

Deanna cleared her throat. "I'm sorry, but we need to go."

"Hang tight. I love you, and I'll fight to get you home," Aunt Val said, her eyes filled with tears.

"I love you," Mika said, her voice choking. She broke down in the hallway, and Deanna had to help her to the car.

The ride to her temporary housing went past the city library. Any other time, she'd be on the edge of her seat and begging to go inside but not today. Everything had faded to dull, like her insides. She was just a pool of nothingness.

Her temporary housing was an apartment on the tenth floor of a building overlooking Calgary. She had a room by herself with a comfortable single bed, a desk, and a soft fabric rocking chair. She didn't give a damn that it was nice: it wasn't home.

The apartment had two full bathrooms for her, four other

teenage girls, and two counselors. No one forced her to talk or sit, and she could go to her room whenever she wanted, which was a lot because she didn't want to be there and become friends with anyone.

There were big windows that let in plenty of sunshine, but the main apartment door was always locked except for supervised group events. She went to the gym with the group some days, but mainly exercised in her room. Aunt Val called a couple of times, but one of the counselors had to listen in. And after every call, Mika would go to her room and cry. Why couldn't she talk to Willow? She missed her so much.

There was a knock on the door. She sighed, knowing that they'd just talk bullshit to try and cheer her up, and opened it. They were nice and didn't physically abuse her like at the camp, but they were keeping her from going home, and that felt like a different kind of abuse.

"Mika, I'm so sorry about what you've gone through. Hiding in your room and not talking to anyone isn't going to solve anything. Socializing will help your trauma."

"You don't know what it felt like. I don't want to play games or talk to anyone. And you can't make me talk to the therapist that comes in the afternoon."

The counselor smiled. "Do you realize those are the only words you've said since coming here?"

Mika hung her head. "All that matters to me is home."

"I understand. Do you feel like the Zoloft isn't helping?"

"It helps a little. I wish you'd let me take it on my own instead of dishing it out like a nurse in a psych ward."

"Okay. We'll be doing a short interview with you soon. It's mandatory, but how you interact with the group is also being evaluated. Please eat dinner with us tonight at six."

Mika nodded, and the counselor turned to walk out. "Wait. You're Amanda, right?"

"Close. I'm Miranda."

"Thanks, Miranda."

"You're welcome."

Mika walked into the dining room a few minutes after six and sat in the empty chair at one end of a long table. The food was awesome and there was loads of it. But no matter how delicious or how often they switched up variety, it didn't compare to home.

"Good evening, Mika," Miranda said. "Since this is your first time, it's a custom to go around the table and give a short introduction. I'm Miranda. I graduated from the University of Calgary with a master's in social services. My hobbies are horseback riding and photography."

Everyone said their name and a hobby. They all seemed too comfortable here. Had any of them been abused or sent to a camp like Mika? A memory of Wyoming flashed in her mind. Would any of those kids ever get out?

"Mika, it's your turn now," Miranda said.

"I'm Mika Lavigne from Ithaca, New York." She paused, then cleared her throat, deciding how much to say. *Fuck it. They're getting the truth.* "I'm stuck here because my grandparents sent me to a conversion therapy camp in Wyoming for my seventeenth birthday. Yeah, happy birthday to me." Each time she outed herself, she felt stronger, and she needed extra strength to get through this. "My aunt rescued me, but Canada is holding me until she can disprove my grands' false accusations. I miss my girlfriend and my aunt. None of this is fair. No one harmed me but that camp and my grandparents. And if I don't get out of Canada soon, I'll miss the start of college." So much for short. She looked up. "I want to go home."

Miranda nodded. "Thank you for sharing."

A few said encouraging words. No one acted mean or seemed pissed that she was gay.

There was a planned group outing the next day. When it turned out that it was ice-skating, she focused on having fun. But going home was always on her mind. What if she didn't get out of here in time for college? The chance that Willow would go to the city without her made Mika's stomach hurt. She hung up her skates early and watched from the sidelines.

The next day, Mika pulled up the covers when the morning sun shone through the curtains and slept in late. Around noon, she woke up and realized where she was. God, was she ever going to get out of here? What if Willow got tired of waiting and moved on? Hunger finally got her out of bed, and she headed to the kitchen.

After making a peanut butter sandwich, she grabbed a bag of chips and an apple, then looked in the fridge for a drink and saw a jar of caramel sauce. Dipping cut-up apples in the sauce would be tasty. She took out the sauce and looked through the kitchen drawers. No sharp objects, and a butter knife wouldn't work. She'd never hurt herself, but she wondered how many girls had passed through here that were suicidal.

"Good morning. It's order out night, and we're trying a new Italian restaurant. Let me know what you want." Miranda smiled and slid the menu toward Mika.

"Thanks. Ah, but don't you always order out for us? I mean, no one ever cooks in here."

"The food is home-cooked from the cafeteria across the street and delivered. They're closed tonight. Also, we have a cooking class there once a month. The next one's in a couple of weeks, but hopefully, you'll be going home by then."

That nugget of hope made Mika feel a little better.

Miranda pointed to a woman wearing a light green shirt. "Zoe's the court-appointed psychologist who has to interview you. You don't have to say anything, but I hope you'll talk to her."

"I'll just say the same things again." She looked at Miranda through watery eyes. "I can't believe my dad's parents did this to me. It's sick." She backed into the refrigerator as the memory squeezed her insides. "I have to be with Aunt Val."

"Okay. You're going to be okay." Miranda came a little closer but didn't touch her. "Eat your lunch. Then we'll talk."

Mika nodded and wiped her face with the sleeve of her shirt. The fabric was soft. When she'd first arrived, they had let her pick out some clothes at a store nearby to supplement what little she'd brought into Canada. One of the shirts she'd chosen had long sleeves and the emblem of the Calgary Flames to remind her of hockey games with her dad. They'd had so much fun. Sadness settled in her chest, and she wished he was here to hold her. Now more than ever, she wanted to hear the truth from Aunt Val. Mika finished her lunch and put her dishes in the dishwasher.

Miranda and another woman walked up to her.

"Hi, I'm Zoe."

She shook Zoe's outstretched hand. "Can we talk in the bedroom? It's more comfortable than the conference room," Mika said.

"Sure."

Mika eased down into the plush rocker. Zoe sat in the desk chair and pulled out a pad of paper and a pen.

"Do you mind?" Miranda pointed to the bed. "I'm here as an observer."

"Go ahead." How many times did she have to tell the authorities? "Look, it hurts to talk about it." Her voice choked up. "This is the last time I'm telling my story." Every time Mika had to talk was like reliving the sleepless nights, the bag of rocks, the beatings, and the isolation.

"I understand. The judge might ask you a few more questions, but I'm the last psychologist you'll see." Zoe smiled. "What you say influences our decision enormously, but it has to be truthful. Do you understand?"

"Yes," Mika said.

"Tell me a little about your life in New York, your friends, and what you like to do," Zoe asked.

She asked easy questions initially, but they became harder over time, and Mika spilled her guts. She shed tons of tears as she explained how her aunt had taken care of her after the death of her parents, but she didn't reveal that Aunt Val was her bio mom. She talked about Benjy and their gaming. Then Zoe's questions dug into her personal life and what Willow meant to her.

"Who decided to start an intimate relationship?"

"Me or her. Both of us. I can't remember. We were making out here and there, and then it just happened. What does it matter? It's our choice. I'm not a little kid."

"I agree, but you're still a year shy of being an adult under Canadian and U.S. law." Zoe cleared her throat. "Sadly, I have to ask this question, but I need to know if it was solely your choice, or if any adult pushed you."

"Aunt Val didn't push me into anything. I had feelings for Willow before my parents' death. She's so kind, smart, and beautiful, and she's got loads of talent. Her paintings are gorgeous. I wanted to kiss her for so long and almost did, but I'd chicken out every time. Then she kissed me, and it was just lit." She wiped her eyes. "We're supposed to go to college together in late August in New York City. My grandparents wanted to ruin everything."

"I saw that you'd been accepted to numerous universities. But Columbia University is one of the best. That's exciting," Miranda said.

"Yeah, but Canada has to let me go, or I won't make it in time. Look, Willow's my girlfriend. No one *made* me gay, and no one can make me straight. That camp is horrible. It was fucking torture. And before you ask, my aunt has never touched me sexually, no matter what my grandparents have said. They're messed up, not Aunt Val." Mika couldn't stop her lip from quivering.

"I'm done with my questioning. Is there anything else you'd like to add?" Zoe asked.

"How much longer?" Mika crossed her arms.

"The interviews of other people, like your teachers, are coming to a close. Your case is moving fast. No one has corroborated the story your grandparents have told the authorities."

"Even Aunt Pauline?" Mika clamped her jaw shut before she

spilled exactly what she thought about her.

Zoe nodded. "She testified to not knowing about her parents' intent. And while she doesn't approve of homosexuality, she never thought your aunt would ever cause you physical or sexual harm. She argued for placing you in a Catholic girls' high school."

"In other words, Aunt Pauline wants to put me into a religious place that nicely preaches that homosexuality is immoral." Mika felt like laughing. Aunt Pauline would be pissed if she ever discovered that Jenn had been having sex for two years with her boyfriend, the guy Aunt Pauline thought was such a "wonderful and respectful young man" from church. Mika sighed. "Again. How much longer?"

"I'm in no position to promise anything, but we're trying to get you home as soon as possible. Your case has drawn the attention of the media," Zoe said.

Mika wasn't sure if that was a good or bad thing. She turned to Miranda. "There's still one thing I haven't been able to do yet."

"What is it? I'll try to help," Miranda said.

Mika bounced her leg up and down. "I want to call Willow." There were times she thought she wasn't enough for Willow. She needed to hear Willow's voice and those words, I love you, again to believe it was real.

"Let me check if I can let you call. If so, I'll probably have to listen to your conversation. I'm sorry."

Mika rolled her eyes. "Like, what are you expecting? Do you think Willow's going to fly up here on a magic carpet and get me out of the apartment through these giant windows that only open a few inches?"

"Well, you never know. She could be a magical fairy." Miranda winked and left the room. A few minutes later, she came back and plugged a landline unit into the wall.

Mika punched in the number while she bounced her leg up and down. Her spirits sank when Willow's voicemail came on. At the beep, she said, "Hi. It's me. I'm in Canada, and they've let—"

"Mika, are you okay? Are they treating you well?"

"Yes." Her eyes watered at the sweet sound of Willow's voice.

"Sorry I didn't pick up right away; I didn't recognize the number."

"Just to let you know, you're on speaker. My Canadian counselor, Miranda, has to listen in. She's great."

Miranda smiled.

"I've been so worried about you," Willow said.

Mika could tell she was about to cry. "Hey, that camp was hell, but I'm out of there. Now the Canadian courts just need to muddle through the grands' shitty claims against Aunt Val."

"I love you so much, Mika."

"And I love you so much that it hurts not to be able to see you, but hearing you say those words means the world to me. *You* mean the world to me. Thank you so much for the drawing and note."

"You're welcome. Everyone's helping to get you home. Some people were interviewed, and all of your friends and a bunch of teachers wrote letters to the Canadian government on your behalf."

Mika smiled even though she was crying too. "That's great. Hey, when I get out of here, I want to take you to dinner, then I want to lay on a blanket with you and gaze up at the stars."

"Only stargaze?"

Oh, how Willow's tone revved up Mika's body. She blushed when Miranda cleared her throat. "Okay. Lots of hugs and kisses. Don't forget Miranda's listening in."

"Yeah, sorry. I'd love to see your beautiful crimson face right now." Willow laughed.

God, it felt so good to hear her voice. They talked for another fifteen minutes, then Miranda twirled her finger.

"Close it up."

"I have to go. I love you, Willow."

"I love you, beautiful. Sending virtual hugs and kisses. See you soon."

"Bye, Willow." Mika pressed the button to end the call. "Thanks, Miranda."

"You're welcome." Miranda unplugged the landline unit and left.

God, it felt so good to hear Willow's voice. Now, the legal system that was holding her down needed to finish whatever was taking so long. The Zoloft calmed her a bit and talking to Willow was a big plus, but every delay felt like she was sinking that little bit further into the darkness.

Chapter Thirty-Nine

Early August

MIKA STARED AT THE calendar in her room: August the thirteenth. Thirteen—Taylor Swift's lucky number. Mika could use some luck now. She opened the closet and pulled out the suitcase that Aunt Val had given her after she'd been rescued from the Wyoming camp. The few changes of clothes in the suitcase were enough along with the clothes the Canadians let her pick out. But there was one new T-shirt in the suitcase she hadn't worn. It was a gift from her aunt that Mika planned to wear for the first time when she was on her way home. And Aunt Val had left a note.

She opened the suitcase and ran her fingers over the new T-shirt with Mars and statistics about the planet on the front. It was a perfect gift. She reread the note: *When you read this, you'll be free and on your way home.* Clearly, her aunt never thought a problem would pop up when going through the Canadian border. Mika still needed the truth about her birth, but she could never thank Aunt Val enough for her rescue and the hard work being done to get her *home*.

Home. She sighed, frustrated with the whole process. The Canadians were really nice to her, but this wasn't home. She had to get out of here. Her mom's birthday was August the twenty-fifth, and Mika wanted to take flowers to her parents' grave. If this whole process took two months, she wouldn't be home in time. And if it dragged on further, she'd miss the start of college.

"Mika." Miranda tapped on the door. "Can I come in?"

"Just a minute." Why was Miranda so early? Mika cracked

the door only enough to peek out. "I'm still in my stinky exercise clothes."

"You have a Zoom call."

Mika leaned her forehead on the door jam. "I look like a mess to face a judge or any other official. Can we postpone it for ten or fifteen minutes?"

"I have the app open on my computer right now. I think you're going to want to take this one." Miranda smiled

Mika swung the door open. "Come on in." She sat on the bed and Miranda sat beside her. "I wasn't kidding about my stinky clothes. You could catch a disease from me."

Miranda laughed. "I'll survive, but you might want to isolate them in a plastic bag until you can wash them." She entered the Zoom full screen on her laptop and handed it to Mika.

When Aunt Val's smiling face appeared, Mika sat up tall.

"The judge has ordered you released to me," her aunt said and gave her a huge smile.

"Yahoo!" Mika thrust her hands in the air. "Sorry. Didn't mean to bust your eardrums."

"We're staying at a hotel along the Bow River, not far from your temporary housing. I'm standing on our hotel room balcony. The river and the Calgary skyline are beautiful from here." Her aunt panned the camera around.

Brie walked into the picture, waved, and put her arm around Aunt Val. "Hi, Mika. We're in a one-bedroom suite. Hope you don't mind the sofa-sleeper."

"Hell, I'll sleep on the floor if it means going home." Mika grinned. "When do I join you guys?"

"My American lawyer had a Canadian counterpart working with us. Her name's Ms. Scott, and she'll pick you up around eleven." Aunt Val wiped her eyes. "I'm crying tears of happiness for a change because you're finally free."

"When do we leave?"

"Brie booked a direct flight to Toronto tomorrow, then we'll drive home from there. I miss you and can't wait until you're here."

"That's great." Mika smiled. Thirteen was lucky. "But why Toronto? Why not New York?"

"There aren't any direct flights to Syracuse. We could have flown into JFK. It's almost the same driving time to home, but it's a longer plane ride and the traffic is crazy compared to Toronto. All that stacks up to a longer day."

"Got it."

"The court already faxed us paperwork," Miranda said. "We'll make sure she's ready to go, Ms. Hayden."

"Get packing, Mika, because I want to hug you as soon as possible. I love you." Her aunt blew a kiss.

"Me too. See you soon. Love, you." Mika handed back the laptop. She laid out one pair of jeans and her prized T-shirt on the bed. "I should shower. Don't want to ruin my Mars T-shirt."

Miranda laughed. "Afterwards, I challenge you to a game or two of foosball before you leave."

"Okay. But I leave the second Ms. Scott arrives."

After several games, Mika settled on the sofa, watching the clock more than the TV. Her leg twitched, but she suppressed the urge to bounce it up and down. Ms. Scott arrived around eleven-twenty and apologized for the delay.

As they stepped into the elevator, Mika sucked in her first breath of freedom. Outside, she stood still for a minute with her head back and arms stretched out, letting the sun shine on her.

"The homes associated with our child services are tops. Did you have a bad experience?" Ms. Scott pinched her eyebrows together, forming a deep V.

"No." Mika smiled at her. "It's just good to be outside without being part of a group and having other adults watch you like a hawk."

"Ah, I see. This is us." Ms. Scott pointed to a red Lexus parked nearby.

"Nice wheels. Um, can I ask you for a favor?" Mika sat in the passenger seat.

"Yes, I'll try my best."

"Can I call my girlfriend? She's back in New York."

"Of course." Ms. Scott started the car and brought the phone app up on the dashboard.

It rang six times before Willow picked up.

"Hello?" She sounded unsettled.

"It's me. I'm in the car with the Canadian lawyer."

"Mika, it's so good to hear your voice," Willow said.

"I'm coming home."

"That's terrific. I have lots of hugs and kisses for you."

"I can't wait." She felt safe in Willow's arms. "I'm so freaking lucky to have the world's sweetest and caring girlfriend."

Willow laughed. "Pour it on, but we haven't even had a fight yet. Mom says I can be stubborn when I get mad."

"I bet you're even more lovely when you're mad." Mika smiled as she looked up through the car's panoramic moonroof at the skyscrapers and the light reflecting off the glass panels of one building. "I'll call you again after I get settled at Aunt Val and Brie's hotel. Love you. Bye."

"I love you, Mika. Bye."

Mika hit the end button and turned to Ms. Scott. "Thanks."

"You're very welcome."

They left the downtown area, and Mrs. Scott parked along the curb in front of an old two-story mansion. If it hadn't been for the sign and the restaurant in the center lower level, Mika never would have guessed it was a hotel.

When Mika saw Aunt Val in the lobby, she ran into her arms.

Her aunt rocked her back and forth. "It's so good to hold you, Mika. I love you with all my heart."

"I love you," Mika said softly. "I can never do enough to pay you back for rescuing me." Although there were still questions to be answered and a hard talk ahead, she knew Aunt Val would always be there for her.

"Hey, Mika," Brie said.

"Hi." Mika hugged her. "Your friend Dutch was great. Thank you for saving my life."

Her aunt wiped her eyes and looked at the smiling young lawyer. "Thank you, Ms. Scott."

"It was a pleasure to assist Sidney and be your legal representation in Canada. It was his hard work that pushed us over the finish line. Here's a copy of the paperwork releasing Mika to you. I wish you all the best and a safe journey home."

"Thank you." Her aunt placed the paperwork in her handbag.

"Thank you, ma'am," Mika said, "especially for letting me call my girlfriend."

"My pleasure." Ms. Scott smiled and left them to it.

"It's lunch time. Are you hungry? Or we could take a walk along the river. It's beautiful." Aunt Val took Mika's hand.

"Can we order in? I'd like to talk."

"Sure." Her aunt's smile faltered for a second.

"Hey, there's a great barbeque nearby. How's that sound?" Brie asked.

Mika nodded.

"I'll go get it and take the long way so you can have some privacy. Be back in an hour." Brie left them standing in the lobby.

Aunt Val motioned. "The stairs are this way."

They'd have more time if they talked when they got home. But the questions bouncing around inside Mika's brain were driving her nuts. She was finally going to get the answers she'd been wanting for years.

Chapter Forty

"THIS IS NICE." MIKA looked around the hotel suite.

"We picked it because it feels more like home than a modern hotel." Aunt Val sat on the sofa. "I'm not sure where to begin. Sit and ask me whatever comes to your mind."

Mika sat on the opposite sofa and stretched her arm over the back of it. "Is anyone going to do anything to my grandparents and Aunt Pauline for what they put me through?"

"When I first talked with Pauline, she claimed she had no knowledge of your grandparents' plan. I didn't believe her, but then she flew out to Wyoming with Sidney and testified against them."

"Maybe she did it just to save her ass." Mika's words spilled out like nails.

"I thought the same thing until I read the transcript that Sidney provided."

Mika rubbed her forehead. "What'd it say?"

"She testified she didn't approve of homosexuality, but she was against conversion therapy of any kind. When it came out that they'd punished you–"

"Abused me. Go on." Mika twirled her finger in the air.

Aunt Val wet her lips. "Did you know you were videoed during your initial interviews with the Canadian authorities?"

"Yes. I signed papers."

"The videos were played after Pauline testified and shown only to the judge, your grandparents, and the lawyers. Sidney and his paralegal represented me. He said it was emotional, and that your grandparents broke down. I only read the transcript, but it brought tears to my eyes. Afterwards, your grandparents testified that they thought it was just a strict religious camp and that they didn't know about any punishment or abuse. The judge gave them a huge fine and ordered them to do twelve months of community service. Pauline went home. That's about it. Do you want a drink?" Aunt Val got up, brought two bottles of water back from the bar fridge, and handed one to Mika.

"Obviously the claims of you grooming me fell through. But the grands should've gotten slammed for lying about that."

"The judge lectured them about that as well."

They drank from their bottles in silence. After a few minutes, Mika cleared her throat. "I've wondered my entire life how come I was so lucky to be adopted by Mom and Dad. They were great, but I'd also wondered what my bio-parents looked like, if I had siblings, if we had anything in common. Stuff like that. But mostly, I wondered why my bio-Mom gave me up." Mika looked at her. Now was the time for Aunt Val to come clean, but silence continued. "I know you're my birth mom and Dad is my bio-Dad."

Her aunt's hand trembled as she raised the water bottle to her lips. "I figured you knew as much when I got the email to Blue28. Who helped you do a DNA test? Jenn?"

Mika nodded. "She manages her mom's tree, and Dad's DNA was attached to it." She gritted her teeth. "Why didn't anyone tell me?"

"Your mom thought you'd handle it better when you were eighteen and out of high school. I agreed to her wishes. Then... they weren't there anymore."

Aunt Val had been by Mika's side since her parents died. They had shed plenty of tears, and she didn't want to be the cause any more, but she wanted the truth. "I also found Mom's old phone and charged it. I read her text messages. She was pretty fucking angry. You said you weren't bi, but it sure looks like you cheated with Dad."

Her aunt's head whipped up. "It's not what you think. I didn't abuse your mom's trust and cheat with your dad."

"Then what's the story?" Mika's tone was harsher than she intended. "I'm just fed up with being in the dark." When Aunt Val stood and started to walk to the bedroom, Mika grabbed her arm. "That's it. You're going to walk away and not tell me!"

"I...I need to get a few more documents to..." Her aunt lowered her head and steadied herself by grasping Mika's shoulders. "They'll help explain things. I promise I'll be right back."

Dammit, why did Aunt Val and her parents think she was such a baby that she couldn't handle the truth until she was eighteen? Mika paced back and forth. It seemed like an eternity before her aunt returned. Her eyes were red and swollen from crying, and she gripped a small bundle of papers like a life raft.

Aunt Val sat back down. "I went through everything a couple of months ago when I first thought about telling you. Then I brought them when we flew out to rescue you. I thought if the police stopped us that they'd help along with my guardianship document. And I did show them to the Canadians." She unclipped the papers and gazed at the first one. "Mika, your parents wanted a baby so bad, but your mom had damage from endometriosis." She handed the document to Mika. "This is from your mom's medical file."

Mika scanned the paper. "Her doctor recommended four cycles of in vitro fertilization?"

"Yes, and they tried six. Only one showed promise, but the baby didn't survive. The doctors at the clinic said your mom's only hope was adoption or surrogacy." Aunt Val wiped her tears with the palm of her hand.

"Surrogacy? They implanted you with Dad's sperm?" Mika raised an eyebrow. "I can't believe Aunt Pauline never let anything slip about this. Her mouth's as wide as the Grand Canyon."

"Your parents hid the truth from everyone because they didn't want to upset either side of the family or leave the church."

"That doesn't make sense. Why would it upset anyone? It was way before anyone knew you were a lesbian. And what does religion have anything to do with this?"

"The Catholic Church believes adoption is the only option for couples with fertility problems. The church views IVF and surrogacy as unnatural and immoral, and you know how your grandparents' conservative views would have caused problems. That's why your parents kept it a secret."

Mika picked up the fertility clinic papers. "The clinic was in Buffalo, and my birth certificate and passports list Canada as my birthplace. That's the only part that makes sense."

"How so?" Aunt Val wrinkled her eyebrows.

"Because I love ice hockey."

Her aunt's laughter lightened Mika's mood over the heavy shit she had to process. "Did you volunteer, or did Mom ask you?"

"She didn't want the surrogate to be a stranger. She begged me to do it. At the time, I worked for a research firm in Toronto, who'd paid for part of my master's. I couldn't walk away from the program."

"Tell me about being born in the back of the car."

"How'd you know that?"

Mika rolled her eyes. "My mom's phone."

"Oh, right, the texts." Aunt Val took a drink of water from her glass on the coffee table. "So the plan was for my girlfriend to drive me to Buffalo when I went into labor. But you didn't wait. You woke me up in the middle of the night. On the way to Buffalo, I could feel your head crowning. You were born in the car just on the Canadian side of the border." Her aunt pointed to the papers. "Here's your original birth certificate, and the New York one with your parents' names. All adoptions modify their records."

"Yeah. On the original, you're the mother and Dad is listed as the father. Why?"

"Once we'd been taken to the hospital and checked out, they asked for a father's name. I was in a daze and exhausted. Since you were born in Canada, I knew there'd be an extra process to get you adopted to my sister and Andrew. So, I said his name, thinking that it might speed things up."

"Mom and Dad were liberal, so what got you two so heated up?"

Aunt Val took a breath and blew it out. "You deserve the truth, no matter how brutal." She took another deep breath. "Mika, I never dreamed it'd be a big deal when I promised to have you. Just nine months of discomfort and a little bit of morning sickness, which sucked." She smiled. "But feeling you move inside me was a little bit of magic. And you were so adorable when you were born."

Mika straightened up. "Hey, I'm still adorable."

"Yes, you are."

"I became emotionally attached as you grew inside of me. And let's face it, you popping out in the back seat was an event I'll never forget. I also had you for almost a year while the final paperwork went through." She wiped her eyes.

"I lived with you for a year?"

"Ten months. You were automatically a Canadian citizen since you were born there, but your parents being American added an extra layer of complication." Aunt Val closed her eyes for a second. "When the time came to sign the final papers, I didn't want to give you up. But I kept my promise, and I couldn't hurt my sister and Andrew."

Mika took in that kernel of raw emotion while her aunt sobbed. She just assumed that Aunt Val had lied and had an affair with her dad.

"I know this is all a shock. It's okay if it makes you angry." Her aunt sipped her water.

"I'm not mad at you. It's just weird. I love my mom and miss her, but I love you too, just differently. And you were sisters that looked totally different. Please don't tell me Mom's adopted."

Aunt Val sputtered, and water dripped from her chin. "No. Not everyone of European descent has the same skin tone or eye color."

Mika took a breath and sighed. "Look, I understand how you could have intense feelings for me. When did you, ah, you know, get over the feeling of being my mother?"

Tears streamed down her aunt's face again. "Never. It's part of the reason I stayed away. Leaving you behind after every visit was like another stab to my heart, and I was afraid I'd say something. I never stopped loving you for one minute. I tried time and distance, but then everything roared back when I became your guardian. I'm not your mother. My sister is. But I do feel like your mom sometimes."

Mika nodded. "Early on, did anyone catch on to your feelings? Or did you talk about it with Mom?"

"Shortly after my debacle with my old high school girlfriend, your mom asked me to leave early and to stay away. She thought I was showing you too much affection." Aunt Val chewed on her lip before continuing. "It hurt so bad for her to ask me to leave, but we sort of made up within the year."

"Sort of?" Mika wrinkled her brow.

"For five years, she wrote short letters but refused to talk on the phone. Even after speaking and a few visits, letters remained her main way of communicating. Your dad also wrote letters, but we talked more frequently." Her aunt wiped her eyes with a tissue.

"Please tell me about the letters."

"I'd receive six or more a year along with photos telling me about your school achievements and your overall progress. I could see that you were looking more and more like me each day, but you had your dad's beautiful eyes. When I moved back from Germany last year, your mom called me several times. She was upset when I couldn't make it for Thanksgiving after being gone for so long."

"Good thing you didn't." Mika sighed. "Both sets of grandparents killed the mood with their talks about cultural issues. It was a zoo."

"I decided to come home for Christmas, then we both got slammed with the heartache of a lifetime."

Mika picked up a tissue, wiped her eyes, and blew her nose. "Yeah, it's been a fucked-up six months, except for Willow and you." Mika waited until Aunt Val looked at her before continuing. "Thanks for taking care of me, helping me get ready for college, and for getting me out of that fucking camp. I do love you, and—" She hid her eyes and bit her lip until it almost bled. She let her tears flow. "I'm grateful for everything. And I'm sorry I wrongly accused you of cheating with my dad."

"I'm not trying to replace your mom. She loved and cared for you for many years. You asked for the truth, and I've given it to you. I love you more than a niece, but I accept that my sister is your mom."

"I thought Mom and Dad picked you as my guardian because they guessed I was gay. There was one of Dad's voicemails on the phone, then the texts between you and Mom sounded like you were arguing. Was Mom upset that I might be a lesbian?"

"No. She was not upset with you. Mika, they were so proud of you and your accomplishments. They wanted you to be happy, and if that meant you being with a girl, they wouldn't have cared."

"Did Mom tell you she didn't want me graduating high school early?"

"No, your dad did. He thought you were ready, but your mom worried about your anxiety."

Mika stood and walked over to the large bay window to look into the hotel's courtyard. "Mom would love this garden." She turned around and leaned against the window frame. "Do you still have the letters?"

Aunt Val nodded. "They're in a box back in Ithaca."

"I need to go for a walk. This is a lot to digest." She headed to the door.

"I know the area. I'll go with you."

Mika stopped and rubbed her forehead. "Okay. But I want silence. I need to absorb this."

They walked to a cool bridge with crisscrossing red supports. A sign read the Peace Bridge. This had to be their time to find peace after all the shit they'd been through. Mika stopped in the middle. She'd always wanted to know about her conception and birth, but this was fucking mind-blowing. Hannah was her mom, but she loved Aunt Val more than an aunt. Aunt Val was hurting too, and maybe she needed to hear those words. Mika put her arm around her aunt's shoulders, and in return, Aunt Val put her arm around Mika's waist, and they looked out at the water. "I'm sorry about my attitude and all the crap I've put you through."

"No need to apologize, sweetie. You're much younger and—"

"Hear me out." She turned and placed her hand on her aunt's shoulder. "Yeah, I'm younger, and damn, I've made a ton of mistakes. I love my parents and miss them so fucking much." Her voice shook, and she took a few calm minutes to find her courage. "You made one hell of a promise to them, and I exist because of that. And even though I gave you a tough time, you've done so much for me." She pulled a napkin from her pocket, wiped her eyes and blew her nose. "After all we've been through, I've grown to love you more than an aunt. I mean, my mom's my mom, but you're kinda like a mom to me. And I feel how much I mean to you." She lowered her head. "I'm screwing this up."

"I get it, and it means a lot to hear those words." Tears gathered in Aunt Val's eyes.

"Thank you for making that promise."

They hugged and walked back, arm in arm. After stepping off the Peace Bridge, she looked back at the calm river flowing below. It was going to be okay.

Chapter Forty-One

MIKA ROLLED OVER ONTO her side. It was close to six thirty a.m. and quiet. Aunt Val and Brie's bedroom door was shut. They might have had a good night's sleep, but her night had been hell. She'd tossed and turned and was wide awake around two a.m. When she couldn't sleep, she noticed the headphones that were paired to the TV. Bad decision. After being glued to it for three hours, she turned it off and sat up in the sofa sleeper with her knees pulled tight to her chest, her mind whirling out of control. Sometime in the early hours, she miraculously dozed off.

A tear rolled down Mika's cheek, and she curled up like a baby. She needed Willow. Her head hurt, and she was so tired, but her mind took off again. When she finally calmed down, she grabbed the set of clean clothes and showered then went downstairs. The dining room was busier than she expected.

"Room number or last name, please," the hostess said cheerfully.

"Ah, I'm staying with my aunt. Sorry, I didn't know a reservation was required." She started to walk away.

"Miss, it's not. I'm required to input the info into the computer."

"Oh. My aunt's Val Hayden." Mika stuck her hands in her pockets. "Maybe I can just get a to-go coffee."

"It's dine-in only, and I see your aunt has a reservation for eight a.m. Also the buffet is prepaid. I can seat you now if you'd like."

"Hi, Mika. You're up early."

She turned to see Brie. "Hey."

Brie put her hand on Mika's shoulder. "I heard you in the shower when I went out for a walk. Have a seat. I'll wake Val, and we'll come down soon, okay?"

"Sure." Thankfully, Brie didn't mention the dark circles under her eyes.

"Hang in there. We go home today."

The hostess seated her at a table with a garden view. She zoned out with a coffee and watched the birds. When Aunt Val and Brie joined her, Brie tried to joke around but Mika wasn't in the mood to laugh. She was hungry and wolfed down a cheese omelet and a waffle.

"We should get ready for the airport," her aunt said.

"Sit and enjoy your coffee." Brie rose and kissed the top of her head. "I'm going to call Dani and recheck the flight times. I'll see you upstairs soon."

Mika perked up. "Can I drive us home from Toronto?"

"Nice try." Brie lightly slapped Mika's shoulder. "You have to be twenty-one to drive a rental. But my sister and her husband volunteered to pick us up."

Mika watched Brie leave, then she shoved her plate aside and wiped her mouth. "This hotel is really fancy. The headphones next to the TV can be paired so that you can watch a show late at night without disturbing anyone."

"You wouldn't have woken us." Her aunt sipped her coffee.

"I caught part of the late-night news then watched Netflix." Mika looked for a reaction.

Aunt Val's hand stilled, and she set the cup down. Mika was glad the tables had emptied out around them. This wasn't shit she didn't want anyone to overhear. "They showed footage of the camp being raided and said all the teenagers were taken into protective custody. Canada was good to me, but I'll never set foot in Wyoming again." Mika folded her arms.

"You have a right to be sad and angry." Her aunt put her hand on top of Mika's.

"They also showed my school picture." Mika's temples throbbed.

"We haven't said anything, and I don't know how they dug stuff up. It's possible that Pauline or your grandparents carelessly said something to their friends."

Mika shrugged. "However it happened, they got their hands on a high school yearbook. My picture's probably all over the internet." She bit her fingernail.

"Don't look. It'll just be depressing. Hopefully, it'll blow over quickly."

"Do you know if there's anything else going on?" She searched for an answer in Aunt Val's eyes, but she'd thrown up her poker face. "Tell me."

"Days after you went into Canadian housing, Naomi called. The media found Willow and reporters were trying to get a statement from her. I didn't mention it to you because I didn't want to upset you."

Mika put her head in her hands. "Willow didn't mention it on the phone. Is she okay?"

"She's fine. You've got a real spitfire for a girlfriend. An LGBTQ organization wanted to interview you and Willow for a documentary against conversion therapy. She agreed to talk to you about it. She's been very protective."

Mika smiled through tears, but even thinking of Willow didn't cheer her up this time. The vivid images that she'd tried to push out of her mind kept coming back. "It'd be cool if my story helps others, but I need some downtime first. It's raw." She stared at her aunt. "Do you know why I watched Netflix?"

"I'm guessing it's not because it's the number one streaming service. I love you. Naomi and I will get you and Willow settled into college, and everything will be fine," her aunt said softly.

"Will it? Or are you making a promise you can't keep?" She hadn't been in the camp long but feared the disturbing dreams would follow her for years. She wet her lips. "The news mentioned a show on Netflix called *The Program*. That's what I watched for three hours solid. It's about private schools for 'troubled teens.'" She made quotation marks with her fingers, then sat back and shoved down the pain. Thankfully, Aunt Val didn't interrupt her silence or try to tell her everything would be all right.

"It was close to what I suffered. But no matter how much it bothered me, I kept watching." Mika rubbed her eye with the heel of her hand. "It's sickening that some parents send their kids off for years. One kid was fourteen when she went to that fucking school. And the woman who made the documentary... Do you know what trouble she caused to get sent away as a teen? She got caught with a Mike's Hard Lemonade. That's it." She sniffled, and Aunt Val handed her some tissues. "No one regulates these so-called schools. And when one shuts down, the owners go to another state or even to another country to do their evil shit." She wiped her eyes, then pounded her fist on the table. "Maybe not every conversion therapy camp or troubled teen school uses violence and brain washing, but it doesn't make it right." She covered her face with her hands.

"I'll always listen to you, but I think you should also talk to Iliana."

"After we get home, I will." Mika dropped her hands. "Do you know there were eight complaints against the camp I was in? Two were from kids that escaped. Why didn't anyone believe them?" She took a deep breath and blew it out. "I've been lucky to have a great family, but it hurts that a lot of kids don't. Thanks for being there for me." She squeezed her aunt's hand.

"We had to get you out. I love you, and I always have."

"Getting me out was huge. I'm so grateful because they almost broke me. How many of those schools are out there hiding under God's word? We have freedom of religion, and I'm all for it, but not when it hurts. The US should be like Canada and ban conversion therapy." She wiped her eyes again. "A small part of me wants to run away and hide, but a bigger part of me wants to fight. I've decided that if anyone asks, I'm not going to sugar coat it. I just hope telling my story helps others."

"That's very courageous." Her aunt's alarm chimed on her phone.

"We should get ready for the airport." Mika stood. A piece of her felt relieved to get it all out even though her drained body and jumbled emotions were a wreck. "And I need to put on my new Mars T-shirt. Thanks for the present. It's perfect. Hope you don't mind me wearing it a second day."

"Not at all, and you're welcome."

As they walked up the steps, Mika couldn't stop thinking about the documentary. "They were all brave."

"The kids in your camp?"

"Everyone in the documentary. It's a shame more people don't understand what goes on in their own backyard. I hope more people watch it."

Mika didn't say one word during the taxi ride to the airport. Slowly, she began to relax...until they reached security.

"Miss, step through the scanner, please. It doesn't hurt."

Mika stepped inside, raised her arms up, and closed her eyes. A female security motioned for her to step forward.

"Wide stance with the legs and arms straight out to the side, please."

The blood drained from Mika's body as the officer patted her down.

"You're good to go."

She didn't move.

"Miss, you look faint. Are you okay?" the officer said.

"Mika, do you want to sit down?" Aunt Val asked.

She stepped away. "No. At least it's not a body cavity search. One in a lifetime is enough for me."

Brie gathered their carry-on bags, and they headed for their gate.

"Let's go home." Her aunt put her arm around Mika's shoulders. "Window or aisle?" she asked as they boarded.

"Window." After settling in, Mika looked out over the airfield. In the distance, she could see the Canadian Rockies. She'd return some day and hike the mountains and canoe on Lake Louise.

"Here." Brie passed Mika her iPhone and wireless headset.

"Our ticket comes with high-speed Wi-Fi."

"Dope. Thanks Brie." Once they reached altitude, Mika connected and browsed her favorites on Apple Music.

Hours later, Aunt Val tapped her on the shoulder. "You need to disconnect. We're landing soon.

"Thanks." Mika handed back Brie's stuff and nudged her aunt. "It's interesting that we're landing in the city where I was born."

"You were officially born in St. Catharines, Ontario, near the border."

"Do you want to visit Ontario another time with me and Willow?"

"I'd love to."

They'd spent nearly six hours between the taxi to the airport, arriving early, and the flight. Her aunt looked tired, so Mika slowed her pace as they walked to the luggage carousel.

"There's Dani," Brie shouted and waved.

"Oh, no," Aunt Val said.

Mika looked in the direction of her aunt's gaze. A crowd of reporters rushed at them. One man pushed a microphone in her face.

"We've heard you were abused in the camp. What happened? Or did you make it all up?"

Mika wouldn't move when Aunt Val tugged on her arm. She balled up her fist and glared at him, but Brie pushed him back. "They withheld food and didn't allow me to sleep for several days. Do you think that's okay?" Mika shook off her aunt's arm and stepped toward him. "And I didn't confess to their so-called sins. So they made me stand for hours in the corner of a room with a heavy bag of rocks on my back. When that didn't work, they hit me with a belt. They're the ones that're full of sin."

"The camp denies those things," the man said.

"The camp is lying," Mika yelled.

A hush fell over the crowd, including those walking past the reporters. It was like the entire airport had stopped functioning, and everyone was looking at them.

"Mika, I'm sorry you went through that horrendous ordeal. I'm from the Canadian office of the International LGBTQ+ Alliance, and we support you." The tall woman handed Mika a card. "The US number's on there as well. Call if you need anything. Safe travels home." She turned to the crowd of reporters. "Please back up and give them room."

"I can't believe airport security didn't have a handle on this," Brie said.

"Hi, guys." Dani waved. "Ryan's out front. Let's get out of this zoo."

A few people snapped pictures along the way, but no one invaded their space again.

Dani sat up front with her husband Ryan and motioned for Aunt Val and Brie to take the middle set of seats. "Mika, take the back row—we brought you a present." Dani grinned.

Mika glanced over and saw a lump under a blanket. She scrambled in the back and pulled it away.

"Surprise." Willow pulled Mika down for a lingering kiss.

"Wow, Dani, you work miracles," her aunt said. "Ahem. Young ladies, you might want to be more discreet until we get home because of the media."

Mika popped her head up and gave them all a huge smile.

"Okay, but I'm keeping my arm around her all the way home. I'm never letting her go," Willow said.

"Ditto." Mika kissed Willow's forehead. "Thanks for the surprise, guys. Hey, I didn't eat any food on the four-hour plane ride. Can we stop for a burger? Maybe there's a Five Guys around here."

"I'm sure." Ryan grinned at them through the rearview mirror.

"I'll search," Dani said. "Oh, there's one twenty minutes away." She punched the address into the SUV's GPS.

Mika ordered the big bacon cheeseburger with a third patty and a large cup of Cajun fries.

Aunt Val turned around. "Any chance I can have a fry?"

"Sorry." Mika held up the crumpled empty bag.

"There's no way you could have eaten it that fast?"

Mika grinned with her mouth shut, chewing.

"She ate most of the fries and only gave me one bite of her burger." Willow giggled.

"It's good to see you smile," Aunt Val said.

"Your aunt said you've had some rough days, but she didn't give me any deets," Willow said.

"Yeah. Maybe we'll talk about it later." Mika put her arm around Willow. "But seeing you is the best shot of medicine. We're going home and moving to New York City soon. I'm lucky that you're mine." She shed a few happy tears when Willow put her head on her shoulder and began to talk about the city's music, museums, pizza, and street food...

"We should get tickets to the *Kelly Clarkson Show* or *Saturday Night Live*. Wouldn't that be lit?" Mika asked.

Willow's face lit up. "That'd be fantastic."

"I have to take you to a Rangers' hockey game." Mika twirled a strand of Willow's hair.

"Okay, and at Christmas, we have to go ice skating at Rockefeller Center's rink. I want to see their huge tree and kiss you under its lights," Willow said.

Mika's fingers stilled, and silence filled the SUV.

"I'm sorry. That just popped out. I know Christmas is hard for you."

"Yes, I'd love to go ice skating with you." Mika swallowed. "I went with Mom and Dad one year. Everything was fine until the end." She gazed off and smiled. "I raced to catch up with Dad. He saw me and speeded up, but not like me. I took off like a speed demon and wiped out hard around the corner."

"Did you hurt yourself or someone else?"

"No. But it was against the rules, and they kicked us out. I had to apologize, and Mom was upset." She looked into Willow's eyes. "Dad usually played by the rules, and he wasn't going that fast. When Mom said his rebel streak encouraged me, he winked at me."

"Sounds like it all ended well."

"Yeah. After he'd checked that I was okay, he took my hand and said his usual, *Woulda, coulda, shoulda. Move on.*"

Aunt Val patted Mika's knee. "You'll move on to Columbia and do great things."

That old song her parents liked, something about getting by with the help of friends, popped into Mika's thoughts. She was surrounded by people that cared for and loved her, and at the top of the list was Aunt Val and Willow. It was up to Mika now to accept and give love, gratitude, and help because in life, there was no save and restart option like with her games. There was only the here and now. Yeah, life could be messy and hard, but there was hope and possibilities with Willow and Aunt Val by her side. The only hard part left before college was visiting her parents' graves.

Chapter Forty-Two

Mika woke up in her room. She rolled onto her back in bed and drifted off into a half-sleep. The bathroom door creaked open, and the scent of sunny citrus made her stir. Was she dreaming?

"Hey, sleepy head. Get up, and let's have some breakfast."

Mika opened her eyes, and Willow smiled down at her.

"You dropped like a rock last night." Willow glided her soft fingertips over Mika's cheek and kissed her lips tenderly.

"So, I'm not dreaming. It's over?"

"Yes."

"You smell fantastic." Mika squeezed Willow's hand and smiled. "And you're in a bathrobe with wet hair."

"And you're deliciously naked."

Mika glanced at the door.

"Why do you look worried?" Willow kissed her breast.

"Aunt Val."

Willow ran her fingers through Mika's hair. "Seventeen is the legal age of consent in New York." She kissed Mika deeply. "Plus your aunt and Mom are letting you sleep over at my house tonight. Now get up and shower so we can have lunch before I go."

"Why?" Mika pulled Willow down on top her.

"I have a Zoom with my CUNY advisor at one." Willow played with her hair.

"You can Zoom with your college from here," Mika said.

"I'd love to, but the paperwork we need to discuss is on my home computer. Spend the afternoon with your aunt; she missed you so much." Willow smacked the side of her butt. "You need to shower."

"I'll shower if you hop in with me."

"I just showered." Willow rolled her eyes. "But for you, devil woman, I'll do it. You better make it worth my while."

"I promise."

The steam from the warm water and their two hot bodies fogged up the bathroom pretty quick. Mika gently caressed every inch of Willow's body. She lingered on her soft breasts, taking them into her mouth. And as she did, Willow put her hand between Mika's legs.

"Open up for me," Willow said.

Mika gasped in pleasure as Willow glided over her clit. She came pretty quickly. After catching her breath, she looked at the teak shower bench and nodded for Willow to sit down. She got to her knees and pushed Willow's legs apart. She wanted Willow bad and began a faster than usual pace. As Willow came, she grabbed Mika's hair and pulled her in.

"That was the best shower of my life. But I don't think you actually got clean," Willow said.

"Wash me." Mika placed the sponge into Willow's hand.

"I will."

After getting dressed, Willow put on some light makeup.

"You look gorgeous without it, you know," Mika said.

"Thanks." Willow glanced back at her through the mirror.

Mika cleared her throat, and Willow turned around. "Mom's birthday is next week. I wanted to take flowers to my parents' grave."

"I think that's a great idea. Your aunt's probably thinking the same. Have you talked to her?"

"Not yet." Mika sat on the bed.

"Well, that's one thing you could bond over. Um, what day is your mom's birthday?"

"Friday. The day before we leave for the city." Tears came to Mika's eyes. "In Canada, I'd sit in my room and think about what I wanted to say to Aunt Val and to my mom if she were here. There's so much, but it's like my brain freezes, and it's hard to think, let alone talk to anyone." She looked up at Willow. "Lately, I'm happy, then it's like whiplash into sadness."

Willow sat down next to her. "You weren't like this before the accident, and Iliana never put you on meds."

Mika bit her lip and hung her head. "There's something I have to say." She looked into Willow's eyes. "I never thought it was a big deal before, so I never mentioned it. I hope it doesn't upset you."

"What?"

Mika sighed. "I was first bullied in seventh grade, then things got worse. Mom and Dad took me to our doctor and a therapist briefly. They said I had an anxiety disorder but was high-functioning, meaning I look like I have everything under control, but inside, I'm second guessing, overthinking, and worried a lot. They put me on Zoloft. That helped, then the camp messed everything up. I didn't have my medicine, and they terrorized me. I'm back on it now, but it has to be increased slowly. My dosage before was one hundred milligrams once a day. So I'm sort of broken."

Willow placed her hands on Mika's cheeks. "Cut yourself a break. You're not broken, and I'm not mad that you didn't tell me before. But you might want to see Iliana before you leave, and I'm sure that Columbia offers good therapy services."

"Yeah, I want to continue therapy." Mika took a deep breath and let it out. "I'm anxious now because I haven't been to my parents' grave since the burial."

"Oh."

"Aunt Val has, but I haven't. I really need to go this time. I'm ready."

Willow put her arm around Mika's waist and leaned her head on her shoulder. "I'll be there for you."

"Thanks."

After a few minutes of silence, Willow took Mika's hand. "Let's eat lunch."

Mika didn't move when she tugged. "I..." Tears came to her

eyes. "There's a lot that went down at the camp. I heard about the LGBTQ+ organization wanting to interview us. I'd like to sometime, but I don't think I'm ready to even tell you."

"I get it. And so you know, I read the things you said to the reporter in Toronto airport." Willow kissed her hand. "You don't have to talk about it until you're ready and only if you want to. Taking time isn't a bad thing."

Mika nodded and stood. "What are you going to fix me for lunch? I'm hungry."

"Me? I thought you were my personal chef." Willow laughed.

Over lunch, Willow filled her in on what everyone had been doing while she was gone. All too soon, it was time for Willow to leave.

"Spend time with your aunt," Willow said again. She kissed Mika and left.

Mika shut the door. The house was too quiet. She looked around and found her aunt in the sunroom. "You're tucked in a corner out of sight."

Aunt Val put her book and reading glasses on the end table. "Best of all, it's the farthest from your bedroom. Did you have a good visit with Willow?"

"Great." Mika could feel her skin heat up from the blush spreading over her face. She looked out the window at the cleaned-up garden. "Who planted new flowers and pruned all the bushes?"

"I hired a company. There's still some work to be done. Seems like pulling weeds is an unending job."

"It's perfect. Mom would have loved it," Mika said softly. "Mom's birthday's next week. I want to put flowers on their grave before we all leave for New York."

"That sounds perfect, Mika. I'd like to do that too."

The chirping of the birds were the only sounds for several minutes.

"Sometimes I feel like I never knew them because of all the

information they kept from me. You mentioned you have a box of letters." Mika looked at her aunt. "I'd like to read them."

"Many of them are personal. We argued in some and swore at each other in some."

"Mom cursed? I never heard her."

Aunt Val smiled. "She'd drop the F-bomb sometimes, but I would make a sailor blush."

"Can you pick out some just about me? Please."

"Sure." Her aunt placed her hand on Mika's forearm. "Give me an hour."

"I'll take a walk." August was hot as always, but today wasn't bad with the fluffy clouds and the breeze. After six blocks, she turned around. When she returned home, her aunt wasn't in the house. Mika looked in the backyard to find her pulling weeds and wearing her mom's old knee pads and garden gloves. Mika fixed her a glass of lemonade.

"You've got a water bottle, but I make a great lemonade." Mika handed over the plastic glass.

"Thanks."

Sweat beaded on Aunt Val's brow, and her T-shirt was damp across the middle.

"Maybe you should take a break and come inside."

Her aunt took off the gloves and knee pads and led Mika into the gazebo. "There are some letters in there that I thought you'd like to read." She pointed to a small box next to a tissue box in the center of the table. "And you might need those too."

"Thanks."

"I needed an hour because I knew I'd cry along the way. Why don't you read the first one while I'm here? Then I'll give you some privacy."

Mika removed the lid, and on top of the pile was a picture of her as a young child helping her mom in the garden. She had a trowel in her hand and a lot of dirt on her clothes and face. She unfolded the letter.

Dear Val,
Hannah and Michaela are planting in the garden. It's
hard to believe that she'll be six soon. She's a sweet
child and curious. We don't push stereotypical girlie
ways on her, and she'll go for the Hot Wheels at
the toy store over a Barbie any day. She made a
make-believe city out of some thin cardboard boxes
that we hadn't busted up for recycling. She cut them
to size, colored them, and taped them to a piece
of plywood in the garage. Then she used my scrap
lumber to make roads for her cars. You can imagine
my surprise and delight in finding her creation. She
also likes Legos. I think our kiddo's going to be an
engineer someday. I thank you every day for our gift.
Love,
Andrew

Tears flowed. Mika grabbed a handful of tissues and cried.

"Oh, sweetie." Aunt Val rubbed her back and pulled some tissues out to dab her eyes.

"It's good. This is what I wanted. Thank you. Can you leave me alone now?"

"Sure."

Mika watched her aunt walk across the green grass to the corner flower bed before picking up the next letter. A picture of her and Dad on skis was attached this one.

Hi, Sis,
I'm sorry about what I've said in the past. I miss you.
I know you said it was hard to see Michaela for a
vacation then leave, but I wish you'd come and visit.
It's hard to believe that she's in the middle of seventh
grade. Like you, she's super good at school and
likes math and science the best.

She's also a tomboy, tall with an athletic build and likes lots of sports. I think she leans towards individual ones. Right now, she's into skiing with Andrew. Her first period was last month. She's not happy is an understatement. She asked me if the doctors could do something because she never wanted a period and doesn't ever want to have a baby. I wasn't sure how to answer. I chickened out and said she could ask the doctor at her next physical. While she seems adamant about children, I hope she changes her mind someday. I'd like to be a grandma.
I've written this last part so many times in my head, but I think I'll say it anyway. Thank you for promising to carry her. I didn't think about all the complications, not the paperwork, but the complications to your heart. I know it was hard to give her up. I've come to terms that you love her as a daughter, even though you don't see her much. So someday, maybe you'll be a grandma too.
Love,
Hannah

"And I still don't want one popping out of me," she mumbled as if her mom could hear. She wiped away her tears, but they flowed so fast.

The next letter didn't have a photo.

Dear Val,
I mentioned the other day that our kiddo might be gay. Hannah thought I was making a hasty assumption, and that we should wait and let things play out. She did say that her biggest concern was Mika's happiness. Val, you know we aren't homophobic. I think Hannah wants Mika to tell us when she's ready.

But I have to tell you, I worry that Hannah fears our parents' reaction. You don't need to worry because Hannah and I won't allow anybody, including our parents, to shame our child.
Love,
Andrew
P.S. At fifteen, I guess I need to stop calling her kiddo, but she'll always be my baby.

Mika had always thought it was easier to talk to Benjy rather than her parents. And when she realized she wasn't straight, reading queer books or searching the internet had been her main source of information. But God, she wished she could go back in time.

The last letter was from her dad right before Thanksgiving, and Mika had to stop a zillion times to wipe away tears and blow her nose.

Dear Val,
I've rewritten my will and other essential papers with the help of a colleague. The other was done when Mika was four. Hannah will say the new one is unnecessary, but I know she'll sign it. You're the logical choice for Mika's guardian, but Hannah has favored my sister in the past. Let me explain before you get angry. Mika is close to Pauline's daughters, but Hannah doesn't want Mika moved from New York. In the past, she's argued that you could move back to Europe at a moment's notice. She's also worried that you're a workaholic. Confess. You are. Still, you deserve to be Mika's guardian after giving us such a beautiful gift. None of us are sick, and I plan on living to a hundred, but I like being prepared.
Love,

Andrew

Mika closed the box, tucked it under her arm, and walked out to Aunt Val.

"Thanks for sharing these."

"You're welcome." Her aunt brushed off her pants. "I'm done here. But I'm sure I'll have more weeds to pull in a week."

"Do you mind if I share these letters with Willow?"

"Not at all. And I'm spending the night at Brie's." Her aunt winked.

Mika grinned.

Aunt Val put her arm around her. "It'll be exciting to see your face when you check in as a college freshman, but I'm going to miss you. You can expect a lot of visits from Brie and me."

"I'm counting on it. And I promise to call a lot."

"I'm going to the florist tomorrow to order flowers for our visit to your parents' grave. Brie's coming with me. Do you know what flowers you'd like to take? Or would you and Willow like to come with us?"

"Mom always liked yellow roses. Could you pick a bouquet that has some of those?" Mika held back the tears.

"Of course."

They walked some more in silence.

"What will you do after I go to college? Will you go back full time and move?" Mika asked.

"I'm in charge of your trust, which means I have to take care of the college fund and the house." Aunt Val shook her head. "And I haven't a clue why your parents chose twenty-five as the age for you to inherit it all. I can only guess they thought you'd be more mature."

"Maybe they thought I'd have my master's and be employed by then." Mika smiled through her tears. "The will says you're free to stay here until the house is turned over to me. It'd be easier if you stayed, and I hope you do. Brie could move in." Mika shrugged.

"The way things are going, you two could be married next month."

Her aunt raised her eyebrow. "I'm enjoying the relationship, but let's not rush the marriage part."

"I like to poke you because you're fun to get a rise out of."

"You're too much like your dad, prankster." Her aunt rubbed her hair.

"Yeah, I am." She swallowed. "And for once, it makes me really happy. Let's enjoy the following days before Friday, 'cause that's really going to hurt." Mika teared up again, and Aunt Val held her hand.

Nothing in life was perfect or guaranteed. She was lucky Aunt Val had come back into her life, and even luckier to find a girlfriend as smart, sexy, and caring as Willow. She was going to hold on tight. Now more than ever, family was everything.

Chapter Forty-Three

MIKA LOOKED AT WILLOW, curled up on her side and sleeping soundly. God, she was gorgeous. With no makeup, her freckles stood out, and Mika wanted to kiss every single one. After coming home, she and Willow had spent every spare minute together, planning their future in New York City.

Exposure to the city's culture, art galleries, and other artists would further Willow's talent. Columbia would be a fantastic beginning for Mika, and she'd found a job in a used bookstore on the Upper West Side. They vowed to work hard in school and their jobs to make their dream of living together a reality. But as bright as their future was, Mika still suffered from bouts of sadness, and the significance of today hit her hard and sucked away that joy.

A tear rolled down her face as she watched Willow sleep. How could she be selfish enough to think about their future when today was one of the saddest of the year? August twenty-fifth, her mom's birthday. She would've been forty-eight. Controlling her emotions today was going to be tough. She slid out of bed and into the bathroom. Soon, she felt Willow's arms wrap around her.

"I'm with you, always. I love you, Mika Lavigne. Remember that, even when we're apart."

Mika closed her eyes tight to hold back the tears. She could never get enough of those words. She turned around. "I love you too, Willow Parker."

Willow rested her forehead on Mika's. "I think your parents are with us today and every day."

"Yeah." Another tear rolled down Mika's cheek. She put her hands on Willow's hips and drew her closer.

"Good morning," Aunt Val said from outside the door. "Let's have a light breakfast before heading out."

"Give us fifteen minutes, please," Willow said.

Mika led Willow to the shower. There was no playfulness, just plenty of tender care as Willow ran a soap-filled sponge over their bodies. Willow was right: Mika could do this. She had to do this.

Breakfast and the forty-minute trip to the cemetery whizzed by as she zoned out. When the car stopped, her tears flowed again. Willow helped her out. Brie and Aunt Val walked hand in hand. Brie held a floral bouquet in her free hand. God, Mika didn't even remember picking Brie up.

Willow kissed her cheek. "Remember, I love you. I'm with you, always."

Barely able to see through her puffy eyes, she inched closer to the headstone.

Mika's parents were buried in a plot next to her Lavigne great-grandparents in Saint Patrick's Cemetery. Her Hayden grandparents were buried with other ancestors in Trumansburg, but that town was the opposite direction.

"Mika, I hope you don't mind or think it's weird, but I want to say some words to my sister and your dad out loud."

"I was thinking the same thing. Go ahead."

Aunt Val took part of the floral bouquet and placed it in the permanent vase. She stepped back and squeezed Brie's hand. "Hello, sis. I miss you. I'm dating this wonderful woman named Brie Owens. She's settled me down. I love her." She dabbed her eyes with a tissue. "Hannah, you were so damn bossy at times, but you were my loyal and fiercest friend growing up and the best sister anyone could ever have." Her voice faltered. "I'm sorry we disagreed at times, and so sorry that I let work consume me. You were a wonderful mother." Her body shook, and she lowered her head. "Andrew, you were always there to talk sense into us and bring us together. You were a fantastic husband and father."

Mika's heart squeezed as Aunt Val glanced over at her. She

had to tighten her grip on Willow to keep from falling over.

Aunt Val wiped more tears away and briefly touched the headstone. "I'm sorry I wasn't there as much as I should have been, but I'm making up for lost time. Being Mika's guardian was a little hard at first, but we got through it. She's an amazing young person. You'd be proud of her for getting accepted into Columbia. Thank you both for picking me to help give life to her. And it meant so much to me when you kept the name I gave her at birth."

Mika threw herself onto her aunt and hugged her fiercely. They clung together and cried. When Mika regained control, she took the other half of the bouquet, kneeled on the ground, and placed it in the vase. Willow dropped next to her and held her hand. It gave Mika some strength as she faced the headstone. Although the sun beat down on them, seeing her parents' names carved in granite was like a cold knife through her soul.

"I miss you, Mom and Dad, so freaking much." Mika turned and kissed Willow's cheek. "I got pretty lucky too. This is my girlfriend, Willow. She's the best." Mika briefly squeezed her eyes tight. "Dad, you were always the coolest in the world, a total softie. Mom, I loved you so much, even though you were the enforcer in the house. Looking back, I needed my ass kicked every now and then." Mika sniffled. "And Mom, I can't thank you enough for asking your sister to give me life. She's doing great, considering I gave her hell. And it'll be damn hard, but I promise not to kick over the Christmas tree this year. Aunt Val's become special to me. I love her more than an aunt, but you'll always be my mom." Mika rose and hugged Willow, then Aunt Val. "Thank you for loving and taking care of me. I'm so grateful you came back to Ithaca."

"I think I needed you as much as you needed me." Her aunt blew her nose.

"I still need you." Although Mika had cried an ocean, the love inside pushed through, and she smiled.

"Me too, sweetie." Aunt Val kissed her forehead.

The warmth of love spread through Mika, helping to dry the

tears. Her mom and dad were her parents. They nourished her soul and helped her grow. Mika loved Aunt Val almost as much as she'd loved her mom, the wonderful mother she grew up with. She knew that her aunt would always be there for her, no matter what tough challenges she faced. Aunt Val had proven that when she rescued her.

Willow and Brie joined them for a group hug. They were a chosen family. Mika would miss Aunt Val and Brie when she moved to the city. Yet every choice she made was a chance to learn something new. She was ready to follow her dreams, and she believed she and Willow would be one of the few lucky couples that stayed together. Silently, she vowed to work hard to make that happen.

She and Willow trailed behind Aunt Val and Brie as they headed back to the car. On the way, Mika glanced up at the sky, and felt her parents' presence. She tugged on Willow's hand.

"Do you want to go back for a few minutes?" Willow asked.

Aunt Val and Brie stopped.

"No. It just hit me," Mika said. She looked at Willow then at her aunt. "I hated English and couldn't remember things when I needed to, but a quote that Dad liked from Ralph Waldo Emerson just popped into my head. *What lies behind you and what lies in front of you, pales in comparison to what lies inside of you.*" Mika removed a tissue from her pocket and blew her nose. "It's like he's wishing me well with my future and giving me a push forward."

Aunt Val smiled through tears. "That sounds like Andrew."

"And I know you have strength and intelligence to make it." Willow placed her arm around Mika's waist.

"With you by my side." Mika pulled Willow in and kissed her cheek. "I love you," she whispered.

"I love you too."

Chapter Forty-Four

14 years later

MIKA PULLED HER WINTER jacket tight around herself as she walked toward the church. It had been many years since she'd seen her Lavigne grandparents, even after they'd confessed that it was their sole decision to send her to that camp. What crushed Mika the most was they hadn't believed her story until the video of Mika telling the Canadian authorities surfaced in the courtroom. Her grandparents had made numerous apologies since, but Mika had brushed them aside and refused to see them.

Over the years, her Lavigne grandparents abandoned their harsh views, joined PFLAG, and donated significant money to LGBTQ+ charities. But Mika's deep emotional wounds kept her from trying to reform the tight relationship they once enjoyed, and she'd only made contact through letters.

Mika slowed her pace to the church as she recalled her conversation with Willow yesterday. "Sweetheart, did you know your grandparents are speaking out against conversion therapy in Binghamton?"

"So?" Mika jammed the leftovers in the fridge.

"Just wanted you to know." Willow kissed her cheek and dropped the subject.

If it hadn't been for Willow, Mika wouldn't know half of how her grandparents had changed. But Willow never pressured her. Later that night, Mika made her decision to go. And now, here she was.

She stared at the Binghamton Unitarian Universalist Church and blew out a deep breath. The vapor lingered in the air before dispersing. Part of her wanted to go in, and part wanted to flee. Why, of all places, had her grandparents chosen to speak here? And two days before Christmas too. The mixture of memories flooded her mind, but it was time to forgive. Mika slowly moved toward the doors.

She entered and sat in the far back corner as her grandparents were introduced. Her grandmother appeared to be in great shape, but her grandfather shook, even when sitting. Mika's heart sunk. Grandmother was eighty-seven, and Grandfather was ninety-four. He had to be helped to the podium as he staggered along on his cane. They each took turns speaking, and she was pleasantly surprised at how their convictions had flipped. If only they'd been so loving and accepting when she was a kid.

The audience applauded politely, and everyone's questions were respectful except one critic. He voiced several barbed comments, not seeming to care that they were elderly. As the moderator calmly addressed the man, her grandfather hobbled with his cane and the assistance of a younger man to the podium. Mika noticed her grandfather's back was now humped.

"Don't be like how I was." His voice shook. "I thought the camp was the way toward our granddaughter's salvation. I lost her love because I was full of religious fervor and ignorance." He repeatedly jabbed at his chest sharply with his index finger.

Mika was too far back to see tears, but she heard his voice choking up.

"I never knew they were abusive, and never in my wildest dreams did I ever imagine the lengths they'd go to. They were sadistic."

The sound of the sorrow in his voice was unmistakable. He hung his head, then Mika's grandmother stood and rubbed his back. It seemed to give him strength, and he stepped from behind the podium with his head held high and the assistant on one side holding his arm and her grandmother on the other.

"I don't know if our granddaughter will ever forgive us fully because of the emotional and physical abuse she suffered. But even the camps that are not as rough shame those we should love. It's not right, and I was wrong. My granddaughter is who God made her. She's a beautiful person."

"God has room in his heart for everyone," Grandmother Lavigne said. "I love my gay granddaughter, her wife, and her family. They have a right, just like anyone, to live happily and freely. And they have a right to have children."

Their solid support shocked Mika so much that she sat still for several seconds before joining the audience in a standing ovation. When the program ended, Mika remained in her seat, watching her grandparents chat with others. Then she saw Aunt Pauline walking toward her.

"Hello, Mika," her aunt whispered.

"Hi." Mika had forgiven Aunt Pauline because she'd alerted Aunt Val about the camp and had testified against her parents for their deception and actions. "I haven't heard from Jenn lately. How's she doing?" she asked without taking her gaze from her grandparents.

"She loves her job in Portland. I thought she'd be the partyholic in the family, not the workaholic."

"Me too." Mika grinned. She never would have guessed her cousin would turn out to be a hotshot real estate agent on the West Coast. "And Carla? Is she okay after splitting with her long-term boyfriend?" The jerk had cheated on Carla after they'd lived together for two years.

Aunt Pauline chuckled softly. "She's happy and moving to Los Angeles next month with her new love, Rachel."

Mika's head whipped around. "You're kidding?"

"Nope. They've been going back and forth between LA and New York for months, and now they're engaged. So, Mother and Father have two gay granddaughters." Her aunt smiled broadly.

Mika had never seen that coming. "And how'd they react to that?" From Aunt Pauline's grin, it seemed she welcomed her daughter's happiness.

"They introduced her to Carla last year. Rachel works for Equality California. She's wonderful and adores my daughter."

"That's great." Wow, everyone had changed dramatically for the better.

"Thank you, Mika. You made it easier for Carla not to be afraid to be herself." Aunt Pauline squeezed Mika's shoulder, then pointed to her parents. "It'd mean the world to them if you'd say hello."

Her grandmother looked over in their direction. "Mika, dear," she said and moved swiftly while her grandfather shuffled along with his cane and his assistant.

They hugged, and Mika's rough exterior fell away.

"It's so good to see you, sweetie," her grandfather said.

"It's good to see you too. I listened to your speech. Thank you for being so supportive. I'm sorry that I didn't come to see you sooner."

"And I'm sorry it took me too damn long to come to my senses. Is your family with you?" He glanced around.

Mika felt guilty for telling Willow she wanted to come alone tonight. "They're not here, but we're staying with Aunt Val and Brie."

"Good, good. Maybe you can drive down to Binghamton one day and visit before you head home to Maryland," her grandfather said.

"You're welcome anytime. Mother and Father are staying with me for the holidays, but I'm trying to talk them into moving here permanently," Aunt Pauline said.

"That'd be lovely. I'll call. Well, I should get going. Goodnight." Mika put on her coat and kissed them goodbye.

Outside in the crisp, cold air, she took a deep breath. Willow's updates on the grands were never pushy, and Mika had thought about healing the gap several times, but she just hadn't been able to overcome her anger. The snow crunched under her boots with every step. It wasn't deep, but her legs felt heavy. Her grandparents didn't have much time left and hadn't even met their great-grandson yet.

She stopped. Her parents would be appalled at her for waiting this long to make up with the grands. She turned around and swiftly made her way back. Aunt Pauline and another man were helping her grandparents toward the car. "Hi, again." She waved.

Her grandparents' withered faces looked up in surprise.

"Would you all like to join us for Christmas?" The smiles that adorned their faces ignited a flame of happiness inside Mika.

"Oh, yes, dear." Mika's grandmother hugged her. "That would be so wonderful."

Her grandfather smiled through tears. "Thank you."

"What can I bring?" Aunt Pauline asked.

"Nothing. We have plenty of food. Show up any time after ten." Mika cleared her throat. "I also want you to understand my feelings." She fisted her hands inside her coat pockets. "My parents were the best. I love them always and forever. But I also love Aunt Val for everything she's done, then and now." No one had said much since learning *that* secret.

"We understand," her grandfather said. "We're no longer against IVF. It gave us you, and it helped you and Willow create a family. I can't wait to see my great-grandson."

"Great. See you soon." Mika's footsteps were lighter as she walked to her car. "Hey, Siri, call Willow."

"Hi, how was it?" Willow asked.

"They're joining us for Christmas lunch."

"Good. I'm happy that you're finally coming to peace with the past. I know things still haunt you, but moving forward helps everyone."

"Have I told you what a wonderful wife you are?"

"That's right, sweetheart. Butter me up." Willow sighed. "Clint and I were looking through a photo album a couple days ago. I skipped the pictures of you with your grands. That made me very melancholy. Afterward, my already overflowing hormones got the better of me, and I almost invited them, but I knew that wasn't my decision to make."

"Thank you. I love you so much."

"I love you too."

Mika leaned her head back against the headrest. "Do you think it's too much for them to be around Benjy's parents?"

"You might want to mention it so Shabana and Garrett aren't surprised but stop worrying and start thinking positively. Things will fall into place. Now, save some of your energy. I need one of your fabulous massages when you get home."

"Yes, ma'am." Mika smiled as she drove away. But there was one tiny glitch. How in the world were she and Willow going to explain to their four-year-old son why his grandparents had never visited? Kids were full of curiosity, and Clint more than excelled in that department. Oh well, they'd say something that was age appropriate, but she'd never lie to him.

For once, peace settled over Mika's body. She glanced up through the car's glass roof at the stars and moon. The tears that followed were more joyful than sad. Somehow, she could hear her parents whisper to her through the night sky, *We love you and are so darn proud of you.*

Chapter Forty-Five

Christmas Day

"MOM, GET UP."

Mika reluctantly opened her eyes and looked at the clock on the nightstand to see it was only a few minutes past six. "It's too early. Go back to sleep."

"You know he won't stop until we get up," Willow said as she inched out of bed. "What time did you go to sleep? You look more exhausted than me, and I'm eight months pregnant."

"I don't remember," Mika said. Although Clint went to bed around nine, the adults stayed up drinking well past midnight. The partying ended somewhere around two, but Mika and Brie's young brother, Jasper, stayed up at least another hour putting the finishing touches around the house to show Santa had been. Mika was a little hung over and wanted more sleep but knew damn well that wasn't possible.

"Mommy, wake up Mom," Clint said.

"Oh, not like that," Willow said just as their son landed on top of Mika.

Mika drew in a sharp breath. "You're getting heavier, big guy."

"Mom, it's Christmas. Grammy and Grambe are up. Get up." He whacked Mika's arm.

"That's war, Clinton Andrew Lavigne." Mika grabbed her son and tickled him vigorously. He giggled and squirmed as she tickled every inch of his stomach. She tickled the bottom of his feet when he tried to get away.

"Stop, Mom. I need to wee."

She quickly released him, and he jumped out of bed and turned around. "Fooled you. Now, get up." He pointed his finger at her and giggled again.

Mika couldn't help but laugh along with his infectious energy and good vibes. She rose out of bed. "Good morning." She kissed Willow and bent down to kiss her big belly. "How are you, little one? You should be coming into the world soon." She smiled as the baby kicked.

"She let me sleep last night, but she started her aerobics about an hour ago." Willow yawned. "Please stop jumping on the bed."

"It's fun." Clint bounced up and down.

"Let it go; it's Christmas," Mika whispered. She put her finger under Willow's chin. "I wish you'd agreed to Aunt Val's offer to let us sleep in their downstairs bedroom."

"I thought you loved this room. Your aunt and Brie did a superb job with the renovation."

"They did." Mika put her arm around Willow's shoulder and glanced around. Sleeping here was a little sad because it was her parents' old room that her aunt had combined with the small guest room. But mostly, Mika felt comfort. Her relationship with her aunt had grown stronger and having her and Brie living there felt right. She pointed to the artwork on the one wall. "I love your painting next to Mom's favorite watercolor. They both capture the landscape around Cayuga Lake perfectly."

"And this is the best bed." Clint continued bouncing.

Mika and Willow smiled at each other.

"I also wish we'd stayed downstairs because it would've been easier on you. You've had more morning sickness and seem more fatigued with this pregnancy. I read that girls are smaller, but your belly looks—" Mika stopped when Willow quirked an eyebrow.

Willow lightly shoved Mika, but a corner of her mouth ticked up in a smile. "Choose your words carefully, babe, or you'll be sleeping elsewhere."

"Beautiful." Mika smiled. "Every inch of you is beautiful."

"I'm more tired than usual, and yes, my belly's bigger, but the doctor says it's nothing to worry about." Willow lightly patted her belly. "She's healthy and almost six pounds, right where she should be. But I'd be grateful if she'd let me sleep a little more in this last month. The stairs don't bother me. It's our energy monster, Clint. Oh, watch out."

Mika grunted when Clint jumped from the bed onto her back and wrapped his arms and legs around her.

"Mom, hurry up. Brush your teeth and give me a horsey back ride."

Mika bent over so he wouldn't fall off, and he drummed his hands on the top of her head. "Please don't do that, Clint." He stopped and rested his head on top of hers. "I'll give you a ride later. Please get down."

He fell back onto the bed but sprung up and looked up at Willow. "Mommy, you can sleep more if sissy needs it."

"Sissy also thinks it's time to get up. But I'm not sure about Mom. She's recuperating from her night of merriment." Willow glanced at the closet, then back at Mika.

"The delivery's complete." Mika winked. She'd managed to sneak the last two of Clint's presents out of the walk-in closet while Willow slept. But she had no idea how she and Jasper got the extra-large train set and table downstairs in their wobbly, drunken state. Benjy had made it and shipped it over a month ago. The fleeting thought brought sadness with it. It was too bad he couldn't make it this year. She'd miss him.

Clint chattered about toys, preschool, and everything under the sun as they moved into the en-suite bathroom to freshen up.

He tugged on Mika's hand. "I kind of like Mommy best because she makes good cookies."

Willow winked.

"But when you make pizza, Mom, you're the best."

"Uno chef." Mika thumped her chest, then tousled Clint's mob of dark hair. "Grazie."

"But Grammy and Grambe have the best house and make the best hot chocolate. I like their house better than ours in Merryland. It's big. Can we move here?"

Mika picked him up and sat him on the edge of the vanity so they were on the same eye level. "I love this house too. You know I grew up here."

He nodded, his deep espresso eyes filled with innocence and love.

"Our jobs are too far away for us to live here. Visiting is the best we can do."

"Can we visit more often?"

"We'll try." Mika wished she could promise more, but they were busy with their careers.

"But there's more room here to play hide and seek, and Grammy and Grambe have less rules."

"Can't argue with that." She smiled at Willow. Despite Clint's perception, she and Willow weren't hard on him because he was a good child and full of joy, and he didn't seem jealous of his imminent baby sister. He was so precocious. When people referred to all three grands as grandmother, he'd correct them. Mika silently laughed remembering the first time he'd done it. He pointed to Naomi and Aunt Val and said, *She's Grandma, and she's Grammy.* Then he'd point to Brie. *She has the best name. It's Grambe.*

"I need a few minutes alone. You two get out of my sanctuary." Willow kissed them, then gently pushed them out and shut the door.

"Mom, why does everybody like to kiss? It's wet."

"Because it's a way of showing how much we love one another." Mika squatted to his level and kissed his forehead then blew a raspberry on his cheek.

His big eyes widened. "I don't like the sloppy kisses."

"Since when?" She kissed him multiple times all over his face as he giggled.

"Surrender," he yelled, and she stopped.

"Mom, how does sissy do it?"

"Do what?"

Clint looked at her with a surprisingly serious face. He cupped his hand around his mouth and pressed up against her ear. "Go wee and poo inside of Mommy. And how is sissy going to get out?"

Mika suppressed a laugh. "Um, let's ask Mommy later, but not today. It's Christmas."

"Okay." He ran down the stairs.

"Dodged that damn bullet," Mika whispered to herself.

The smell of strong coffee and the piney smell of the five-foot-tall Balsam fir tree filled the air as Mika descended the stairs. The tree stood much taller with its root ball in a container. She remembered when she kicked the old fake Christmas tree over. She'd hated celebrating Christmas for years, but the season's joy took over little by little, and the birth of their son brought back the magic. She liked Aunt Val and Brie's new tradition of buying a live tree and donating it after Christmas to be planted in the nearby forest.

"Good morning," her aunt said. Brie and Naomi waved from the large sofa in front of the fire.

"Morning." Mika waved back. "You're here early," she said to her mother-in-law.

"I left at a reasonable time last night, unlike you party animals." Naomi smirked.

"Oh, trust me, I'm feeling it today," Brie said. "And I bet Dani and Ryan are too. It was Mika and Jasper who stayed up the latest."

"How'd you sleep?" her aunt asked Mika.

"Not bad for a couple of hours until someone woke me." Mika made a funny face at her son, and he made one back. "Willow will be down soon. Is that cinnamon rolls I smell?"

"Yes, ma'am. Mini ones to get us started." Jasper walked in and set the plate on the coffee table next to carafes filled with coffee and hot chocolate. In a flash, Clint grabbed two.

"Put one back, Clint." Willow appeared and swung her arm

over Mika's neck.

He gave them his trademark "I'll die if you don't let me do what I want" look.

"Listen to your mommy," Mika said, and Clint put one back. She turned to Jasper. "Don't you have other pajamas to wear besides that vintage psychedelic outfit? It's hurting my eyes."

"More like your head. Looked like you were drinking your wife's share last night." He grinned.

"Stop showing off, old man," Mika punched his bicep.

"I'm only fifty years young. And if you want to continue receiving freebies at Java Heaven, you'd better respect me." He grinned like a kid.

The doorbell rang. "Mika, can you and Clint please get the door? I saw Shabana and Garrett at the store the other day and told them to come early," her aunt said.

"Let's go, Mom. Benjy's dad makes cool things, and his mom is the best cook."

Mika looked at him. "Hey, big guy. I thought you said Mommy and I were best." When Clint dropped his roll, put his sticky hand in hers, and pulled with all his might, Mika sighed and looked at the adults over her shoulder. "I hope one day he discovers napkins." She moved too slow for her son, and he broke loose and bolted for the door. She unlatched the deadbolt lock, and Clint yanked it open.

"Surprise!" Benjy, his wife, Maya, and their five-year-old, Austin, shouted. Their two-year-old daughter, Alice, was soundly asleep in Benjy's arms.

"It's Uncle Benjy and Aunt Maya," Clint yelled over his shoulder. He grabbed Austin's hand. "We have rolls." And they took off at the speed of sound. Surprisingly, Alice didn't move an inch despite the noise.

"Come in. I can't believe this. It's so great to see you." Mika opened the door wider.

Everyone hugged, with Benjy getting the last one after placing his daughter on the sofa. Mika hung on extra tight. "It's so good to see you, my friend. I thought you were staying home in Colorado this year."

"And miss seeing Clinton's mommies? No way. I juggled some things around, and the new manager I hired came up to speed fast," Benjy said.

"I might have pushed him too. He's been working too much," Maya said.

The noise volume exploded as Austin and Clint chased each other, giggling.

Mika put her hands over her ears for a second, then shook her finger at Benjy. "You boys are too wild."

"Tell me about it." Maya rolled her eyes.

They watched the grands bribe the boys to settle down to breakfast. It wasn't hard with mugs of hot chocolate, scrambled eggs, and Jasper's oatmeal pancakes.

"What are the recipes for today? Can I help?" Maya asked Jasper.

Mika clapped Benjy on the back. "We got lucky in the food department, dude. You married a star chef, and Brie's brother's coffeehouse and bakery just got named one of the best in the northeast by Food Network."

"And I'm bigger because of Jasper," Willow said. "I swear the extra weight is his fault. If we don't stop by Java Heaven when we visit, he comes to us with all kinds of goodies. And when we're home, he ships us a FedEx overnight package almost every month."

"Clint's grown a lot. How's sissy doing?" Benjy asked.

Willow took a deep breath and blew it out. "She's well but kicking the daylights out of me. Want to feel?"

Benjy placed his hands on Willow's belly. He glowed, and Mika swore she saw tears in his eye.

"Me too." Maya rushed over. "Oh my, that's a strong kick." She grinned then pointed at Mika. "Aren't you thrilled I talked you into this?"

Mika nodded.

"My wife can be stubborn sometimes." Willow winked.

"Guilty as charged." Mika winked back. When they'd first told Maya and Benjy about their thoughts on starting a family, Maya suggested that Benjy be the sperm donor. Benjy and Willow were on board immediately, but Mika needed convincing. The emotional journey between her and Aunt Val made her reluctant at first, but it was the best thing that had ever happened. They were one big happy family with no secrets, and all four adults agreed that their unique family would be explained to all the kids once the youngest child reached age five.

"When can we open presents?" Clint tugged on Mika's pajama bottoms.

"Go finish your breakfast, please," Willow said to the boys. "You can pick one present, but we can't open the others until after lunch."

"Oh, Mommy." Clint stomped off.

Willow turned to Mika. "I was over zealous in getting up. I'm more tired than I thought. Do you mind if I go lay down?"

"Are you okay, honey?" Mika rubbed Willow's neck.

"Uh-huh. An hour away from all this noise should help me and the baby."

"Rest in the downstairs guest room," Aunt Val said. "I had them put acoustic insulation in the addition to reduce most noise."

"Thanks. I'll take you up on it this time." Willow walked slowly across the room and shut the door.

Mika chewed her bottom lip.

"Relax. Didn't you say the doctor okayed the car trip?" Benjy asked.

"Yeah. Doc wasn't thrilled about her going at 36 weeks but said she and the baby were in great shape." Mika sighed.

"Stop worrying," Maya said. "Trust me. The last month of pregnancy is nothing but being tired."

"Okay." Mika ran her fingers through her hair. "Benjy, your parents might have said something already. I made up with my grandparents. They're coming over."

"Mom told me. It's wonderful. I'm happy for you."

Mika cleared her throat. "I don't know if my cousins or Aunt Pauline ever told them about you and Clint," she whispered so the kids couldn't hear.

"They're not blind. You and Willow send them pictures with your letters, and Clint's not exactly your shade or Willow's." He smiled.

"From everything Willow's told us, they've changed and regret what they did to you. What's there to worry about?" Maya asked.

Mika looked between them. She jammed her hands in her back pockets and rocked on her heels. "They were also xenophobic and never liked you, Benjy. I don't know how much that's changed."

"Mika, that was a long time ago. Give them a chance. I'm not worried." Benjy put both hands on her shoulders. "I'm betting that the spirit of Christmas love will carry the day. How's work at your fancy Goddard Space Flight Center? Hey, is it true that we're close to colonizing Mars?" He sat near the fire beside his wife and motioned for Mika to sit.

"I hope so, but my division studies exoplanets." She puffed up her cheeks and blew the air out slowly. "With climate change, we need to look beyond our solar system and get there as fast as possible. Mars is a stepping stone."

"Whoa. It's Christmas. Don't kill the mood. We can talk about climate change, war, and earth extinction another day."

"Sorry, you're right."

"Willow mentioned you've gotten a lot of job offers. Are you thinking of moving?"

"The offers have come in as I get close to finishing my PhD, but right now, Maryland's the best for my family. They've slowed me down, but in a good way." Mika smiled. "I'm so blessed. Willow's still painting, and her pieces sell well through several galleries. She's planning to return to part-time teaching this summer. I'm just worried that something's different with this pregnancy. It didn't seem to slow her down until a few days ago."

"Hey." Benjy slapped her knee. "It's going to be fine."

Mika nodded, but the thought kept nagging at her. Willow was the one who insisted on the drive home. Mika hoped it wasn't a mistake.

"Mom, we're done eating breakfast. Can we open one present now, please?"

Clint always melted Mika's heart and knew just how to wrap her around his finger.

"Sure." As the boys tore open their gifts, Mika noticed Clint had picked out the one Benjy placed under the tree. She whispered, "I hope Santa picked something age appropriate and quiet, or I'll kick Santa's butt."

He snickered, mimicking the best dastardly villain of any Disney movie.

Clint leaped into the air. "It's a remote-controlled car."

Benjy loaded the batteries and showed Clint how to work the controls.

"Look, Mom. It even honks." Clint pressed a button several times, and the little car made an irritating noise.

"I see." Mika approached Benjy and whispered, "St. Nick, you're toast."

Then Clint grabbed everything and ran toward the bedroom. "I'm going to show Mommy." He was inside before anyone could stop him.

"So much for Willow's nap. When we collapse at the end of the day, the rug rats will still be playing with the noisy remote-controlled car." Mika shook her finger. "You'd better make it up to us."

"I'll take the kids to the park tomorrow when they get up and let everyone sleep in," Benjy said.

"Mom." Clint ran out of the room without the car. "Mommy's making funny sounds like she's hurt. She told me to get you."

Mika and Naomi ran to the bedroom.

"I'm having contractions. They've subsided for now." Sweat

beaded along Willow's brow.

"Are you sure?" Mika held Willow's hand.

"I'll call the ambulance," Naomi said.

"No, Mom. It's nothing. Even if it were labor, I'd have plenty of time. Clint caused me hours of pain before his grand entrance."

Mika felt helpless as another pain hit her wife.

"Here's a heating pad and some towels, just in case." Aunt Val handed them to Mika.

"Who's watching the kids?" Willow asked between deep breaths.

"Brie, Maya, and me," Benjy called out from the living room.

"Honey, we need to go to the hospital now," Mika said.

"It's too soon. I'll be fine. If my contractions get closer, we can go to the hospital."

"I'm not sure that's a good idea," Naomi said.

"Mom, I'm—" Another contraction hit Willow. She squeezed her eyes tight. Then she looked at Mika. "Don't worry. Remember how long it took with Clint?"

Willow's contractions with Clint had begun in the middle of the night, and she didn't wake Mika until sunrise. Fifteen hours of labor later, and Clint entered the world. But this seemed different.

"Will you read to me?" Willow asked.

"Sure." Mika hustled out of the room and came back as quickly as possible. When she began reading *The Hitchhiker's Guide to The Galaxy*, Willow laughed.

"At least it's entertaining. I suppose I should consider myself lucky that you're not reading me *One Hundred Years of General Relativity*. Can you rub my belly with some cocoa butter?" Willow asked.

Mika ran back upstairs. She looked in three places but couldn't find Willow's favorite cream. Regular hand cream would have to do. When she reentered the room, she dropped the tube. Willow's breaths were fast and short. Her knees were bent, and her legs spread wide with Aunt Val positioned in between. "Oh, my God."

Mika rushed in and brushed back Willow's hair and stroked her forehead. "I love you."

"You're doing great, dear," Naomi said from the other side of the bed as Willow squeezed her mom's hand tight.

"Willow," Aunt Val said, "remember two steps forward, one step back. It's natural for the head to recede a little, but she'll make her way out with a few gentle pushes. Just breathe. Mika, come here, please."

"What can I do to help?"

"I need another towel, and Willow needs you to calm down. It looks like your eyes are going to pop out of your head," Aunt Val said softly.

Mika glanced at her aunt's hands. Where did she get the latex gloves? Willow's cry snapped her attention back, and she rushed into the bathroom for another towel.

"Gentle push. That's it. Rest. A few more pushes, and she'll be here," Aunt Val said. She looked up at Mika. "Want to catch the baby? I'll be here with you."

"Here." Brie dangled a pair of latex gloves over Mika's shoulder. "I sterilized some scissors with rubbing alcohol. Tell me when you need them."

When did Brie enter the room? Everything was a blur. Mika slipped on the gloves and stood where Aunt Val indicated. Their daughter's head pushed out slightly with Willow's next push. *Okay, this isn't so bad.* Then Willow screamed louder with the next push and frightened Mika to death. Worry was replaced by wonder as the baby's shoulders emerged. Then the rest of their daughter's body, along with the cord and fluid, shot out like a rocket. Mika gazed in amazement as their baby cried louder than Clint ever had.

"She's going to give Clint some competition." Mika smiled at Willow, who nodded with a broader smile.

"Want to cut the cord?" Aunt Val asked.

Mika nodded. Then her aunt helped her wrap the baby in a

towel.

"Show your amazing wife her newest bundle of joy." Aunt Val winked.

Mika placed their daughter in Willow's arms. "She's gorgeous like her mommy." She was in awe as Willow positioned their daughter to breastfeed, and the baby immediately latched on. A few minutes later, she fell asleep on Willow's chest.

"Looks like you did fine without me."

Mika turned. A woman with a stethoscope draped around her neck and a bag in her hand stood nearby.

"This is my gynecologist, Dr. Carmen Richardson. She lives around the corner, so I called her," Brie said from the doorway.

Everyone left the room giving Willow and Mika some privacy with the doctor. After a quick check, Dr. Richardson pronounced Willow and their daughter in good health with no complications.

Mika kissed her wife and baby. "I guess we need to figure out a name. How about your middle name, Marie?"

"How about Joy Marie, since she's our Christmas present that's sure to bring us joy?"

"Perfect." Mika played with Willow's hair.

There was a commotion in the living room. The door popped open, and two paramedics rushed in.

"You're late to the party, ladies and gentlemen. This feisty girl wouldn't wait," Dr. Richardson said. They wanted to whisk Willow and Joy Marie away, but they left after the doctor assured them everything was under control. "Willow, I'll return later to check on you and little Joy Marie. In the meantime, don't hesitate to call me. Brie has my number."

After she left, Benjy and Maya peeked through the cracked door. "We wanted to catch a glimpse of the baby."

"Come on in." Willow said. "And like Clint, the best part is her beautiful looks from her bio-Dad."

Benjy beamed with pride.

Aunt Val poked her head inside the door with Clint latched

onto her hand. "He'd like to see his sissy."

They waved him over, and he let go of Aunt Val's hand and tiptoed inside. His eyes were wide, and his mouth hung open.

"This is your little sister, Joy Marie. What do you think?" Willow asked.

His lip quivered. "Mommy, I'm sorry I woke sissy up making noise with my toy car."

"No, it wasn't your fault, big guy."

"If she's sleepy, maybe Mom can put her back in."

Mika laughed, unable to contain herself. Benjy made a couple of soft snorts trying his best not to snicker. Clint looked at them wide-eyed.

"Never mind Mom and Uncle Benjy." Willow cupped her son's face. "Your baby sister wanted to join the party and meet everyone." Willow smiled. "But you could turn the noise down a notch."

He nodded. Mika picked him up, and he wrapped his arms tight around her neck.

Aunt Val came back into the bedroom. "All the grands are here. So is Pauline. We've been chatting and filling them in on the action."

"Bring them in," Willow said without hesitation. "It's a big room."

As Maya and Benjy turned to leave, Mika grabbed Benjy's arm. "Please stay." She handed Joy Marie to him and helped Willow sit up better.

Benjy rocked Joy Marie in his arms, humming a lullaby. When the grands entered, he placed Joy Marie in Willow's arms, took Clint's hand, and stepped to the back of the room.

Shabana held onto Grandmother Lavigne, and Garrett came behind with Grandfather Lavigne. Aunt Pauline entered last. There wasn't a dry eye among them, but they all had bright smiles. It looked like her grands and Benjy's parents had been friends for years. They took turns whispering their well wishes. Joy Marie cried on and off. Willow finally quieted her with breastfeeding.

To Mika's surprise, her grandfather motioned to Benjy.

"Clint's a fine young tot and handsome like you." Grandfather lifted his frail hand and patted Benjy's arm. "Well done, son."

"Thank you." Benjy nodded and glanced at Mika.

She shrugged. Clint was clinging onto Benjy's leg like a life raft and probably didn't understand. She'd have to say something to the grands. "And this handsome young man is Clinton Andrew Lavigne." She bent down to his level, ran her fingers through Clint's thick hair, then pointed at her Lavigne grandparents. "Clint, these are your great-grandparents. That means they're your grandfather's parents. Remember I told you stories about your Grandfather Andrew and them?"

Clint nodded.

"We can talk to them more in the living room." Mika knew her grandfather couldn't stand very long.

"Congratulations, she's beautiful." Aunt Pauline blew a kiss to Willow and waved to Mika.

Naomi entered. "I'll stay with Willow. Go visit," she said to Mika.

In the living room, Mika sat with her grandparents and Clint, who clung to her side. He warmed up to his great-grandmother but was cautious with his great-grandfather. Aunt Pauline was a short distance away with Maya and Benjy's parents while Benjy played with Alice and her toys on the rug.

As everyone chatted, Clint leaned his head on Mika's shoulder, listening but not saying much. "Mom," he whispered in his not quiet at all kid way. "Why does he shake like a tree?"

"Because he's nearly one hundred years old." Mika watched as Clint's eyes got bigger and bigger. "Great-grandfather Lavigne likes you, big guy."

Clint looked back and forth between them. Mika didn't know what to think when he ran off, but he returned with his new car. He jabbered away about what it could do. The warmth of love blossomed in Mika's chest when her grandfather marveled over Clint and his remote-controlled car. Soon, Clint waved bye and ran off to play with Austin.

When Shabana and Garrett came over, Mika excused herself

and left to find Aunt Val. As she walked down the hallway, her aunt came out of the powder room.

"Are you hungry? Lunch will be ready soon. I've been helping Jasper in the kitchen," Aunt Val said.

"It can wait." Mika gently took hold of her arm and led her toward the bedroom where Willow and Joy Marie rested.

"Oh, we shouldn't disturb them."

"It's the best time while everyone else is hanging out together." They entered the bedroom, and Willow appeared to be asleep with Naomi beside her, cradling Joy Marie.

"I'll give you some privacy," Naomi whispered. She handed Joy Marie to Mika and left.

"Sit down and hold your granddaughter," Mika said to her aunt.

Aunt Val teared up as Mika slipped Joy Marie into her arms. "You've come a long way since I moved here. I'm so proud of you and Willow." Aunt Val smiled down at Joy Marie and rocked her back and forth.

Willow sat up and stretched. "Honey, snap some pictures of Grammy and little Joy Marie."

Mika took several pictures with her iPhone.

"Val, thank you for being who you are. And I'm grateful to you and Mom for giving us a chance," Willow said.

"Agree." Mika knelt beside the rocker and cupped Aunt Val's face. "You gave me life and took care of me at the most horrific point in our lives. I was suffering, but so were you. But you did it. You rescued me, and you've been there every step of the way since." She kissed her baby's forehead, then looked up at her aunt. "Willow and I planned for two children, and we decided that you'd be the first to know after the second child." She delicately smoothed out Joy Marie's hair. "Clint was conceived using Willow's eggs, but Joy Marie was conceived with mine. You've always been special to us, a special grammy in Clint's eyes, and now you know about your special connection to Joy Marie's genetic side."

Tears fell down Aunt Val's face. "Thank you." She rose and

placed Joy Marie in Willow's arms, then kissed Willow's forehead. "This is the best and most beautiful Christmas present ever." She turned and hugged Mika.

After several heartfelt seconds, Mika put her hands on her aunt's shoulders. "I got lucky and had two moms. Clint and this tiny precious soul wouldn't be here if it wasn't for you. And it started years ago with your promise. Thank you."

The accident that shattered Mika's life had taken a heavy toll. Aunt Val, Willow, and their family and friends had pieced her heart back together and made Christmas her favorite holiday once again. She knew there'd be many more wonderful Christmases to come, but none would be as magical as this one. As she gazed at her daughter and wife, Mika said a silent prayer to her parents in heaven. *Thank you so much, Mom and Dad, for making that promise.*

~ THE END ~

If you enjoyed The Promise, maybe you'd like my contemporary adult romance, Cabin Fever. And I'd love if you were able to spend a few minutes writing a review for me on Amazon!

Other Great Butterworth Books

Cabin Fever by Addison M Conley
She goes for the money, but will she stay for something deeper?
Available on Amazon (ASIN B0BQWY45GH)

Back to Back by Jo Fletcher
."When Fred and Ruby's worlds collide, can love rise from the rubble?"
Available on Amazon (ASIN B0D6M499K2)

Heart of the Storm by Ally McGuire
Sometimes a storm is just what you need to clear the skies ahead.
Available on Amazon (ASIN B0CYTSQXWW)

Sanctuary by Helena Harte
Passions ignite and possibilities unfold. Welcome to the Windy City Romance series.
Available from Amazon (ASIN B0D4B42RRW)

Brave Enough to Love by Valden Bush
In a dance between truth and sacrifice, can they rewrite the rules of love?
Available on Amazon (ASIN B0CQP8PMVB)

Dead Ringer by Robyn Nyx
Three bodies. One killer. No motive?
Available on Amazon (ASIN B0CPQ8HFK7)

Medea by JJ Taylor
Who will Medea become in her battle for freedom?
Available from Amazon (ASIN B0CK2FB7GW)

Virgin Flight by E.V. Bancroft
In the battle between duty and desire, can love win?
Available from Amazon (ASIN B0CKJWQZ45)

Fragments of the Heart by Ally McGuire
Love can be the greatest expedition of all.
Available on Amazon (ASIN B0CHBPHR6M)

Here You Are by Jo Fletcher
.Can they unlock their hearts to find the true happiness they both deserve?
Available on Amazon (ASIN B0CBN935ZB)

Stunted Heart by Helena Harte
A stunt rider who lives in the fast lane. An ER doctor who can't take chances. A
passion that could turn their worlds upside down.
Available on Amazon (ASIN B0C78GSWBV)

Dark Haven by Brey Willows
Even vampires get tired of playing with their food...
Available on Amazon (ASIN B0C5P1HJXC)

Green for Love by E.V. Bancroft
All's fair in love and eco-war.
Available from Amazon (ASIN B0C28F7PX5)

Call of Love by Lee Haven
Separated by fear. Reunited by fate. Will they get a second chance at life and love?
Available from Amazon (ASIN B0BYC83HZD)

Where the Heart Leads by Ally McGuire
A writer. A celebrity. And a secret that could break their hearts.
Available on Amazon (ASIN B0BWFX5W9L)

Stolen Ambition by Robyn Nyx
Daughters of two worlds collide in a dangerous game of ambition and love.
Available on Amazon (ASIN B0BS1PRSCN)

Breakout for Love by Valden Bush
They're both running from their pasts. Together, they might make a new future.
Available from Amazon (ASIN B0CWHZ4SXL)

The Helion Band by AJ Mason
Rose's only crime was to show kindness to her royal mistress...
Available from Amazon (ASIN B09YM6TYFQ)

That Boy of Yours Wants Looking At by Simon Smalley
A riotously colourful and heart-rending journey of what it takes to live authentically.
Available from Amazon (ASIN B09V3CSQQW)

Sapphic Eclectic Volume Five edited by Nyx & Willows
A little something for everyone...
Available free via the Butterworth Books website

Of Light and Love by E.V. Bancroft
The deepest shadows paint the brightest love.
Available from Amazon (ASIN B0B64KJ3NP)

An Art to Love by Helena Harte
Second chances are an art form.
Available on Amazon (ASIN B0B1CD8Y42)

Music City Dreamers by Robyn Nyx
Music brings lovers together. In Music City, it can tear them apart. Available on Amazon (ASIN B0994XVDGR)

Let Love Be Enough by Robyn Nyx
When a killer sets her sights on her target, is there any stopping her?
Available on Amazon (ASIN B09YMMZ8XC)

Dead Pretty by Robyn Nyx
An FBI agent, a TV star, and a serial killer. Love hurts.
Available on Amazon (ASIN B09QRSKBVP)

Nero by Valden Bush
Banished and abandoned. Will destiny reunite her with the love of her life?
Available from Amazon (ASIN B0BHJKHK6S)

Warm Pearls and Paper Cranes by E.V. Bancroft
A family torn apart by secrets. The only way forward is love.
Available from Amazon (ASIN B09DTBCQ92)

Judge Me, Judge Me Not by James Merrick
One man's battle against the world and himself to find it's never too late to find, and use, your voice.
Available from Amazon (ASIN B09CLK91N5)

Scripted Love by Helena Harte
What good is a romance writer who doesn't believe in happy ever after?
Available on Amazon (ASIN B0993QFLNN)

Call to Me by Helena Harte
Sometimes the call you least expect is the one you need the most.
Available on Amazon (ASIN B08D9SR15H)

What's Your Story?

Global Wordsmiths, CIC, provides an all-encompassing service for all writers, ranging from basic proofreading and cover design to development editing, typesetting, and eBook services. A major part of our work is charity and community focused, delivering writing projects to under-served and under-represented groups across Nottinghamshire, giving voice to the voiceless and visibility to the unseen.

To learn more about what we offer, visit: www.globalwords.co.uk

A selection of books by Global Words Press:
Desire, Love, Identity: with the National Justice Museum
Aventuras en México: Farmilo Primary School
Times Past: with The Workhouse, National Trust
Young at Heart with AGE UK
In Different Shoes: Stories of Trans Lives

Self-published authors working with Global Wordsmiths:
Steve Bailey
Ravenna Castle
Jackie D
CJ DeBarra
Dee Griffiths
Iona Kane
Maggie McIntyre
Emma Nichols
Dani Lovelady Ryan
Erin Zak